# Georgina

## A Song Of Youth

## Cedric Paul Foster

The Book Guild Ltd

First published in Great Britain in 2016 by
The Book Guild Ltd
9 Priory Business Park
Wistow Road, Kibworth
Leicestershire, LE8 0RX
Freephone: 0800 999 2982
www.bookguild.co.uk
Email: info@bookguild.co.uk
Twitter: @bookguild

Typeset in Adobe Caslon Pro

Printed and bound in Great Britain by
CPI Group (UK) Ltd, Croydon, CR0 4YY

ISBN 978 1910878 835

British Library Cataloguing in Publication Data.
A catalogue record for this book is available from the British Library.

MIX
Paper from
responsible sources
FSC
www.fsc.org
FSC® C013604

# 1

Now Georgina's a fine looking wench; there's no doubt
about that. Even at fourteen years of age, the heads
of males would turn in the street to admire the curves,
which were to develop to voluptuousness within the next
two years. Such is the miracle of Nature that turns mere
pigtailed, freckle-faced girls into women almost, it seems,
overnight. But Georgina's contours were not the only things
appreciated by men (and some women), there was this
gorgeous, 'georgenious' thick, ripe-corn coloured hair that
was indeed a crowning glory of light, golden sheen, which
flowed from her high forehead down in a superb sweep
to her waist, a veritable mane of hair. Once in a while,
the silly little kids at school would give it a tug and say
something foolish – well, you know what children are like –
and Georgina then would turn and spit like a cat, her bright
green eyes afire. Let the little beast not come too near! For
the fine arms had strength, too, by Jove, and to see her thus
flushed and angry, the sculptured arm and hand descend
and strike was a treat for the eye and heart. Ah, Georgina!
That's what her mother called her, Georgina. But no one

else called her that. Everyone else called her 'Gina' for short and very close friends knew her as 'Georgy'.

(Enter mother) "Georgina! How many times have I to tell you not to leave your clothes and toys strewn about the room?" The 'not' of this was heavily emphasised. "And another thing: your cycle's in the road again. Go and bring it in immediately!"

"Yes, mother."

"The last one disappeared or was stolen or something." (*with mock resignation*). "Well, it's your own bike, and I'm not going to buy another, that's for sure." (*Exit mother*). Gina rises with an exaggerated expression of exasperated patience from her seat in the garden where she had been reading to fetch the cycle, unconscious of her beautiful form as she did so, in mind still a child.

Is that not a strange thing, now? When I come to think of it, her mother is small and dark, pale of face, the eyes set close either side of her nose like those of a bird. Yes, she reminds me very much of a bird.

She's prim, with a big collar and a tight uniform of a dress in dark brown over the flat chest; a Miss Pringle indeed. Her manner, as she goes, is cool, yes, but not cold. She reminds me of the matrons in many wards of many hospitals, kind but firm. "No nonsense, now, Mr Tittleweed, if you please! Take off your trousers. This won't hurt!" Women are easily able to distinguish real pain from morbid self-pity. How erect she holds herself! How aristocratic the tilt of her head as she makes for the front door! A noble woman, this, but there's not a trace of Gina to be found in her no, not anywhere. And there she is, our sweet, young thing, near the fence at the bottom of the garden. And who is this on a warm summer evening but young Charlie Samuels from next door. "Hello," says

Charlie as he pushes his long snout through the conifers, which divide the two gardens. He has black hair and a sallow complexion and eyes like those of a mouse, sharp and quick with a mischievous glint in them. Georgina is amused by his sudden, cheeky appearance through the branches and to her he looks so funny, framed as he is by the green foliage, like a wood imp in the fairy tales she had read. The girl laughs.

"I'm going to the flicks tonight –wanna come? It's gonna be good." Charlie's manner is exactly that of his father, a dapper, very successful Jewish salesman. The boy's voice, too, has the same timbre as his father's, and the same persuasive cadences. Georgina and Charlie have had some jolly romps together in their childhoods. Now they are growing up, and their friendship has ripened into a real understanding of one another.

"Ray's been; he says it's good."

"Okay," Georgina replies, and is pleased with the idea. "But I'll have to ask my Dad."

"Do so, do so." the imp bids, unconsciously but accurately adopting the encouraging free-to-decide-for-yourself tones of his father, habitually used when he, the father, knew he'd softened his client almost to the point of purchase. At such a juncture, the customer was gently exhorted to 'think it over'. To have gone a step further would have been a step too far and so ruined the chances of a sale. The manner assumed in such circumstances and beautifully conveyed by the innuendo of what we know of today as 'body talk' that of 'of course, no intelligent individual could possibly waive the unique opportunity now open to him.' This technique usually worked, though not on every occasion; there were unfortunately unintelligent people.

The idiom was not lost on Georgina either, and she

3

smiled as the face disappeared as quickly as it had popped up amid the green fronds. 'He and his father,' she thought, 'were as alike as two peas.' She said to herself how she would like to get out for a while, since school had been pretty hectic over the last few weeks. TV was a bore and anyway she was always obliged to watch what her parents or her older brother wished to see of an evening. Yes, she would ask her father about a possible trip to the cinema, although he had been oddly ill-inclined to let her go anywhere recently. It was strange. Brother, mother and father seemed these days to be in conspiratorial league with one another. They conspired together and saw to it that she would be at home for longer periods and in bed before ten. It was embarrassing. 'What was the idea?' she asked herself.

Father arrived home later that day at 6.30 pm and, as usual, his arrival was something of an event, aye, a significant event, a full stop as it were to the working day, to the day that had passed and so a prelude to the evening that was now to begin. He was never what you would call friendly at such a time, his manner being invariably formal; he gave and received kisses of greeting at this time with cool grace and equanimity, like that of a sovereign. Each of his subjects, his wife, his daughter, Georgina, his son and even Georgina's little sister, Sarah, who had even stood guard in the front garden to wait for his approach, had received a formal hug in turn, and each thereafter went about the business of making him comfortable as if galvanised into action at the pipe of a bosun's whistle.

Sarah had shrieked "Papa's coming!" and everyone had turned to clearing the decks after their welcome.

"Is dinner ready?" Our lord would then ask as mother and Georgina took his light jacket, placing it on a coat hanger in the hall, while Patrick, Georgina's brother, supplied the daily newspaper, and Sarah fussed with his slippers.

In answer to this routine question, mother simply raised her eyebrows in affirmation and then received the short, sharp kiss he bestowed on her after the manner of a South American generalissimo would on another of his kind in honour of faithful service.

"Good!" he said. Mother returned to the kitchen to the most alluring aroma of a freshly-cooked dinner. Dad turned to his subordinates, "Thank you," he said, this bright, very bright, blue-eyed man in his middle fifties with his red, squire-like face and his full, gently receding red hair combed impatiently from the noble forehead.

For ex-Colonel Henry Hennessey, DSO, VC, straight as a poker, twice mentioned in dispatches, formerly of the Irish Guards, had served in two world wars. In the first he had been a sapper and in the second a professional soldier. As you can see, he was twice decorated and had even earned the distinction of the Victoria Cross. He had also been wounded, which also accounted for the slightly mechanical way he moved his left arm. He sired his children late in life and now stood before them and his wife, and signalled again that he was hungry.

"I'm hungry," he said and marched away with an obedient retinue into the room in which he was to dine.

"Good!" he said again in his clipped, military manner, seated himself at the table, and began to tuck the serviette under his chin. The others took their places quietly. It was a strictly observed custom in this house never to speak until father had spooned his first mouthful of soup and pronounced his "Ah, good, very good." Only then would anyone dare to refer to the day's events. Colonel Hennessey would never ever have broached a theme of his own accord himself, and would have sat through the whole meal without saying anything more than his large, appreciative 'Ahs' and 'Goods'. On these occasions, it was usually mother who turned to the course of the morning or the afternoon, and father would always look at her then as he was doing now, beaming between spoonfuls of soup as though at a distinguished guest, a brigadier perhaps or someone from the Foreign Office, or even, let's say, a member of the royal family. The look was engaging, infinitely polite over the spoon, and he would respond to mother's declarations –whatever their content – with an 'Oh, indeed?' and a 'Really?' And if mother's observations were interesting or invited comment, he would say 'How odd!' or 'How interesting!'. All very English, this, and undoubtedly acquired in British Army officers' messes throughout the world. But woe betide anyone who assumed that our man had not heard correctly or for all this superficial courtesy had perhaps not understood the import of what had been said to him. It was then that the Irishman would come forth, the spoon crash into the plate, the colour flush the cheeks, and our colonel's eyes sparkle like blue diamonds. At moments such as these, everyone would cringe and hope, holding onto their chairs that the volcano would not spill, for the colonel when angry could be terrifying. But such occasions were rare. If ritual was observed at dinner, for example, the proper approach, such as the respectful enquiry, the preparatory compliment to further comment, the appreciative nod in response to his remarks, the introductory attempt at humour – all these were a means to his heart, and his heart was noble and generous, even if tradition and habit had pickled his brain somewhat. Ritual with him was everything. Once you knew the ropes of the ritual, you could pull as it were, and the women knew well from instinct and experience how to work them, while brother Patrick, a mere man, had a harder time of it. With him, skirmishes with father were frequent.

Moreover, as far as father was concerned, there was no better example of the love of man needing first to pass through the stomach than with our Irish Guardsman.

After the meal, he was always more equable and indulgent, this father of theirs, than at other times, and it was even possible to disturb his subsequent perusal of the newspaper to crave a boon.

Georgina came forward.

"Dad?"

"Yes, my love," (head still in the paper).

Georgina (quickly), "I'd like to go out tonight to the cinema – with your permission of course. Henry's fiery moustache quivered slightly behind the paper. "Ugh?"

"Well, there's a good film on, and I'd like to see it."

"What film?" asked the voice from behind the paper curtain.

"It's called '*Spartacus*', and it's about Roman slaves in revolt against their masters," Georgina said hurriedly.

"Really?" said the newspaper. "Well, perhaps. What time does it finish?"

"Ten, I think," said Georgina.

"And your mother, what does your mother think? Ten is a little late, isn't it?"

Georgina thought quickly. "You'd approve, Dad. I heard about it at school today."

"Oh, really?"

After this, there was quite a long silence. Gina waited. She knew the ropes.

Then, "Well, we shall ask your mother," the father said with a broad wink appearing behind one edge of the paper. "But not later than 10.30 pm Understood?" It was settled.

Mother would be amenable, but these days she was curiously concerned about her daughter and to Georgina's surprise, Dad even followed her into the kitchen where mother was busy with the maid attending to the washing up. It was as though he wanted to supervise the request. Mother looked up at him, and father winked again reassuringly, but this time at mother. So it was agreed. Gina was pleased to be allowed go, but she could not help feeling that their attitudes were a bit... well, queer.

'Whatever's the matter with them?' she asked herself.

And so an hour passed, and the time came for the visit to the cinema. Young Charlie Samuels was at the corner of the street with a red, conspicuous scarf round his neck, although it was already March and really quite warm for the time of year. The scarf was an emblem, his particular signature. He, like Georgina, was growing up. Identity was important. Gina joined him, linked arms with her escort, and took the roads that led into town, and soon the queue outside the cinema loomed into view.

"We'll have to wait: 'Hey, look! There's 'Nosey Parker!'" Charlie cried. And so it was. 'Nosey' had not received his nickname because he was particularly curious by nature. Rather he was so baptised because he had a very large nose and his name happened to be Parker. They greeted each other, as adolescents will, and with much explosive, noisy guffaws so that members of the older generation in the queue turned serious faces towards them. 'Nosey', who was tall and who from time to time displayed a dignity of bearing that was later to become part of his adult composure, was also endowed with integrity and a considerable sense of humour. He surveyed Georgina for a second or two and then said, "Hey, did you know Sandy Perkins is keen on you?"

"I hadn't noticed," said Georgina with affected indifference. (It was a lie). She knew very well that Mr. Perkins was addicted to her.

"Ach, get away! He's daft about yer!"

"He's daft anyway," Georgina retorted. 'Nosey' smiled.

"You know," he mused, looking at Charlie for male assent. "These women have got no idea. Here's a young feller, full of pep and go, an athlete forsooth, a strong, muscular man indeed, deep-chested with powerful arms, tall…" 'Nosey' was in his element…

"Oh, shut up!" Georgina's eyes flashed.

"What's wrong with him, then?! 'Nosey' enquired, affecting to be hurt by her demand. He waited.

"I don't like blond men, that's all. And anyway, he's not my type," Gina said simply. 'Nosey', who in fact liked Sandy Perkins, shrugged his shoulders as if to say, 'Well, there's no accounting for lack of taste' when, to his surprise, Georgina snapped, " All right, how would you like to walk out with Linda Jones? Now there's a good, sweet young girl, just right for our Mr Parker…" She expertly affected 'Nosey's' manner. The latter threw up his arms in protest.

"So you see what I mean," said Georgina, clinching matters.

"Yes, but Linda Jones…"

"Well, Sandy Perkins?" Georgina returned confident of her logic.

Charlie, following the discourse with relish, laughed at this deadlock. Aye, who can fathom the 'antipathies and affections of the human mind'? Handsome Perkins was not loved by Georgina Hennessey, nor Linda Jones nor Mr Lawrence ('Nosey') Parker, and that was that.

The film was good and the three of them emerged a few hours later from the thrilling brutalities of antiquity into the balmy air of an early spring evening. They drank tea in a small restaurant off Derwent Street and then took their separate ways homeward. All of them were expected home by 10.30 pm and tomorrow was another day a school after all.

*Spartacus.* Georgina dreamed of him, of a muscular Kirk Douglas, crucified along the Appian Way with other rebels against Roman authority. How cruel! That beautiful body! Those eyes! How she longed to lie in those strong arms and gaze up into his deep, blue eyes! Her heart beat quicker as she lay in the folds of her warm bed. This was a man, the man of dreams. Wonderful. These were the first feelings she had sensed with regard to men. Only a few weeks ago, she reflected among the soft sheets of the bed, she had felt little about them. And as for her peers, she felt nothing for them. They were children, either stupid brutes or fools. But Kirk Douglas – what a man! And with this thought in her mind, she turned to fall asleep again, and all too soon the school day was upon her.

The weeks passed. Examinations came and went and then, at last, came the summer holidays. Then, suddenly, her period arrived. She was sixteen. "That's quite late," her mother had said. This she knew. Other girls had had their first flow of blood much earlier, even some at twelve, and when it came Georgina was glad of it. Somehow, she felt grown-up for the first time.

A glow passed through her body. She was a woman at last. She could have babies and the idea made her happy.

Children? And then, how strange! What is it like to have a baby? And who would be the man? He would be tall and strong and noble like Kirk Douglas.

And kind. He would look after her and she would be happy, wonderfully happy for the rest of her days. She would have lots of children, yes she would. For him whom she worshipped, yes, lots of children. It would all come true. She knew it would come true. One day.

But life, dammit, seems not to concern itself with our desires. Instead, it presents us with problems and tasks, which are often our quite alien to our wishes and inclinations. Mother again:

"Don't make any arrangements for August, Georgina."

"Why not?" Georgina had wanted to visit her pen friend in August with the money she hoped to earn as an assistant saleswoman at a nearby shop in the first weeks of the summer holiday.

"Because we're off to Ireland."

"But I don't want to go to Ireland. I know where we're going, and I've seen all those folks before." Her mother's face reddened slightly. "Your relatives, I suppose you mean? Don't talk of them in that tone of voice to your father, my girl."

Georgina resented the 'my girl'. She was no longer a girl. She was a woman.

The kid's days near Burton Port in Donegal were over. Good, they had been fine, but now they were over.

"And don't forget your dental appointment for this afternoon," her mother called after her as she flew down the stairs. She had forgotten. She wanted to forget. "Damn." Another afternoon spoiled by a dental appointment. "My teeth are quite all right," Georgina hazarded, but her mother ignored her. Dental appointment. Holiday in Ireland. And the wretched sea's so cold there! So no swimming. She longed to swim in a really warm sea. That was adventure. Evelynne, her French pen friend, had repeatedly invited her over to stay for at least three weeks. She lived in the southwest of France not far from the sea, a warm, beautiful sea. She had written about it in her letters. There, the sun shone all the time. Every day. Not like in Ireland. One day on, one day off. And then rain. And more rain. This year Georgina had planned to experience a new world in France. Tourism was in. Everyone went abroad these days for their summer holiday. Not just to English-speaking Ireland, but to real places abroad. Now all that was a dream, crushed by a visit to Ireland, Papa's odd relatives and the same old routine. What a bitter disappointment! Dental appointment! Bah!

The dental appointment, however, proved to be an experience of a kind she had not anticipated. Firstly, there was this young man who had looked at her in the waiting room from the corner of his eye, and then had looked away again as though he had been merely temporarily distracted from a picture in the magazine he was reading, one of some village or other in the Thames Valley. *Country Life* was the name of the magazine Georgina noted. She watched him slyly. The picture he was scrutinising could not have held so much interest as he was at pains to display, she concluded. Then she noted that he was really looking at her, secretively casting a glance at her and then returning to the illustrations of the magazine with exaggerated attention. On the third occasion of his looking, she tossed her flaxen hair for him in a gesture of slight impatience at such curiosity. He didn't look any more after that and she discovered to her surprise that she was disappointed. Anyway, he was too old for her, she assured herself. At least twenty-five. But... interesting nevertheless.

Then there was the dentist himself, Mr. Adams. He was a man in his fifties, married to the hilt, father of two sons, themselves dentists in other towns. Mr Adam's manner, it seemed to her as she took her seat in the adjustable dentist's chair, had changed. He was, well he was... what was the word their English teacher had taught them recently... 'ingratiating'? So ingratiating was he that Georgina was glad to find some relief in a short exchange with his female assistant, an older girl she had known since childhood. It wasn't of course, that Mr Adams didn't do his job properly. On the contrary, he was most thorough. Most attentive. He enquired, moreover, after the well-being of her parents at least twice during his attention to one tooth in particular, and twice used her dad's full title. No, it wasn't that. He was professional enough. "Is Lieutenant Colonel Hennessey enjoying his relative retirement these days? I mean from his active engagement with the army? Nice to see more of him at home these days, I suppose?" These were questions which she could only answer with a deep 'er' from her throat. She felt silly. Mr Adams went about his business of selecting this and that and nodding or saying something very briefly to his assistant before addressing himself to his patient with another volley of questions as though she were in the street.

"I suppose you'll be leaving school soon?" The buzz of the drill. She nodded as best she could in response to his enquiry.

"Now keep, still, my dear, it won't take long." Buzz. Georgina hated it.

"Swill."

And then she had been moved by the automatically operated chair to a slightly lower position in order to complete the job being done on her tooth.

And then, well, what could she say? It seemed that Mr Adams was leaning over her with, well... with delight. Yes, there was a dreadful glint in his eye as he prepared to probe the offending tooth again. Or so she interpreted this surgical procedure. Dreadful. He and she followed the same trajectural path downwards as the seat moved towards the floor. She was reclining and he was following. Ridiculous of course. But this eye, not a lustful eye, no, not that, but a delighted eye, the assistant being absent at that moment on some other administrative errand. Georgina wondered greatly. Mr Adams bored conscientiously. His eyes were not unlovely, Georgina thought as she looked into them. Kindly eyes. There was humour in them, too, she noticed and closed her own. It was the only practical means of self-defence at her disposal.

"Open wider," said Mr Adams, "That's it." He was busy pressing the amalgam into place. A moment later, Georgina was relieved to realise that Mr Adams' medical assistant was there again to offer a hand in drying the buccal cavity of its saliva. Georgina observed Peggy, the assistant, doing her job routinely. Could she possibly know what was going through her mind? As a woman, had she had a similar experience? Nothing could be detected in Peggy's practised movements. Swabs were tucked between Georgina's cheeks and gums. There was a conspiratorial exchange between the surgeon and his assistant, and the patient was left to feel silly and abandoned there on the chair, couchant, with a suction pipe protruding from her pretty mouth.

Then it was all over and Georgina was mightily relieved to regain both the upright position and with it, her dignity. Now Mr Adams was his old sober self again, businesslike, yet kind in his professional way. The scene had changed entirely.

"Peggy will make the next appointment for you," he said as he accompanied Georgina to the door. He smiled formally. Had she been dreaming?

"Another appointment?" she enquired, surprised.

"Another small filling, that's all. Nothing serious, I assure you," he added, the smile broadening. "Goodbye, now, and please convey my best wishes to your mother and father."

"Goodbye, Mr Adams, thank you." The door closed.

As I think I've said, Georgina was a well brought up young woman, but on the way downstairs from the surgery's waiting room to the hall where the appointments were made in that house, there was a nagging question in her mind. It was incommunicable, vague, and turbulent and demanded an answer. She wanted to talk to Peggy about it. But about *what* precisely? She reflected. About Adams? About Ralph G. Adams, dental surgeon, 12 City Walls. She longed to take Peggy aside and say...

"Would the 24<sup>th</sup> of October be all right? That's the only day I can book you in unless you have toothache," Peggy said. Her attitude was matter-of-fact. She smiled her professional smile and Georgina smiled back. Did Peggy even guess her thoughts? Georgina was then handed a slip of paper on which the day and time of the next appointment was written in Peggy's neat handwriting.

"Goodbye, Georgina," Peggy said simply.

"Goodbye, Peggy."

Peggy knew Georgina knew she knew.

The encounter between her and Mr Adams came shortly before the school holidays and in no time at all or so it seemed, the terminal examinations at school were over. The summer had arrived and the sun shone. Georgina had done well in her school tests, so well in fact that her form mistress had suggested university study after leaving school.

Trudy Johnson was about thirty, and not so very far removed from Georgina's young world, despite that fact. She was not, for example, like the other chaste sisters that taught at St Mary's Catholic Convent School to which her father had sent her. Georgina felt that those folks today were from another universe. Moreover, the two women liked each other. Trudy was a teacher who never lost her patience, although, God knows, she had ample opportunity with twenty-seven adolescent girls to deal with every day. No, Trudy was self-possessed, open minded, mature and – this Georgina valued in her above all – fair and just. She could also take criticism and she did so with dignity and good humour. These qualities, as I say, endeared her to Georgina and not only her. The other girls in Miss Johnson's class acknowledged her maturity. Moreover, Trudy was always well dressed, up-to-date, alert and sensible.

"Let's see, how old are you now, Georgina?" she had asked one afternoon when the two of them had finished going through Georgina's examination work. It was a rhetorical question, designed to deepen personal contact.

"Nearly seventeen."

The teacher admired the peach-like skin of her protégée's face. It was a second's observation: the skin had been recently kissed by the sun. Trudy also noticed the full, sensuous lips.

"This work is good, and if you continue like this until Christmas, you could easily qualify for the university entrance examination."

Georgina had never given the university a thought, even for a moment.

"What would you like to be in life?" Trudy asked gently. Georgina looked out of the window for inspiration and noticed the willow waving in modest glory in the light of the sun.

"I don't know; never thought much about it," Georgina said finally. She turned her green eyes towards her mentor. Miss Johnson noticed the beauty of these eyes and was moved. "Well, it's time you thought about it. Time moves on very quickly," she added with a smile.

"An air hostess, I think," Georgina said, suddenly inspired.

"For that you will need a good mark in your school

leaving certificate and a bit of luck. It's certainly within your possibilities." The teacher smiled again.

"But you're clever enough for something more demanding," she went on, "even though it's a tough job being a stewardess. What about biology in which you've got very good marks or even medicine in view of these?" Georgina felt warmed by the compliments and yet was still confused. While she was glad to find her efforts assessed so highly by someone she respected, she nevertheless didn't quite know what to make of her teacher's remarks. It was true, she supposed, that it was time she made up her mind about the future. But a doctor? A biologist? She had never really considered such things. The truth was that our heroine was almost sweet seventeen and had never been kissed.

That night, Gina lay in her bed and thought about these things. Was it possible that she was retarded in some way? The girls in her class had practically, without exception, had some experience of men. Far from merely being kissed, some of them had even been to bed with a man. 'What was it like', she wondered as she lay there. She reflected on the men she knew. Most of them were boys, she concluded, and she felt not the slightest attraction for any of them. She thought of her brother. After all, he was a man. She contemplated her brother for a moment. From her point of view he was a very self-centred young man. He was both the apple of his mother's eye and his father's minion, already well in the process of being manipulated into an army career. What did this young man possess that could make him sexually attractive? She didn't know. All she knew was that he had always received a great deal of attention and that he was soon to train at Sandhurst to become an army officer. No such educative thought had been spent on her. She realised that now. As far as a career was concerned, she was a non-runner.

She thought on. The army officers she had come into contact with via her father and brother were not the kind of men she would like to live with, and she saw very clearly now that the men to whom she had been introduced were not so much men she conceived as men, but simply father's colleagues. Somehow, for her they all seemed to lack something, but just what was lacking she could not say. By contrast, the image she conceived as a 'proper man' rose in her mind. He would be strong and protect her, but he would also be gentle and, above all, he would love her. That was a man.

'And what would he look like?', she asked herself. She honestly didn't know – Kirk Douglas perhaps?

That night she slept fitfully and, rising early in the morning, went to the window and there watched the light of dawn slowly fill the garden. How beautiful the trees were! As she watched, a feeling of great happiness came over her. 'What a wonderful thing it is to be alive!' she thought. The sun's light had caught the hedge at the bottom of the garden and turned it into a reef of diamonds. The lawn, too, was a carpet of light. She opened the window to be nearer this expanding glory, and the scent of early morning met her nostrils. She was so captivated by this that she put on her light dressing gown and ran down the carpeted stairs and through the house in her bare feet and from there onto the lawn. Here, she watched the sun climb into the sky above the hills a mile or two away. Then she sat down on a damp bench at the lawn' edge and recalled how many happy days she had spent her as a child together with her brother and with other children in the neighbourhood and with their dog, Sammy, who, alas, was no more, but very much a part of that happiness. 'Poor

Sammy,' she said to herself. 'Where is his doggy soul now? Does he still remember us all?' Despite her happiness at the wonder of dawn, her eyes filled with tears at the thought of Sammy's fluffy coat, his never failing, uncomplicated, demonstrative affection, his patience when he fell ill and at the last his quiet acceptance of his oncoming death.

The air was invigorating and she took in great lungfuls of it as she sat there. feeling the health that was in her pulsate and filling her body with vigour. The tears for dear Sammy fell onto the dewy ground, here to join the million jewels in the grass at her feet. Somehow, she knew he was all right. It was strange, but she knew this with absolute certainty. Heaven, she assured herself, had room enough for their pet.

She was never to forget this early morning and the very private communication she had with the dawn of that day.

Two weeks passed after this event and it was raining hard in Ireland in July.

Gina, her brother and a friend were on a long walk in the middle of it all.

"It's not the rain that's at fault," the friend had said, "It's all a matter of having the right clothes on. It's great then!" He was right, she supposed supposed, as they sloshed on through the damp, summer fields, saying 'hello' now and again to the resigned, dripping cattle and the fat-fleeced sheep huddling in their pens. They climbed the cloud-hung, purple hills bordering the sea and finally returned for tea at their tightly thatched house.

There, Georgina heard talk of the land and ate hot toast and jam at the fireside as if in winter, heard the kettle whistling on the coals and the big, black cat purring on the rug. All of it was the Ireland she remembered as a child. It was as it had always been, a relaxing experience, homely and wonderful in its way. Of course, father's relatives were there, too, some of the officer clan and others of the same ilk, but, she had to admit, it was not as bad as she had anticipated. No, it was not so bad, only... only she longed for young people of her own sex, longed for an intimate chat, longed to ask them questions that were untrammeled by school and all that went with it, and longed to hear what they would say, to hear it all 'in your own key' so to speak. Her brother's company was all very well in its way, but he was beginning to take an interest in things that didn't interest her at all, like farm tractors and the ins and outs of animal husbandry and so on like the other men hereabouts. Here, all the talk was of farming and of horses in particular and old times and how old so-and-so was doing these days and of how such-and–such had lately joined his father. Cancer of course. Dreadful business. And of Gina's cousin, twice removed, who had married at last now nigh to dotage and of another, much younger woman who had borne a sixth child. How John o' Toole and Henry Donovan had made good in the United States, and how little Tobias Mahoney had ascended to the fifth grade at school and was clearly a mathematical genius. And then there were the MacPherson girls still going strong now in their mid-sixties down at the Post Office in the village, and of old aunt Hennessey (no relation) now 102 and who would probably live for ever, and what a terrible shambles Park Farm had become in less than a couple of years. And did the visitors know that Bill Tipton – no, not the Tipton on Foley's Hill, but the other one near Loseby's Lodge, you know, the one with a cast in his eye – had been run over by an errant tractor somehow and was still half in heaven and half in his hospital bed deep in a coma at Everton Infirmary. And so on.

And so forth.

All of it delivered with such wit and charm that she always enjoyed these conversations and narrations. However, she was a listener for the most part, and rarely allowed to take part in these reminiscences herself. For most of the time, it was strictly a family affair, and perspectives stretched back some fifty years.

How was the colonel's daughter to know about these things?

Then the sun would shine again, and they would go out and ride down the cosy little lanes and from thence into the wide plains of the valley towards the blue-hazed mountains, happy in the steaming meadows and the smell of the earth of an Irish summer. The bedraggled mists would become snared and snagged among the trees. Now and again, they would hear the cry of the corncrake and the pheasant in the late wheat and the cries of the purling buzzards high in the sky. The sea was never far away, and then they would gallop at full tilt along the empty beach and, breathless at the end of such a sprint, watch the fretful ocean change colour in response to the moody skies above. They were good days, happy days.

"Georgy's form mistress has suggested that she might do well at university," her brother announced at tea-time a day or so later. The tea was poured in silence at hearing this. It was as though her parents and the neighbour who was with them on this occasion had not heard her brother's remark. After a short pause, Patrick continued so as to stimulate a reply, "I think it's a good idea, actually," he said.

"Well I don't," said her mother promptly. Father sucked the tea at the rim of his cup. Georgina turned to him in silent appeal. He smiled very faintly, but she read in this that he did not sanction such a thing, so she pre-empted his answer.

"Why not?" she asked. There was a pause, and then

Father pronounced, waving his hand in negation to her plea, "Because a young woman has to marry some time. It's all in the natural way of things."

"I can get married after my studies, surely, mother. Anyway, I don't know anyone I'd like to marry. I've never even thought about it."

"But we have," her mother said briefly as though to end further discourse.

"Oh, you have?" Georgina asked, half in a tone of defiance and half in astonishment,

"We have," her father confirmed quietly and with a complacent smile of satisfaction over the rim of the cup.

Georgina was both flabbergasted and annoyed at their presumptive demeanour. "Now you don't want to go studying," her father continued, putting the cup to the saucer with thoughtful deliberation. "Wasting the state's money. You'll never use the knowledge you're invested with at the university and you'll probably end up getting married anyway. That's the way it is in life." There was a pause. Then her father went on, "Let the plain ones go in for a career. That's their consolation." His son laughed loudly at this, and Georgina was about to protest when father held up his hand.

"Now a beautiful young thing like you shouldn't go wasting three, four or possibly more years at university, when she could beget children during that time."

"Beget children?" Georgina echoed in angry amazement, "I don't want to *beget* (she emphasised the archaism) any children. "If you want to know, I can't stick the noisy, messy creatures. Ugh!"

"But you'll love your own," her father consoled her, smiled and looked across at his spouse knitting at the fireside. Mother acquiesced with a wise nod of her head. "More tea, dear?" she enquired of Georgina's brother from this position. "Your cup must be empty." Little Sarah giggled at something or other. The neighbour affected not to have heard anything of the exchange.

"Well, I'm damned!" Georgina exploded, using an expletive she had picked up in the stables. Her mother was horrified.

"Well brought-up girls don't use language of that kind!" she scolded. "No daughter of mine uses that kind of filthy language and in that tone either!"

"It isn't filthy," Georgina countered and added hotly, "I've heard a lot worse than that this week."

"GEORGINA!" her mother and father cried in unison. Georgina, despite her anger, was still in possession of herself. Her fair countenance was flushed and her wonderful green eyes were bright. "And may I ask who this person is you have up your sleeves as my prospective husband?" The visitor shifted his feet uncomfortably in embarrassment.

"Never mind," her mother said with exaggerated calmness. She, too, knew how to make use of the occasion.

"So you think I don't have a right to know? Well damn me – that's the limit!"

"Georgina!"

Her father rose to his feet. "Don't you dare speak to your mother like that! I won't have that in my house. Such harlot's talk. Her father was angry now and the carotid artery beat fiercely at his neck, his face red to the hairline.

An angry Colonel Hennessey was a figure terrible to behold.

Georgina backed down, giving her brother a straight look. After all, he was responsible for this skirmish, and in the next moment, Georgina was up and off upstairs to her room.

Meanwhile, in the living room downstairs, consternation

and embarrassment settled like a paralysing narcotic over the little tea party.

Nobody had anything more to say. Even Sarah, the child, suddenly became as sober as an owl.

After a minute or so, the neighbour left discreetly with effusive thanks and with a 'don't trouble' and a 'thank you so much' and 'so kind' by the back door. After another five minutes or so, brother Patrick opened up with: "Mother, I will have another cup of tea, if you don't mind." Without a word, the strong brown potion was poured into the Wedgewood cup, and again silence descended, so that, later, the rattle of the empty cups was eloquence pure. After the crockery had been cleared away, and father had ensconced himself in his room, Patrick too took the opportunity to go upstairs. He knocked on Georgina's door.

"Yes?" came the irritable response.

"It's me, Patrick."

"Come in."

Georgina opened the door. She was in her underwear. "Are you going to bed?" Patrick asked a little bewildered, and noticing for the first time how desirable his sister had become. 'Well rounded', he called it later, and had to admit in the following few seconds while his sister retreated into the room to put on her jodhpurs, that she was a good-looking woman. He noticed as men do that her breasts were high and full, that her figure was firm and beautifully shaped. He could not help but notice, as she slid energetically into her riding hose that the curves of her youthful legs were another thing that he quite overlooked in the past. In addition to these matters, he noticed as well that her toenails had been painted bright red, and recalled in the same moment that mother had expressly forbidden her to do this.

"So you're going out riding?" he enquired.

"I have to," she retorted, "to get away from the stifling atmosphere of this place." Patrick looked a little dejected. "I'm sorry for bringing up all that," he said apologetically. "I thought I could mention the fact that you had done so well at school with impunity... promote you a bit, I mean. I hope you understand. You see, I feel you deserve a university education."

Georgina, who was fond of her brother, despite his faults and his infallible self-assurance, walked towards him. "I know that," she said gently, stroking her hand through his hair. Passion and anger had left her eyes. "Do you want to come with me?" she asked. He hesitated, then, "OK, we'll ride to Scarr Point and back."

"Good, let's go!"

And so they left the house and rode the five miles to Scarr and, inevitably, the subject of the tea table was revived.

"They're only thinking of your good, I suppose," said Patrick in response to Georgina's indignation at what had happened. "They just want to marry me off; that's what they want to do," Georgina said emphatically. Patrick reined his horse a little and said nothing in reply. "Like a prize heifer," his sister added and Patrick laughed. "All very well for you to laugh, Georgina cried, slightly piqued by what she considered to be tacit agreement, judging from his manner.

"Good God!" he said.

"Well, isn't it so? I don't know any eligible men, and have little experience with the other sex in any case. I have just had my first period and no doubt they take this as a sign for me to start reproducing as soon as possible. It's ridiculous: I'm not interested. I want to live first. Do you understand?"

Patrick was a little daunted by the mention of

biological detail, but that was the way his sister was fashioned. She had always been scrupulously open, honest and straightforward in everything. That was her nature. He liked her for it and at that moment he was warmed by the realisation that now they were two adults. They had a right to their own opinions, and he admired her for her candour.

"I imagine they're a bit short-sighted about it, I mean terribly traditional. That's the way it's always been done here: marry off your daughters as soon as possible to some well qualified suitor and so on. Nineteenth century stuff, you know. Ireland's a traditional country after all." Patrick scanned the horizon.

"Well qualified?"

"Well, money and all that."

"Money?"

"So that you never need to work," Patrick said by way of clarification. She looked at him. He hurried to explain in detail. "Never to be in need. 'To live in circumstances similar to those to which my daughter is accustomed,'" he added, ably adopting his father's upper-class accent and its tiny Irish nuances. At this Georgina couldn't help but shriek with laughter. Patrick was a good mimic. Then, just as suddenly, the smile fell from her face. It was a characteristic of hers.

"Well, I'm not going to be a baby machine. Not for anyone. And who's to be my suitor? Do you know that, Patrick Hennessey?" At this juncture, they were obliged to halt before a very narrow bridge spanning a stream.

Patrick did not answer immediately

"Come on, now; you know who they've got in mind, I'm sure."

Patrick was glad of the moment or two that they needed to negotiate the bridge in order to collect himself. He was very different from his sister in one respect, and nearly always chose to take either the least line of resistance or seize upon an opportunity to change the subject.

Others, too, had noticed this trait in him, but his reluctance to tell the plain truth, as now, almost invariably arose from a desire not to cause pain. He was a born diplomat this brother of hers. But he knew that he didn't stand a chance with his sister; he could hide nothing from her.

Once they had come to the end of the bridge, she drew her horse to a halt and turned to look at him squarely.

"Who is it?" she challenged him.

"James Rourke," Patrick said quietly.

"*What?* Jimmy Rourke! You must be kidding?"

"He's a nice guy – or what?" Patrick protested, astonished by his sister's reaction. "A nice guy? Firstly, he's about thirty-five, as old as the hills, and, well, just look at him, that beard and all…"

"What's wrong with his beard?"

"I hate men with beards."

"But you don't know him."

"Don't want to either. What I've seen of him is enough for me, drooling idiot!"

"Drooling?"

"Yes, he's a slimy as they come. All that 'sir' here, and 'sir' there when he talks to Dad. And that big, red, stupid face of his. Smokes like a chimney, too."

Patrick was nonplussed. It was his first encounter with female logic. For him, Jimmy Rourke was an admirable man, a splendid horseman and cricketer and a good raconteur. How many times had he, Patrick, laughed at his tales and jokes in the last few days? Moreover, he was tall and strong and versed in the ways of the world. Georgina's view of him was altogether beyond comprehension. Beard? What was wrong with his beard? Many naval officers had beards, didn't they? And as for his respectful bearing towards his father, this was only natural in view of their rank and experience. It was all quite acceptable. It wasn't 'slimy' at all. So far as Patrick could see, he wasn't trying to seek his own advantage with father either. 'But was he so keen on his sister?' he asked himself. Patrick hadn't noticed. So he tried to pacify his sister. "Oh, well," he said a moment later, "Perhaps it'll all come to nothing."

"You're too damn sure it will!" Georgina said resolutely, looking out towards the sun, which had begun to set over the sea. He had often seen this look of hers, this gaze into the distance as if seeking support there. He knew it meant determination. Inwardly, he shrugged the matter aside, and the two of them rode on for home, racing with one another from time to time along the shore for the last few furlongs. It was quite like old times and they both knew it, though neither said a word about their mutual feelings.

In the second week of August, the sun shone down upon Georgina's thick mane as she relaxed on the balcony of her small room. There were wonderful lights in her hair and it shone like finely spun gold. She always wore it loose over her shoulders so it reached the middle of her back.

Her mother, who kept her own hair closely cropped about her ears, was never tired of telling the girl to have it cut, since, in her view, it 'wasn't moral' to wear her hair so long. "Who do you want to impress with it?" she would ask, and Georgina would say quite honestly, "No one, why should I?" Georgy didn't even understand the implication the question carried. Her parents were for ever making a fuss about the length of her hair, but at the same time realised that to force her to have it cut short might lead to serious repercussions, and so they resorted to regular nagging and niggling until his lordship, James Rourke, RN, said one day by way of polite, casual observation, that he liked it as it was. Thus, the matter was dropped for a time.

And then there were these eyes that occasionally looked at the sun. Green, they were as I have said. But what a green! Call them cat's eyes if you will, and I will ask you what is wrong with cat's eyes? But that's neither here nor there. No, these green eyes were never cold as cat's eyes can sometimes be. No, here I am speaking of a phenomenal colour, a deep green that could change according to its owner's mood. They could laugh and smile at you or flash with fire. They could be loving and tender as happened this week when she played with the spring lambs at John Spooner's farm or as they looked now, delighting in the sun's pleasurable warmth. When you looked into these eyes, you were not only moved by their splendid colour, but also by the way she used them to engage you in her thoughts and feelings. There were depths in them as well as mere changes of mood. She said almost everything with her eyes. Now and again, just every now and again, there was a tinge of sadness in them. It was as if she suspected that the lambs were for the knife and that she knew that all things change and that everything was busy changing into something else, and that neither the flowers she so admired nor her own beauty would last for ever.

See her now as she holds her face to the sun, the straight, noble nose and below, her full, voluptuous lips that laughed to show you a perfect row of very white teeth. You will notice if you are a good reader of character that she also possesses a firm, well-developed chin above the soft neck. You can't fool around with a person who has a chin like that. She knows what she wants, this one, and she'll probably get what she wants as well.

Some time later, we find our friend sitting on the sunlit balcony adjacent to the bedroom in her bikini, although if her mother and father knew that she possessed this 'trio' to cover her essentials, they would be furious. No bikinis in this house. She may wear a bathing costume yes, but only at the sea when she intends to swim.

"Afterwards, you are to change into 'something decent', do you understand?" Though just at this moment as we watch her, she is sunning and thus sinning, but the Irish sun doesn't mind at all.

But let's leave this truly delightful scene for the moment and proceed to the 10th of August, three days after this sojourn on the balcony and a fortnight after the memorable tea party.

The table is laid again, for today is Georgina's birthday. It is the eighteenth year of her age. Guests hover at the door. Three neighbours, Mr and Mrs Leonard Earl, two English settlers in Ireland, retired people of substance and fortune, Mrs Molly Devlin, sixty, spinster of this parish, a charmingly dear lady who was for years in the service of the late Lady Elverstone, also of this parish; two officer gentlemen of the Royal Irish Guards, by God, forty-three years and fifty-one respectively, tall, upright, each with a trimmed moustache, the one fair and the other dark, Mr. Stanley Browne, aged fifty-six, small and red-faced with ferret's eyes to match, a 'fat, sleek-headed man who sleeps o'nights' in his expensive lawyer's hole at the other end of the village and the colonel's advocate. A Sir Charles Hill, fifty-nine, was there, too, a friend of the family, local MP, Justice of the Peace, one-time zinc prospector in Australia, married three times, divorced three times, even now a handsome piece of work, meticulously attired in tweeds and tie, Georgina's brother, Jane, the girl next door – and who is this – Mr. James Rourke himself. Almost all the company hold drinks of various kinds. At a tinkle somewhere in the throng, and an announcement to toast to the beautiful Georgina in their midst, everyone except

Mr Browne who cannot drink because of his high blood pressure, lifts a glass to her good health and long life. Eighteen! Goodness me!

They are a happy company indeed as they take their places at the fine, solid mahogany table that our colonel once purchased twenty-five years before in Singapore. Georgina is demure, happy to let the circumstances of her birthday take their course. Her father saves her a place at table next to Mr Rourke, and the two of them sit first to take their places followed by the rest of the guests. Port wine is poured. Outside, the sun shines upon the just and unjust with its usual indifference, and only her brother is aware of what might be going on in the birthday child's head.

Most of the folks around here indulge in some sort of agricultural activity, but mainly as onlookers and so the talk naturally turns to matters bucolic.

Mr Devlin, for example, an authority on pigs, opens play. "I understand, colonel, that you want to invest in livestock this coming winter?"

"That is indeed the case," the colonel replies jovially, "but we must have a clairvoyant in the neighbourhood. How did you know that?"

"Nothing of the kind," replies Mr Devlin, "I was talking to Willis yesterday, that's all, and it didn't appear to be a state secret."

"No, no, it isn't, and I recall mentioning it to Willis now. He knows the proper people of course."

"Of course," Devlin concurred, "he's a clever old fellow. Always in the know. Never puts a foot wrong when it comes to right judgement. He purchased ten sow for me last year, the best I've ever owned. I gave him something for Christmas for his trouble. Good man, Willis."

"Some more wine, Captain Rourke?" Mrs Hennessey

appears with a bottle in her hand. Captain Rourke gladly accepts the offer, surveying Georgina as he holds his glass towards his hostess. Georgina sits, smiling at the various compliments paid to her.

"Well, well," one of the guardsmen remarks, "sweet eighteen!" He means well, and his cheerful smile hides no implication other than a happy benediction. But Georgina is all too aware of the sequel to this observation. For a moment, it stings her. She asks herself deeply, 'Why hadn't she been kissed?' Then she immediately answers her own question: 'because she's never been in a position to be kissed. She would liked to be kissed and for a moment she looks at the guardsman and likes him. He's a friendly, good-natured fellow. She knows more about him in fact that he would like her to know.

It takes a woman but a few seconds to look into the soul of a man, believe me.

"What has become of your posting?" Mr Browne enquiries, "didn't I hear that you're off to Egypt?" Captain Rourke is embarrassed for a second or two, and can only bring forth a "Well, ah…"

"We've seen to that," the colonel says tactfully, and Mr Browne smiles a knowing smile, not much of a smile, but a knowing one, the smile of a man who knows the world.

The insinuation, however, was not lost on Georgina, who felt like those poor people must have felt in the Middle Ages and at other barbarous times who were walled up alive on occasion. Another brick had been set in position.

It is now Mr Earl's turn to harp upon the rural string. "And did you know that Jack Stockton has bought another 200 sheep for Haddon Farm?" he asked the colonel. The colonel didn't know, and for a second or two didn't realise that it was he who was being addressed,

"Oh really? Must be doing well," he replied.

"Oh, he's got all he wants in life, you can be sure of that," he added.

"Such a nice man, I always think," says Molly, hoping that the conversation will take a new turn, "always picks me up if he happens to pass by the bus stop. Such a sense of humour, a real gentleman, too."

At this point one could not be quite sure what was going on in the men's minds. Perhaps they are thinking that it's merely a female point of view. They had not thought of Jack Stockton as particularly 'nice'. For them, he was merely a canny individual, a man who knew for sure on which side his bread was buttered. And if he really had a sense of humour, they hadn't noticed it. Most people were possessed of a sense of humour in these parts. After all, one could go as far as to say that humour was the salt of all their exchanges. If it was true that 'speech was given to man to hide his thoughts' in other places, humour here was certainly that which gave speech an unerring truth. The gentlemen nodded politely at Mrs Devlin's comment and returned to matters in hand.

"They're Leicestershire, aren't they?"

"Aye, they'll fetch a good price at the end of the season in wool and meat. Fine bunch they are."

While they continued very much in this vein, Georgina reflected on this last remark. She recalled how, as a little girl, she had watched with horror and fascination as the poor creatures were laid one after the other on their backs while a man came along with a very sharp knife and slit their throats. Just like that. On that occasion she was where she should not have been and had observed the dreadful process through a fissure in the door at Fazeham slaughterhouse, had watched how the little hooves had paddled in the air after such treatment as though they were walking, and how, later, their pretty fleeces were peeled off their backs and slung to join others piled up to be taken off somewhere. For days afterwards she had had nightmares, and her parents had been very concerned. The little boy who had watched all this with her was sick on the spot and from that time on never touched lamb or anything else slain by the hand of man. Indeed, Georgina had never forgotten what she had seen on that day, and even now, seeing sheep dotted in the fields around was always reminded of their end.

She wondered if these casual conversationalists knew what was to follow after their flock had been herded up the lowered tailboard of the visiting cattle truck. She was sure they did.

The Earls talked about their neighbours. Molly Devlin's Irish treble weaving in and out of the conversation with a 'now there you're absolutely right, to be sure' and 'didn't know that at all?' and 'well, now, isn't that interesting?' Mr Browne, for his part, talked long with her brother, the guardsmen in trio with Captain Rourke, her father chipping in from time to time, while her mother chatted with Sir Charles, and so she was left more or less with her own reflections. She didn't like his moustache, she thought to herself, surveying the captain from the corner of her eye as she tackled the cake that had now been served on a plate before her. Nor the colour of his hair for that matter. True, he was tall and strong, no doubt of good physique, and yes, he looked nice in his uniform. And it was true that he could be charming when it suited him. She liked him to be charming. They had walked out together now for three weeks, always with John Appleby as chaperon with his pony and trap at a discreet distance behind them. But Appleby and his commissioners need not to have worried. James Rourke had never stopped to kiss her. Already, she thought, he takes me for granted. It was this that she resented more than anything else.

He had his feet under the table, this fellow. Perhaps he would be promoted on being posted to Egypt in command of a new frigate and was already a prospective relative. 'Was she in love with him?' she asked herself. 'No, she was not.'

And she had other things in mind, this green-eyed beauty with her thick, corn-coloured hair.

"I'm sure you would like another cup of tea, Sir Charles?" her mother enquired an hour later as they had now left the table to seat themselves at various places in the room.

"Don't mind if I do, by Jove," he returned, "Thank you Mrs Hennessey, thank you."

'She would go to the local hop, she would' Georgina thought to herself as she watched Sir Charles receive the tea. And she knew already with whom.

Not with James Rourke, no, but with Peter Belmonte.

Peter Belmonte was an acquaintance with whom she had spoken to gaily on many an occasion in the last few weeks. Peter had that something, which she could not define, but of which she was very sure.

Now Peter Belmonte was not, as might be imagined, a foreigner in these parts, despite his abundant, raven-black hair and his flashing dark eyes.

No doubt he was of Spanish extraction, since, hundreds of years before, the Spaniards had been blown this way with what was left of their Armada and their aspirations to conquer the larger, neighbouring island of Britain. They had not been successful, and the capricious sea and the boisterous, irresponsible winds of these parts had foiled their attempts to land – not to speak of a well-prepared British fleet under Sir Francis Drake and his associates with their disastrous fire and pitch. This, and the good seamanship of the latter had put the Spanish dream of conquest quite out of countenance. What remained of this badly mauled fleet of theirs was blown first ever northwards, where, in an attempt to negotiate a course to the west and south, it was battered to shreds on the sharp rocks of the northern Scottish coast. The Scots, for their part, murdered them like lambs. A few ignominious survivors finally reached the relatively calmer waters of the Irish Sea to the west where they were only too glad to set foot on *terra firma*, exhausted as they were after their arduous feat of rowing. The Irish received their fellow Catholics with open arms, glad, too, no doubt that they could entertain an English enemy. And so this is where young Belmonte had acquired his name and his looks. He knew that he was good-looking. He was older than Georgina and he knew about girls. Or so he thought. Anyway, there was no doubt about his experience with young women. Georgina fell for him. Every time she saw him, her heart beat a little faster. 'He's as handsome as a film star,' she said and was never tired of looking at him.

This young man, Peter, worked for her father as an ostler and Georgina used to ogle him secretly as he worked competently with the horses in the stable and courtyard. She admired the way he handled them, so strongly and firmly, but never harshly. He knew just what to do. That's what she wanted. She wanted him to take her in his strong arms and... and, yes, kiss her. Like they kiss in the films she had seen. 'Why had she never been kissed?'she asked herself again. It was time, was it not? It was high time.

"Georgina! Father has asked you a question! Are you deaf?"

"Yes, mother?"

Mother turned apologetically to the company. "Where are your thoughts, girl?"

"Oh, oh, sorry, mum, nothing," Georgina said mechanically.

"Nothing?" said her mother. "You see, she can't even say 'nowhere'"

Georgina then looked at her father with an enquiring smile.

"I asked you, dear," said her father gently, "whether you would care to join us on a visit to Dublin on Thursday. Sir Charles and I have business there and you could come with us if you wish."

Georgina noticed that Captain Rourke had already acquiesced. Yes, she did wish. She had never been to Dublin and felt that if she had to be with Rourke, at least the taciturn, all-seeing Appleby would not be present. The visit could even be enjoyable, she told herself.

"Yes, Dad, I'd love to come." She had allowed herself the familiar 'Dad' in company, and it seemed that he was not put off by the endearment.

And so it was arranged. The conversations remained more or less in the same gear, and Georgina fell back into thinking about Belmonte. She hoped beyond hope that they'd be back home by Saturday. Saturday was the night of the hop.

Ah, yes; the truth was that Captain Rourke didn't stand much of a chance with Georgy. He did his best, it must be admitted, while in Dublin to please the girl, was kind even generous. They visited places of interest together, took long walks as a couple and talked with one another, but the young woman's heart was not melted in his favour. Let us say this at once: Captain Rourke was in no way an incompetent suitor. He tried to interest the girl in his tasks on board ship and, in addition even to interest her in sport. He introduced her to tennis at one point on visiting a celebrated sports club in the city, gently and firmly placing her hand on the racquet and showing her a stroke or two. He was very patient. In the afternoon he rowed on the lake with her, and at her request also taught her how to row.

This brought them both a good deal of pleasure. His splendid uniform was soaked on this occasion, but he exhibited no annoyance and showed not the slightest bit of irritation at her clumsy efforts to row them any distance. On the contrary, he showed not only forbearance, but also a good deal of humour in all this. Later, he talked to her good humouredly about his job and his ambitions, introduced her to strong drink at an expensive bar, which to be honest, she hated, enthused about polo and updated her on naval history. He was tactful, cordial and well mannered, honest, thoughtful and intriguing. Nor was he a fool. He could see that he was not the man for her, but was man enough and gentleman enough to keep this to himself.

The only thing which really interested her was their mutual interest in horses. On this topic they were united in their enthusiasm and it was here that our young officer entertained a spark of hope. On all other subjects, though, he could see that her thoughts were elsewhere. Devastating, but there we are.

The colonel was annoyed. He had been watching them carefully when they were all together. "Can't think what the matter is with the girl," he protested, seeing that his plans were going awry.

"She may warm up, lad," he had assured Rourke on his reporting that Georgina had no plans to join him in wedlock. "Give her a chance," he had said, patting his younger colleague on the shoulder. "Early days yet."

Stiff upper lip and more. The seafarer as I have said, kept his disappointment to himself. For Captain Rourke, the trip to southern Ireland's capital was not only a disappointment, but a farce, and on his return home, he was actually eager to get away for a while and join his strong-armed rowing brethren at the club. There, he found solace among old school ties, a bottle of Scotch whiskey, officers and gentlemen. Men, after all, are easy to understand, are they not? Not like women who are such strange, unfamiliar creatures.

Meanwhile, Georgina, having returned on Saturday morning from Dublin, immediately sought the company of Mr Peter Belmonte on the pretext of the need to currycomb her horse. Belmonte, to her infinite satisfaction, was there at his place of work. She affected to ignore him, while at the same time keeping a strict eye on him. He, however, knew the game she was playing, but she, alas, did not know. The one question, which burned in her mind was: 'Would he be there on Saturday night?' After much earnest combing, she appeared on the other side of the horse so that she was in his full view. He had his hands full at that moment in urging a large, black, stubborn horse back into its box. This gave her opportunity to pause and watch. She watched how firmly he handled the animal, noticed the resolute, determined manner to get the upper hand of something at least ten times as strong as he.

"Whoa! There's my boy. What's all the fuss about? Eh? Come, come, my friend, gently does it..." and he firmly grasped the bridle and led the animal into the stall. Gina caught herself admiring the man's broad shoulders and his small, tight behind. She had never felt such instincts before, and drew herself up. She wondered in the same second what the good sisters at school would have said at such thoughts. Would they not have crossed themselves and spoken of the devil being present at such moments? But Georgy's heart warmed with delight as she saw him in the doorway after returning from the chore of fetching a yard brush.

"Morning, Miss."

"Morning, Peter. She called him 'Peter' deliberately and not 'Belmonte' as she might have done. He was known by his surname, as were all personnel here. To call him 'Peter' was to transgress and unwritten law of class distinction, a distinction, which was quite clear to all those who employ and those who were employed. In short, the one is responsible for the continued existence of the other, a fact that should not be forgotten and a law that should not be flouted.

The opening ploy was not lost on Peter Belmonte, who was more in control of the immediate situation than our Georgina.

"You're up early, Miss. Didn't you sleep well?" Belmonte enquired with a twinkle in his eye. He could take such liberty, because he was a lot older, because he was good at his job, and because he was appreciated by her father. 'A ready young feller' was the way he was described in and around the village.

"Oh yes, thank you; I slept well and you?" He laughed at her naiveté and didn't answer the question. Instead, he wordlessly helped her to saddle 'Beauty' the mare she had just groomed and made ready for her morning ride.

"Will you come away with me?" she asked, careful to mask her enthusiasm.

"I have to do here for a while yet, Miss. Later if you like."

"Good, I'll help you finish, then," Georgina cut in.

"It's not the amount of work so much; it's just that I have put in so many hours of stable work before early evening, and I've lost some time this week due to my mother being ill."

"Oh, really," Georgina replied. "Nothing serious I hope?" Here, she used her father's phrase and commiserative tone without realising it.

"Not much wrong, but the old lady took to her bed last

week, and I had to look after her." Georgina noticed the 'old lady', an epithet she wouldn't use to describe her own mother. She smiled and hoped that it was a loving one.

She found him interesting, and an hour later they were astride their respective steeds riding out into the countryside together.

"I love it here," the girl said with emotion; "it's wonderful." She was looking out towards the horizon as was her wont, and he looked at her during this short interval. The difference in station did not prevent him from admiring her firm breasts filling her riding attire with feminine abundance, nor the riding breeches stretched tight over her thigh and her hard, ample buttocks.

He desired her.

"Would you like to live in Ireland, then, Miss?" he asked.

She thought of him and his proximity "Yes," she said. "Don't call me 'Miss'" she added softly, looking him in the eye. "Call me Georgina."

"Georgina," he said, engaging her look. For a moment, there was a rapport between them, which would be difficult to describe in a few words. It had something to do with the balmy winds of those parts, the odours of late summer, the warmth of the horse's back, the way her thick hair danced to the breeze's caprice, her personal magnetism, her health, his youth and manliness, his clear eye and the way he did things, so surely and sensibly. And then there was the way he sat on his horse, squarely, horse and man as one, his hands as he held the reins – all this and indefinably more. For a long moment they looked into each other's eyes, and each knew what the other was thinking. He wanted to take her in his arms, and she wanted to be taken, but the moment had not come for this. Instead, they veered off to the left, took a woodland route and talked of the weather and the views presented to them as they rode along.

"If only there were more of this," Georgina sighed, "just riding like this: the wind, the sky, the freedom."

"Don't you feel free, then at other times, Miss?" She looked at him

"I mean 'Georgina' It seems so strange to be familiar to you. I mean, if your dad heard me calling you 'Georgina', I'm sure he wouldn't approve." She chose not to comment on this, and sought to answer his question.

"Free? I don't know. No, I don't think so. School's a bind. Three times a week attendance would be all right and quite enough, but five and half days a week. Ugh!" He smiled at this.

"Then there's the family and my father in particular. I've recently learned that he wants to marry me off."

"Like they used to in old times?" He said this with genuine sympathy.

"Yes."

"And what about the suitor?"

"Totally *un*suited," she replied, stressing the first syllable."

They laughed. "And you, Peter?"

"Well, I suppose riding's my love. One day, I'll have my own stable and hope then to be able to charge for my services, instead of being paid for them."

They rode on for quite some time without speaking. The terrain required their concentration. Then she asked, "Don't you want to travel, see the world and all that`?"

"I'd like to visit the USA and also Peru in South America."

"Peru? That's odd. Why Peru?"

"Don't know exactly. You're right; it's a bit odd. Perhaps I want to get away from things a bit. Dunno. But I would like to see that marvellous ancient civilisation I've read about. I'd like to see the remains of their culture."

"The Incas, you mean?"

"Yes, that's right." They negotiated a steep descent, the horses slipping a little on the scree underfoot.

"What's your favourite colour, Mr Belmonte?" she asked then suddenly, smiled at him.

"Red. And yours?

"Red and gold are mine."

"When were you born?" she asked as the horses slowed down at the bottom of the slope.

"19th May at 9 am. Time for work. A sensible hour, don't you think?" he bantered.

"That makes you Taurus. I'm Leo. Just had a birthday."

"When?"

"Tuesday last."

He raised his eyebrows at this, and noticing, she asked, "And… ? But he interrupted her.

"Leo folks are proud people. They are kings; everyone else is a subject."

"Well," she corrected, "they're independent, if that's what you mean. Can't stick folks breathing down their necks."

They rode on. Clouds were gathering. The farmhouse was coming into sight.

"Are you walking out with Captain Rourke?" he asked suddenly.

"Yes, why?" She hoped somehow that he would ask. It would clear the air. She could tell him then that she was not particularly interested in Rourke, but before she had a chance to say this, the farmyard dog came racing towards them and his attention was diverted for a moment.

There was a row at home about Georgina's determination to go to the local dance. "Your duty is to stay at home now that you have a man who wants to marry you," her mother said loudly so that father, who was in the next room, could hear. Georgina was invariably annoyed at this dependence on "father's final word" in all matters of decision. Why did she have to be so servile? Couldn't the woman herself determine what was to be done?

"He might want to marry me, but how do you know that I want to marry him," she retorted. "Anyway, he hasn't said anything about marriage – not to me at least." Georgina raised a face of protest towards her mother, and at this, her father appeared in the doorway. "She wants to go dancing this evening at that low place down the road," her mother declared.

"You're not going," Colonel Hennessey replied peremptorily.

"But Dad!"

"That's enough!"

Now Georgina was generally a brave girl (sorry, young woman), but this was the last straw. The unfairness of it all. She was a prisoner in her own house, their house. She was something that could be sold to satisfy *their* desire to have a daughter married to someone of *their* choice and class. She had no feelings for this someone and little in common with him either. She said as much and added, "I'm young and want to enjoy myself. Just as you did when you were my age. Why shouldn't I go dancing?"

"Enough!" her father said again.

"We don't want you to mix with the riff-raff of the village, young people who get drunk and vomit – even the girls these days – and all that noise and dirt," her mother said, and added," We're respectable people. What will they think of us, seeing you there?"

"Now I hadn't thought of that one," Georgina remarked sarcastically with tears in her eyes.

Her father was furious at this affront and his red face was suddenly redder.

"Go to your room, you impertinent young hussy! First you swear like a trooper and now you think you can treat your mother like a servant girl.

Go!" he commanded, pointing to the stairs.

At the seventh hour, her brother Patrick appeared in the living room and was met by silence and two glum faces. In the first few minutes of his arrival, he busied himself with removing his wet shoes and with shaking the rain out of his hair. Returning to the living room, he asked cheerily, "What's up? Is there anything wrong?" It was a purely rhetorical question and quite ridiculous in the circumstances. Mrs Hennessey looked into the fireplace without a word and Patrick appealed to his father with an enquiring look and received the response, "That sister of yours wants to go dancing at that awful... awful." He indicated somewhere in the direction of the wall, irritated by the fact that he couldn't recall the name of the place that deserved so much contempt. "The Trocadero you mean perhaps," Patrick suggested helpfully.

"Yes, that dirty place."

"Oh, Dad, it's really not that bad," Patrick contradicted and, pulling off his jumper, placed it to dry before the fire, for although it was late August, the evenings were already cooler. The fire, moreover, added a certain cheerfulness to the place.

His father glared.

"No, really Dad; looks much worse on the outside than it actually is," Patrick said lightly.

"You've been in that hole?"

"Yes."

"Ugh!"

"It's quite nice inside," Patrick persisted. His mother listened morosely, ensconced in her chair.

"No kidding, Dad. Georgy will be bitterly disappointed." Here, brother Patrick used his maturity to take a little liberty both with the word 'kidding' (for the colonel a contemptible Americanism) and that of 'disappointed', which might have been construed as a tinge of admonition in the way it was intoned.

"Trocadero. Ugh!" his father puffed, and at this Patrick could not but for the life of him recall the sound apes make when dissatisfied with something or other. He laughed inwardly.

"Don't call her 'Georgy', Patrick. It's a ridiculous diminutive. And what do you mean by 'disappointed'?" he probed peevishly.

"Well, Dad, she's young. By the way, I hope I'm old enough to go?" he asked with a friendly, engaging smile.

"What? To that flea-pit? What will folks say of us?" his mother then asked from the hearth.

"Tom Hall's going. And Steven Hollis – at least three of us. It'll be nice to see some women for a change in our respective professions, either marching with other fellers or at sea for months – and outside a church," he added with a air of conviction, smiling at them both in turn with a salesman's self-confident acumen.

His father puffed again and his mother rose to attend to something.

Colonel Hennessey kept his fingers curled on the arms of the chair he then lowered himself into, "You know what she's like," he said under his breath, almost in a man-to-man tone, a question in his manner. Patrick lifted his eyebrows. "She'll be all right if she comes with me, now won't she?" he said, turning his thick pullover over to toast on the other side in front of the flames of the fire.

"Mother!" Hennessey roared, and mother appeared immediately from the neighouring room, teacloth in hand.

"Shall we let her go with her brother? He's promised to look after her, hasn't he?" and here he looked meaningfully for a long second at Patrick "And be back at ten!"

"Eleven."

Father's look blazed at this prompt amendment, and Patrick, who knew his father all too well, added quickly, "The dance finishes at eleven, you see, Dad, and I want to be there at the end. It's only reasonable, after all. It's a happy get-together for everyone who has taken part and there's the distribution of some prizes for the best dancers." Throwing up his hands in a dismissive gesture, he concluded, "You good folks worry too much. I'll see her right."

"10.30."

With a sigh of exhausted patience, Patrick turned to them." Look Dad, Mum, she's getting on; she's eighteen, not thirteen."

"All the worse!" the colonel asserted loudly, "You let her be kissed or mauled by one of these country knaves, young feller, and I'll wring your ruddy neck."

Father and son looked at each other like two boxers while the clock ticked audibly on the mantelpiece.

"Understand?" the colonel bawled.

"Yes, Dad. Of course. Please don't worry. I'll take care of her as I've always done." Mother squeaked disapproval from afar. Father relaxed a little at hearing this assurance

"What was that about a church, Patrick?" Mother called from the kitchen.

"Oh, nothing, mother, nothing of any importance," and he leapt up the stairs to tell Georgina the good news. Her door was closed. He knocked three or four times before she opened it.

Her face was red with crying, he noticed, and she merely left the door open for him and ran back into the room, throwing herself face down onto the bed. Patrick closed the door quietly behind him and whispered,

"It's OK, girl; I managed to get round them." He paused between her sobs. "But we'll have to go together. I think you ought to do something about your face right now. It's 7.30pm."

Georgina turned and half raised her body from the bed. "Oh, Patrick, you're an angel!" She jumped up and threw her arms around his neck. Patrick, a little daunted by this show of emotion, pulled her arms from his neck gently saying, "OK, OK, get changed and I'll see you downstairs," he said, a trifle ruffled from the fray.

When, perhaps twenty minutes or so later, Georgina appeared at the bottom of the stairs, she looked truly beautiful. Her youth was mainly responsible for this of course, the roundness and curves of young womanhood did the simple but elegant dress justice. Her mother looked at her with mixed feelings, pursed her lips in reluctant acquiescence and then said, "You'd better wear a mac or something. It's still raining." Nothing else occurred to her as she stood there in the presence of her daughter's overwhelming beauty. Georgina moved towards the door. "Bye, Mum, bye Dad," Georgina cried, leaving two still slightly disgruntled parents. Father seated himself, coughed his brief, impatient, cough, and took up the *Shire News* without another word.

And so off they went, brother and sister, into the soft drizzle of an Irish evening, and arriving at the Trocadero, they discovered that the foyer was already crammed full of young people and the air thick with tobacco smoke.

Patrick bought tickets for the two of them, and gradually they entered the fierce light of the ballroom proper. Georgina was tense. Would he be there? She looked around nervously. She couldn't see him. Our girl (there we go again) was intent on one thing only this evening. She wanted to get as near to Peter Belmonte as possible. If she had a dream at this moment, then it was to be in his arms and dance with him through the night. As it happened, she was asked to dance by several youths during the evening and nevertheless enjoyed herself greatly. At last, she felt free and happy. But where was he? Would he come at all? Perhaps not. An hour passed and then to her joy she spied him laughing in the company of four young lads at a table at the edge of the dance floor. And – he had seen her! She pretended not to have noticed him, and made as if she were thoroughly enjoying herself in the arms of another, which, I might add, delighted her partner. Then, a few minutes or so later, HE was there, asking her to dance with him. He proved to be a good dancer and in the hour that followed, she was happier than she had been for years.

The two of them danced for the rest of the evening, and Patrick, her brother, often looked towards them across the hall through the spinning, twisting figures on the ballroom floor, through the whirl of dresses and the hot, flushed faces, through the thin, blue smoke under the dappled, rotating, coloured lights above and the vigorous sound of the eleven-piece band, playing for all it was worth, watched through the dust of clothes, through the heat of that place, hearts beating, lungs panting, eyes bright, souls stirred to the excitement of African rhythms.

When they had finished dancing, Georgina looked for him, trying hard to single him out in the noisy crowd and wondered what he was thinking. But she didn't really care; she was enjoying herself. And wasn't he wonderful, this man, this man to whom she already felt attached? Was she falling in love? She believed she was. After the dance and its celebrations, she walked home with him, the two of them along the tree-lined lane that led for two miles to the farmstead.

"Look, there's the moon!" Georgina said, pointing through the trees above them, as it appeared for a moment behind the ragged, scurrying clouds. "They say people do funny things by full moon," she added, looking at him in its sudden light. He stopped a moment and turned to her looking rather earnestly into her eyes. She wondered and rather hoped that he would stop and kiss her now. It was the right moment. But he walked on with her in silence. As they neared home, he said, "I hope no one's abroad at this hour." His eyes scanned the dim outlines of the farm in the distance. 'What did it matter?' she thought to herself. Her heart was so full.

"We shouldn't be seen together, that's all," he whispered.

"Why? Are you ashamed of me?" she asked with a giggle to hide her true feelings. He smiled in the moonlight, but she was a little disappointed by his reserve. Yes, she was in love; she knew it. Then they had reached the farm's gate and the two of them stood there, saying nothing. Now was the time to kiss her if at any time, she thought. He turned his face to her. "Good night, Georgina," he said almost formally. And she, too, rising to the unwelcome occasion, said "Good night, Peter. We'll see each other in the morning."

"Yes. Tomorrow. Good night. Sleep well."

"You, too," he said and slipped away down the road to the cottage where he lived with his mother. Georgina watched him disappear into the gloom, and then wandered into the yard, happy, but a trifle disappointed. A light was burning in Patrick's bedroom, she noticed, as she neared the house. He was waiting for her. As she made for the front door, Sasha, their dog barked at her briefly before coming to greet her, rubbing his sturdy body against her legs and putting his wet nose into her palm. "Good boy, there's a good lad, but hush for God's sake, hush!" The dog then trotted the rest of the way to the door with her.

She threw a small pebble at Patrick's window, but Patrick had heard the dog and was already at the door with a torch as she made to open it.

"You've left it a bit late. It's already midnight," he said.

"Do they know?" she whispered.

"No, they're out," Patrick hissed. "Come in quick! I will wait up for them, and you're lucky, my little sister, by God, you're lucky! Why do you take such risks?" He looked a little annoyed, his handsome face full of concern as he closed the door behind them. *I have to carry the can, not you.*"

"Oh, I'd get it in the neck as well, you know that," she answered.

"Come," said Patrick, "this is no time for argument. Get off upstairs. Good night!"

"Good morning!" she giggled. Patrick turned, saying, "I'm going to get myself a drink. Off with you." She kissed him affectionately on the cheek. "You're a brick. Thanks, my wonderful brother," she said and flew upstairs as the sound of tyres could be heard outside on the gravel. Belmonte's instincts had served him well, she thought as she undressed in the darkness and threw herself into bed without troubling to wash.

It was now late August and the sun was weaker than it had been through the earlier part of their holiday. From time to time, there was a cool wind sallying in from the sea, sweeping over the beach and up against the green mountain foothills. These winds were the first scouts of winter. The mornings were quiet and crystal, as if the world had stood still for a while. Georgina loved early autumn. And she loved Peter Belmonte as well or thought she did. She wanted more than anything else to be kissed by him, and that before the holidays were out. To this end she had laid her nets in which Mr Peter Belmonte would be caught. Instinctively, she knew what to do.

Not many days after the dance, the stable lad had a day off, and it was on this day, too, that Georgina would also take a 'day off' as it were, and see to it that she would be at his disposal on that day. She planned that on that day she would ride with him to Roscoe, some twelve miles away, far from the farm on a day when she knew that the colonel and his spouse had business for a day long in a nearby market town in the other direction. With great tact, she broached her proposal to Peter, who quickly agreed to the suggestion, and so it was.

The day came and the two of them set off for their destination as soon as their elders drove off in their car for the busy market town of Cork.

The autumn sun shone warmly on their backs as they rode, in the fields and woodlands around. It was good to be alive. They picnicked together, laughed in each other's eyes and at 2.34 pm, to be precise, it happened. They had been talking about the films they had enjoyed until that moment when suddenly and without warning, without even so much as a prelude to the act, this Belmonte laid his lass on her back and fastened his mouth on hers. In the first few seconds she enjoyed the position and was glad to submit to anything he had mind, but also surprised. Emotions followed one another in chain reaction. He was heavy; his breath smelled from a recent cigarette; he had pinned her down so that she could not move; she could hardly draw breath. She felt the hardness of his erection on her thigh. She tried to say something. For a moment, she didn't know whether the attack was pleasant or unpleasant, but a second or two later she realised that his tongue was in her mouth and knew that she wasn't ready for this. He pressed his lips so hard against hers that it hurt. She made a noise of protest in her throat and then a huge effort to move, but movement was hardly possible. He was now fully on top of her and she was no longer sure of what was happening. His hand searched for her breast, which he took roughly, pinching the nipple and gripping the organ with such pressure that she cried out in pain. Still he didn't let go and his mouth was fixed to hers like a clamp. Seconds passed in this horrible clinch until, as suddenly as before, his hand passed swiftly between her thighs. With all the force she could muster, she used her strong legs like a lever and threw him off as a wrestler would.

"What the hell... ?" she shrieked, but he grabbed her again and threw her back into a soft patch of grass, this time deliberately pinioning her arms above her head, looking down at her, his hard penis on her *mons pubis*. His eyes were wild and full of intent, and again he descended to kiss her, but this time she turned her head away before he could do so. For the first time, she noticed his nicotine-stained teeth.

"What the hell do you think you're doing?" she yelled. "Get off!" Her blouse was open to fully reveal her breasts, since she was not wearing a bra.

"You look good," he said to her surprise. 'What the devil does he mean by that?' she thought. 'The fool! I don't look good for him.' Then he made a thrusting movement with the lower part of his body and she panicked.

"GET OFF AND STAY OFF!" She screamed, but he remained in the same position, smiling an unpleasant smile, his strong arms still fixing her to the ground, and enjoying her anger and vitality.

"LET ME GO, DAMN YOU!" For a second or two longer he held her in check and then his face clouded to a mixture of anger and disappointment. He rolled off her, stood up and walked over to a nearby log, sat down, and lit up a cigarette, completely ignoring her.

Confusion reigned in Georgina's mind as she buttoned her blouse, noticing as she did so that a button was missing, and knowing, too, that her mother would be the first to notice. She searched for it in the grass, but in vain. Her dress was well past her lovely knees, revealing her strong legs. In the bright sunlight, she noticed that they were covered in very fine, smooth hair and recalled, absurdly in the circumstances, what her biology teacher had once said in class about all mammals except whales are covered in hair. Her legs were scratched and her dress creased. It bore witness of the struggle where it had come into contact with the damp, dirty ground. She straightened herself up and settled her mind and turned her attention to Peter, who seemed to have forgotten that she was there. Her breast hurt where his fingers had grasped her and she was not inclined to open the conversation. She felt that he should apologise to her. A full ten minutes passed while a bird sang in the thicket. Both of them heard the sound, but neither listened because they were so preoccupied with their own thoughts. At last, Georgina went towards her horse, the silent champing witness to her first kiss, put a foot in the stirrup, mounted and turned the animal's head towards the path leading homewards. Coming abreast of Peter, she paused, looked down at him and waited for a response. He looked up for a moment and they looked at each other in silence. He was downcast and seeing his dejection, she asked, "Are you coming?"

"Yes," he answered with wearied resignation, and trudged to his own horse, swinging himself easily into the saddle. She watched with stifled admiration at the easy firmness he managed the mare and together they rode slowly through the glades of early autumn, sometimes alongside each other and sometimes in single file, according to the lie of the ground, both of them in deep reticence.

It was almost an hour later when they passed Oak Lake and a 400-year-old monumental tree nearby and they paused for a moment. They spoke for the first time.

"Why?" she asked quietly

"I'm sorry."

"*Why*? She asked again emphatically.

"I mistook your signals all morning, that's all, "he replied.

She looked at him comprehendingly. With a little irritation in his voice, he said, "All this 'come on' stuff and 'try to kiss me if you dare!', this gay laughter, all this mock coyness and so on. I thought you were asking for it."

This was offered with some self-justification as though to say 'It serves you right; you shouldn't do such things'.

"I wanted you to kiss me," she said simply. "That's all I wanted. Just a little tenderness." He remained silent.

"I thought you wanted sex.

No," she said." Not that."

"Oh," he said, his voice very small.

"Love comes before sex," she said, surprising herself with such wisdom. "Anyway, I've never had sex, "she said.

"No one?" he asked in surprise.

"No one." Silence. They rode on. When the cry of the gulls came within earshot, he reined his horse in and pulled at her sleeve. They looked at each other again. "I'm really sorry," he said, and she could see that he meant it.

"Me, too. I mean that our holiday had to end like this. He looked miserable, and his fine, sun-tanned features confirmed what he said. She felt compassion for him and added, "Peter, dear, you just didn't understand my 'signals' as you call them, that's all. She smiled and looked at him kindly, lovingly. He nodded. "Guess so," he said resignedly. It was then that she desired so intensely to kiss him and feel herself loved in return so that it hurt behind her bruised breast and much more keenly than the bruise, but she knew that she was now in no mood to make what he might consider another move towards him, and so they rode on into the waning afternoon.

The sea came into view in the distance for the second time, and when they had come to where the wood bordered the beach, she pulled up her horse and turned to him again. He seemed unwilling to pause and she knew that he was willing to leave her. This, too, made her sad.

"You were just far too impatient." She began to cry.

"I would have given you everything, but not like that. Not so soon."

She could sense his eagerness to go, felt that he didn't need to be lectured, knew that he didn't understand. Nevertheless, she turned to him to ask,

"Do you understand what I mean? It's important for me to know."

"Yes," he said meekly, and paused a second before asking, "You won't tell your father?"

"Oh, Peter, what kind of a person do you think I am?"

"I'd lose my job, you know."

She spurred her horse and cantered towards the beach. Anyone who could be so uncomprehending, she thought to herself, is past anything I can say to him. If only he could show her that he understood her feelings, the afternoon could have been saved, despite what had occurred, and perhaps her love for him could have even deepened. But not now. It was over. Suddenly, she was looking forward to the tea her mother would be preparing in an hour. At least that was some consolation.

They said no more to each other for the length of the journey home, and 200 yards before their arrival at the farm, they said goodbye to each other. It hurt her more than she had expected, for inwardly she knew that she would never see him again.

That night she lay awake considering the farce that had been her first kiss. More than a farce. It had been a truly horrid experience. And she had been on the point of falling in love with this ruffian! Bah! What a fool she had been.

# 2

Dear Gina!,

Greetings, greetings greetings! *Bise!* I embrace you. But what has become of you? For many months I have not heard from (of?) you. Oh, my English!

Do you live now in England or Ireland? – *très belle la côte irlandaise.* You will come to (and?) see me soon? I hope so. I look forward to my friend's visit this summer, but she says *Non. Quel domage!* Please write to me quickly. How is it you come for *automne*? Yes? *Merveilleux!* I expect you. Come soon.

*Avec des salutations très affectueuses,*

Your Evelynne

PS: I buyed a little cat – he is wonderful. His name is Tommy. You will love him.

EV

Georgina read this excited epistle several times before putting it in her drawer. This is where she placed all her precious things and which she kept locked. She turned the key in the drawer and then popped it into her handbag before going over to the window where she stood quite still for several moments, taking in the scene. Below, on the terrace, she could hear Mrs Tucker, their housekeeper, collecting the dishes after the evening meal.

Beyond this terrace was a long, wide stretch of lawn, flanked at intervals by fine, old trees and, halfway down it length, a tennis court, and at the very end of the garden a small house where in an earlier generation, the gardener used to live. But that was a long time ago. Today, this little house was divided into two apartments, each with a separate entrance to the road outside, and occupied during term-time by two students who lived their own lives, and who were only encountered on rare occasions. Father had long entertained the idea of apportioning part of the large area now occupied by the lawn to an outdoor swimming pool, but the plan had never materialised.

The one thing Georgina loved above all about this garden was its huge, 250-year-old cedar of Lebanon, which at the moment stood fifty yards away to her right. She loved this tree, and truly it was a majestic plant over 200 ft high.

The evening was warm for the time of year, she noted, and it was extremely unusual for them to have eaten outside on the terrace in the second week of October. The nights were drawing in, it was true, but the warm weather was holding.

On her return to England a week before, Georgina had taken matters into her own hands and applied to London University to study biology. What she would do with a degree in biology, she was not sure, but felt it better to qualify in something, rather than merely seek employment to gain a certain independence. After all, she assured herself, she had a brain, why, then, should she not use it? The insecurity, which accompanied the contemplation as to what she should do later as a qualified biologist was dismissed by her strong will as a concession to her father's conviction that she marry as soon as possible.

Elated by good examination results – she had passed in physics and chemistry as well as mathematics – and to further consolidate her independence of mind as well as put the wishes of her parents beyond the possibility of realisation in the near future, she had, on the recommendation of an older, male friend, applied – 'just for the hell of it' as she said later, to the university's school of medicine. To avoid parental discovery, she had given her friend's address as her permanent one.

Three weeks or so after her application the telephone rang in the hall at the bottom of the stairs where she happened to be at that instant. She lifted the receiver. "Georgina? It's me, Gerald. There are two letters waiting for you here. Do you want to collect them or shall I bring them over?"

"No, wait a moment." Her mother was on the carpeted stairs not far from where she was standing.

"We could meet somewhere if you like?" Her mother had paused in her ascent and was listening to what was being said. "We could meet somewhere if you like?" Georgina said again weakly. She was disturbed by her mother's proximity. "Where do you suggest?"

The good Gerald, however, was quick to apprehend the situation, and added: "Let's say Luciano's Coffee Shop in Sheep Street, say in fifteen minutes. That's not far from your place. I'll wait for you. All right?"

"Yes, that's fine. Thanks!" Georgina put down the phone.

"Who was that?" her mother asked, halfway up the stairs.

"Oh, that was Gerald, an old friend of mine," our blonde replied nonchalantly.

"You mean Gerald Monroe, the art teacher at the college?" her mother asked.

Georgina was taken aback at this, since she didn't suspect for a moment that her mother would know Gerald. "Yes, why do you ask?" she said, and her expression wore a quizzical look.

"He's far too old for you. At least thirty. What do you want with him?" her mother pursued narrowly. The enquiry, as well as the way it was conducted, irked her daughter, and Georgina turned on her mother and said slowly and carefully, so that her mother would have no doubt as to the import of her communication, "Gerald is *not* a suitor. Gerald is just an older *friend*, an educated gentleman whose company I enjoy from time to time over a cup of tea or coffee as the case may be and whom I've known since I was twelve years of age and who, by the way, is very married." She said this slowly and succinctly. Mother was not pleased by this pedantry, but indicated by her manner that she had accepted the facts of the situation. She proceeded upstairs. At the top of the stairs, she called out, "Back at 9.30 pm sharp!"

This, if you like, was a show of arms, a rattling of the sabre. Her father at this time was in the library, playing cards with three of his clan and was safely out of the way for at least another two more hours, she considered, but for all that, it was still another demonstration of the ultimate upper hand for Georgina, and she had come to resent this rein on her independence more and more. Why? Other young women of her age had 'steady' boyfriends, yes, slept with them, even went on holiday with them, did wonderful things with them, were grown up, self-assured, lived either alone or with their respective beaux and planned their futures together while she, *she* had to be home at 9.30pm. Peeved, she turned to the coat hanger in the hall, donned a light jacket and made for the door without replying to the monitory figure at the top of the stairs. The door slammed behind her.

When she arrived at Luciano's Place, as everyone called it here, Gerald was already at a table, sipping a cup of hot chocolate, his favourite beverage. Entering the café, Georgina was quick to spy his florid face and the rapidly greying hair swept back from his forehead. Gerald, she knew, was homosexual, and Georgina had always considered this strange in one, who, was married to a good-looking woman of the same age and who had sired two children. Had he turned to a new habit of living in the last few years, she asked herself as she made her way to a small table at the end of the room. Gerald rose to greet her. He was tall and slim and his manners were impeccable. The nice thing about Gerald, she told herself, was that he was not merely polite, but also sincere. One could trust him. One felt good in his company, and he had a great sense of humour. He helped her to a chair, and as he did so she wondered who else in this town would show such consideration. After she had sat down, she looked round and noticed that people were staring. This habit among some people was beginning to annoy her. Gerald, though, beamed and asked her what she would like to drink. "*Cafe au lait*," she replied promptly. It was a social habit these days to drink coffee as well as the traditional tea on this island, although, strictly speaking, she was averse to coffee. Gerald ordered. She noted the capable, strong hand and the gold ring on the fourth finger as he turned to the waitress. He had a smile for the waitress, too, this dear, sensible, collected Gerald.

"Hope it's good news," he said as he produced two buff envelopes from his inside pocket. Before releasing them from his fingers, he added, "What's it to be, biologist or doctor?" He grinned broadly.

"I don't mind so long as I can study. Get away from home," Georgina said bluntly.

"Is it so bad?" Gerald asked, an expression of concern passing across his handsome features as the *café au lait* arrived. Georgina said nothing, but confirmed his enquiry with a grimace as she tore open the letter.

UNIVERSITY OF LONDON

SCHOOL OF MEDICINE

RE: YOUR APPLICATION FOR A PLACE OF STUDY, DATED 6TH SEPTEMBER, 1955

Dear Miss Hennessey,

The Board of Commissioners has considered your application and is happy to inform you that your qualifications are appropriate for acceptance into the school of medicine at this faculty, and that a place has been provisionally reserved for you. This is subject to an interview which will take place at 10 am in Room 114 on 18th October.

Yours sincerely,
W.S. Cornfield
(Registrar)

Georgina turned to her friend, "I've been accepted for interview at the medical school on 18th October," she proclaimed with joy. People stared.

Gerald smiled his celestial smile. "Good girl. I'm sure

you'll flit through the interview. And you've got the brains and what it takes to complete the course, I know."

"Thanks, Gerald, You're so encouraging. I like you so much for that. And something else. You know how I am." She was embarrassed all of a sudden.

"I have to say things outright." He smiled again. "You're so grown up, Gerald, so on top of everything; I noticed this even when I was quite small when you came to talk to us about art at school. It was so enthralling. I don't think anyone has forgotten that talk. It was really great."

"Well, thank you, and if compliments are in the air, Miss Hennessey, then you are worthy of a few yourself. Not only are you a brain, but a lovely young lady into the bargain." Georgina noticed the order of these observations. She was pleased. Gerald was very attractive and mature and so this, coming from him, was a compliment indeed. She felt very flattered.

"Aren't you going to open the other letter, then?" Gerald asked in mock surprise, "and so disappoint the illustrious department of biology by your indifference?" Georgina made it clear from her attitude that an interview in this case was highly unlikely, and commented, "Firstly, I'm a woman, and secondly their standards are very high. I noticed this from their application form.

"Well why don't you open the letter and see if your prejudices are valid?" Gerald insisted. Georgina tore open the envelope.

UNIVERSITY OF LONDON

DEPARTMENT OF BIOLOGICAL STUDIES AND TROPICAL MEDICINE

10TH OCTOBER, 1955

Dear Miss Hennessey,

We thank you for your application of 8th September this year, and are pleased to inform you that you have been considered for interview on 17th October at 4.30 in the afternoon. Room 10 in the John Schofield building.

If possible, we would like to take a look at your schoolwork on this occasion and also learn of any fieldwork done, since notes, reports and results will be useful for us in making a decision.

Enclosed is a sketch of the building. Please use door A and proceed upstairs to R. 10 which is on the left hand side of the corridor.

Yours faithfully,
Secretary to Prof Ronald Dray, Head of Faculty

My God! I've been accepted here, too," Georgina exclaimed, and she got up, went over to Gerald and embraced him. People stared. "Gerald, what shall I do now? Suppose I get in at both faculties, what then?"

"Then you'll have to choose," Gerald said simply. He was highly amused and delighted into the bargain at her success. "Will you tell your folks about the interviews?" he asked.

"No, not yet, they're only interviews. Later, if I'm taken into faculty, I can spring it upon them as a *fait accompli,* you know." Gerald knew. "I taught your mum at night school for a term, do you remember?" Gerald said.

Georgina remembered.

"Yes," he said inwardly, recalling the acquaintance, and for a second or two he was oblivious to everything else.

"Was she a good student?" Georgina asked mischievously. Gerald thought back soberly. "No free movement. Terribly strung up. Always wanted to hear how the others in the class were faring. In fact, she seemed more concerned about them than about the subject of her painting. Odd."

No, not odd," Georgina contradicted. Gerald raised his eyebrows at this.

"She's intensely curious," Georgina explained. "Always sticking her nose into other people's business, and then telling them what to do. Damn cheek!

Gerald received this information in silence, not wishing to acquiesce in such a harsh judgement, recognising at the same time that the conflict between Georgina and her mother was deeper than he'd expected.

"I'm sorry," he said.

"Oh, it's all right. Maybe she'll grow up one day, and see that other people have feelings, too," Georgina said lightly. Gerald smiled wisely, but said nothing. Then the two of them fell to talking about other matters. They talked of Gerald's part-time activity as a painter, and his forthcoming vernissage. Georgina was interested. As I have said, she was an intelligent young woman just coming out into life. It is conceivable at this stage to imagine that she now go on to university, study, and make a thoroughly good biologist or a doctor or what you will and so go further on to enter the cultural life of the city, marry, raise children, Georgina, the happy, the respected, the suburban. Everybody does something of the kind. But life, fate, destiny, karma – whatever you will – had other designs for her, not to mention the part to be played by her own strong will and temperament.

Within four or five weeks of this pleasant interview with Gerald, Georgina was twice interviewed and twice accepted by the university, which, of course, landed her promptly in a quandary, so that Gerald was once more called upon to give his advice.

"Gerald?"

"Hello, Georgina, How are you? Nice to hear from you again."

"Gerald, I've got in at the biological faculty *and* the medical school! They told me in both cases at the interview itself already and said that an official letter of acceptance would be 'forthcoming'. Isn't that marvellous?"

"Yes, it is and congratulations indeed!"

"Thank you, dear Gerald, but what shall I do now?"

"Well, that's not really for me to say, young lady; it is you who have to decide." Gerald's mellifluous tones flowed down the line. "And there's one letter for you here on my table, by the way. It's one of the official notices I suppose. Looks as though it's from the medical school. Let me see, yes – shall I open it?"

Yes, do, please."

"Very well, then, with your permission… er. Wait a moment, where's the opener – ah yes"

There was a rustle of paper as the envelope was slit open and the letter extracted. "Just a sec." More rustling.

"It's from the university's medical school and reads as follows:

Dear Miss Hennessey,

We are now pleased to inform you officially that, in view of your qualifications and with respect to the recent interview, we are able to reserve you a place of study at the faculty for medicine in the new term. (Oct. 1955-56).

Please make arrangements with the registrar as to the payment of fees, student accommodation, and the requirement of a student pass and an enrolment number.

An informal meeting of staff and students will take place on Thursday, 12th October in the senior common room of the medical faculty where new students will be warmly welcomed.

We look forward to seeing you there then, and take this opportunity of wishing you every success with your studies.

Yours truly,
(Prof. Martin Robinson, MD, MSc. FRCS)
Registrar and Head of Surgical Dept.

"Now isn't that nice, Miss Hennessey?" Gerald commented. He was fond of calling her 'Miss Hennessey'. She liked it, too. In the first place, it gently emphasised Gerald's role as an older friend and mentor, and also gave her a sense of dignity in the matter of self-identification. This was important to her at the moment. There was a pause on the line.

"Are you still there?" Gerald asked after a second or two.

"Yes, I'm still here," Georgina sobbed. "I'm crying; I can't help it."

"I know how you feel. I'm very pleased for you, though." (Pause while Georgy wiped away her tears and returned to the mouthpiece.)

"Well, what are you going to do now?" Gerald asked, "become a brilliant woman surgeon or a famous woman biologist? We all want to know."

"I don't know, and that's just the problem. They have to have my confirmation next week. Term starts in late October."

"Well, what does Mrs Johnson say? I mean, she knows you well enough to judge I would think." Gerald went on, referring to her former teacher at school.

"She's taken a year off to look after her ageing mother in Southampton," Georgina replied.

"Well, you could go down there, couldn't you?" Gerald's voice was encouraging

"I don't know. My parents wouldn't let me. Can you help, Gerald?"

"Yes, I could, I suppose. I'll talk to a colleague in the careers advisory dept. in the town, and you and I can meet after the talk in the usual place on Tuesday. I finish early on that day, say, around 11am at Luciano's?"

"Thanks, Gerald, that's really nice of you. I'll see you then.

"Good, see you then. Bye."

On the Tuesday in question, Gerald had medicine to recommend. He tested Georgina's aptitude for the subject in a number of ways, by asking her to fill out short questionnaires, which he sometimes used for other students. On reading her answers, he was soon able to tell her that she was well fitted for the medical option, and at lunchtime said that the only thing to do now was broach the whole thing to her mother and father and inform them about the way matters had developed in the last few weeks. This, he said, would certainly unveil deceit on her part, and only she knew the correct reaction to what he referred to as 'likely turbulence'. Georgina felt very uncomfortable. Her enthusiasm, like drunkenness, had impaired her sense of reality. "There's no way round it, my dear," Gerald advised, "you'll have to put your cards on the table. They're paying for the whole caboodle!" He smiled kindly. "And they will, I'm sure."

"Pay?"

"Well, yes, for your further education." Georgy had not considered this aspect, and was struck dumb for a moment or two.

Gerald continued, "Medicine's quite expensive, but pays off in the long run. All of you must make an arrangement about this. They'll understand, I'm sure. They should be delighted at your success. For goodness sake!" he exclaimed happily.

"But they may not want to pay at all, and in any case I shall be in their debt again. Damn! Isn't there a grant for students?" Georgina cut in.

"Yes, there is of course, but if you'll excuse my saying so, dear girl, not in your case, since the grants committee will probably deem your father to be capable of undertaking the costs – although he's retired.

Gina's mouth opened a little. "In other words," Gerald continued, "you're not poor enough to be endowed with a grant. At least I don't think so."

Georgina's face dropped.

"Oh, that's awful," she said, and she foresaw the next five years of study as a financial thralldom, followed later by the requirement to repay this debt to her parents. The idea appalled her. Tears appeared in her beautiful eyes.

"Come, dear," Gerald comforted her, rising and putting an arm round her shoulders. "It's too soon for such assumptions. One thing at a time. The main thing is that you've been accepted. The next is to apply for a grant and wait for an answer. First of all, you must go home and face the music. Remember that it's an honour to have been accepted. Show them the letters. They'll be impressed. Third party as it were. Your folks will certainly appreciate this, even if the whole thing comes as an unpalatable surprise." Georgina had never heard the word 'unpalatable' before, but quickly deduced its meaning. Despite her distress, she had to smile at the idea. It was very like Gerald to find the right word for a situation, and he had often made her laugh with this aptitude in their conversations. He was adept, too, at understatement. She loved him for this especially. He squeezed her shoulders for a moment longer and then said, "Come, my young friend, '*de la confiance!*' Into battle; it has to be done." He looked at her, pausing before adding kindly," Like having a tooth out, eh?"

Georgina immediately thought of Mr Adams, and then rose to her feet. It was 12.55 pm, she noticed. Lunch would be ready.

Hurriedly, she thanked her friend, hugged him and the two walked towards the exit. "In a few minutes, I'll be in the lions' den. Keep your fingers crossed for me," she said weakly.

"Of course I will," Gerald returned, "Do right royal battle, Miss Hennessey!"

Then they shook hands formally at the doorway, and on leaving Gerald gave her the 'thumbs up' as a final gesture of encouragement. He watched her trim figure retreat, the incredible mane of hair playing with the sunlight as she went to 'do battle'. He wished her well.

Even before she entered the house, the smell of roast lamb wafted around her nostrils from the kitchen. It was good. Molly, the cook, certainly knew her business, Georgina thought as she let herself in at the front door. No one greeted her as she flew upstairs to make herself presentable for lunch. 'It will be a memorable one,' she thought to herself grimly as she combed her hair in front of the mirror in her room. In what state of mind would she be in two hours from now? She asked the reflection in the glass.

Her fair hair carelessly proclaimed the spring of life, falling in joyous undulations over her shoulders and above them framing the heart-shaped face, the cheeks, full and tinted with rose from subdued excitement and the fresh air from the walk home. The voluptuous lips parted slightly, and the fair, slender neck curved in a graceful line to her fine shoulders and firm bust. All of it was an affirmation of life's vitality and an almost wanton gaiety, an irresponsible flourish of nature and a resounding retort to age, infirmity and death. Indeed, the image in the glass spoke of purity and joy, yet at the centre of this abandon there was the smallest expression of apprehension. The tantalising green eyes had for once assumed a tint of seriousness. Even this was ravishing, a note of poignancy in a chord of beauty.

Finally, she stood up and left the bedroom to join the company downstairs where everyone was about to sit down for lunch. Her father nodded to her with a friendly smile. Patrick said grace: "May the Lord be thanked for this, our meal."

"Amen."

The atmosphere this afternoon was charged with a special *bonvivre*. Even when little Sarah spilled some of her soup, the matter was soon attended to, the mess mopped and the child forgiven. Father for once was in the mood to talk. Patrick, too, related an anecdote he'd heard that morning in the Officer Cadet School mess. He attended this school prior to his enlistment as a potential army officer subsequent to his twenty-first birthday. He talked about a certain Captain Smythe who on a certain very wet and windy day in March was taking parade when his hat suddenly sailed from his head on a gust of wind only to descend a moment or two later and be blown under the wheels of a passing army vehicle. The driver had been quite unable to make the necessary manoeuvre to avoid the hat in time. A most unfortunate affair. However, he stopped, retrieved the crushed hat from under his jeep and marched, cap in hand, to the sergeant major on duty at the parade, and presented him with the mutilated headgear. This was then relayed to Captain Smythe with an apology. Taking the cap and looking at it, he remarked bleakly, "Washed *and* ironed, I see."

Even the duty sergeant major couldn't help but smirk at the remark.

"Yes," said father, relishing the story, which, in fact, he'd heard before.

"He was always a bit of a card, Smythe. I knew him as a young feller, of course. Is he still there?"

"No," Patrick replied. "He's one of the senior officers at Sandhurst today. Major or even a full colonel, I believe.

"Is he, by gad? Good for him."

Georgina felt very uncomfortable about all this. It was disarming. She hated the idea of spoiling the rest of the day for everyone, as she certainly would do in a moment or two. A good scrap in a mean atmosphere would have suited her better. It would not have had the flavour of treachery. Dessert was served. Molly retired and Georgina took this as her cue.

"Dad, Mum," she said as an opening, nodding to them respectively. "There's something I'd like to report," she began.

"Oh, yes?" Her father looked up from the cherries and cream, "What is it, dear? Can't it wait until we've finished our meal?" Georgina nodded, and her mother knew at once that something serious was afoot, but said nothing. Patrick looked at his sister admonishingly across the table. The courage Georgina had screwed up a moment before for this encounter had deflated like a pricked balloon. She felt thoroughly dejected. The rest of the meal was finished in silence. Mrs Tucker and the cook cleared the table, and Patrick excused himself, despite signs from Georgina that he stay. Little Sarah returned to her dolls in the next room. Both these actions, Patrick's absence and Sarah's proximity, only added to her sense of uncomfortable exposure.

"Now, dear," said her father, "What's on your mind?" Mother sat still to listen to everything. In a split second,

Georgina decided then and there on telling her parents bluntly about everything that has happened, rather than preparing them gently for a final *coup de grace*. It was more in keeping with her nature.

"I've applied for university and have a place to study medicine. Term begins in a week."

Father didn't explode. Instead, he just stared at her. It was possible that he was more preoccupied with her deception than with her decision.

Then, mother said, "Well, well." For the moment she could draw on no further reserves. Her father's face was like a rock. It passed through Georgina's mind that this was the expression he wore when, at other times, he had to make serious decisions during battle or in the case of administering punishment to a miscreant. He was quite cool as he said, "Why didn't you inform us of your intention to study medicine?"

"I had no intention; I just applied," Georgina returned.

"The intention comes before the application, doesn't it? Come, on, that's not logical."

"I applied for biology as Mrs Johnson suggested last term and a friend said I could apply for medicine as well, so I did so just for fun."

"Just for *fun?*" said the colonel, incredulous at such blithesomeness.

"Well, yes, just to see what would happen," Gina said, losing her nerve and feeling already that she had lost grip of the situation as a whole.

"And the authorities saw fit to accept such an unconsidered application?" the colonel asked.

"They considered my exam results and thought I was good enough," Georgina said stalwartly. Her father relaxed his position and turned to her mother. The two of them stared, as though they had heard of the death of a near relative. "Was it Gerald Monroe that put this nonsense into your head, girl?" her mother asked.

"He did suggest medicine as did Mrs Johnson. Is it 'nonsense'? I would like to go to university, and I can't see anything wrong in that."

"Well, you're not going," her father said, and banged his fist on the mahogany table. "It's simply a waste of public money. Ugh!"

"And you'll be about thirty before you start practising your profession. Your chances of marriage will be about nil by then," her mother added. "Just nil."

Then it was her father's turn, "I'm over fifty-five, young woman," he said, "and I want to see some grandchildren some time. In five or even six years' time, when you'll be pleased to settle down to life – if you ever settle to having children at that age – I might be dead or too old to enjoy them." Georgina was silent at this. She had not expected an attack from this angle.

Her father looked at her long enough for him to be satisfied that what he had said had sunk in. Then he continued," Your mother's of the same mind. "It's no use waiting for Patrick to produce grandchildren.

"Anyway, he's not allowed to marry before he's thirty. This is an unwritten law in the army. And a man must see a lot more of the world before he takes a woman as his wife. So that's out."

This was an appeal, quite a different kind of vice in which she found herself squeezed. She said feebly, "But Dad, I don't want to marry yet. I'm not ready for it." After a brief, contemptuous look at his daughter, Colonel Henry huffed and turned again to his wife.

"The captain wasn't good enough for you, I suppose," said her mother meanly. Georgina was already familiar with this ploy, and shot back, "It wasn't that he isn't good enough; I didn't love him, that's all."

"You didn't give him half a chance, young woman. It would have been an ideal match," the colonel added. Georgina could think of nothing to say to this. After another dramatic pause, he went on, "Well I'm not sending you to university to waste your time and that of others, so you stuff that in your pipe and smoke it. If you are not going to marry and thus comply with our wishes, we, who have so far lavished so much on you, will require you to earn your own living. You'll have to work as other people have to; I'm not having you hang around here."

It was a command. He had spoken. For the second time that year, Georgina broke down. She sobbed bitterly and quietly to herself, while the grandfather clock in the dining room ticked away imperturbably and her parents looked on without a word. After a minute or so, Georgina slowly sobbed her way to her room where she sat in a chair and cried and cried.

Some time later, she heard Patrick arguing loudly with his parents downstairs. It was unlike her brother to raise his voice. She had heard him do this only once before when the gardener had accused him, wrongly, of breaking a glass pane in the conservatory. She recalled the gardener as a funny old stick, and his manner on that occasion was quite out of keeping with the mishap. Patrick, she remembered, after polite protest, then resorted to loud remonstrance of his innocence. And now it was happening again, but this time with her dad. She could hardly believe her ears, and listened intently to the raised voices issuing up the stairway "Maybe, Dad, maybe but she's a great girl. You should be proud of her achievement, I feel."

"We don't want her gallivanting about the university. And as for her marks at school, I'm amazed, I can tell you." It was her father's voice. "She never was one to sit down and work like you, so what makes you think she'll do that now?"

"Because she's an adult now, dad; she's not a kid any longer."

"A 'child' you mean," his father corrected him. "I don't like this cheap, American word."

"The *child*," Patrick replied irritably. "You must get that clearly into your heads," he added.

"We don't need to be lectured by you, young fellow," said his mother. The temperature in the room was rising rapidly. "I'm not lecturing, mum, but it annoys me to see you ignoring your daughter's needs, and simply and exclusively concentrating on *your* plans for her future. It's a kind of neurosis, really it is."

Colonel Hennessey's large red face reddened visibly. "You cheeky, young pup! Who do you think you're speaking to?" he demanded. Patrick retreated a step from his position.

"I'm sorry, Dad, but we all have our fixed ideas, I suppose, both young and old. Me too. Everyone suffers to some extent from blinkered vision and all that." He said this more or less in a tone of apology than as an acute observation. The colonel, for all his annoyance, couldn't help smiling at the phrase, coming as it did from one so inexperienced and addressed at two people that had seen most of the world and its ways at some time or other. He knocked his empty pipe in the fireplace, sat down, and began to stuff it slowly. Then he looked at everyone in the room squarely in the eye.

"She's not going to train as a doctor," he said very slowly and deliberately, looking at his wife and son individually to see if they understood the import of this sentence. "Qualifications or no qualifications; acceptance or no acceptance, I hope that I won't have to say it again in this house."

Lieutenant Colonel Henry Hennessey wore a blue blazer with the badge of his regiment sewn on the breast pocket. Under this, he wore a white polo jumper and below, grey flannels. On his feet were immaculately polished, black shoes. In this get-up he was a figure authority. Every member of the family knew that to go beyond the point now reached would bring all hell down upon the household. His keen, blue eyes in the red face surveyed his son carefully, the unlit pipe in his half-raised hand was also an ominous signal not to say another word other than to agree with this dictum.

Mother was simply afraid, and Patrick had not yet learned how to deal with his father's rage.

It must be said, though, that Patrick did not back down for fear of opposition, but because he feared more for his father's health on such occasions. When he, Patrick, had won his spurs, he would tackle his father with more justification at his back. For the moment, it was better to let the matter stand, he concluded, and so merely nodded at his father's declaration.

The colonel rose to light his pipe in a manner, which suggested that the whole affair had been resolved amicably and sensibly. He stood in front of the fireplace with his feet a little apart, as though on the deck of a ship.

Elizabeth, his wife, made a movement of resignation with her mouth. Sarah, who had crept in from next door, looked wide-eyed from behind one of the comfortable, winged chairs of the living room. No one had seen her. The colonel struck another match and set to in an attempt to relight his pipe, puffing gently at the latter. The affair was over. "I would like a coffee, I think," he announced, and then seeing Sarah, "Ah there you are, you sweet little thing! Come into daddy's arms."

Mother left for the kitchen, Patrick for the garage, ostensibly to retrieve something from the pannier of his motor cycle but in fact for a breath of fresh air. It was almost four o' clock in the afternoon. Mother, fumbling with some glasses in the kitchen, felt nevertheless that something was wrong with the way the altercation had taken, although she also felt that her husband's clear stance had cleared matters up more or less satisfactorily. It wasn't completely satisfactory. Not at the moment. She looked out of the window and felt sorry or her elder daughter. It saddened her to see Georgina's wings thus clipped. Wings were there to fly with, were they not? She recalled the confinements and restrictions of her own childhood, the weight of an authoritarian tradition, which accompanied her tender years and which she had been led to believe was necessary for the development of her character. Discipline was good for the character, she was convinced of that, and there was a need to make sacrifices in the process. Such was inevitable, she consoled herself. But then a moment later, she wondered if this view had not hardened her over the years. Deep within her, there were others factors at play. Yes, there was resentment at seeing her daughter denied what she had deserved by dint of effort and native intelligence, and at seeing her desperate helplessness at the mercy of a man. Yet, concurrent with ancient feelings, those of the knowledge that the man's strength was the source of her existence, she struggled hard with the compassion she felt for Georgina. Instinctively, she knew that to resist his will or to abandon caution would be to risk her own existence, and this basic fear had the upper hand in her life.

For the first time now she realised the truth of these reflections.

She took the coffee into the lounge.

Georgina sat still in her room, listening for tell-tale sounds from below.

But there was nothing. Patrick, she knew, would be

away on his motorcycle soon to attend his cadet course, and she knew how much he enjoyed these events. He would be doubly pleased now to be out of the house and away from the tensions midday had brought. A few minutes later, she heard his machine purring along the gravel path towards the road. As for Patrick, although he was travelling south to his course and his friends, he was still with his sister. She was somewhat younger than he, and yet her attitude to life was different to his, he mused. Many things were quite different. She didn't care for class or money and neither did she want to be regarded as a 'baby machine'. What did she want and how could he help his sister to attain her heart's desire? He wondered whether her wish to go on to university was a genuine desire to study or whether it was an excuse to leave home.

'You couldn't be sure with women', he thought by way of conclusion to this train of thought as he rode along. 'You could never be sure of what they were thinking. Why hadn't she found Captain Rourke interesting, for example?' For Patrick, this was a complete and utter mystery. Such a great lad, Captain Rourke, he pondered as the cadet building came into view.

"I bought some bread and sausage which you might like," Mother said apologetically. "We have no cheese and biscuits, I'm afraid. Cookie forgot to buy cheese today."

"Oh, that's nothing. Excellent, excellent," her husband said with emphasis, and partook of one of the 'Viennese' sausages on the plate with one of the small forks provided.

"Almost as good as those I sampled once with John Pendleton before the war. The Germans can do a lot with sausage. Whatever became of Pendleton? Nice young chap. Bit callow for sure, but a good man. Probably grown into something useful by today."

The colonel's mind flitted back to a café on the banks of the river Spree in 1937. That had been before either of them were married. It had been a good time. He wondered vaguely whether Pendleton had ever married, and said aloud: "Wonder how the young chap's doing?" But at that instant, Hennessey realised that eighteen years had elapsed since then and that 'young Pendleton' would shortly be due for retirement, if, that is, he had survived the war.

The thought struck him like an arrow. "Eighteen years!" he said to himself. "My God!" Realisations of this kind were occurring with ever more frequency these days, he noted to himself. As an unconscious consolation to this reflection, he stabbed another sausage.

The next morning, Georgina went with Mrs Tucker, the housekeeper to help with the purchase of groceries and other household articles. They took a number 24 bus into town, and while there, Georgina took the opportunity to ring the registrar's office at the university in London. She wanted to enquire about a grant to study.

"Yes. Thank you. My name's Georgina Hennessey. I'm eager to talk to someone who can help me with getting a grant."

"One moment, please, I'll put you through to the Grants Commission. Hold on." There was a click and a buzz. Then: "Grants Commission. Can I help you?" Georgina repeated her request and asked for an interview. She received an appointment for the following afternoon. The building and room were explained to her. "Thanks!" she said, and, pleased with this development, rejoined Mrs Tucker in the store's restaurant.

"Did you manage, deary?" Mrs Tucker asked kindly. "Yes, thank you," Georgina replied, taking a seat next to her and pulling the tea that Mrs Tucker had thoughtfully provided for them both towards her.

There will never be a plaque to commemorate Mrs

Tucker's virtuous life, which is a pity, for she had long ascended the heights of heavenly love and kindness, which, perhaps, most religious people can only aspire to. In a word, she was a delightfully good person. Georgina looked at her now in the simple coat she habitually wore, and under which, she knew, was an immaculate white blouse, topped by a cameo just beneath the top button and worn every day like a badge. And then there was this kindly, round face and the faded, loving, blue eyes, which were always full of good cheer.

"Yes," Georgina repeated, "thank you Mrs Tucker, I think everything will be all right."

"I'm sure it will, dear," Mrs Tucker said encouragingly. To all but her parents, this good woman was known as Mrs Tucker. Her parents called her 'Elsie', but the children were not allowed to call her by her Christian name. Elsie always seemed to be able to enjoy both good health and good spirits. Georgina had never seen her in a bad mood or seriously put off by anything. Whatever the crisis, she could always deal with it.

'Cool', they would call it today, because Mrs Tucker was quite 'unflappable'.

However, the presence of mind usually described these days by the word 'cool' was in her case always accompanied by a cheerfulness that was quite indomitable. What endeared her to everyone was that, whatever the crisis, she was always careful to preserve the integrity of others involved in it and maintain a sense of balance.

Everyone, even Higgins, the cross, pernickety old gardener, loved her. Indeed, Georgina had only seen Mrs Tucker flustered for a moment, and that was on the occasion when there had been a gas leak in the kitchen. She had shoo-shooed everyone out of the room and clambered heavily upstairs to tell her employers and the two guests who were dining there at the time, and then turned to dash as best she could downstairs again to open windows and see to the leak herself so as to avoid an explosion, not to mention being overcome by gas fumes in the process. The action was truly heroic and she took a considerable risk.

Georgina knew that she could trust Mrs Tucker and together they drank their tea in the pleasant atmosphere of the café. Georgina looked better this morning, but the signs of her sadness and disappointment hung about her.

"You all right, dear?" Mrs Tucker asked between sips of tea. "You seemed very sad yesterday when I brought the dessert." Mrs Tucker looked kindly at her.

"Ach, it's mum and dad, you know; they want to keep me chained up at home. I'm sure you've realised that." She paused a moment to look her partner in the eye. "I'm just not free, you see," Georgina added with feeling.

"Well, it's all very natural to feel as you do at your age," Mrs Tucker said thoughtfully. "You want to spread your wings, but they don't want you to come to any harm, you see."

"Well I've got to get into the air some time," Georgina countered, taking her cup and putting it resolutely to her lips.

"You will, I'm sure, my dear; it's just a phase. Unconsciously, your parents want to be assured that you can fend for yourself. It's natural. You'll be all right. Everything will be all right. You'll see." Mrs Tucker smiled.

"They want to marry me off to someone of their own choice, that's what they want to do," Gina replied heatedly, so that Mrs Tucker raised her eyebrows a little. There was a slight pause, and Georgina went on, "I'm sorry, dear Mrs Tucker, if I'm still all strung up about it, but I'm young and want to get out and about a bit before being cooped up with a man and oodles of messy, noisy children." Mrs

Tucker smiled again. "I think I know why your mum and dad are so particular about you," she said, nodding her head wisely. Georgina's face was one question mark. "Why?"

"They know the world; they know your worth, and they know you're, well, dear, to put it simply, that you're stunningly beautiful." Mrs Tucker laughed lightly at her own revelation, while Georgina just stared, not knowing whether to laugh or cry. Mrs Tucker knew how she felt, so she decided to continue. "The truth is that there are a lot of unscrupulous people in this world who would like to take advantage of your beauty." Georgina listened carefully, so that Mrs Tucker was given the cue to go on, and her expression became suddenly earnest. "Have you ever heard of Eleanor Roosevelt, dear?" she asked. "Yes, I think so," Georgina replied. "Well, Eleanor Roosevelt once said something that I feel is very important. She said that we not only have the right to be an individual, but also the right to be as you are, whatever that individuality might involve and that we can't make a useful contribution to life unless we recognise this."

Georgina was impressed. "So you have to go your own way," Mrs Tucker added. "That's important, but you have to be careful of those who would want to exploit you. Men are all very well, bless them, but rather dull when it comes to understanding us women." Elsie took another appreciative sip of her hot tea. "They tend to devour what they see. Gobble it all up and don't think much about anything else."

"Gobble it all up?" Georgina asked incredulously.

"Yes, if we're not careful they will eat us up," Mrs Tucker emphasised with a good-natured smile. Georgina still looked stupefied, and Mrs Tucker felt the need to elaborate a little, so she went on, "They're thinking of one thing when they're young," she said, looking Georgina in the eye.

"Oh yes," Georgina concurred, painfully recalling her own experience of this fact while in Ireland. "Why are they like that?" she asked curiously.

"Well, it probably has something to do with sustaining the species. An ancient instinct in them all. I can see, too, that it was very important 20,000 years ago when anything could happen any time, if you see what I mean. But today, things are very different. It isn't so dreadfully important to maintain the species in view of a dangerous environment, but the instinct remains as though this were still true. I feel that today the time has come to reduce our numbers so that we can preserve our standard of living. What do you think?" Georgina nodded, impressed both by Mrs Tucker's wisdom and her expression. "So you see, dear, the poor things are thousands of years out of date and we women have to tame them. Your mum and dad don't want your heart broken. And they don't want to see you come to any harm either. That's understandable." Mrs Tucker sighed. "Dear girl, it's not so easy to be beautiful. You've got to look out!" Mrs Tucker nodded several times, looking archly at Georgina as she did so. Then she said, "Oh, dearie me, here am I lecturing you love, I'm sorry."

"Oh, Mrs Tucker, you're so sweet. You're not lecturing me at all and I see what you mean." Mrs Tucker nodded again and was pleased that Georgina had understood. She took another sip of her tea and added, "None of us want to see you hurt, my dear, so go your way, but just take care. I'm sure you'll be all right."

Georgina smiled and said that she would think about what Mrs Tucker had said, and then it was time to go. They paid and left with their provisions and caught the bus home.

That evening her mother and father left the house to

attend a public meeting in the town. Patrick was out at the cinema with a friend. The staff had gone their various ways to their homes, and at 7pm the house was empty. Georgina lay on her bed in her room pondering on the conversation that had taken place at Kingston's restaurant earlier that day.

So she was 'stunningly beautiful'. She thought this over to herself. It was a great compliment. Up to that moment she had been innocent of the charms, of her beauty and of its effect on others. She wondered, as well, that two of her best friends, now young women themselves and whom she had known since childhood, had never said anything of the kind to her, much less her young companions at school. Brenda Dawling, the closer of the two, was truly beautiful in Georgina's opinion. And then there was Doris Harting. Doris was lovely, too, in her bonny way. Doris was a sportswoman and half her beauty was bounding good health. She was also a nice person, Georgina reflected. What had happened to Doris? she asked herself. Tomorrow, she would try and contact her. In addition, it would be a legitimate excuse to go out in the evening. Her parents never minded female company and they knew Doris personally.

With this decision, Georgina then slowly took off all her clothes and inspected herself closely in the long mirror in her room. The last of the sun's rays illuminated what she saw in the glass. Her eyes, she noticed, had lost their apprehensive look, but were still serious. It was as if they were watching her, looking at her thoughtfully, considering her objectively and entirely oblivious of the song of youth, which radiated from every other part of her. She was not for a moment put off by this new aspect of herself. In all the many times she had stood in front of the mirror, she had never detected this strange detachment before, this someone, this presence watching her. She regarded the eyes and the face intently. What was it that stared back at her? She stroked a cheek with her finger. The light from the window revealed very fine, light hairs on her cheek, which were only discernible at this angle. Turning her face now towards the light brought her straight, well-formed nose into profile. Yes, she had a good nose, she noted. From the root of this nose a clear forehead rose to her hairline and from thence to her hair, which, today, was swept back 'put of the way' as her mother had urged her to comb it. This was because Georgina had helped in the kitchen. 'Cookie' was away for a week. Georgina pulled out her hair ribbon and shook her incredibly abundant hair which then fell around her head and shoulders, making a very gentle sound as it did so. She raised her head and shook it, noted the face below, framed by the hair with its full, red lips and the firm chin. She opened her lips ever so slightly to reveal part of the line of very white, even teeth. Then she swept her hair out of her face, almost impatiently it seemed, and looked at her smooth neck and her small, shell-like ears, which were then revealed. She looked very long and very critically at each of her features, as women are wont to do. 'Yes,' she said to herself, 'not bad.' After this inspection, her hair fell back into place again round her shoulders and over her back. Then she took her breasts in her hands and lifted them and felt their weight and firmness with her fingers. She was pleased with her breasts. They looked well now, she thought to herself as she regarded them, first frontally and then, turning, from the side. She took her nipples between thumb and forefinger and excited them, watched the tumescence and was herself excited. 'Yes,' she mused, 'she could easily compete with any of the girls she had seen from time to time in the glossy magazines and at the beach.'

She was glad, too, that her breasts were not a

hindrance when she rode or when she ran as was the case with some of the girls she had known at school. She noticed how fine the skin of her breasts was as she ran a finger lightly across the contours of one of them, wondering at the incredible softness and rotundity of the organ, wondering at the way the chest and the breast joined each other insensibly, perfectly. She remembered how quickly they had formed when she was about fourteen. It had seemed only a few months at the time and then, suddenly they were there. How strange, she thought to herself. Nature is miraculous. Her nipples had now subsided and she inspected them again, looking carefully at the protuberances in the area around them. She stepped back so that the entire woman came into view in the mirror. It was the figure of a woman of which she could be proud, and of which others could be jealous, she thought. Below her waist, her hips flowed out into two symmetrically perfect lines in an uninterrupted curve to her knee like a drawn bow. From her knee, the line took a shapely curve to her neat, small feet, the symmetry continuing into the perfection of her toes. She turned to one side again to admire her full, body profile and noticed the straight back and its feminine hollow, and the elegant sweep of her firm bottom to join her thigh. She noted the slight swelling of her belly, the poetic line followed a perfect curve over her *mons pubis* of tight, thick golden hair, there to vanish beneath her. Again, she turned in full view of the mirror and brushed her abdomen very gently with her hand as one sometimes brushes a table surface briefly before setting a clean plate on it. She looked at the shield of hair beneath her belly and wondered again at Nature's consummate work of art. Then she passed the flat of her hand instinctively over the mound of pubic hair and took the two lips of her sex between her fingers.

Here, as with the rest of her body, there was fullness, turgidity, and at her touch the lips opened and were moist. Her breathing was a little faster. For the first time in her life up to now, she longed to be caressed there. Her other hand passed through her hair. 'Who would love this body one day?' she asked herself, the hand descending and running over her breasts to her waist and hips, and from there to her haunches, and from there to her belly again. "I want someone to love me and make love to me" she said audibly "I'm ready." And she knew that she had spoken the truth. In that moment she would have given herself up to the act of love. Looking again at the shape in the mirror, she asked, "What's it all for, if not for love?"

Then, in what for an onlooker, would be a rhapsody of movement, she tripped to the bathroom and showered. After a few moments, she re-appeared and without retrieving her nightclothes from the drawer at the side of the bed, got into bed nude.

This was the first time she had done anything so 'sinful', but she loved the kiss of the bedclothes around her, and grabbing a book from the bedside cabinet, settled to read for an hour until the sun had quite disappeared behind the poplar trees. "It was good to be alone for once," she said to herself. "One needs to be alone now and then."

"I'm afraid I can't do much for you this year, Miss Hennessey. You see, grants have already been allotted. Term starts in a day or two. I'm sorry." And Mr Ailsworth of the Grants Committee Office looked sorry. Georgina felt that if he could have done something for her, he would have.

"Does that mean that I have to wait another whole year?" she asked in utter astonishment.

"I'm afraid so," Mr Ailsworth replied unhappily. "However, I'm certain we could arrange something for next year, should your father still be unwilling to support you."

"But what about my place in the medical school? Would that still be valid?"

"I really cannot say; we'll have to consult the secretary there to verify that.

I should imagine so, but cannot say for sure. Shouldn't pose too much of a problem, I think."

"Do you mean that they could keep me on the list, so to speak, for enlistment next year?" Georgina asked without much hope.

"Yes," Mr Ailsworth replied. "We very occasionally have problems of this kind."

"When you say that you 'might be able to arrange something', Mr Ailsworth, what do you mean exactly? Would I be eligible for a grant?"

"Yes, I believe so, if you can prove that you are no longer in the care of your parents. "

"And living alone, you mean?"

"Yes."

"I see. And do you think I could live from the grant awarded to me?"

Mr Ailsworth smiled.

"Of course. You would be warmly advised to live in hall, though, not in digs in the town. We have to keep costs down, since the sums incurred in training a student in medicine are quite considerable, as you well understand." Mr Ailsworth moved towards a set of tall, green, steel drawers. "Shall I give you a form to fill in? That would be the first step in the procedure."

"Please."

"The next step after that would be for you to trip over to the medical faculty and explain the situation, and if they have no objections about keeping you on their list of potential students, we can take it from there."

"Thank you, Mr Ailsworth, you've been very kind." Georgina said in conclusion, pulling her leather handbag towards her over the polished table.

"Not at all, Miss Hennessey. I will do whatever I can to help," Mr Ailsworth replied and he meant it. There were some applicants about whom he couldn't care less, especially the arrogant ones, but this one, let's be frank about it – wow!

So our Georgy left the marble halls of the Registrar's Department containing the Grants Committee offices and made her high-heeled way to the medical faculty. En route, heads turned in appreciation. Having arrived, she acquainted the secretary there with her business and was shown to the office of Professor Well who was then head of faculty. There, she was asked to take a seat and wait a moment. She looked around the room. It was furnished in the style of the late nineteenth century, and Georgina caught herself thinking of Sherlock Holmes and the films she had seen, which sported this kind of furniture as a background. Shelves of books ranged from floor to ceiling. She glanced nervously at some of the nearest of these heavy tomes, many of them bound in red with gold lettering: *The Lancet* 1947-1950 and next to this row. DISEASES of the EYE. The room in general was sombre in dark oak or something similar. Dark, but comfortable. Opposite her, behind Professor Well's voluminous chair was the bust of an unknown man with a beard, the whole set in a niche in the wall at the back. The two looked at each other, the stern, uncompromising features of some nineteenth century physician and the young fair-haired woman. Minutes passed. At last, there was a noise at the door, and Professor Well, a very large man with a leonine head, appeared in the room, quietly closing the door behind him. He shook her hand vigorously and settled his huge body into the leather chair that immediately swung towards his desk.

Everything about this man, Georgina concluded, was powerful, a potential that was at odds with his gentle, engaging manner as he spoke to her.

"I hear from the registrar that apparently your parents are not willing to support you in your aspiration to become a doctor?" he asked with a smile.

"Oh yes, and I'm pretty bitter about that," Georgina almost blurted. The head of faculty brooded for a moment.

"I'm sorry too, young lady. Perhaps they will change their minds."

"I don't think so," Georgina said, surprising herself by the confidence of this assertion. The head of the school of medicine raised his eyebrows.

"Regrettable, regrettable," he said to the desktop. There was a pause while Georgina waited for him to go on in the vein of 'Perhaps I can have a word with your father... the marks here are really very good...', but nothing of the sort was forthcoming, and finally they shook hands formally and she left.

Clicking away in her high heels along the corridors of that place of learning, Georgina revised her situation. Actually, what right did her father have to interfere so radically in her life? Good, he had sired her and he and her mum had been good to her, but they didn't have a right to her future. That was hers and hers alone! She stopped at a staff café on the way, ordered a cup of tea and sat down with it to continue champing on the problem. The more she reflected, the more hopeless the felt. Then, like someone turning on the light in a dark room, she had an idea. Evelynne! Yes! She would take advantage of Evelynne's invitation to visit her. This would get her out of the house for a time, provide a diversion in sunny France at this time of the year and give 'them' (her parents) a break to ponder upon their iniquity. And perhaps Evelynne would have a good idea. They had got on like wild fire with each other last summer. Yes! Why not? Clearly, it was time to talk to Gerald again.

They had agreed by phone to meet in the city's park near the bandstand this time as it was still very warm for the time of year.

"I'm seriously thinking of spending a year down in France with Evelynne, if I'm not taken on," Georgina announced.

"Nice idea," Gerald said smiling. At this Georgina was slightly surprised. She thought that he would take the conventional view that 'she should think twice about undertaking such a long trip,' and 'who's going to pay for it?' and 'just think of the long, long trip and the inconvenience', and perhaps Evelynne 'is just being polite,' and what not.

"You really think I could go?"

"Yes, why not? Travel broadens the mind, does it not?" he added, his eyes smiling at the cliché. Georgina loved him for this. Within seconds, her mind had cleared of all the harboured doubts that had accrued about 'distance', a 'foreign country', 'the language barrier' and so on that she knew would be held like a shield. After all, she assumed logically, Evelynne had managed to survive the trip to Britain, so why not the other way round?

Gerald interrupted these conclusions. "A trip to France might nicely bridge the waiting time to enter medical school. Your parents don't need you to come to any decision and, who knows, your absence might finally spur them on to help you."

"Do you think so?" Georgina said almost plaintively. Gerald smiled his angelic smile. "Don't be so pessimistic, girl; you're young and life's your oyster. I'm confident that something positive will come up for you. And as for a trip to France, well, there's nothing to stop you. You're eighteen, and you tell me that you've got your own money to get you down there, then make up your own mind and go. You neither need them nor me in making that decision. Tell 'em where you're going and go." This was said with a confidence that made Georgina feel like a human being again. Gerald was a golden friend, she thought to herself. After enjoying the autumn sunshine together and talking further of this and that, they drank tea at the pavilion café and went their separate ways. She would tell him of her decision, she said as they shook hands and parted company.

A glorious evening closed the day and Georgina had decided this time not to beg for help or even ask for it. No, she would announce her decision to visit her friend, speak of train times, say for how long, what it would cost and would add that it would be good for everyone if she were absent for a while.

Yes, Gerald's suggestion was a good one. Inwardly, she had made up her mind to join her friend and, dammit she would go, regardless of their inevitable objections.

15TH SEPTEMBER

Dear Evelynne,

Many thanks for your letter. Yes, I'd love to come down to see you. How long may I stay? I've made some enquiries and there's a train from Paris via Orleans to Bordeaux on Thursday, 25th of this month leaving Paris at

1.55 pm and arriving in Bordeaux at 7.55 pm. Would this be all right for you? Oh, and can you pick me up at the station?

Lots of love,
"Georgine"


Bordeaux
France
22nd Sept.

Sweet Georgine!

Yes, yes, come soon to see me! I'm longing to see you again. I am there at the time you say. It is nothing to pick you up.

From Tommy and me.

A kiss and hug.
Evelynne

This reply clinched things for Georgina, and she informed her brother of her intentions clearly and resolutely. She mentioned date, time, distances, connections, arrival and the approximate time she would be absent. This was man's talk, she knew, and he was suitably impressed by her manner.

"Oh," he said, quite disarmed by her precise articulation, which had left out nothing in its discourse and so waited for his reaction.

"Umm," he added, looking at her, weighing up this decision, and then, "Well, I suppose you'll have to tell Mum and Dad that you're off?"

"The answer to that, dear Patrick, is 'no!'"

"Well, you can't just buzz off like that and say nothing, can you?"

"Yes, I can and I will." Patrick paled a little. "You can tell them," Georgina added with the air of a 'take it or leave it'.

"Me?"

"Yes, you. Or leave them to enquire where I am."

"So I'm left holding the can?" Patrick asked helplessly. He took a deep breath, surveyed his sister and shaking his head, said, "You know what you are? You're a hothead and you worry me."

"Why?"

"This hotheadedness is going to lead you into trouble one day, I reckon."

"Well, be that as it may," Georgina replied coolly, "I'm off on Thursday early to London and then to Paris. The tickets are booked and nobody's going to stop me." This remark implied that Patrick wouldn't let her down by snitching to her folks.

"And you want me to explain it all?" he said, lighting a forbidden cigarette and moving from the lounge towards the orangerie. Georgina followed.

"I'll send them a letter when I get there and say that I wasn't going to stay for another denial of my freedom. "*Fait accompli*" and all that. I'll be in good hands and there's absolutely no reason for them to complain. It's my life, not theirs."

"Well, damn me!" was all that Patrick could say, and Georgina left him to chew over the matter.

When the day arrived for her departure to France, the sun was shining with gusto as she left the house surreptitiously around 7 am. She had decided to walk to the station, entering its nineteenth century portals well in time

to catch the first train to London. As she settled in the seat
of her carriage, feelings of contrition settled upon her as it
lurched out of the station. "Your parents will be furious,"
one part of her was being warned, while the other asked
what did they think they were doing by denying her a visit
to a friend. "But you could have told them; left a letter or
something" the other voice chipped in, while another voice
took her part in the argument: "Don't worry; you're old
enough to look after yourself, aren't you?" and so similarly
and contrapuntally for practically the whole of the journey
to the capital. The ticket collector came and went, and
soon her mind was distracted by the backyards of the
houses bordering the railway line when without warning
she realised that the train was sliding into Charing Cross.
From here she would have to buy tickets for Dover for a
ship to cross the Channel.

It was beginning to be exciting, she thought to herself.
She bought buns to serve as a breakfast, crossed London,
and boarded the train for Dover. The distance to the coast
was covered quicker than she had anticipated, and as she
set eyes on the sunny white cliffs of that town, she was
confirmed in her decision. All she had to do was board the
ferry and then catch the train to Paris.

Evelynne was there at Bordeaux's main station as promised
to pick her up, and as Georgina disembarked from her
carriage, the sun warmed her in a way that reminded her of
her mother opening the oven after baking a cake. It was still
very hot for English veins and this was the first Georgina
noticed as she moved to Evelynne's waving arms.

"Oh, you are come. Marveilleux!" she said happily and
hugged Georgina for a full half minute. As for Georgina,
she was happy too to see her friend and relieved at last to
have arrived. To tell the truth, she was a little tired after her

long journey and was glad when they had reached the taxi to take them to Evelynne's place.

"It ees not far. The suburbs, you know. I like it. Eet is qui-et."

Georgina wondered at this for a moment, but soon they fell to discussing their last meeting, then how she had managed to get away. Evelynne's bright eyes shone, on hearing what had happened before Georgina left home. "Oh you are naughty, but I love you for it! It's good that you are here. Very good. And you weel en-joy eet. The sea is not far away and you will enjoy this too. I know." The taxi was slowing into a small road at the end of which was a fine house standing in its own ground. "Oh what a lovely house!" Georgina gasped. "This is your parents' home isn't it?"

"Er, no, it is mine," Evelynne said simply. "I am glad you like it. But come, come inside. It is better inside." So saying, she paid the driver, exchanged a humorous word or two with him, whisked up Georgina's baggage and moved towards the large iron gate to the garden. Georgina noticed how swiftly her friend tapped out the code to open the gate, and soon they were tramping the long, lightly gravelled path towards an imposing front door ahead. It was now very hot and the two young women were glad to find the shadow of the porch as Evelynne opened the house door.

"Voilà! Now for a coffee – or would you prefer tea?" Evelynne asked, kicking off her high-heeled shoes when they were in the cool shade of the hall.

"Water," Georgina said in a mocking tone of hoarseness, and they both laughed.

"Ah yes, you are thirsty of course," Evelynne said understandingly. "I will get a bottle," and she moved off into the kitchen, followed by Tommy, leaving Georgina to look around the parlour where she now found herself.

The room was large, airy and orderly. It was not what Georgina had expected.

What had she expected? That it would display the traits of her hostess: be hopelessly untidy, careless, perhaps even slipshod. Or was that unkind? She knew Evelynne as a happy, spontaneous being, quick in repartee, generous and seeing the funny side of everything. Somehow, this room reflected nothing of the characteristics she would have thought typical of her. Everything was ordered, or so it seemed. All its furnishings were clearly expensive. Everything had been dusted and spoke of regular attention in these matters. There was also an expensive painting of an eighteenth century girl and a dog with a farmhouse or some such building in the background, and beyond this a rich, unspoiled countryside. Georgina looked intently at the girl's face.

"Here you are, fresh from the well. Drink it slowly, it's pretty cold," Evelynne said, seating herself on the quality sofa with a coffee, Tommy in her lap. "How long are you staying, dear Georgine?"

"I haven't thought about that," Georgina answered truthfully.

"Good!" Evelynne said, her very dark eyes twinkling with good humour.

Evelynne, unlike Georgina, was small with a round face, a dark complexion and long, thick black hair well below her shoulders, which she was fond of shaking in different directions. Her hands and feet were petite, her figure neat and perfect, her voice warm and musical. As Georgina surveyed all this, she also took in Evelynne's composure and the way she sat there, her back as straight as a die, the blue-and-white dress that fitted her so well, and the loving way she stroked her pet.

"It's a super house, this," Georgina said, surveying the large living room.

"I'm glad you like it, dear," Evelynne replied in that winning, simple way of hers.

"I mean…" Georgina continued, searching for words.

"You mean you are surprised because it is so beeg?"

"Well, yes, and that it is so very nicely furnished, if you don't mind my saying so."

"Of course not; the 'ouse itself belonged to my parents, and I've kept it like they would 'ave it."

"Oh!" Georgina said quietly, and because her friend was also a well-mannered young woman, she didn't press for further information.

"Come, I show you the garden too now it's getting cooler, "Evelynne said after a long pause in which they finished their drinks.

"Goody!" Georgina enthused jumping up. Tommy miaoued at this sudden movement, and then they all went through the kitchen next door and on into the sun-soaked garden. The fact was that it was still very warm. The garden was large and bordered by mature trees with a high fence on three sides. There were no neighbours as far Georgina could see, and at the end of it was an impenetrable wood, thick with tangled undergrowth. To her right, superb French countryside with rocks and gorges that rose in a splendid panorama of green and beige.

"It's wonderful here," she said appreciatively.

They visited the pond, which was long and deep, one that sported carp and goldfish and Georgina noticed steps with a handrail at one end of it.

Suddenly, she felt an overpowering sense of refreshment and freedom as she stood there with her friend watching the fish ease through the water.

"I'm glad you like it," Evelynne said for a second time.

"I can see it's already doing you good," she added, smiling that wise smile of hers.

Georgina, like every woman, was able to receive and process varied information from several sources at the same time. She loved the garden. She had noticed the apple trees now heavy with fruit, the form, style and colour of the house. She heard Evelynne telling her of their only neighbour, a priest who lived alone about 100 yards away. She stroked Tommy and looked into his eyes and knew at once that they were friends from now on. She felt good. She felt free, and breathed in the scents of the garden deeply. She knew that Evelynne was sincere, and she was happy to have her as a friend. At the same time, she wondered about this smile that accompanied her description of the pastor. It was sincere. Of this she was convinced, and yet there was something in this enigmatic smile of hers, something displaying a depth or a secret knowledge that Georgina was unfamiliar with, and a trifle at odds with her otherwise exuberant, bubbling personality. She hadn't noticed it on their previous acquaintance. It wasn't disturbing either, no, but it was interesting. Then, Georgina suddenly realised that it was also fleeting. Evelynne was smiling now, but the wraith of the occasional deep maturity in her face had vanished.

"… and 'e keeps a mistress, I'm sure he does," she was saying with half serious conviction. "Perhaps 'e keeps 'er in the cupboard or in a drawer!" And Evelynne exploded into a mischievous peal of laughter at this unlikely possibility.

It was infectious, this laugh, and Georgina couldn't help laughing, too. Evelynne turned to her companion: "Look, I show you something. Come." She took Georgina's hand and led her to a small gate laced in flowery growth in the fence at the end of the garden, unlocked it and tripped forward a little ahead of her. To Georgina's surprise, there was a sandy path that circumvented the wood which led them up towards a small hill about half a mile away. Here, as they went on, the land was sparsely wooded with fir trees. At least that's what Georgina called them and, climbing the hill and a little out of breath, she cried in wonder and delight, "There's sea! The sea!"

"Yes, that's the Atlantic Ocean, Gina. Wonderful isn't it?" Evelynne remarked, her dark eyes scanning the upheaval of blue and white along the shore. "It's a bit choppy today for some reason, and the yellow flag is flying.

"That means we should keep our distance today, but we'll come back for a swim tomorrow, eh? You'd like that, I think?" she said, looking at Georgina.

"Oh wouldn't I just!" Georgina replied, delighted at the prospect.

After admiring the slow descent of the sun for a few moments, the girls sauntered back along the sandy path the way they had come, and, reaching the garden once more, Evelynne announced that now the time had come to devour the delectable water melons she'd bought that morning in preparation for their evening meal. Georgina was shown her room, which, again, she admired for its expensive furnishings, the quality of the bed, the fine, thick curtains at the windows, the *en suite* bathroom and again she wondered how Evelynne had garnered so much money for so many beautiful accessories. Last summer, she had given Georgina the impression that she was an impoverished student. It didn't add up. She would have to learn more about this, she said to herself.

The evening meal was one of the best she had ever tasted and she said as much. Evelynne was clearly flattered and after washing up together, the two of them decided to play badminton in the court outside. This afforded them much amusement until the sun went down around 9.30.

Georgina was tired, she had to admit and was glad when Evelynne suggested they retire.

The next morning dawned and threw its light in Georgina's bedroom with such gusto that the young woman thought it was already midday. She jumped out of bed, splashed some water on her face, pulled on her clothes as quickly as she could and went in search of her friend.

"Evelynne!, Evelynne!" she called, and not finding her in the kitchen, went out into the garden to discover a completely nude Evelynne walking over the grass towards her. "Evelynne, oh!" Georgina gasped, "You're here."

"Yes, why not?" Evelynne asked simply, the morning sun shining on her lithe body. "Did you sleep well, dear Georgina?"

"Yes, like a top."

"Like a what?"

"A top, oh I see. Well, that's what we say. A top. I dunno. Top. It's just what we say."

Evelynne smiled. "I reckon it's about time you learned a bit of French," she said playfully and the two laughed. They went inside and Evelynne availed herself of a dressing gown hanging behind the door. Putting it on, they proceeded to the lounge where, at the small table where they had dined the previous evening, breakfast was ready to receive them.

"Oh, how wonderful!" Georgina said enthusiastically. "That's super-duper! I'm hungry."

""Well I'm glad I didn't prepare all this for nothing, then," she said in that simple way of hers. "Supeer-dupeer," she repeated, apparently fascinated with this new linguistic discovery.

"It's slang, I suppose," Georgina informed her.

"Well let's get on with eeting," and with this she sat down to pour the coffee.

"I like coffee," she said in French. Then, in English, "I ope you do, too."

Georgina nodded. She had always drunk tea at home. Coffee was something exotic. She watched as Evelynne poured the black liquid into her cup.

"You can take milk weeth eet, you know," she added, detecting Georgina's serious mien.

"Oh, thank you," Georgina said politely as she would have done at home, sitting up straight just as she had been told to do in partaking food at table.

Evelynne smiled and sipped at her *Jacques Varbes* coffee with obvious pleasure.

There was silence between them for a moment or two as they enjoyed their respective breakfasts, broken at last by Georgina who asked rather as a child would, "Can we go swimming this afternoon, Evelynne?"

"Naturally. We depart, say, at about 2 pm. Then the sun is not so strong."

"Oh it can be as strong as it likes for me," Georgina replied brightly.

Again, Evelynne smiled and thought of how many English people she had seen on the beach that had blithely exposed themselves to the sun and had later nursed painful sunburn on their white skins for days after.

"*On verra*," (we'll see) she said in reply like a knowing mother.

In the forenoon they visited a market on a tandem that Evelynne possessed, having rescued and dusted it from the shed. It was great fun for them both to ride the two or three kilometres to the small town where they shopped for provisions. The variety of different products from those at home were most interesting for our Georgy, who peered and poked and listened with fascinated interest at the way people talked to each other, met neighbours, was able to nod and say the occasional *"Oui"* in acquiescence to she knew not what, but it was fine nevertheless. She was taken seriously and she loved it.

After lunch, Evelynne suggested they cycle to a cove she knew of and prized for its seclusion, and so the two of them rode a-tandem for about five kilometres, coming at last to a hill of sand speckled with hardy bushes. At this point Evelynne said that they would have to heave their bike over the low steel barrier between road and sand dune and manhandle it down to the beach below. Once there, they found it deserted and idyllic. They laid out their respective towels on the sand, undressed and looked at each other.

"You're very beautiful," Evelynne told her companion, sizing her up with unreserved appreciation.

"You're not so bad yourself, mademoiselle," Georgina returned, blushing slightly at the observation.

"I'm too small," Evelynne said, smiling, but convinced of the statement.

"Too small for what?" Georgina asked jocularly.

"For the catwalk," Evelynne replied promptly.

"You're perfect," Georgina contradicted, and they both burst out laughing and didn't know quite why. The sun was still high in the heavens.

"You must use some cream," Evelynne suggested.

"Oh, no, I don't need that; I get brown quickly," Georgina replied.

"No, no, you must use some cream; you're not in Brighton, you know," Evelynne insisted, and taking the small tin of cream she had with her, she opened it, dug her fingers into it and was already applying it to Georgina's back. As she rubbed it in she informed her friend of its need.

"I 'ave seen no end of these Eenglish girls 'ere with red backs and arms, and you don't want that, eet's ug-ly and painful. Come!" So saying, she continued to embalm

Georgina's superb back while she, Georgina, enjoyed the treatment, closing her eyes and looking up into the sun.

She was surprised when Evelynne extended her massage to include her breasts and abdomen, continuing to her thighs and knees. She said nothing to about this.

"Now you can fry – that's the word, isn't it?" Evelynne asked, amused at the prospect.

"Yes, that's right," Georgina confirmed, wondering at this moment whether Evelynne was "one of them". She observed her friend as she packed away the cream in a light wicker bag they had brought with them.

"Aren't you going to cream yourself?" Georgina asked.

"Not yet. I'm much browner than you are and so won't burn so easily, but you absolutely must protect yourself for the next day or so."

Georgina nodded. Perhaps Evelynne was right. For a while Georgina was silent as she watched Evelynne run off breezily into the frothing, crashing waves, calling to her friend to join her. After perhaps a minute Georgina followed and the two frolicked like children amid the rise and fall of the troubled waves. Georgina had to admit as she left the sea that this was one of the happiest moments she had ever experienced. She was pleasantly exhausted after her battle in the ocean and for the rest of the afternoon the two roasted in the balm of the autumn sun. At 5 pm, Evelynne announced that it was time to recover their cycle and ride for home. Even this was a refreshing experience for Georgina. She was free at last, really free! On the way as they streamed through the village, Evelynne greeted the neighbours she knew and Georgina smiled and waved. What freedom! What happiness!

They arrived and leaned the cycle against the outer wall.

"Won't it be stolen?" Georgina asked.

"Stolen? Why no. Who would want to steal our tandem?" And she laughed.

Georgina laughed too, but didn't know why. She liked Evelynne's 'our tandem' and felt at home. She was getting to like her more and more.

Half an hour later, they were sitting at table again, and again Evelynne had prepared a light meal, which Georgina found delicious. Four or five days passed more or less in the same way and on perhaps the sixth day or even after a week, she felt that the time had come to talk about the future – her future. In the intervening period since her arrival they had enjoyed the same warm friendship each day, neither of them getting on each other's nerves, both of them getting along with each other without a hitch. Both of them had commented on this.

"Guest and fish stink after three days!" Evelynne said with a serious mien one evening some time later, and for a second, Georgina perked up in surprise and consternation.

"But that ain't the case with us, is it?" Evelynne added with a laugh. Greatly relieved, Georgina readily agreed.

"No, it's wonderful. And where did you get that proverb?" Georgina asked with a giggle, "It didn't sound like you at all." At this, Evelynne simply burst out laughing.

"I don't know. I just picked it up somewhere; it's a Spanish proverb apparently."

"Well, I hope I don't stink," Georgina added, turning down her lips and pulling a face at which Evelynne once more collapsed into laughter and the two girls hugged each other out of sheer fun. It was some time before they could recover themselves. Then Evelynne said between attempts to recover herself, "I would have thrown you away a long time ago if you did," which only made them laugh even more. They rolled from the couch and onto the floor together, quite helpless with laughter and then over and over each other until they were quite out of breath. Shaking her hair into place and sitting up at last, she said seriously, "I suppose I have to go back sometime."

Evelynne raised her eyebrows, "Why?" she said.

"Well I've got to earn some money and keep myself. Go somewhere. Can't expect my parents to keep me for ever." Evelynne was silent. Then, "I don't want you to go. You can get a job here. Improve your French. On some days of the week I could talk to you only in French. You'd soon pick it up, you know."

Georgina nodded. "That's OK, Evelynne, but I'm officially here on holiday. I can't stay on indefinitely, can I? I mean, it's heaven here, but it can't go on, can it?" Strangely, Evelynne was silent. She rose and took the empty dishes to the kitchen. Suddenly, she had become the other Evelynne, the serious, mature Evelynne, the one Georgina didn't understand. The latter watched as the capable hands packed the dishes and cutlery carefully in removing them to the kitchen table next door. Every movement was preconsidered, exact, correct. Then she returned, took a chair opposite her friend and turning to Georgina, she said, "I'd like you to stay." She paused to let this sink in. "There's no reason why we shouldn't continue to get along together. We have a house to live in. I have more than enough money for us both. Think about staying. What's in the way? Your own independence?" She said the last word in French.

Georgy considered for a moment.

"Yes, dear Evelynne, I suppose it is that finally. Isn't it awful? Sounds like ingratitude."

"No, it doesn't at all. I understand how you feel and it's perfectly normal. Of course you want to feel independent of me. I have my independence and so I respect yours. I know you're not ungrateful. There's no question of feeling grateful anyway. *We* (she emphasised the word) are enjoying being together. Let's see how we get on for another week, shall we? Then we can think of a future for you."

Georgina noted Evelynne's maturity again, and wondered how she had managed to understand so much at twenty-three, but said nothing. She only nodded. They washed up together in silence, afterwards retiring to the lounge for a glass of wine. Georgina had learned to enjoy these late evenings over a glass of red wine.

"Evelynne?"

"Yes?"

"May I ask you a personal question?"

"Well, of course, ask away. You know all about me in any case."

"Physically perhaps, " Georgina smiled, "and you me, since we spend so much time walking around the place and garden with no clothes on and then spending our time at the beach in the same attire."

"'Attire', what does it mean?"

"It means 'clothes', but I mean it ironically."

"Oh, I see. Ah yes, 'attirer'. Same as French. You get it all from us anyway" She laughed heartily at her own observation. Then they both laughed.

"But seriously, Evelynne," Georgina continued, "although I know you well from that angle, I don't know about your background."

"I 'ope I look good from every angle," Evelynne said with mock remonstration.

"No, be serious. Tell me about yourself."

Suddenly, Evelynne again resumed that serious vein and her answer was measured as if she were under oath.

"I lost my mother five years ago. Meningitis. No hope. She died within a fortnight and everything changed here."

"So you lived here?" Georgina asked gently.

"Yes. My father could not bear being alone without her."

"But he had you," Georgina interrupted.

"Yes, but that was not enough. He returned one day to South America – to his homeland in Argentina. For me, that was a catastrophe. I was your age and quite alone. Except for Madame Levrois next door, I would not have managed." There were tears in Evelynne's eyes.

"How could he have left you in the lurch like that? That was wicked," Georgina pronounced.

"No, he was a lovely man, and he still cares for me. He just couldn't manage without Mummy. He was totally out on a limb. My mum did everything for him. Although he had a good job here, he always spoke Spanish and was never really any good at French. His friends were all either Spanish or South American. He never really integrated with the folks here. He was just like, 'ow you say, a feesh out of the water. When 'e went away, it was aw-ful, but you 'ave to get on with things, you know. I understood him and now I can forgive 'im. I see 'im once every year over there, you know. 'E's a good man. I love him."

Georgina was silent.

Evelynne continued, "He looks after me. Every month I 'ave a lot of money. He is very *genereux*. I 'ave no problems. I help Madame Levrois, because she's poor. 'Er husband died a year ago. Sad. The 'ouse here is mine, too, but I am alone, and that's not nice. I 'ave a few friends, one very good friend, but ee is a man. You know what they are."

Frankly, Georgina didn't know, but appreciated Evelynne's sentiments nevertheless.

"And you?" Evelynne asked. It was odd that the two had not considered their respective futures.

"*Je n'sais pas.*" She had already learned this phrase. Evelynne smiled. The truth was that she really didn't know now what would happen to her. She had left her homeland in a huff, and had been told that she would have to wait a further year for any chance to enter university. It was as though her young life had been temporarily shelved.

"I wanted to study medicine, but I have to wait another year before this can be realised," she said honestly. "My parents don't want me to study anything. All they want is for me to marry. But I don't want to marry any old man or someone they choose. Why should I?" Evelynne nodded.

"Then stay here." Evelynne said conclusively. Neither of them said more, but drank more red wine than was good for them.

"I'm tired," Evelynne said after a long pause between them.

"Me, too," Georgina said, "Let's go to bed." At this, Evelynne rose and walked towards her companion, taking her in her arms for a long time. "Don't go, dear Georges. You are 'appy 'ere." Georgina shared her friend's feelings perfectly and the two stood in an embrace for a full minute or so. Georgina allowed her comrade's hands to run over her back and buttocks. It was good.

"You are wonderful," Evelynne whispered. "Let's go to bed."

Because they were pretty drunk or because both of them had freed their hearts of a burden, they fell into Evelynne's, the nearest bed together and, like two small children, were soon fast asleep in each other's arms.

The next day dawned cloudlessly, and by eight o'clock the sun was shining brightly through the kitchen window at two sleepy girls making coffee and cutting and pasting their breakfast bread with butter and jam.

"Shall we go for a swim again today?" Georgina asked her friend.

"Yes, and we'll lunch at "Le Corsair." It's cheap and good even if a bit cramped."

"Super!" Georgina said, leaping up to rescue her egg

from the saucepan, in case it became too hard. "I think the fresh air and the exercise does us a world of good."

"I hadn't thought of that," Evelynne said nonchalantly, "We get so much of it down here. Anyway, it's nice swimming with you. You're a good swimmer, you know, Georgy."

"I've had a lot of practice at home and at school, I suppose," Georgina replied.

"I love to see you swim," Evelynne continued, "So elegant and powerful, and then this lovely form as you step out of the waves. A great sight!"

"You talk like a man!," Georgina said, amused. "And anyway, you're perfect yourself." They set to and hungrily devoured the rolls that had been left at the door earlier by the baker's lad.

"Scrumptious!" Georgina proclaimed.

"What?" her companion asked.

"Oh, doesn't matter," Georgina mumbled, her mouth full.

"Scroomchess!" Evelynne ventured, and Georgina nodded her head vigorously in approval, making noises through the egg and the bread.

It was Friday again. They swam until 11 am, lounged in the sun for another hour and then visited "Le Corsair." As Evelynne had said, the food was delicious and after their respite they rode home again happily. It was one of those very quiet autumn days, and the afternoon was hot and sultry.

"Thank you for inviting me again, dear Evelynne. You are very kind, and I feel that I'm much in your debt," said Georgina as she flung herself onto the settee.

"Oh, don't bother about that," her friend replied, taking off all her light clothes and joining Georgina quite nude on the sofa. She smiled lovingly at her friend. "Aren't you going to join me?" she said with a mischievous laugh.

Nobody's going to see us, and in this hot weather it's the best thing to do. I never wear clothes when I'm at home, anyway," Evelynne added.

"Yes, I've noticed," Georgina said laughing, stripping off the rest of her garments at her friend's suggestion.

"I would like to say it again, Evelynne. It's so nice of you to invite me all the time. I do appreciate it. I wish I could reciprocate some time."

"What?"

"Reciprocate; it means pay my way by asking you out for a change, but…"

"You've no money. Yes, you told me." Evelynne said, affecting boredom.

"I feel rotten about it," Georgina persisted, "you mustn't go on paying for everything. What shall I do?" At this Georgina seemed perturbed and made to get up.

"Sit down, dear girl, and relax," Evelynne ordered, pulling at Georgina's arm. Georgina sat heavily. Her firm breasts bounced slightly as she did so.

"I don't want you to go," Evelynne declared. "I'm selfish, I suppose, but life here with you is wonderful. Let's not spoil it by talking about money."

"I agree, oh I so agree; it's wonderful here, "Georgina concurred, "but sooner or later I must have some money myself."

"Yes, I know. We'll see," Evelynne said sympathetically, "Per'aps I could get a job for you. I 'ave friends, good friends and they will 'elp you I'm sure," Evelynne assured her. "I'll see what I can do."

"But that would be wonderful. Of course. But then there's my father and mother.

"They aint 'ere," Evelynne said flatly.

Georgina's reception of this grammatical liberty and her expression on receiving this simple assurance must have resulted in such a wreath of questioning complexity on Georgina's face that Evelynne laughed out loud.

"Oh, my pet, you are so concerned about these people that want to marry you off to some military, socially acceptable booby. To the devil with them."

"But they're my parents!"

"Yes, but you're a *beeg* girl now. It's in the natural way of things to go your own way."

"I owe them my life and my education. Everything!"

"You don't owe them anything. You don't need to offend them, but go your own way. And for heaven's sake don't allow them to put obstacles in your way – or do you want them to succeed in marrying you off like a piece of merchandise to some chinless wonder?"

Georgina was surprised by Evelynne's apparent sudden command of idiomatic English; she hadn't suspected this aptitude in her friend. It was disarming. Again, she felt herself confronted by a more mature mind than her own, and fell silent. Evelynne had snatched a book from the small table at one side of the sofa and had ostensibly begun to read in apparent complete disregard for Georgina's state of mind.

After a time, Georgina opened fire.

"You don't seem to care!" she said petulantly. Evelynne for her part reacted calmly to this provocation.

"Oh that's where you're wrong, *mon amie,* I know what you're in for if you go back 'ome. *You* return to middle-class existence that you hate, and *I* lose a friend. There aren't any complications here or am I wrong?

"Well, there's the money thing. That's the first obstacle," Georgina replied.

Evelynne put her magazine down with exaggerated patience and stood up in her wonderful human nakedness as though to emphasise her remarks.

"I've told you I've got good connections haven't I?"

"Yes"

"And I also told you on the beach that I'll make arrangements soon?"

"Yes"

"Well, why don't you believe me?"

"Because I don't know what you're referring to. Who or what are these 'connections' you mention?"

Both women were standing now, talking to each other as though they were in the market place, quite oblivious of their respective nudity. For a male observer happening upon the scene, it would have inspired a work of poetry or the finest of paintings!

"Just be a little patient, that's all," Evelynne said gently. "The time will come naturally. Let's eat something." As usual and always to Georgina's surprise, Evelynne made what seemed to her to be one or two perfunctory movements in the kitchen only to produce within a matter of minutes a dish of the most delicious food. How she managed this day after day was a mystery to her. Then she would say without exception, "Let's eat," rather, Georgina thought, like a clergyman enjoining his congregation to join him in "Let us pray." And indeed there were so many occasions where she, Georgina, would then sit and enjoy her food as though it were something of a holy ritual. Georgina pulled on a pair of long pants and sat down at table – one didn't sit naked at table – whereas Evelynne remained as she was, but remembered to tie a serviette round her neck as was proper in a French household. They set to.

"Good?" Evelynne asked with that mischievous look of hers that Georgina loved, but still didn't understand. Her mother would have described it as 'canny' she thought to herself. Yes, that was it. Her friend was canny, a treasury of secrets, a wise bird indeed.

"I just don't know how you can whistle up such delicacies within a few minutes just like that!" Georgina remarked, clicking her thumb and middle finger as though summoning the proverbial white rabbit from a hat.

Evelynne smiled her enigmatical smile and Georgina mused.

They drank a little less red wine than on the night before and settled themselves on the couch again. By this time it was about 6.30 pm, but still relatively warm for the time of year.

"Aren't the evenings superb?" she said and noticed that Evelynne had placed her arm round her shoulders. Both of them felt sublimely relaxed and comfortable. Georgina enjoyed Evelynne's proximity and turned to smile at her friend when Evelynne kissed her very gently on the neck, passing both her hands over Georgina's shoulders and back as she did so. Georgina did not protest, but took Evelynne's face in her hands and looked long and deeply into her eyes. Evelynne's eyes were dark and liquid, and Georgina noticed that the enigmatical smile was there again. It was a playful, ingenuous smile, and particularly endearing, bordered now by her long, curly, black hair.

"You've got lovely, strong hair," Georgina whispered. Without answering, Evelynne passed her hands down Georgina's arms and over her breasts. Georgina shuddered with pleasure. "Are you a lesbian?" Georgina asked softly, bathing her companion in a loving smile.

"I'm an admirer of good things," Evelynne replied, giving Georgina another exquisitely gentle kiss, this time on her forehead. "I know that life and youth are very short. I know that I feel good. I know that you are beautiful and that I have the privilege of having you here. I just want to show you how I feel." So saying, Evelynne hardly used her voice at all, and Georgina felt herself simply melting in her friend's embrace. She was sublimely happy. It was good. Very good.

They remained clasped in each other's arms like this for several minutes. There was great mutual understanding between them, which made them both very happy. Georgina had never felt such bliss as this ever before and revelled in the new discovery. Then because of this tide of happiness that quite overwhelmed her, she took the initiative and pressed Evelynne firmly against her and kissed her face, to which her companion responded warmly by winding her legs around Georgina's waist and pulling them tight, so that the latter felt strangely captive. "This is wonderful!" Evelynne said under her breath, "let it last." The fact is that this embrace lasted for thirty minutes in which both females fondled each other tenderly. At last they unwound, as it were and Evelynne suggested they go for a walk through the darkening woods outside. It was now blessedly cool, and after dressing, they set off through the garden for the shade of the wood and the path that would eventually take them to the beach. They had remained silent for a long time when, not far from the sea, Georgina said, "This is something new for me. I didn't know such happiness existed."

"Yes, it's wonderful, isn't it?" and taking Georgina's hand, ran with her towards the tumbling waves. "Shall we go in?" Evelynne asked excitedly, kicking off her light shoes and pulling her blouse over her head. "Yes, yes," Georgina cried, "but we mustn't swim far away from each other now it's getting dark."

"Good," Evelynne complied. "We'll stay here," and she plunged into an approaching wave and was gone for a second or two. Emerging with the water streaming from her hair and shoulders, she called over the commotion, "Oh come, it's lovely and warm," but just at that moment she was buried by another oncoming wave. Georgina swam out to her as best she could and thereafter the girls were forced to hold hands for mutual support, so strong was the cascade of waves crashing down upon them, effortlessly sweeping them off their feet like skittles. It was only with the maximum strenuous determination that the two eventually fought themselves free from the ocean's insatiable appetite. Once on the shore, both of them were pale. They recognised that although the sea was warm and inviting, its strength could easily prove to be fatal. They sat, knees drawn up to their chests and viewed the sea's agitation like front row spectators.

"That was near," Georgina shouted to her companion. Evelynne was still pale beneath her tan. She nodded. She knew only too well how many people lost their lives each year in doing just what they had done, and felt slightly guilty. "At this time of the year it gets a bit choppy," she said with that air of underestimation she had experienced during the war when people she had cowered with in air-raid shelters had commented on the hell of bombs outside as "a bit noisy". She smiled to herself. Evelynne for her part looked petulantly at the boiling waves like a child having just received a smack.

"It's a bit more than 'a bit choppy' don't you think?" she asked. "Anyway that's a good word. Where did you learn it?"

Evelynne, rallying, replied that she read a lot of English and must have seen the word in a magazine somewhere or perhaps had heard it from a tourist. She didn't know for sure. Georgina smiled.

"Choppy means there's plenty of low-level movement. This lot's swirling murder!" she added, watching the falling, churning, heaving water a few feet away. It was now cooler and since they had no towels with them, they decided to pick up their clothes and walk for a bit along the beach.

"Next week it'll already be November," Georgina remarked as they walked away from the tormented ocean.

"So what?" Evelynne said, shaking her thick black hair free of water.

"And then Christmas. Gosh! I've been here six weeks."

"*C'est fantastique!*" Evelynne rejoined.

"Yes, but I really must contact my parents and tell them I'm in safe hands, and that I want to stay. I really can't let them stew without their knowing that."

"There you go again," Evelynne returned, her black eyebrows raised to signify that Georgina should notice at last that she was repeating herself.

"I know you want to contact them," she went on, "that's proper. Good, contact them, but just let them know how you are and stay on."

Georgina was quiet for some time, weighing up this alternative.

They went home to eat and freshen up after their rough dowsing from Father Atlantic and it was then that Georgina decided to accept Evelynne's suggestion that they drive to a town about thirty miles away to make the phone call to her parents from a public phone box. This would preserve their anonymity, Evelynne had suggested. They arrived in the sun-drenched town about 3.30 pm and after drinking a coffee together at a nearby café, they squeezed themselves into the café's telephone cubicle.

"International," Evelynne said to the operator in preparing Georgina's call.

"Give me the number. I will spell it out to her. Just a moment."

The numbers were given and the line burr-burred for her companion.

"Here!" she said, "you're through."

"Hello, mummy; this is Georgina. Can you hear me all right?"

"Yes – Georgy – where are you?"

"I'm still here in France with Evelynne." There was a click on the line and silence. Then, "Can you hear me?"

"Yes, we can hear you," said her mother. "How are you?"

"Oh I'm fine, thank you, just fine. What's the weather like up there?"

"It's raining, dear, and cloudy. Can't expect much at this time of the year."

"Is papa all right?"

"Yes, he's all right, but worried about you. Why don't you come home?"

There were more noises on the line, and the next voice Georgina heard was that of her father's.

"How long do you think you're going to stay down there for, young woman? We're expecting you home. Don't forget that you are still under our parental care until you are twenty-one, and I demand that you come back home at once! Do you hear? At once!"

"He's terribly upset about your absence from home." It was her mother again.

"Why? I'm OK down here with Evelynne; she's looking after me very well, and we get on marvellously together."

"Well, dear, I know, but you must come *some* time. You've... (there was another ear-splitting interruption and Georgina and her mother were obliged to wait until it cleared)... been down there now for nearly eight weeks."

"Yes, I will of course, but for the moment I'm on holiday here. It's lovely and the weather is great."

"Umm, the weather. We'll expect you home at Christmas – at the latest."

Then the phone was suddenly dead. No word of

enquiry as to just how good it was "down there" or what she was doing, how she felt, how she got on with Evelynne. Nothing. Not even a farewell. Georgina replaced the receiver with tears in her eyes.

"They only think of themselves," she said, turning to her friend.

Evelynne's face was serious. She didn't like her friend to suffer. She said,"Well it's time you thought of *yourself, n'est ce pas?* "But for Georgina this judgement was hard to accept and they walked on through the streets of the shadowy little town in silence and sadness.

"The bus doesn't leave before 6.30 pm," Evelynne announced miserably, and seeing her dejection, Georgina smiled and put her arm around her shoulder as they walked along aimlessly through the narrow streets.

"Hey, there! What super young females! Hi. I like that dress of yours, darling, how about a bit of a pow-wow. I'll invite you both to a coffee."

The speaker was a young man of about twenty-one or two in tight, black trousers, an impeccable white shirt and sleek, oiled hair. He was accompanied by another as swanky as he and as predatory. "Keep your hands off!" Evelynne said furiously. He had already taken her by the arm and was attempting to pilot her to the small café on the opposite side of the street, while the other stood ostentatiously in front of Georgina and sized her up with undisguised appreciation as though she were a new candidate for his harem. "Oh, really superb! Super!" he said coming nearer. Georgy was a little scared, and took a step backwards. "A real beauty. Just look at that fair mop!" and the young gigolo put out his arm to take a lock of Georgina's hair. But before he got that far, Evelynne had come between them, her face reddened and her eyes were afire.

"You piss off, you miserable piece of shit!" Evelynne hissed.

"Very ladylike, I must say," the young man returned and unhindered, made a second attempt to touch Georgina.

"Gerroff!" Evelynne screeched, her eyes blazing. "Get away, you thug!" The young man, who was well built and much taller than Evelynne retreated slightly. The other boy now joined in and tried to accost Evelynne. The latter was ready for this and swung her handbag with considerable accuracy into the assailant's face from which he withdrew from the fray with a small cut above his eye.

"Little beast!" he said as he took himself off to nurse the wound. At this, Evelynne took advantage of the moment and, seizing Georgina by the hand, pulled her away from the other young swain with all the force she could muster.

"Try again and I'll kick the balls out of your pants!" she cried vehemently as a Parthian shot to the first amorous candidate.

"Nasty little slut!" the lad replied and commiserated with his stricken friend who was still dabbing at his head with an immaculately white handkerchief.

The whole engagement took place in a rattle of machine-gun French which, fortunately, Georgina couldn't yet understand, but was nonetheless quite aware of the tone in which this unhappy exchange took place, and, we must admit, was somewhat stunned by Evelynne's tiger-like reaction. The two ladies then left the scene of the encounter and made for the nearest café.

What was all that about?" Georgina asked, still a little shaken by the episode. Evelynne paused just a second or two before answering.

"*That,* dear girl, is what beautiful women like us are faced with every day in this country. All they're out for is to have us on our backs as quickly as possible. They've no interest other than to satisfy their own lust. *Animaux!*"

"Whatever did you say to the taller one, Evelynne? He looked a bit put off by what you said." Georgina enquired.

"I told him to leave us alone," Evelynne replied simply

"Was that all?

"Yes."

"He must have said something pretty insulting to you in the first place for you to have thrown your bag at him," Georgina pursued, but Evelynne showed no inclination to enlarge on the subject and sat stone-faced in front of her coffee. It was clear to Georgina that Evelynne was considerably upset by the interlude, so she tactfully sipped at her own coffee, relieved that the brutal episode was behind them and said nothing more for several minutes.

'Would those boys be waiting outside for us?', Georgina thought to herself, and 'not only the two of them, but a party, and what would we do in such a situation?' It was now only 4.30 pm. Their bus wouldn't leave for another couple of hours. Suddenly, Evelynne recovered enough to say, "You 'ave to be firm with them. Don't ever give an inch, because if you do, they'll take advantage of you. Mark my words: not an inch!"

Georgina listened quietly, "Best thing to do is to make it perfectly clear to them at the outset that you're married or waiting for your 'usband or something like that. Never listen to what they say, but walk on and ignore them."

"I didn't realise that they were such a menace," Georgina said quietly, "and thanks for telling me. Good that they weren't on the beach."

"Oh they would have raped us in seconds, believe me!" Evelynne interrupted, "but for some reason they don't go along the beach, I don't know why. Perhaps they feel more secure in the town."

"What shall we do now? Do you think they're still around?" Georgina asked nervously.

"Probably not; they're not violent usually, and I don't think that tall one will come for more. If he tried again, I would definitely report him to the local police or the gendarmerie. They're always on our side, and these fancy boys know it."

"The one was quite good-looking, I thought," Georgina ventured.

"Less than before we met him," Evelynne said with a wicked smile. "He won't come for more. Anyway, one of these days I'll show you a real man. At home though. Not in the street. No! Never."

Then changing the subject as the waitress approached, she turned to Georgina to ask,"Do you like toasted cheese sandwiches?"

"Sure, they sound very good, why not?"

"Good. Since we don't have to watch our waistlines, let's 'indulge' as I think you English say?"

"Super, let's." So they 'indulged' and felt the better for it, added cups of tea to their indulgence and were well satisfied. So satisfied were they that Georgina felt moved to ask Evelynne what she had meant a moment before by 'a real man'.

"Oh, nothing," Evelynne hedged.

"Nothing?"

"No. I mean 'yes'. Nothing."

"So, no man."

"That's right."

Georgina the Beautiful laughed, and it was at such times that she was at her most attractive. Her guileless laugh was bell-like. When she laughed, she exposed her perfectly white teeth to match the poetry of her lovely head of thick, blonde hair and playful green eyes. Aye, at times like these she was a veritable goddess. One could almost feel sorry for the hapless aspirants to a closer association of an hour ago. At least they had shown good taste in their choice of quarry. Sexist? Not a bit of it! Georgina's attractiveness was something no one could overlook. If you couldn't appreciate that, you were certainly in need of a pair of glasses! And the nicest part of all this perhaps was the fact that our young woman didn't overdo things. She knew now at nearly eighteen that she was a handsome creation, but was far from showing this off. The naturalness of her person was one of her most winning qualities, and it was precisely this that Evelynne prized in her friend and wanted to protect.

"No, you've something up your sleeve," Georgina coaxed.

"Sleeve? What's that?"

"I mean you're hiding something from me?

"No. Of course not."

"You don't want to tell me then?" Georgina pursued.

"Well," Evelynne began, "It's not a secret or anything like that. I just want to say that these street men are not what I call real men. They're mere boobies, little boys. For them, we're just something to exploit, use, and then throw away like an apple core."

Georgina was tickled to bits with Evelynne's serious mien and delighted with her apt comparison. She listened. "I have a friend that comes over now and again from Bordeaux to visit me."

"Well, well," Georgina said wide-eyed, "you never told me anything about that! So you've got a boyfriend! What's his name?"

"Jean-Luc. He's much older than we are. He's forty-six." Evelynne replied simply.

All Georgina could say this time was "Oh" in the tone her mother used to use when Georgina had been obliged to own up to something. Evelynne understood the meaning of the intonation perfectly, and added hurriedly,

"He has absolutely no effect on our relationship. He's just in the background, that's all, and it would be nice if you could meet him. I'd like that." Georgina remained silent. For some reason she couldn't fathom, the prospect of Jean-Luc disturbed her. He was suddenly a totally unnecessary foreign body in their relationship that she didn't want to meet. In that moment, she questioned herself. Was she jealous? Did she secretly envy Evelynne her male friend? But why?

Evelynne sensed what she was thinking. "It's all right. He's very nice. He's not going to come between us," and she put her hand lightly on Georgina's.

"I've no right to have any reservations, dear Evelynne, and you have every right to a boyfriend."

"He's hardly a 'boy'", Evelynne said with a smile, "and when I talked of a 'real' man I was thinking of him."

Georgina nodded.

They left the café and sought the bus station. The 'street men' were not in evidence and both women were heartily glad of the fact. The bus was on time and they arrived home somewhat after seven o' clock. The sun was setting earlier each day or so it seemed to Georgina. Winter would soon be here, and she wondered again whether she should go home.

They sat down to a light supper in relative silence. The events of the day and their subsequent conversation occupied their thoughts. After supper, Evelynne slipped into the garden for something, leaving Georgina to wash up and tidy the kitchen. It was now almost dark except for a full moon climbing into the sky. After five minutes or so, Evelynne appeared in the doorway. She had cut some autumn flowers and was now arranging them lovingly in a vase on the kitchen table. Georgina watched her.

"They're wonderful," she said as Evelynne continued to primp and preen a leaf here, a flower there, her back towards her. "We don't have such flowers in Britain. I've never seen anything like these before."

Evelynne then put down the scissors she had been using, turned, and came towards her. Evelynne hugged her friend tightly for a long minute while tears came into her eyes. Georgina was moved, too, and responded warmly to her embrace.

"Let's go to bed," Evelynne whispered, releasing her. Georgina nodded silently and the two met a few minutes later under the shower. The warm water and the reciprocal soaping they gave each other did them a world of good. As they dried themselves, they laughed and chattered like birds, and later fought each other in the bedroom with their respective pillows, wrestled on the bed, laughing and shrieking until they were quite exhausted. Thus, the tensions of the afternoon evaporated in a swoon of youthful sleep until dawn.

Tommy had received his cuddles from both ladies during the day, had purred appreciatively, having eaten his food and spent the daylight hours on his favourite chair. But now it was dark. He jumped from his cushion, stretched expansively, tore at his mat with his needle-like claws and took measure of the kitchen with eyes and nose, satisfying himself that all was well here before finally moving off towards the cat flap in the kitchen door and out into the night. At last, thank goodness, it was cool and he revelled in the night scents of the garden flowers, laced with the salted air from the sea. First, he would inspect that small mousehole he'd seen yesterday. The mouse would probably come out soon, he calculated. He would wait awhile. Yes, he would wait. Tommy yawned and sniffed very gently at the opening in the earth. Yes, the mouse had been here recently. He waited. Above, the moon rode upon the swift autumn clouds flying eastward. He could hear the sea crashing on the shore hardly a mile away. The trees above him swayed slightly in the light breeze. Somewhere an owl hooted. The cat looked up, seeing the branches silhouetted against the sky. Everything in movement. Everything was in motion; everything was changing, changing into something else. Now and for ever. Sometimes slow, he knew, sometimes quick. Now! Quick! Pounce! A moment's struggle. The mouse is dead. Tommy tears off its head and eats part of its trunk, although he's not really very hungry, leaving the rest to become one with the earth and the other to pass through in his gut, change with time and then join the rest of the mouse in the muck of the garden. Sated, Tommy moves on among the grass and flowers, eyes bright to see and claws to kill, paws and teeth to rend, his black shadow blending as easily with the night as water fills the contours of a vessel. Sleek. Silent. Deadly. The roosting birds see him, but stir not. The owl notes his progress. Tommy's soft paws tread lightly over last year's leaves that, a year ago, had gathered on the branches by the hundred thousand with their fellows to bid welcome to the sun in joyous green so high in the trees of yesteryear, but now how great their fall! Now they were brittle, dry and brown, the skeletons of past majesty, breaking under a cat's paw. The owl swoops. Tommy, ready, claws unsheathed, eyes ablaze, strikes, but he's not quite as swift. He slashes out at the soundless feather, but misses and the bird flies on unperturbed. Tommy knows the Game of Creation, all about death and re-creation, and he knows very well that the price for keeping alive is constant vigilance, of eating and of avoiding being eaten. He knows the eternal rule of change that is indissolubly linked with creation. He knows that death is part of this perennial cycle with no beginning and no end. He knows that life leads to ageing and death and that death in its turn leads to life and that the two are one in an alternating, endless parade. It is all acted in the guise of coming and going, of being and not being, a royal game of infinite change.

He has no words as we have words to soften the incontestable truth of this unfathomable pageant, but he, aye, even he understands the nature of this magnificent Symphony of Time, this ineffable manifestation for which there are no words.

It is Saturday again as the morning light invades the heavy curtains of the girls' bedroom. Evelynne is awake first and tiptoes from the bedside towards the bathroom to prepare herself for the day and arrange breakfast. Looking out of the kitchen window, she notices that it had rained in the night. Heavy clouds hung over the garden and most of the leaves had now been swirled from the branches of the trees. In three weeks it would be Christmas. And next week her birthday again when she'd be twenty-four. What a thought! How time raced.

Georgina appeared a few minutes later, and the two settled to breakfast in good spirits. "That was real fun last night," Georgina said happily. "I think I've made up my mind to stay," she said.

Evelynne turned from withdrawing a slice of bread from the toaster and said in that simple fashion of hers, "Of course, you're going to stay, my dear."

"But I have to get a job. Something. Somewhere," Georgina cautioned.

"Yes, I'll help you there, "Evelynne reassured her, "Jean-Luc will certainly be over before Christmas and he's a pretty influential man in his world. *You*, dear Gina, must keep up your French. The better French you speak, the more likely you will be to find a job," Evelynne said with conviction.

"You said my French is improving."

"Yes, it is of course, but you need daily practice."

"Anyway, what does Monsieur Jean-Luc do for a living?" Georgina asked with interest.

"He's the Bordeaux editor of *Mode pour Toi* and has a lot to do with the fashion world."

"Oh."

"Yes, and he helps beautiful women like you. I just know he'll appreciate you. You could make a fortune," Evelynne added in French.

"That's not the important thing," Georgina replied, "I must *do* something worthwhile."

"Yes, I understand," Evelynne said. "We'll see when the time comes."

For the next three weeks, both women worked hard and systematically on Georgina's French: They even worked on Evelynne's birthday, only spending an hour or two in Bordeaux where Evelynne bought herself a new pair of shoes, and Georgina spent her last sous on flowers. This gesture was greatly appreciated by Evelynne incidentally who noted it inwardly, and who had made up her mind to help her English companion in every way she could. Evelynne also proved to be a very competent teacher, one with an iron will and high standards of perfection, and Georgina a willing, conscientious pupil. Generally speaking, they put what Georgina had learned in the morning to practical purposes in the afternoon when Georgina would be allowed to fend for herself ("to be thrown to the lions", as Evelynne called it) during visits to a nearby village or town and sometimes even as far as Bordeaux.

During these weeks, the two women came even closer to one another, learning to respect their differences and their strengths and to appreciate each other generally. Georgina also learned how to cook well under her friend's guidance, and this very much pleased Evelynne, so that in March of the following year, Georgina could more or less stand on her own two feet for all practical purposes and – much to Evelynne's delight – could speak, read and write passable French. She could go shopping regularly on her own now, ask questions (and understand the answers) as to quality, volume, contents, price and even bargain when it came to it!

It was on her return from one of these excursions late one morning that she entered the house to discover that Evelynne was apparently not at home.

She called briefly, and when there was no response, she concluded that her friend was in the garden. She kicked of her shoes in the hall and wandered barefoot into the kitchen. No one. She went out into the garden. There was no one here either, so she assumed that Evelynne had gone over to see how her neighbour was faring, as she did from time to time. Turning towards the hall again, she noticed that spring sunshine was trying to enter the drawn curtains of their bedroom and was just about to go in and draw them when she noticed that Evelynne and a man were locked in sexual embrace on their bed as she reached the door. Georgina stood still in her tracks fascinated by the scene, but the lovers themselves were quite unaware of her presence. After a moment, she turned and left for the kitchen, unpacked her purchases and, with shaking hands, made herself a cup of coffee, looked desultorily at the paper, washed the cat's bowl, and waited.

After what seemed to her to be an hour, but in fact was only a few minutes, the lovers appeared, dressed and tousled, and seated themselves at the kitchen table without a word.

"Coffee?" Georgina asked blandly.

"This is Jean-Luc," Evelynne said quietly. Georgina stretched out a hand, mumbled her name and added that she was pleased to meet the new guest. She looked at Evelynne.

"Jean-Luc came just after you had gone," her friend said sheepishly.

"Oh yes?" Georgina replied ridiculously. The three sat silently. After perhaps two long, minutes, Jean-Luc, a man in his mid-forties, broke the icy meditation over morning coffee.

"May I introduce myself more fully?" he asked in polished French, "I feel we owe you an apology, *mademoiselle*, and I would like to take this opportunity of doing so. Moreover, I would also like to add that we did not deliberately take advantage of your absence – I would like to emphasise this point – but that I quite surprised Evelynne here this morning. She didn't expect me. Please forgive our, er… indulgence." He smiled.

Georgina smiled back, saying nothing. Evelynne fiddled with her hair.

"I'm sorry, too, dear," she said very quietly.

"And I'm sorry if I've given you cause for offence, Georgina, which I'm sure I have," the gentleman hurried on to say.

"Not at all, I was surprised, that's all," Georgina said and stood up. "More coffee?" she asked going over to the coffee machine.

"Oh yes," the other two said almost in unison, and both noticed in that second or so that Georgina not only exhibited beauty, but also a fine dignity of manner as she poured out their beverage from a large flask. It was this that Jean-Luc appreciated most in this embarrassing interval, and felt kindly towards Evelynne's friend.

"Thank you," he said warmly on receiving the coffee. Georgina, picking up this wavelength, nodded in acknowledgement. The coffee was poured, its pungent aroma reaching all their nostrils.

"You make good coffee," Jean-Luc announced, sipping at the cup's rim.

"I too have to apologise for coming in so abruptly. I had no idea…" Georgina said, finding words at last.

"Not at all. Most regrettable," Jean-Luc swiftly responded, dismissing Georgina's need to apologise. "I should have rung to say I was out this way today," and then, changing the subject, he observed, "Lovely weather we're having." The sun's rays were pouring into the kitchen.

"Yes, lovely today," Georgina agreed. There was a brief silence.

Then, Georgina enquired, "Have you known each other long?"

"About two years, I'd say." Evelynne said, answering for him.

"Yes, about that," Jean-Luc confirmed, smiling at Evelynne.

"Evelynne has mentioned you from time to time, but I had no idea that you were such a 'close' friend," she said with a dagger in her smile. They all laughed at this, and the tautness of the atmosphere relaxed considerably.

"I would like to make a suggestion," Jean-Luc said, standing, "I would be honoured if you two ladies would be my guests for lunch. Would that be acceptable?"

"Very good idea," Evelynne said, turning to Georgina for confirmation. The latter acquiesced. "But give me a minute or two to make myself a bit more presentable," she added.

"There's plenty of time," Jean-Luc said, looking at his watch. "I think I'll take a round in the garden while you two get ready," and he and Tommy went out into the welcoming sunshine outside.

Jean-Luc knew of a good restaurant in the neighbouring countryside and surprised Evelynne, who had never heard of either the village or the restaurant, and yet was convinced that she knew the names of all the restaurants in the area. The weather being clement for the time of year, they were able to sit outside on the terrace which was naturally integrated with the garden, where a large, white dog lay basking in a pool of sunshine. The food was indeed very good, the service friendly.

Jean-Luc proved to be excellent company. He was a good raconteur with a veritable treasury of appropriate *bon mots* that made them both laugh. Georgina noted the athletic body beneath the impeccable light-grey suit, the well manicured hands and nails, his tanned face from which a pair of kindly blue eyes flickered with wisdom and good humour. Yes, this man was a *charmeur,* but, Georgy felt, a sincere individual nevertheless. She liked him. He seemed to have everything in hand. None of his movements was hurried; none of his remarks came too soon to cut off another's opinion. It was as though this early afternoon was all there was in the world, that time didn't matter, giving one the impression that he had somehow been appointed to listen. He made you feel relaxed in his company and that your opinion was the only thing that counted. She noted, too, the lines of worldly experience on his face, the slightly thinning hair, now slowly beginning to grey. She was curious to know more about him, and would ask Evelynne later.

Their host also generously paid the bill, leaving a large tip, Georgina noticed, and around 2.30 pm they were in the car once again, heading for home over the springing green fields. On the way, Jean-Luc spoke of the political situation, of the trouble he'd had a week or so before with the car he was driving, the price of the repair and the price of things generally, especially in the cities, and finally, of his intention to drop by again soon. They had arrived at *rue du nord 45*. Alighting first from the car, Jean-Luc opened the door for the ladies and, after kissing Evelynne affectionately, addressed himself to warmly shaking hands with Georgina.

And then, waving goodbye from the car, he was gone.

"Well! Quite a day so far!" Georgy declared to the garden while Evelynne followed searching for the key to the front door.

Evelynne smiled ever so slightly. It was that enigmatic, *Gianconda* smile again, and Gina didn't know again what to make of it. Evelynne hadn't said much during the meal or for the rest of the afternoon for that matter, and Georgina wondered whether there was another reason for her reticence.

Suddenly, she was there with a question: "Did you understand everything he said?" she asked.

"Yes, for the most part; I felt very proud of myself," Georgina said lightly with a smile.

"Good!" Evelynne said encouragingly. "You're so intelligent, *ma Georgine*. I'm so proud of you." The two women let themselves into the house and once in the lounge, sat heavily on the sofa. Somehow, the day had been as strenuous as though they'd been swimming.

"Let's have a glass of wine," Evelynne suggested, rising to go to the sideboard. "This here is an especially good year," she added, drawing out a bottle from one of its cupboards.

"What again?" Georgina half-protested, "We've already swilled down no end at the restaurant. Especially Jean-Luc. I wondered now and again at table whether he'd ever be able to rise from it later with dignity! Then the driving on top. I was scared I tell you."

"He can take his alcohol all right," Evelynne replied assuringly and poured Georgina a glass of red wine that caught and brilliantly reflected the afternoon sun. "Nice guy."

"Nice guy! What does that mean? Sure he's a 'nice guy'. I think so, too, but I assume he means a bit more than that for you," Georgina said with a laugh.

"He's a lovely man, then, put it that way," Evelynne conceded.

Georgina said nothing in reply, smiled and sipped at her wine.

"He's a good friend, a very good friend," Evelynne repeated a moment or two later.

Now, as we have said, Georgina was a well brought-up young person and English to boot, so that she did not pursue the issue and so cause embarrassment, but rather hoped that Evelynne would meditate on the matter of her own accord and in her own time. Nevertheless, she was intensely curious.

After an interval, Evelynne, feeling the warmth of the wine in her stomach, continued. "Jean-Luc is what I call 'a real man', you see. He comes over now and again and we make love, because we both need it, but he would never demand my body. He accepts me as I am, and our lovemaking is simply a natural consequence of his friendly feelings for me."

Georgina listened intently. There was a pause.

"Do you love him?" she then asked gently.

"Love? No, I don't think so, anyhow not in the usual way."

"Usual?" Georgina queried.

"Yes. I mean I don't want to serve him in any way or

spend the rest of my life with him. Anyway, he's too old for that."

"How old is he, then?" Georgina enquired.

"He's forty-six."

"Umm, I see what you mean. But you can give yourself to him wholly like today without getting involved?"

"Yes. I suppose I love him as a good friend. He has always been kind and generous. He's an interesting companion. He's gentle, kind and considerate. Knows all kinds of things, and I'm sure he's very good at his job."

"Is he married?" Georgina ventured.

"No, so there's no need to lie and deceive. He comes, he loves, he goes and we're both happier for seeing each other. Isn't that wonderful?"

Georgina was silent. Sensing that her companion was astonished at these revelations, Evelynne went on, "We *like* each other, Georgina, that's the main thing. Our friendship is one of trust and mutual respect. He doesn't expect me to give up my life for him. I can give him what he needs when he comes over and he does the same for me. It's a natural part of our relationship. I think you understand me now, *n'est-ce pas?*"

The wine was taking effect. Both women were enfolded in that warm mutuality again that they had enjoyed so much over the last few months. Georgina for her part didn't feel any longer that Jean-Luc had disrupted that feeling or that he was perhaps some kind of usurper. Moreover, she understood Evelynne's sentiments and was surprised at her own tolerance. At first, she might have put Evelynne's independence of mind down to an emotional shortcoming – even coldness. Such an idea had in fact occurred to her, but on consideration she knew that neither applied.

Evelynne then continued, "I know you thought me to be a lesbian, but for me this is just a term. I don't think of myself as anything. I just do what comes naturally. So long as you love, it doesn't matter. Love is the main thing." So saying, she curled up luxuriously with Tommy on the sofa, leaving Georgina to her thoughts and reflections.

Georgina looked into the fire that they had lit, having prepared it a day before against the possibility of a cold evening. The days were fine and warm, but the evenings cooler.

"I want to be clear about one thing," Georgina said, "I'm not criticising you, and I hope you understand me here. No criticism. It's just that I've had a different background, I suppose. That's natural enough, isn't it?"

Evelynne nodded. "Of course."

"And we're all conditioned in our way, aren't we?" Georgina pursued.

"Of course," Evelynne concurred. "Most folks don't even suspect that they're locked in a steel corset of conditioned reflexes."

Georgina was impressed with this remark and also by the way Evelynne had summed up the situation.

"I'll ring Jean-Luc tomorrow and ask him to come round. I don't want to talk about these matters on the phone; you never know who might be snooping," Evelynne declared.

Lt. Col. Hennessey was pleased with himself as he sat down to his evening meal. Tucking in a large, white serviette behind his tie, he announced to his family and a couple of neighbours who had joined him for dinner that it wouldn't be long now before his daughter would be safely ensconced in the house again, "Interpol are on the job. We'll soon prise her from the claws of this damned French woman." One or two in the company nodded.

Mrs Shawcross asked, "What kind of a woman is that?" and Georgina's mother replied for her husband, since at that very moment he was busy sawing at his steak. "A girl she used to correspond with, you know, a penfriend."

"How nice," Mrs Shawcross commented, but was immediately broadsided by the colonel who had dropped some of his potato on hearing the remark.

"Not nice at all. I wish we'd never set eyes on the hussy!"

"Hussy?" General Shawcross, ex-Indian army, now retired, queried. "Have you ever met her?"

"Oh yes," Georgina's mother replied, anticipating another outbreak from her husband. "Seemed a very nice young thing then, small and dark, you know how they are down there."

"Not a hussy, then?" General Shawcross concluded.

"Yes, a damned hussy, Ludwig, if you'll forgive my saying so. Keeps our daughter down there a thousand miles away from home and hasn't the decency to persuade her to come home. Been down there for six months now, she has. Six whole months!"

"But I understand that Georgina has written to you quite often and even telephoned on one or two occasions," Mrs Shawcross ventured pleasantly.

"Perhaps she doesn't want to come home just yet?"

"But she's got no money and no job!" the colonel proclaimed loudly. "This woman is keeping her; she knows all the ropes to carry this out of course and our kid's just a pawn in her hands. Georgina's got no prospects for a job in France and no money to get back up here." More potato found its way back onto his plate.

"Interpol will see to it and you'll know more in a few days, I'm sure, Henry," Ludwig Shawcross assured him.

"Must say I liked Evelynne when I got to know her," Patrick interjected. "Girl could play great tennis. Never seen anything like it, to tell the truth. Beat Ray Fitzgerald once and made him look like a beginner, I remember."

"Oh yes, she's got things tied up all right; she knows

what she's doing, and she'll keep our daughter down there as long as it suits her – or so she thinks – but soon she'll smile on the other side of her face, believe me," Henry Hennessey prophesied. Patrick shut up, but felt a kindly flush of pleasure that Georgy had had the pluck to leave home. Dessert was served.

Jean-Luc arrived two days later, swinging his lithe body up the steps to the house. Evelynne embraced her visitor.

"You have a question, I understand," Jean-Luc asked almost professionally as the three of them sat down to afternoon coffee in the kitchen.

"Jean-Luc," Evelynne began, "I hope you don't mind my asking you to come over, but I think you can help us, and the matter is private."

"I'll be glad to help in any way I can," Jean-Luc returned, smiling.

"I'll come straight to the point – and can you understand everything?" she asked, turning to Georgina. "I 'ave to speak it in French, you know?"

"Of course," Georgina encouraged her, "I can understand most things today."

Jean-Luc smiled at this and listened carefully.

"She needs a job. Can you get her one?"

"Jean-Luc laughed. "Is that all?" he said.

"Yes. That's it," said Evelynne, "but it's a bit urgent – I mean… *soon?*"

"I see." Jean-Luc, looked serious. How soon?" he asked.

"As soon as possible."

"I see," Jean-Luc said again thoughtfully. "You mean in Bordeaux?"

"Yes."

"Well it shouldn't present much of a problem, and I suppose you mean as a model?"

"Anything"

"Anything?"

"Umm," Jean-Luc mused, looking out of the window and at the lively spring wind combing the trees outside.

"I suppose you want to take measurements?" Evelynne guessed correctly interrupting his contemplation.

"Well, yes, but what does Georgina want to do? Does *she* want to become a model?"

Georgina nodded in affirmation.

"Stand up," Jean-Luc said, "and we'll see."

"Hey! Paws off! I'll manage that," Evelynne said, snatching the tape measure from Jean-Luc's hands in precisely the way a mother would from that of a child about to undergo a risk.

Georgina stood up and allowed Evelynne to take her measurements, which she did quickly and with such professional acumen that Jean-Luc had to smile. Georgina blushed slightly.

Evelynne announced the relevant statistical information at each third of her friend's body and returned the tape to its owner.

"Ah yes, very fine," Jean-Luc sighed, rolling up his tape and replacing it in his briefcase.

"Actually you don't need a tape, *mon ami,* you can see for yourself."

"Ah yes," Jean-Luc replied, "but facts are facts and need to be recorded with a photo and laid before a committee. I can only recommend," he explained.

"She will need training, too," he went on, but there was something hesitant in his manner, and Evelynne took him to task.

"Isn't she good enough for you, then?" she asked provocatively.

"Don't be absurd, "Jean-Luc flung back.

"And don't you be so hedgy. Where's the hook?" Georgina couldn't understand every word of this rapid exchange, but by now she knew enough to understand the general gist of things even in rapid, idiomatic French.

Jean-Luc, bloody but unbowed, replied, "She's impeccable of course."

Evelynne threw herself into battle again: "Of course *what?*"

"She's not the kind of doll that can display her charms on a catwalk, that's what," Jean-Luc returned with exaggerated patience.

"And why not, may I ask? Evelynne demanded.

Jean-Luc sighed. "Because I don't want to see this beautiful young woman boiled down to a strutting, titless skeleton, swaying on a catwalk to suit the whims of a rich Bordeaux clientèle

"Boiled?" Evelynne, still warm, enquired.

"I mean that she's too lovely to be reduced to an emaciated norm, and I don't want to be responsible for such a thing either."

"But you're up to your neck in this business. It's your life, so I'm surprised to hear you talk like this," Evelynne noted with remarkable self-composure, her deep black eyebrows raised in ironically surprised enquiry.

"All right, I know, but I just don't want to watch this wonderful example of womanhood bereft of what makes her attractive, that's all."

"So you don't see the ladies you have to deal with over there as 'attractive?'"

"No."

"Well, that's something new. Evelynne was visibly relieved, and it was clear that she appreciated Jean-Luc's reasons, and as for Georgina, she largely understood what the tiff was about, and felt like a prize bull.

Jean-Luc asked for more coffee and fell silent for a few

moments, and then suggested that Georgina could work in another branch that was to be set up soon and which would cater for 'normal' young women. "It has great potential," he enthused. "She wouldn't get the same salary as a top model, but she'd be well paid and earn enough to render her completely independent," he added.

"That'd be wonderful!" Georgina cried, "and I could come to see you regularly, dear Evelynne," she added happily.

Evelynne smiled her smile.

"Aren't you pleased?" she asked her friend, but before Evelynne could answer, Jean-Luc, fatherlike, answered for her. "I'll see that she's properly looked after," he said. Again, Evelynne was relieved. She knew she could trust Jean-Luc.

"Well, when could she start work?" she asked.

"I have to put this proposition to the board. Only thereafter can I give you an actual date," he explained formally. "Let's see, we have the 21st. We usually meet at the end of each month. Depending on their decision, Georgina could start perhaps around this time next month, but I must say again that it's not up to me alone."

"Ok, ok, you said that," Evelynne chipped in not very kindly, and Jean-Luc was brusquely obliged to swallow his clarification, which he did with dignity, but not without noting the rudeness. He maintained his equilibrium, and it was at that very instant that Georgina quite clearly perceived a depth in their relationship, which had not been confirmed by their recent chat. These two were very close to one another. From this one, short exchange she knew for certain that they were much more than the occasional lovers Evelynne would have her believe. It was an exposure. It was like sweeping thick, lounge curtains aside to reveal a hitherto unsuspected magnificent mountain landscape. The insight pleased Georgina. She felt she knew more about her friend. For a moment, perhaps, she had fathomed that smile, and she was more than pleased that she might be financially independent within a few weeks. She jumped up and kissed Jean-Luc on the forehead who sat there quietly holding his coffee cup. He smiled.

These days, it was customary for Georgina to go out shopping for them both in St Laurant, a forty-minute bus ride away from Soulac-sur-Mer. On this particular morning she left an hour earlier than usual, having planned to give herself a bit more time to find something sweet and typically French for her younger sister, Sarah. The weather was fine and warm, and spring well underway. "And if you feel molested, go straight to the police station," Evelynne had warned on seeing her off at the bus stop. It was market day in the town and Georgina felt sure she would find something suitable for Sarah after she had purchased her provisions. She took her time, sought conversation with other women, took coffee and was not molested by predatory, male youth. At midday, she discovered a delightful, hand-made doll, which she thought would very much please her sister and sat down at last to lunch. She had time, and the sun was so benevolent that she revelled in its balm to her face and legs. After lunch and as was her custom, she sought the telephone kiosk she always used on these excursions to ring Evelynne and tell her either how she was getting on or what bus she would eventually take to get home. On this occasion, the telephone rang out for a long time. "Perhaps she's in the garden," Georgina said to herself, replaced the receiver and returned to the town centre. It was now very warm. She sat down on a bench outside the park and desultorily watched the pigeons at the town's fountain. After about half an hour, she felt that she should try again and went back to the kiosk.

"Allo!" she said loudly into the mouthpiece, "I rang earlier, but…"

"Yes, I know you did," Evelynne's voice breathlessly confirmed.

"What's up?"

"Give me the number of the kiosk phone," she ordered.

"What?"

"The number in the phone box, so that I can ring you back. *Don't* ring me here. Stay put."

Obediently, Georgina found the number and recited it slowly to Evelynne.

"Good," Evelynne said. The receiver clicked. Silence. Georgina was alarmed and looked from the kiosk up the sun-soaked road. Most people had withdrawn into the cool shelter of their houses by this time. It was 2 pm. In the distance, she could just see the market people breaking camp. What could have happened? They always enjoyed their persiflage on the phone, where Georgina would muster all the French she knew to impress her friend and where the latter would put all kinds of idiot questions to her and cause a good deal of laughter. Today, things had been short and formal. Evelynne sounded a different person. It was discomforting. A good hour passed by which time Georgina was sweating under the heat from the sun high above her and from that reflected by the buildings when the bell in the kiosk rang.

"Allo, Evy?" Georgina asked tentatively.

"Allo, my love. Jean-Luc and I'll pick you up in twenty minutes. Go to our café. We'll meet there. Kiss!" She was gone.

Georgina made her slow way to the café, found a place outside on the terrace and waited. 'With Jean-Luc? How come?' she asked herself. He would normally be at work seventy-odd miles away in Bordeaux city. Why Jean-Luc? Clearly, there was something wrong.

They had come on motorcycles and had parked these carefully in front of the house, briefly exchanged a few words with each other, inspected the house and its garden with a professional eye, as policemen will and entered, heavy in their road attire, still helmeted, official, unhurried.

"*Bonjour, mademoiselle,*" they had said, "Are you Mademoiselle Evelynne Dumant, perhaps? Perfectly friendly, the one even a little self-conscious.

"Yes, that's me," Evelynne said, surprised to discover their incongruous presence among the striving green and the blossoms of spring.

"*Ah, oui,* we are trying to locate the presence here of a young woman called…" the one paused to get the correct pronunciation of the name, scrutinising a paper he held before him…" er, Georgine 'Ennessey, a British woman of, er, about eighteen years of age. Is she here?"

"*Non.*"

"*Non?*"

"But she lives here apparently?" the one policeman pursued.

"She's gone."

"Gone?"

"Yes, gone home. Yesterday," Evelynne lied.

"And when precisely, please?"

"Yesterday morning. By bus."

"You mean by bus to Bordeaux?" The younger man took the opportunity to look beyond Evelynne into the hall.

"Then you won't mind if we take a look around to assure ourselves," his superior enquired.

"Well, of course. Come in."

Both officers were careful to wipe their shoes before entry. They nodded courteously to Evelynne as she opened the door a little wider for them to enter the house. Their large, blue bulkiness filled the hall.

"This is her bedroom," Evelynne said helpfully. The officers nodded.

"And this was our kitchen, "she added, showing them the sunlit kitchen, noting to herself how glad she was to have washed up tell-tale dishes for two people. The policemen were awake to every detail as their eyes surveyed the kitchen and a moment later the lounge. Evelynne began to feel uncomfortable.

"Upstairs?" the one asked.

"We never used the rooms up there. Nobody's been up there since my mother died two and half years ago," Evelynne explained truthfully. The policemen received this information and murmured their condolences. She was suddenly glad of their diverted attention. Here she was on very secure ground. Georgina had never been upstairs. One of the officers signalled to her that he would nevertheless like to assure himself that there was no one there, received Evelynne's tacit assent and soon his large boots were creaking up the wooden steps to the upper storey. He left his colleague alone with Evelynne, returning after a minute or so to ask whether they might look around the garden and its immediate precincts as well. Evelynne asked them if they would be glad to have a cup of tea, her coffee having been used up that morning. Smiling, they concurred.

The whole inspection, together with the notes they took of this and that, which Evelynne later signed, took not much more than half an hour, after which the two, replacing their cups and thanking her for the beverage, politely took their leave and purred off into the distance. It was a formal encounter after which Evelynne sat down to think of what would be the next best thing to do. Jean-Luc. That was it! He'd have to help here. She hoped against hope that he would be in the publishing house that morning as she dialled his number. It rang a long time. At last: "Beremont."

"Jean-Luc. It's me and it's urgent. Can you come over? Now."

"OK, if it's urgent," Jean-Luc replied evenly, "but you'll have to be patient. I'll come as soon as I can. What's wrong?"

"I'll tell you as soon as you're here. Can't tell you on the phone."

"All right. About an hour." Evelynne suddenly felt cold as she went into the garden.

'So her father means business,' she thought to herself as she viewed the spring flowers struggling through the earth to light. She hated him. What right had he to determine Georgina's life now she was eighteen? Did he want to interfere in their friendship, too? Never! Their friendship and her future were now one and the same. The minutes passed, and the sun was already on the decline when she heard the noise of Jean-Luc's car wheels on the road outside. She rushed through the house to greet him.

"What's wrong? Are you all right?" Jean-Luc asked earnestly.

"I'm OK; it's about Georgina. Let's get into the car and drive to St. Laurant. She's waiting in a café there for us."

"For *us?*" Jean-Luc repeated incredulously.

"Let's go," Evelynne urged, jumping into his sports car.

Jean-Luc complied and the two of them drove off in the direction Georgina had taken in the bus that morning.

On locating the café, Jean-Luc was ordered to park a little further along the road and join them a second or two later at the café. This he did, while Evelynne found her friend and hurriedly told her what had happened that morning. Georgina was furious and already crying when Jean-Luc returned from the car.

"This means that you'll have to go with him to Bordeaux – at least for the time being," Evelynne explained.

"Why?" Georgina asked.

"Because the police will be back again shortly, that's for certain," Evelynne assured her. "And they may even send folks in civilian clothes to spy on us, so the sooner you're away from Soulec, the better, at least for the moment," she added. This was translated in whispers to Jean-Luc, who, with Evelynne, had forged a plan on their way to the café. Evelynne then explained that she had brought some of Georgina's clothes along with her, including her toiletries "to bridge the gap" she said.

And so it was that our heroine was whisked off to a suburb of Bordeaux for her safety and after saying farewell to Evelynne, spent the night in tears and rage.

# 3

## *Bordeaux*

In the days which followed, Jean-Luc proved to be an attentive friend with impeccable manners and good sense. He helped Georgina to feel comfortable in his flat, provided for her every need, including pocket money, and did everything possible to make her feel at home. Every day she heard from her friend, Evelynne, who was anxious to know how she was faring.

"He's a good guy," she said, "he'll look after you, but you will perhaps need to lean on him a bit to find you work."

"I think he knows that," Georgina replied. "I won't push him."

"Sure, he works better when he's not pushed," Evelynne agreed. "I wonder, though, what he's got in mind."

"He hasn't mentioned anything yet," Georgina remarked, "I suppose he'll get round to that later. For the moment he's extraordinarily kind and generous," Georgina went on.

"Hey! You be careful!" Evelynne warned facetiously, "he has a weakness for beautiful things," she said, laughing over the phone. "Anyway, I only choose the best," she added playfully.

"Yes, and you can count yourself among 'the beautiful things'," she reminded her.

One evening not long after her flight to Bordeaux, Jean-Luc informed Georgina that the following day he had an appointment with his boss to learn what the board of directors had decided about Georgina's stay and that she was to accompany him. He was as friendly as usual, but Georgina noted a sprinkling of formality in his manner, and this set her worrying again as to what she should do if it were decided not to employ her. It was then that she resolved once and for all not to go home. She would stay on, come what may.

Léon Courelle reminded Georgina very much of a gorilla. He was large, ponderous, hairy, shirt-sleeved and dominant. As general manager of *Mode pour Toi,* he knew what he knew and said as much. His sentences were short and to the point, and Georgina convinced herself that he would have made an excellent, senior New York police officer. No two people could have been more different, she thought, than these two sitting there on the opposite side of the large, posh, steel and plastic desk, Courelle in his pristine white silk shirt, tie askew, black eyebrows drawn over small eyes, an unshaved jaw set for a possible punch-up, his massive presence filling the room, and Jean-Luc, retiring, thoughtful, obliging, almost self-effacing in his modest green jacket, sitting just a little self-consciously at his side, a pencil in one hand. How these two got on so well with each other, she thought, was one of life's enigmas.

After formal introductions, Courelle opened play. "We regret that we cannot employ you here in Bordeaux, Mademoiselle 'Ennessey, since the police would most certainly trace your whereabouts. We'd like to take you on, believe me, but the risk is too great. For you. For this house. And I can't take the responsibility. If you were twenty-one, we might fight it out, but for the moment you are too young." He smiled slightly. "I'm sorry."

Georgina's face fell and there was a short pause before he added, indicating Jean-Luc, "But we want to help you and I think M. Beremont here has a suggestion which may help you and which I wholly endorse."

As though he had not anticipated the privilege of saying something himself, Jean-Luc made a movement as if roused from a reverie to say, "Ah yes, yes. We have a branch in Italy which we know for sure is looking for a lady of your, what shall I say, er, height and figure – and, oh yes, and for a lady of your hair colour. In fact they have asked *particularly* for these attributes, er, er, and we think we can supply them – if you'll excuse the parlance."

"They're looking for a beauty like you," Courelle summarised, smiling.

Georgina sat there not knowing what to say or think. She felt like goods that powers much greater than she were bartering for, and she felt a deep annoyance that her father's influence had penetrated so far. M Courelle's body language signified that it was time to go and Jean-Luc accompanied her to the door, which he graciously opened for her.

"Evelynne rang a few minutes ago," he announced. "Let's meet downstairs at eleven at '*L'Ourse*' for a drink and I'll tell you more. For the moment I have things I have to see to." Smiling, he retreated into the main office again. This almost formal explanation only consolidated her feelings, so that now she felt even more like a parcel on a shelf to be dealt with later. Slowly, she wandered through the halls of '*Mode pour Toi*', impressed by the businesslike way everyone went about their work. She was met with smiles and 'Can I help yous?' and one of the secretaries actually offered her a cup of coffee. These few moments offered her an opportunity to gain an idea of the size of the place and she was overcome with a mixture of anger and sadness again at her parents' interference with her life. 'Damn!' she thought to herself as she passed office upon office, 'I could have been given a good job here except for these interfering people!'

Jean-Luc appeared promptly at eleven outside on the pavement of *The Bear* as it was called and she was again grateful for this man's unerring reliability. Once seated, Jean-Luc came out with some good news, "Evelynne's coming on Saturday," he said with a smile, "I think you're happy about that, umm?"

"Oh that's wonderful!" Georgina cried. She had never felt the need for womanly company more. Jean-Luc as gentlemanly as ever paid the bill, invited her to lunch, took her out to an interesting exhibition in the afternoon and generally provided for her welfare. The days passed. Then, at last, on Saturday she found herself waiting in the sunshine near a fountain in the park and Evelynne and Jean-Luc were approaching. Crying with joy, Georgina flung her arms round Evelynne's neck. Jean-Luc, as tactful as ever, quietly withdrew.

"He's told me all about things," Evelynne said as she hugged her friend. "Let's walk a little in the park."

"Isn't it absolutely gorgeous weather and that in the first days of April?" Georgina noted happily. "Must be over 20 degrees C."

Evelynne, too, was happy, happy about the weather, the park, the sunshine, happy to be with Georgina again. Not far from where they were was a small pavilion. A band was playing, and all this added to the pleasure of their reunion. The two young women sat down and ordered ice cream.

"What do you think I should do, Evelynne, dear?" Georgina asked in English.

Evelynne's answer surprised her. "Take what they offer; they'll pay you well – or if not they'll hear from me!"

"Yes, but it means going down to Milan, and I don't know whether I want to make another change, another language, other customs and all that. It's all a bit complicated."

"Sure, but you'll be safe and the House of *Mode pour Toi* in Milan is a big, international concern. The idea is almost certainly Jean-Luc's. He's proving a trump card. You can't refuse, darling, you absolutely can't!"

"Why?"

"Because the offer is something you get once in a lifetime, that's why. To turn it down for any reason would be like cutting off your nose to spite your face."

Georgina couldn't help but burst out laughing at this apt phrase, and coming from Evelynne it was especially funny.

"What's so funny?" Evelynne queried, pulling a hurt face, which made Georgina quite helpless with laughter, so that after a moment or so people began to stare. Georgina coughed and spluttered into her ice cream and some of it fell into her lap. The concerned faces of the public began then to ease into smiles, seeing that Georgina was quite beside herself with mirth.

"No, what's so funny, then?" Evelynne pursued. "What did I say?" And so the cycle continued for at least another minute while Georgina caught her breath again, trying hard to recover.

"I like, like the phrase, good phrase... ugh." Georgina applauded, making huge gasps to restore herself to normal conversation. Evelynne waited.

Wiping her eyes and face that streamed with tears, she

finally got herself under control enough to explain, "Oh Evelynne, dear, I'm not laughing at you. Do excuse me." Evelynne relaxed at hearing this and waited for Georgina to continue.

"It's just that you used that phrase, that's all."

"Isn't that correct, then?" Evelynne asked.

"Oh yes, perfectly correct; I didn't know your English was so good, dear, believe me. It just came out of the blue, somehow. So funny!"

Evelynne's dark eyes surveyed the sunny park. Her expression was serious. It was now about 3 pm. She waited for her friend to comment on her remark about the firm, and understanding this, Georgina continued, "Well, I suppose the thing is that I have to learn Italian, and that's just when I'm beginning to get along nicely in French." It was then that Georgina noticed an expression she had never seen before on Evelynne's features. It was a medley of disbelief and, yes, contempt as if she had been told some hifalutin, tall story which, despite its unlikely content could, if one were to see it from a different point of view, could, yes, could just have some truth in it, and yet who would be daft enough to believe in such nonsense? Georgina found the expression fascinating and paused before going on.

"You're not serious I hope," was all that Evelynne could say.

"About what?" Georgina asked ingenuously.

"About the language thing, because if so, you're potty!"

"Potty?"

"Down there they couldn't give a sheep's baa about whether you speak Italian perfectly. Anyway, you'd pick that up as you went along."

"Along where?" Georgina enquired, since, when it suited her, she could be very practical. However, Evelynne was not in the mood for such detail, so she said nothing in answer to what she considered to be a deliberate deflection on Georgina's part. She almost sulked, and for a moment or two there was silence between them.

"I'm sorry, dear Evelynne, I'm very sorry," Georgina said seriously. "Do please go on with what you were telling me. I'm very interested. Just a bit scared, that's all." After a further pause that gave emphasis to her words, Evelynne continued.

"Jean-Luc told me how things went this week in your interview with the boss."

"Courelle?"

"Yes, I'm glad to learn from Jean-Luc that you didn't say anything stupid like you've said to me this afternoon, thank God – about not knowing Italian."

Because there's no need to learn anything if you don't want to. The circle down there is as I've said international and there's plenty of English girls in Milano too. Competition will be the problem, not language. All you have to do is show yourself and make 'em pay for it." Georgina listened politely as Evelynne went on.

"If they accept you after the first introductions have been made, you're in, girl. You will have achieved in one go what every girl dreams of, but hasn't the necessary qualifications – or connections. The one's as important as the other. It's clear that Jean-Luc has put in a good word for you and now Courelle has seen you and he's made up his own mind."

"But I was only there for about twenty minutes, Evelynne," Georgina protested.

"Yes, I know all about it. Jean-Luc told me everything."

"But they don't know me!"

"They don't need to know what you've had for breakfast. They know enough, believe me, and Courelle's suggestion that you go down and work for them in Milano means that you've embarked on a career where you could make a million if you're sensible." Georgina listened. After a moment, she said, "But I'll lose you and I don't want a million." This was said so sincerely that Evelynne was deeply moved and had difficulty in resisting her tears.

"You won't ever lose me, my darling. Of course not. But you'll thank me later – us later – that we've put you on the right track in life," she replied. She meant Jean-Luc and herself.

"Well, if you say so," Georgina acquiesced and turned to the rest of her ice cream.

"I don't 'say' so, I *know* so," Evelynnne said with conviction.

After their interval at the pavilion, the two enjoyed each other's company in the park, later meeting up with Jean-Luc again who, over dinner, confirmed in his own way that Georgina was on the brink of a new life.

# 4

## *Milan*

It was raining as Georgina, accompanied by Jean-Luc, finally rolled into Milan's main station, and the fact was that it had been teeming for most of the day.

"Not a very good start for a new life," she commented to Jean-Luc as he manhandled her baggage down from the coach. He straightened, took his bearings and, steering her by the elbow without replying, moved down the platform towards the exit. "We take a taxi from over there, I think," he said practically as they inched their way along with the crowd from the train towards the ranks of cars at the station's entrance. Beyond the shelter of the station, the rain lashed and slashed about them as they waited for a free car.

Jean-Luc looked at his companion, smiling apologetically while the rain streamed off his hat, "I'm sorry," he said, his shoulders lifted as if to say, 'Well, that's the way it is I suppose.' For some reason, Georgina would remember this gesture for the rest of her life, his standing there, tall, competent in his unobtrusive way, the kindly smile that said so much about him, his gentlemanly concern for her welfare, apologising for the weather.

The next day the sun shone from a clear blue sky as Jean-Luc introduced her to her prospective boss and future colleagues, to Carlo Denti with grey, meticulously coiffured hair above a good-natured face, distinguished and dignified, who held his head as though something would spill, whose immaculate suit was moulded to a slim, athletic body and who moved with them from one office to another where they met Luigi Trento and Martina Cagglioni who managed the place, to Immanuel Laplano in charge of public relations, Kurt Spielmann, a German responsible for the building's general maintenance, upkeep and security, to Enrico Ernesto Salves who, with his son and two technicians controlled the photographic department and were also responsible for the firm's liaison with the publishing section, and Stefano Cotti who managed all the fashion shows and exhibitions throughout the year with Maria Montanini who was generally in charge of the health and wellbeing of the company's models and Emilia Mundi and Carmena Straccola and Joachim Hertz and Carla Putti, and Sheila Murphy and Bettina Cantonolli, Bertha Toppolan, Giovanni Bertolini, Franco Mona, Paolo Pertomicci, Sansolo Carpi, Beate Lupo, José Colon, Umberto Shettsa, Ronaldo Cremona, Hanso Scherzi. It took all morning and Georgina's hand ached. She could never remember all these names. All these people! She felt so small and insignificant. 'Thank goodness,' she thought to herself, 'quite a number of these future colleagues also spoke either English or French,' so that she would not entirely be stuck out on a limb.

Carlo Denti himself invited Jean-Luc and Georgina to lunch and during it the three of them talked of Georgina's future with the firm, whether what she had seen in the morning of the company's staff and premises appealed to her, when she would like to start and whether she thought she would be happy working at the firm.

After lunch, the two men, Georgina and Denti's secretary retired for coffee to the boss's office to discuss salary and the terms of employment, Jean-Luc, of course proving himself an excellent intermediary in these arrangements. When employer and prospective employee were satisfied with the form of the contract, they signed the agreement, said their goodbyes and Jean-Luc and Georgina left for their hotel.

"You're a very lucky young woman," Jean-Luc remarked as they rode in a taxi back to their hotel. Georgina looked at her friend enquiringly.

"I mean to earn so much money as a beginner." Jean-Luc said, "Obviously, Signore Denti was pleased with your manner and appearance."

"I'm glad," Georgina replied.

Jean-Luc didn't stay. At six, he took the next train back to Bordeaux after making sure that Georgina had received all the information she needed for starting work the following Monday. She said farewell to him in the hotel lobby, "Give Evelynne my love!"

"I will, I will. See you again soon. *Au revoir!*"

Georgina turned to use the lift and find her room. Sitting down in one of the ample armchairs the latter afforded, she was overcome by a huge wave of loneliness. Jean-Luc had been the essence of punctuality, thoughtfulness and care, and now he was gone and she was in a foreign country, not knowing its language or its customs or what her work would entail the day after tomorrow. And there was a Sunday in between to deal with. Jean-Luc had recommended a day at the zoo, but if she were honest with herself, she reflected, she had no great desire to follow his proposal.

# 5

## *Work*

Dear, dear Evy,

I feel I have to thank you and dear Jean-Luc for all your help. That was really lovely of you both. Jean-Luc is such a peach. He took care of everything.

I have now been at work for a week. They don't make it easy for me to earn my money. I was very surprised when they told me that I would have 'to go to school' for a month and 'learn how to walk'! I thought they were kidding at first, but I was soon under strict training from a forty-year-old woman called Kristina Paweleska and her assistant, Jenny Nowak. They are nice enough, I suppose, but absolute sticklers for discipline and talk between themselves in Polish and to me in broken English. Sometimes I find this a bit annoying, if not a bit condescending. But there's little time to think about myself and my feelings. I'm obliged to do all kinds of physical exercises, which I find easy, but they always find some fault somewhere. Not enough swing here, not enough 'curve time' there. They mean by this that I have to 'think' about my every movement and their object, they say, is to make me aware of every movement I make. That, they say, is the difference between a model and an ordinary (if beautiful) girl on the street. I know what they mean, but they never let up. I'm in the gym from eight sharp in the morning until ten. Then there's a break of about fifteen minutes. Not more. After that, shootings. This goes on until one and not a minute earlier. One or both of these women turn me around, raise my arms or legs as the case may be, say little, and sometimes I reckon they actually enjoy putting me through the hoop. I can't tell, 'cos they don't say a word that I can catch. It's all in Polish. Mind you, I feel pretty fit even after a week. The one thing I hate is the preparations for photo-shooting. They (and now there are two others, a British bloke, thank goodness and his Welsh wife) who insist on making me up every damn day! I hate this. Goodness knows how my skin will react to all this paste and coloured stuff they rub into my face. I feel like a geisha girl sometimes and then like an over made-up tart on others, but they just simply go ahead, and when I object they both say, "Oh but if we didn't make you up for the camera, you'd look like a consumptive on the photo; it's necessary." So I submit to their treatments, though I hate it. I have to. There's no saying 'no' here. If you brush folks up the wrong way, you're soon out in the street, I'm told. I try to make conversation with these two, of course, and they're nice in a kind of detached way. They certainly don't let themselves be side-tracked on any issue. They say things like, "We take the consequences if we don't get it right." "We're responsible, you know." "You'll learn it in the end; it's all in a day's work," and things like that.

I haven't made any friends yet. Somewhere, there are

supposed to be a bevy of girls of my age, but I haven't seen any of them. I think of you and the wonderful times we had together. These thoughts are my comfort. I miss the wonderful sea, too.

The food's good here; I will say that. Lunch, for example, is always good, and I learned the other day that you can even take a snack from 6pm to 10pm if you're working overtime. There's plenty of choice of food in the canteen and there is even a little wine if you like that kind of thing. It's also all very clean and ordered here as well. There is even a medical centre that's on duty all day.

I have to continue my physical exercises, by the way, for at least a month before I can go on the catwalk or even exhibit myself for public shootings, and every day I learn that they have very high standards here. I have to toe the line. If you do that you're OK.

By the way, the firm will also pay a certain per cent for my digs when I move in next month, and for the moment it's paying for the hotel.

I hope you will come and see me soon, dear Evy. I miss you so much. Come over soon! I'm so lonely.

A bundle of lovely kisses and hugs to you and Tommy! Warmest greetings to Jean-Luc, too, of course, that lovely man, and thank him again for everything.

Love,
"Georgy"

It was July before Georgina was judged to be qualified enough to publicly display clothing. Her face, her figure and her deportment were in the care of experts. Even her diet was regulated. Added to this, someone in the firm's hierarchy, knowing her well and registering her aversion to the need to be sufficiently skinny to swagger on the catwalk, accordingly assigned her to a department where she could exhibit clothes for youthful figures between twenty and twenty-five, and this assignment she carried out with taste and commitment. As the months passed she became popular as someone known for her equable personality. As far as her superiors were concerned, she proved to be obedient, diligent and intelligent. Such was her reputation that she was once called in by general manager Denti and complimented on her progress, Her Italian was also improving, and the fact that she took its study seriously by using it as much as possible and frequently asking for help in this regard endeared her to many. By the time she was nineteen she was also regularly taking part in fashion shows as well as photo shootings, not only for the firm, but by special permission, for external advertising firms. This, in particular, was very well paid. Both *Mode pour Toi* and Georgina benefitted financially from this arrangement.

One of these external companies was an agency, which specialised in nude photos. She learned that she had been 'discovered' and was interviewed privately by representatives of both firms.

Dear Evy,

It seems such a long time since I heard from you. Are you all right? I keep thinking of you and wish you were here.

It's nearly two years now since I joined Mode pour Toi and I don't for a moment regret coming here, but life is very, very full. I don't get a minute to myself. Good, the salary is OK and the contracts they give me by the way have boosted my bank account tremendously, which is also all very well, but I need a break and wonder if you could visit me. I've moved into a nice flat in the via del

Cruto, not far from the cathedral. Number 11. I can take the weekend off on the 20ᵗʰ. Saturday and Sunday. I can cancel everything if you can make it. Why don't you take a weekend off yourself and come over? I can think of nothing better than a lovely chat with you. Do, do come!

A thousand hugs and kisses!
Georgy

That was in August and Milano was very hot on the day Georgina and Evelynne found themselves after nearly a year of absence finally sitting together on the Piazzo del Duomo. It was a happy moment indeed for both of them.

"It's so lovely to see you and to be here, Georgy. I'm so, so happy, "Evelynne declared as they waited for the light beer they had ordered.

"I'm so happy too, dear; you can't imagine," Georgina replied.

"Yes, here we are together again at last!" Evelynne exclaimed joyfully.

"Writing to each other is all very well, but there's nothing to beat a good old gab with each other, what?" Georgina enthused.

"Sure, it's been a long time. *Mon dieu*, this beer is good," Evelynne said, her dark eyes glinting in the strong light.

"It's the weather this year. Makes you sweat like a wrung-out sponge, but it does the soul good. When I think of that English stuff we used to get as a substitute for summer; it was a kind of apology, an excuse from St. Peter for not getting on with the thing properly!" Evelynne laughed heartily at this.

"That's great, an apology. I'd not thought of that. You can still hit the nail on the head, dear! You do the same in your letters. I always have to laugh."

Georgina's smile at this remark was older, Evelynne noticed in that second. Not old in any negative sense, but wiser. Evelynne's extraordinary sharp perception saw in that moment that Georgina had learned a lot in her time at *Mode pour Toi*. She, Evelynne, perceived the work and the commitment in that smile, the maturity and conscientiousness behind it, the sacrifices she had had to make when others found the time to rest and so balance their lives, but also the ironic humour that Georgina was capable of on occasion.

"You told me in one of your recent letters that you've taken up painting," Georgina enquired.

"Yes. Every Thursday I take the bus to Bordeaux for a two-hour session with my teacher as I told you. He's very good and arranges visits for his class to various museums and art galleries. I love it. There are six people on the course, two women about forty or so, one man and three younger females. Keeps me out of mischief." The two women giggled deliciously and ordered another two beers from the harassed waiter.

"And Jean-Luc?"

"Oh yes, he comes over whenever he has the time. Usually at the weekends," Evelynne said a trifle wistfully.

"So you're still 'in touch'," Georgina asked pointedly. Evelynne received the innuendo and they both fell to giggling again like excited children, so that a few people looked their way.

"Oh yes," Evelynne continued with a sigh as she recovered. "We need each other." Georgina, noting this reaction, remained silent, but she was glad that they were still enjoying each other's company. There was a pause between them.

"And how do you manage to steer clear of these Italian beaux with their almost medieval overtures?" Evelynne asked in French.

"Well, to tell the truth, it's easy enough during the day because I'm so hard at work, but they're active in the evening, and I simply have to watch out."

"You haven't fancied anyone yet, then?"

"You know, dear, you'll think it funny, but I really don't have the time. By 6 pm I'm finished. I usually eat in the canteen and then go home and flop down on the bed. Sometimes I read a bit to improve my Italian by wading through a magazine, but that usually makes me even more tired. You can't imagine."

"Oh, I think I can," Evelynne said, nodding. "It's wonderful that you're making progress in the language, too. And your French hasn't deteriorated either from what I can gather."

The fact was that these two as they sat there in the heat of the afternoon spoke a mixture as they had done very often before and without the slightest sense of inconvenience, the one speaking French and the other English. This had often served as perfectly serviceable vehicle to mutual understanding and came quite naturally.

"And there's another offer looming," Georgina announced after the second glass of beer arrived. Evelynne waited for her friend to enlarge on the theme.

"They want to take nude photographs."

"Why not?" Evelynne commented as though she'd been offered a cup of tea.

"Umm. Georgina sipped her beer.

"If they want to photograph that beautiful body of yours, let them."

"Let them," Georgina echoed looking glum.

"Let them pay for it," Evelynne repeated firmly.

"They're offering up to the equivalent of $5,000 a time," Georgina added.

"Wow! Well, why not? And the greater the demand, the bigger the offer," Evelynne calculated.

"But that's crazy," Georgina said. "And I don't know whether I want to be exposed to the world like that."

"Look," Evelynne postulated, leaning towards her friend over the table, "It's simple. They want something. You're that something and they're willing to pay for what they want. Don't make it too easy for them either. A beauty like you is for them like coming across gold or platinum. Gold has to be dug out of the ground, refined, moulded and I don't know what and that takes time and energy. Why should the agency have it so easy? Raise your price if they want to go on shooting. Say $7,000 or $10,000.."

"But that's ridiculous! They'd never pay that amount, and what would I do with all that money? It's indecent."

Evelynne's petite figure vibrated with energy. Her eyes were stern now like a mother on discovering a child's secret misdemeanour.

"Now you listen to me, dear girl. It's only – and *only* – a matter of supply and demand. They want what you've got and you can give them what they want. But they're not going to get what they want for free. Neither are they going to pay the earth for what they want. They have their financial framework, believe me. All you have to do is to strike a bargain. They'll tell you how much they're willing to pay for a shooting. They're not daft. So get on with it. Sign the contract and you're in. How long do you think the game'll last?"

Georgina was moved by Evelynne's enthusiasm. She loved the way she always took her side in whatever issue, and felt flattered by her undivided devotion. Her rhetoric, too, was convincing. She sat silently for a moment, thinking about her heated proposal.

Evelynne for her part said no more, but pretended to show great interest in the resident pigeons picking a living from among the crumbs that fell from the tables. Georgina looked at her friend. She looked at her incredibly thick hair and her tanned complexion, her mind shifting for a second to the knowledge of her companion's white teeth, which were small and regular. She looked at the simple, blue-and-white dress she wore and the bare arms that, she knew, were remarkably strong for her size and weight. This one was a fighter, a woman of courage and temperament. Sitting there, she reminded Georgina strongly of the classical pictures she had seen of Diana, the huntress at dawn with her pert breasts, bow in hand, marching into the woods of ancient time. At last, she said, "But I'm bit worried about their taking advantage of me or exploiting me for pornographic ends. I'm not having that."

"Then say so," Evelynne returned shortly.

"Say so?"

"Yes, that's what a contract's for, isn't it?"

Georgina was suddenly acutely aware of her worldly innocence. "I'm a bit circumspect about the whole thing."

"Circumspect?"

"Yes, a bit uncertain, a bit wary – 'afraid' if you like."

Evelynne's warmth was there again. "Don't worry, dear. Put it like this: these folks you're going to work for aren't going to kill the golden goose that lays their eggs." Georgina laughed spontaneously at this, but Evelynne continued soberly. "They'll make sure you're protected from the slightest male abuse. It'll be a job for you to do like anything else. Just take off your clothes, lie around or take up whatever postures they want you to assume and let them click. Just like that. They love it! And you'll love the money you get for it."

"But I don't necessarily want the world to gaze lustfully at my body," Georgina protested, "Why do I have to show everything?"

"Because the male eye is more developed than the

brain," Evelynne replied simply. At this Georgina nearly split her sides with laughter. Again, coming from Evelynne, there was this delicious incongruence allied to an aptness, which was just irresistibly funny. The tears ran down her cheeks and customers at neighbouring tables stared again.

"The phrase isn't mine," Evelynne said seriously. "I think some film star said it, but it hits the nail on the head as you folks say."

Georgina continued to laugh and, as she did so, it seemed that all the tension and hard work of the last few months abruptly fell from her pretty shoulders. It was so good to watch and hear Evelynne's earnestness, to feel her energetic support, to know that she was understood.

"It's just that I feel a bit unsure, you know," she said when she had recovered enough to speak again.

"*Bien sûr*," Evelynne rejoined, "of course you do, although I imagine that since you're working for two people, they will either not show your face or change your identity in some way, so that people won't catch on that the woman showing the clothes is not the same as shows her body. They'll be particular about that."

Evelynne was sure of herself, and Georgina didn't go further in expressing her apprehensions. She decided it was time to show her friend the cathedral. Anyway, it would be cooler in there than here, she reflected, so they paid the hot-and-bothered waiter and wandered into the shaded precincts of the city's most famous landmark.

Sixty-three can be a critical age for any man, and it was just at this age that Lt. Col. Henry Hennessey of the Irish Guards fell victim to a stroke while on a bus travelling from Gloucester town centre to his home on the city's residential outskirts. His wife was with him at the time. Passengers helped to carry him onto the pavement and a few remained until the ambulance reached the spot. From there, he was transported to the local infirmary where he was treated immediately to prevent the onset of unnecessary complications. Neither he nor any member of his family had expected such a thing, and it came as a shock to them all. The family patriarch had partaken of his coffee that morning at breakfast time, large and loud as always, had read his paper as usual, smoked his cigar as usual, cursed the weather as usual, the 'insufferable' political situation of his country, initiated by these 'Socialist bounders', opined on the general decay of the armed services and, as usual, our loss of India to that 'skinny, insolent loin-clothed upstart'. His patient wife had listened to all this (as usual) with a forbearance that had become a habit over the last twenty years as had his arteries, and his heart, and these, in conformity with an ancient pattern, had obediently responded to the 'alert' signals from the brain and accordingly raised his blood pressure to deal with an archaic order to flee or fight. But neither was forthcoming. Instead, his ageing body was obliged to deal with a sedentary life with little exercise and large quantities of substances foreign to the system such as whiskey and tobacco. Nor was this all. On top of these outbreaks of impatience and irascibility at a world quite clearly sliding into decadence, there was the slow, insidious acid icicle eating away at his nervous system. His disappointment with his eldest daughter was inconsolable, and her conduct nothing less than wilful insubordination. So it was indeed. How *dare* she go against his word? Women were created to marry and have children, and that as early as possible, not embark upon courses of university study to become lawyers, doctors or God knows what, much less leave home and perilously support herself in some foreign country and live alone. Damnation! The very idea was absurd!

As compensation, he would certainly keep a tight rein on Sarah, and had already made up his mind what measures to take when she was of a marriageable age.

But Col. Hennessey's body, long suffering as our bodies are, could not deal any longer with the frustrating conjuncture, "Fight I dare not, but flee I cannot", and nature finally took over and supplied her own mechanical solution to his apparently irresolvable problem: his arteries constricted under the repeated impetus from his brain to act, the flow of blood to his heart was impeded and his muscles seized up. The left side of his face, his left arm and leg were paralysed. It was then that Henry Hennessey gave up. He gave up the unequal struggle and, let go. In the long hours during which he lay in his hospital bed, he came to terms with himself and his world. It was in these hours that he learned to appreciate his wife for her humility and loyalty and for her presence in these last few days of anguish. He expressed his thanks to the doctors and therapists who attended him each day. He even thanked the personnel who brought his food, and though he didn't enjoy hospital fare very much, he ate it without complaint. His wife was more than thankful for this.

"You know, Beth," he said to her one evening,"I've had a damn good life. Can't complain. No, can't complain." Elizabeth, his wife smiled and stroked his head. "It's only…"

"I know," she said. "I know, it's Georgy isn't it? Well, if you'd like to see her, she's waiting in the foyer."

"She's here!" Hennessey exclaimed. "Then why don't you bring her in?" he cried, trying excitedly but in vain to lift himself from his pillow.

"She's very upset to hear what's happened, but didn't know what kind of a reception she would receive. She arrived this afternoon by taxi.

"Then let me see her, let me see her!" the colonel repeated, and Elizabeth asked Sarah, who was also with her this evening, to fetch her sister.

Georgina, who still wore her travelling attire, looked more beautiful than ever as she entered the room, tears in her eyes. Father and daughter kissed one another and she hugged him for a long time before he asked, "And how are you, my darling girl. I must say you look very fine."

"I'm well Dad, thank you," she sobbed as Sarah offered her a handkerchief.

Her father, smiling broadly as best as he could after his injury, said "Well, I must say you look fine. Sarah said that you came up from London by taxi? Must have cost the earth."

"I wanted to get to you as soon as possible, Dad, and the train didn't go before 4.30. So I took a cab."

Her father laughed. "Thank you, my girl, that was sweet of you."

The assembled family, including Patrick were stunned by this reaction. Nobody said anything for some moments. After an interval, it was the same Patrick who remarked how well dressed Georgy looked. "Hey, my playmate, do you look swell! If I may say so, girl, you look like an advertisement for the finest clothes on the market."

Georgina laughed with the others at this. "Well, I should do; I'm in the business," she replied lightly. Col. Hennessey nodded kindly as best he could. Harmony prevailed as they filed out of the ward at eight-thirty. It was beginning to get dark.

Georgina's mother, sensing her daughter's concern and eagerness to talk to her, explained what the doctor had said to her earlier in the evening.

"It will take a long time before he can walk again – if ever he can walk again," she said.

"Oh God," was Georgina's reaction. "I feel guilty that it's happened. It's all my fault," she added, tears filling her eyes.

"I'm not too sure of that," her mother replied. Georgina looked frankly at her mum.

"I'm afraid he himself is partly responsible for what's happened," she said in confidential tones to Georgina as the family walked through the hospital grounds towards the bus stop at its entrance. "Your going to France was what brought things to the boiling point; he couldn't abide your going against his word. That's why he set Interpol on you. He wanted to teach you a lesson and have you brought home as a penitent. I wasn't in agreement with that, by the way." She looked squarely at her daughter as though to underline the statement. Georgina said nothing.

"It's odd," her mother went on, "I felt that you were happy down there somehow, but I would never have tried to convince him with a mere insight or whatever it was. And what's more, I was glad that you had made up your own mind. And what's more, why should you marry someone of his choice?"

Georgina could not believe her ears. "I haven't thought about marriage, Mum to tell you the truth," she said, "I've been so busy; you can't imagine."

"Busy? Doing what?" Her mother enquired.

"Modelling clothes largely. Posing. Going from one interview to another. Photo shootings. Helping to fill the pages of our fashion magazines. Meeting all kinds of people who want to employ my 'talents' in their own interests. Fashion parades twice a week. Advertising work – the hardest by the way. Keeping fit and keeping up with trends. Consulting, going through contracts, sidestepping pitfalls and folks wanting to exploit you, debating issues on fees and taxes. It's mental gymnastics, I tell you and lots and lots of hard work. I don't fall into bed before midnight on any working day of the week. Saturday afternoon and Sunday are free. It's then I get some fresh air and I and another girl go into the park to eat ice cream (which we shouldn't). Then it's Monday again before you're really rested and off we go again with the routine."

"Well I hope they pay you enough for it all," said Elizabeth with a way that required a straight answer.

"Oh yes, I'm paid well enough. Have an apartment of my own and plenty to live on."

"An apartment of your own?" Sarah had joined them as the bus drew up to the stop. They boarded and once settled in their seats, her mother repeated her question.

"Yes, I'm paying it off of course, but it's a necessary refuge."

Her mother and Sarah listened to all this with the greatest interest. "And it's an investment," Georgina added as the conductor took their money. Mother Elizabeth looked out thoughtfully onto the passing fields and villages as the bus negotiated the corners and twists and turns of the road on their way home. Georgina had matured, she thought to herself. Her manner was confident. She knew how to manage her life, it seemed. Well, after all, she was now twenty-one. No longer a child for whom one has to take total responsibility. It was very gratifying to realise that her daughter had found her own way in the world, but Elizabeth knew that there would be other challenges to come and wondered as their home came into view how she would manage these. Being beautiful was not an easy gift to bear.

When they were seated for their evening meal, which Patrick had prepared for them, young Sarah, now sixteen, wanted to know all about her elder sister's life at first hand, and Patrick who had joined them, listened with interest.

Both of them were surprised at the intensity of work involved in Georgina's life. Sarah, for example, imagined modelling to be accompanied by a round of champagne parties and chit-chat with celebrities.

"There is some of that," Georgina explained, "but that's only the flower on the stalk; the hard work's done in the earth below, and we know that these parties are informal interviews for further contracts and very often for marriage."

"How do you mean?" Sarah asked.

"Think of it as a market, then; all these beautiful females in their best attire enticing the interest of wealthy males… there's a lot of undercover transactions going on and not only financial ones."

"How do you manage yourself, Georgy? The competition must be phenomenal," Sarah suggested.

"Oh, by golly it is! I can hold my own as far as looks are concerned, but, thank goodness, I have a super-duper colleague, Helen, to help me out in other ways. She's older and experienced and she and I always go together to these battlegrounds and support each other. I must say I have secured one or two worthwhile contracts this way, but I prefer direct advertisement. It's much easier to say 'yes' or 'no' in that case and such negotiations are always conducted in a sober atmosphere."

Mother Elizabeth nodded. She could all too well imagine to what a nest of vipers her daughter might be exposed to on these occasions, whereas for Sarah such a situation was the essence of delirious adventure. Patrick remained silent, pondering upon Georgina's different, woman's world. For him it was strangely alien, but he did ask about one thing. "I hear the fees are good once you get into the right stream?"

Georgina smiled. "They're good, yes, very good. I will

say that, but your agent doesn't give money away. He or she makes sure you earn it while you're 'on stage' as it were."

At this point Georgina felt that she would like to change the subject. She was not going to allow herself to be manoeuvred into a situation where she would be obliged to say what she did to earn so much money. Taking her clothes off to expose her body had never caused her a moment's embarrassment or inconvenience. For her, this was as natural as putting them on, and her association with Evelynne had done much to confirm her feelings in this regard. However, she was not disposed to share these convictions with her middle-class family. It had nothing to do with them, and they wouldn't understand anyway, so she changed the subject.

"How long will dad have to stay in hospital?"

"About a week, I imagine, dear, or perhaps a day or so longer. Depends on how he rallies and reacts to treatment. But to fully recover – if he recovers – will take at least a year." Elizabeth conjectured.

"A year!" Georgina exclaimed.

The nerves have to relearn the job of co-ordination, and that takes time."

Georgina felt a twinge of conscience that one member of the family would not be present to help him in time of need. She sat silently at table.

"If you won't be here, dear, to help, it doesn't matter," her mother announced as though she had read her thoughts at that moment, "We'll manage and you have your young life to lead. Dad is my responsibility. After all, that's what married life's about." Georgina was astonished by this remark, spoken calmly and sensibly as if her mother were reporting that next week would be Easter and that she must shop in time. And she had twice used an endearment that she had never used in the past as far as Georgina could recall. Her daughter could not help noticing that, for the first time in her memory, her mother was relaxed and even-tempered. It was as though, Georgina reflected, as though she had undergone an operation to change her personality. The meal finished, Sarah asked what Helen was like.

"Helen is quite black," Georgina said simply in answer, pausing for a moment to see how this would be received, then, "She's supremely beautiful from head to toe, has a deep, smoky voice, gorgeous, almond-shaped eyes is very kind, and absolutely reliable. She's about thirty-seven or eight, unmarried and has been in the fashion business for years. She's of Ethiopian origin, grew up in the USA, but prefers to live in Europe. These days she does more administrative work than modelling and also teaches new recruits the business. Although we don't see each other as often as I'd like, we remain firm friends." Georgy pulled out a picture of Helen from her expensive handbag and showed it round. Her mother smiled. Sarah said "Wow!" and Patrick clearly shared her sentiments. Then it was time to listen to the 9 pm news on the radio. Georgina's thoughts flew over the years of her childhood and early youth. She could not recall a more harmonious evening at home than the one she was now enjoying. She kicked off her quality high heels and spread herself in an armchair. Somehow it was good to be home again.

After visiting the hospital the following afternoon together with her mother, the two decided to visit her mother's favourite café in the city. He's quite changed; it's amazing," Georgina began as they sat down among the well-to-do of the town to take their tea.

"It's nothing short of a miracle," her mother remarked,

"and what's so important to me is that he seems to have completely forgiven you for your departure from home."

"Yes, it's quite astonishing, and I feel free from the pressure of being railroaded into a marriage that I didn't want," Georgina sighed.

"I bet you do," Elizabeth replied simply.

This, for Georgina, was another sledgehammer for her to digest. It was so very different from her mother's former stance, where she had wholeheartedly supported her husband's ambitions for her daughter. She mused on her mother's conclusion for a second or two. Georgina realised at that moment that she was no longer a young person that needed parental guidance anymore, but a young woman who had experience of her own, so she ventured, "But you were all for an early marriage yourself once, Mum. What's changed your mind?"

Her mother had assumed an unfamiliar attitude in answer to this. She was still, composed, even wise as she said, "Times have changed. Things are very different than they were in his day. Young people have their own ideas and are freer to implement them. He lives in the past. He's conditioned by his background and his profession. Like a large oak: old, strong, but brittle in a high wind. That's what's happened now. Saplings bend, bow to the currents of the times."

Georgina was flabbergasted by this, not only by its content, but by the way her mother spoke. It was as if she were a different person. There was no pontification in her manner, but a simple statement of what she felt to be the facts of the present situation. She was pleasantly calm, and smiled ever so slightly as she made her philosophical comparisons. It was a manner of total acceptance.

"Will he be all right, do you think?" Georgina asked tentatively.

"Yes, but it will take a long time before he's back to normal – physically I mean."

"And mentally?" Georgina hazarded.

"No, suffering has changed him. Sometimes folks have to suffer to wake up to their surroundings, to learn things."

Again, Georgina sipped at her tea in astonishment at this and to hide her reaction to her mother's equanimity, she said nothing. Moments passed.

"I suppose you intend to return to France, dear?" her mother then asked, changing the subject, and Georgina noted that she had never mentioned her removal to Italy.

"Well, yes, at the end of the week, I suppose."

"That's wonderful. It's lovely to see you again of course, absolutely lovely, but I'm so glad that you have managed to stand on your own two feet. "Parents are always pleased when their offspring manage to fend for themselves, you know. You've not only managed to do that, but also earn well. I'm proud of you, dear."

Georgina wondered whether she was dreaming. Her mother continued, "Tell me about this French girl, what's her name?"

"Evelynne."

"Yes, Evelynne, that's it. I'd quite forgotten."

"Evelynne's a wonderful person. She's wise, full of good humour, very quick at understanding the essentials of anything that's placed before her, whether it's something practical or something abstract. She's highly intelligent, very affectionate, very emotional and a loyal friend."

"Well, that's a lot to say!" Georgina's mother said with a gentle laugh. "It must be lovely to have such a friend. Is she pretty?"

"Yes, you know yourself, Mum, you saw her once."

"Ah yes, I remember, but then she was very young when she came here, about fourteen I think? Tell me more."

So Georgina enthused about her friend and her mum listened with interest.

They ordered more scones. She told her mum about her job and her prospects and her desires for the future. The old circumspection that had always attended their conversations at one time had quite disappeared.

"And I wish you every success, dear," her mother said when she had finished. Then, she added as though it were something of marginal interest,

"Do you intend to get married one day?"

For the first time during the whole afternoon, Georgina felt herself on her guard. It was a very personal question and one she had not had time to consider, and that was the truth.

"I suppose so. One day," was all she could say in reply.

Her mother merely smiled her smile again, but did not comment, and then it was time to leave. In the evening, Georgina asked her family out to an expensive restaurant in the town and the evening went off well for them all.

On her return home Georgina didn't feel tired, although it was well past midnight before she climbed the stairs to her room. The others had all retired to their respective beds, while Georgina on arrival at her own bedroom sat in the comfortable wicker chair of her childhood and reflected on the afternoon's conversation with her mother. Although hard to contemplate, it was quite clear that her mother was relieved by her father's indisposition. Georgina's experience of her mother today was of a different person. She had taken Georgina into her confidence; she had shown tolerance and even interest in Georgina's profession and had wished her well for the future; she had accepted her friendship with Helen without demur – and why not? She had not probed for information, using strategic questions as was her way in past years. She had accepted the fact that Georgina would probably stay abroad at least for some length of time, which was extraordinary. All this had left Georgina in deep surprise, and she now asked herself why. Perhaps it was because her mother had felt free to voice her own opinions after many years – decades – of oppression? Did she still love her father in view of this, Georgina asked herself. Or was this sudden openness and gentle intimacy today the result of her own maturity?

Georgina reflected. She was now twenty-one and instead of experimenting with various men of her age or older as she was sure her peers had done, all she had managed to do in the period since her departure from home was to work. Indeed, she had had no time for much else in that interval. Wasn't it time that she got to know a man more intimately? What was it like to sleep with a man? Or even be kissed and caressed by a man? She was curious. Jean-Luc's embrace of Evelynne crossed her mind briefly.

But now it was time to sleep, she told herself. Tomorrow would be the last day of her stay before returning to Milan. Before falling asleep, however, she thought of her sister and how she was growing up 'behind her' so to speak. She was herself now entering womanhood.

Every member of her family had changed during her absence. Patrick had fully gained the independence of manhood. Father's body had warned him of old age and the diseases that go with it. Her mother had reached an equanimity that only time can bring. Their canary had died the year before. Everything, she thought to herself, everything was changing sprouting as now in April, changing with time, happening at this very instant like plants in the garden growing skywards. In a way, it was a rather frightening insight to contemplate. Yes, it was a bit scary. And she was part of this 'growth', this change in time. Meditation on this kept her awake for at least another hour before she finally fell asleep.

"Don't leave it so long before you come again, dear, and God bless," her mother said the next day as Georgina leaned out of the train window to say farewell to her family. It was Saturday and Patrick was there, too, to wish her well on the first leg of her journey to London and from there to the coast and continent and the long train ride to Milan.

"And let us know what you get up to!" her sister called above the swishing, hissing steam and the banging of coach doors. In this she perfectly echoed their mother's former intonation, and Georgina smiled and nodded. "I'll do my best," she replied as the coach received a bump and moved slightly from its original position. "No, but do," Sarah repeated, "I'd love to hear from you."

"OK, I will, but first I've got to get back," Georgina said, recovering from the lurch. "Take good care of yourself among all these foreigners," Patrick added, tongue-in-cheek, "I hear the men are mighty lovers!" At this remark Georgina had to laugh. "I can deal with them well enough, don't you fear," she returned. It was a beautiful day and the sunshine had sharply illuminated every detail of the station, her family included.

"Take care of Dad," Georgina added, addressing her mother, "and let me know how things go. I'll ring you at least once a month…" And then a whistle blew; the train jerked and was already in motion.

"Bye-bye!"

"Bye, dear, bye!"

The train hooted and puffed heavily out of the station on its way to London where she would catch the ferry to Dover, and from the other side of the Channel the train to Paris. It was raining in Dover and there was a wind, which stirred the waves to a choppy welcome. Georgina's green eyes were serious as she watched them heaving and falling while waiting in the queue to board the boat. Only a few years before, hundreds of thousands of soldiers had left these very shores to take part in the world's second, bloodiest war, she reflected and was struck by the thought that she was now leaving her homeland for good, not, as on her first trip, to get away from tyrannous parents to join a friend for a holiday, but, as far as she knew, for good. She lived and worked and had her being in another country. It was an earnest reflection. She knew now that she was on her own.

The journey was uneventful, but to her joy the sun had become stronger the further south she travelled and this made her happy. She loved the sun.

She arrived in Milan at 10.30 pm and took a taxi home. Tomorrow would be another day of dressing and undressing, posing clothed and nude, of waiting, of being hungry, since very often there were no official breaks during shooting, only innumerable cups of coffee.

The visit to Britain had provided her not only with a necessary physical rest from work, but also psychological contrast and relief for which she was grateful. Georgina had not realised at once that this spontaneous trip to her native land had not only freed her from the intensive daily commitment in Italy, but had also given her an unsuspected mental vantage point. She had 'come up for air' so to speak, and had discovered that she could think clearer. She had now been employed for four years by *Mode pour Toi* and for three of those years concurrently by the photo agency, *Allegro,* and had earned a lot of money during that time, all of which had been subjected to tax percentage, and then paid into her personal account. The management of her financial affairs had been undertaken by one, Toni Catelli, who, like her, worked under contract for *Mode pour Toi* as its financial adviser, but also independently.

He was about thirty when Georgina first met him, a serious young man in a dark suit, formally polite and well mannered, correct, his impeccable tie always in the right position, a man dedicated to his profession as an accountant. Georgina had noticed his manicured hands and the way these counted money, signed and folded documents. Their encounters were usually brief and to the point, and since she lacked the specific vocabulary in the early days of her employment to explain things as she might, their communication was reduced to a few words and many smiles. She liked his smile, and she liked his reliability. He could be depended on; he knew the answers to the questions she put to him and received clear answers and friendly encouragement. Yes, she liked him. On this particular morning, they had met on his suggestion to discuss an investment of some of this accrued money. They sat opposite each other at his private office in the town, she attractive in her best blue business suit, feeling happy and free, he in his formal grey with a select, red tie, cheerfully ready to assist.

"Good morning, Signore Catelli!"

"Good morning, Signora Hennessesy! How are you?"

"Very well, thank you. You would like to talk to me, I think?"

"Yes, that's right. Please take seat." He smiled amiably. "It concerns what you have earned in the last four years, an appreciable sum." He paused to smile again. "Your account..." and here he showed her bank statements for the last month, "now totals, let me see, yes, $351,000 dollars and 36 cents, reckoned in those terms, do you see?" He pointed to the figures at the bottom of the sheet.

"Goodness me!" Georgina gasped in English. Catelli nevertheless understood and chuckled good-humouredly, "That's a lot of work, Signora."

He looked at Georgina and she at him and in this moment no words were necessary. Her heart beat as he smiled at her affectionately. The moment was brief but potent. Recovering, she said, "But you wanted to tell me more, I believe." He, too, recovering, cleared his throat to explain, "Well, you see, we don't normally keep so much on our current accounts, and I'd like to suggest that you transfer a certain amount to a savings account or even invest a percentage."

"Well, I don't know about these matters. What would you as my adviser suggest?" Catelli was prompt with his answer: "I'd bank two thirds and invest the rest."

"Thank you, Signore, but in what and how?"

The next few minutes were taken up with suggestions for investment and clarifications. Georgina looked uncertain. Signore Catelli was indulgent. "You don't have to decide now. Take some of this literature with you and tell me when you're ready to invest. In the meantime, I'll transfer your capital to a savings account."

"Where's the advantage for me in this?" his customer asked.

"Well, young lady," (she noted this and smiled inwardly, knowing that this friendly expression was customary usage) "On your present account there is practically no interest, in the savings bank account roughly 2.5% but in an investment account this can vary from 3 or 4% and even more, depending on a number of factors."

Georgina nodded. "But as I say, take the stuff home with you and let me know when you've discussed the matter with another person in your confidence. He or she will translate the difficult things for you. Do you understand me at least? That's important," Catelli concluded with another warm smile.

"Oh yes, thank you," Georgina replied, appreciating

this smile more than the potential contents of the printed matter he now selected from his drawers.

"Then I wish you a most pleasant day," Toni Catelli said sincerely, giving her his hand across the desk, and privately wishing to himself that he could get to know his client better. Georgina left the office wondering with whom she could confer about such a personal matter as this when, in response to this inner enquiry, Helen appeared in the corridor as if ushered into it by a fairy wand. Helen, tall and lithesome, Helen, an epitome of human relaxation, whose every movement was poetry that flowed gracefully and effortlessly into everything she did, whose smile spontaneously welcomed everyone warmly into her confidence as though one were a long-standing friend. Georgina always felt reassured by her natural, disarming charm.

"Hi there, Georgy, long time no see!" she said in her own inimitable way. She paused before a door. "Yes," Georgina said, showing pleasure at seeing her colleague again, at the same time communicating by her manner that they might now seize an opportunity to talk to one another.

"You got much to do this evenin'?" Helen asked.

"No, I've taken today off to get a lot of admin behind me," Georgina replied.

"Oh yes; I know all about that!" Helen laughed indulgently, widely displaying impeccable white teeth as she did so.

"So why don't you come over and see me? Would be nice to talk to a younger colleague, and I've heard a lot about you." She laughed again.

"Oh really?" Georgina asked, a trifle disturbed.

"Only good, *good* things, don't worry" Helen assured her, dragging out the word 'good' in deep, smoky reassurance. Her wonderful eyes looked heavenwards as she did so.

"Sure, let's meet, but I don't know where you live," Georgina said.

"You don't need to, dear girl, my chauffeur will pick you up 'cos I know where *you* live!" Seeing Georgina's reaction to this remark seemed to cause her much amusement, and the large, red mouth laughed again in unconcealed mirth.

"Oh, all right…"

"Say at seven. Come for dinner. Do you like fish?"

"Yes, I do," Georgina enthused.

"Good, then till later," Helen said happily, and disappeared through the door.

Toni Catelli closed another door in the same corridor about forty minutes later, locked it carefully, and tripping swiftly down three storeys of stairs reached the main entrance of the building and jumped into a waiting taxi. The driver knew where he had to take his passenger and already rejoiced at the tip he always received about this time on a Tuesday morning. After a short journey, Catelli descended and arrived at the front of the car, "*Grazie, mon amico,*" he said to Giovanni Brazzioli, the driver and thrust the generous tip into his hairy hand. 'Real gentleman, that man,' Brazzioli thought as he engaged second gear on his way back to the Piazza Romana. Catelli disappeared hurriedly into a palatial building and covered the first flight of stairs two at a time. The second brought him to more red carpet leading to a large room where there were already quite a number people immaculately dressed like himself. Arriving at the edge of this assembly, he met a friend.

"Saluto, Aldo," he said, seizing this man's sleeve.

"Ah, Toni, you've arrived just in time. Look!" They looked. Above them was a wide, moving screen with what looked like arithmetical data passing from left to right. It was the latest stock market information, an open secret to all except the initiated. Toni studied the repeated information moving on screen without interruption across the room. Like his young colleague, he understood what it all meant. "That's amazing! What you said on Sunday seems to have materialised," he cried in excitement. "It's more than 4.5%!"

"Oh it'll be more than that soon, old feller, you take my word for it," his companion assured him with a convincing smile.

"Well, I'm damned. You were right, and you reckon you'll be right again?" Toni asked.

Aldo leaned towards his friend. They had been to school together, got on supremely well with one another, and confidences were on the daily agenda. They had also suffered losses and fiascoes in their time, too, misjudged the critical moment and duly fallen on their noses. But these experiences had only made them comrades in arms. They shared everything with each other, knew everything about one another like prisoners in the same cell. Both of them had been poor and both relatively rich – "and rich is better" they had agreed, echoing Ella Fitzgerald's remark on one of their singular successes. The truth behind their success was patience, watchfulness and experience. They had just turned thirty, and their apprenticeship in the last few years had paid off. But there was also something else, which was just as important. Neither deceived the other – even when the advantages of deception were considerable. They trusted each other through thick and thin, shared every piece of information and every discovery, every fear, every anticipation – and every success. This mutuality was the key to their success.

"Oh I think I'm right this time again," he whispered.

"Umm," Toni mused as he looked at the ticker tape moving endlessly across the room.

"Whadye mean 'Umm'," his friend asked provocatively, feeling that Toni was in some doubt about his intuition.

"No, no," Toni returned hastily, "No, no, I'm sure you've got the right hunch; I was just thinking…"

"What then? Aren't you going to invest? I certainly am!"

"Sure. I was thinking of helping someone else."

"Who, for God's sake?"

"A young woman friend of mine."

"Oh hell's bells, man, don't bring women into this. You'll fuck up the whole thing!"

"Why? There's nothing wrong with women is there – or what?"

"No, of course not, but they're wired up differently."

"Why can't I help a friend, then?" Toni asked innocently.

At this, Aldo assumed the manner of the cabaret artist, of an elder man answering the artless questions of a younger, naïve stooge. The effect would have been very funny to an observer.

"Why?" he began with exaggerated patience, "because this, my boy, requires a nice, cool, steady head, that's why. Don't bring emotions into a scene where they don't belong. Who is this woman, anyway?" The last question was asked almost fiercely.

"Oh, just a friend. Well, actually she's not a friend at all, but an acquaintance if you see what I mean.

"Make up your mind," Aldo urged, looking steadily into his friend's face and his nose very near Toni's.

"An acquaintance. I do her books," Toni replied staunchly.

"You do?" Aldo raised his eyebrows.

"I would like to help her, see."

"He'd like to help her," Aldo, echoed, appealing to the damasked wall next to them for support. "And how, my friend, do you want to help this female?" he asked, suddenly assuming the manner of an advocate at a court of law. "Have you fallen in love with this person or what?"

"I don't quite know." Toni said, unperturbed by Aldo's challenges. "She has bright, green eyes and thick, flaxen hair."

"Oh Jesus, you're not kidding! 'Green eyes' and 'thick, flaxen hair'?" Aldo repeated theatrically, opening his eyes wide and rolling them to the ceiling. "Well, well, how poetic!"

"She's got a hundred thousand grand to invest," Toni said simply.

Aldo's jaw dropped and for a moment, for just one fleeting moment, he looked like an imbecile.

"What did you say, my friend?" he asked after a brief interval, regaining his composure.

"You heard me, I think, and I'm going to invest this sum for her – that is, if *we* think we're going to get good returns on the job."

"Thank you," Aldo said soberly. "*We* have to decide whether *we're* going to invest at all, and how much. You and I know the consequences of investing such a huge sum. That's 50M lire, Toni. FIFTY MILLION!" Aldo hissed the last words into Toni's ear. "I hope *we* know what *we're* doing, 'cos if we bugger it up, mate, we'll be in jug this time. That's for sure. Think on these things!"

"You, too, Aldo. Like you, I'm a bit scared. It's a hell of a risk, but I think we're really in the right key this time. This is the moment we've been waiting and working at for years. Imagine!"

Aldo, a born actor, listened to Toni's enthusiasm with a face of stone. The face stared into the crowded room, its mouth loudly agreeing at intervals with an "Oh yes," and an "Of course" as though Toni were talking about Milan's recent weather. From time to time, Aldo's expression formally acknowledged another face here and there as men in high-class tailored suits and subdued, matching ties moved off slowly towards the distinguished dining room next door.

"Do you reckon anyone else has hit upon *Geronimo Diesels*?" Toni whispered urgently.

"That we'll have to work on, lad. Very soon," Aldo replied coolly, as the two men joined their business colleagues filing through the doorway to the adjacent room. "Let's have lunch, play it cool; keep our ears and eyes open wide," he whispered before fanning out towards the laid tables. "Drop the vaguest of hints, speak, but say nothing, note every shift – you know the drill," he added.

Toni, the more sensitive of the two, nodded but said nothing. He knew 'the drill' all too well, but today he could hardly disguise his excitement.

"Ah, there you are!" said Helen, who had heard the wheels of the car on the gravelled entry to the house, and stood at its front door to welcome her guest. Georgina, holding a bunch of flowers and accompanied by the chauffeur, arrived at the top of the steps a moment later.

"I'm so glad you could come, my dear. Do come in." Helen embraced her guest. "Thank you, Louis," she added as the driver turned to descend the steps and return to the limousine. He waved his hand in friendly acknowledgement and disappeared into the dusk of the evening.

"Wonderful guy, Louis," Helen oozed, "I just don't know what I'd do without him. He can do everything, mend everything, deal with unsolicited callers, manage the garden, repair the car, paint the stairs – you name it, he can fix it." Georgina stood a little shyly holding the flowers. "Hey, are they for me, you darling? What a lovely idea! Nobody's bought me flowers for a decade I'm sure."

"Not even Louis?" Georgina ventured, eyebrows raised, and the two of them fell about laughing at the possibility.

"Oh, I'm sure we're gonna get on really well with each other," Helen prognosticated. "The girl's got a sense of humour." She took Georgina's light coat, hung it up on a silver hat stand in the hall and ushered her guest into the living room. This was luxuriously comfortable and warm. The nights were drawing in, and there was a slight edge to the air outside. What made the lounge even more inviting was the real fire that Helen had made up at the hearth. It popped and crackled at one end of the room where a sofa had been drawn up in front of it. Helen showed the way to the dining room, garlanded with low lace curtains and displaying shining cutlery and polished porcelain. Here, too, there was a fireplace where the flames reached high and the room was already cosily warm. Noticing Georgina's pleasure at seeing the fire, Helen exclaimed, "Nice and warm isn't it? I could never abide these European winters. Guess I'm really made for the sun!" As she said this, she stroked her dark-skinned arms. Georgina smiled.

"I didn't know what you like to eat, my pet, so I got a lot of things together for you, and I guess it's all on the table for you to choose," she said as the maid came in with tea and confirmed this remark. Georgina just gazed. She was familiar with the French cuisine and had often eaten well with Evelynne, but she had never seen anything like this before.

"I think I'd like a cup of tea," she said modestly.

"Sure you would," Helen applauded, "there it is, girl, just help yourself." But before she had settled herself at table, Anna, the maid, had already filled her cup. Helen sat down opposite her guest. "It's beyond belief. All this super food. I feel most flattered," Georgina protested lightly. "I don't eat much usually, so this is really a feast for me.

"You just wait till you get the wine, boyo," Helen said, winking at Anna. Anna smiled coyly. "She's Portuguese," Helen explained. "Doesn't understand everything yet, but she's comin' on just fine, aren't you, honey," Helen noted, putting her arm around Anna's ample waist. "All ya have to do is speak English; she'll get it. She's clever, our Anna." Helen sat down at table.

"How do you manage to keep slim on all this? Georgina asked, tucking into a fish salad and helped with the sauces by the obliging Anna.

"Gee, girl, I don't eat like this every day, bless you," Helen replied, "gotta look after ma figure, that's sure."

"But I've heard that you don't model as much as you used to?"

"Oh, sure, that's true, but I feel better as I am, model or no model. There are even some days when I don't eat at all. I drink plenty, though. I think that's important. And I exercise – practically every day. And I do that because I like it. I like it and it in turn likes me; does me good."

"What kind of exercises?" Georgina enquired.

"Mainly stretching and breathing, a bit like swimming with no water," she laughed and Georgina smiled. "You'll have to show me; I'm interested," she said.

"Oh, be glad to. You'll love 'em, I'm sure, but let's tuck in first. Anna's done a great job and this is a feast for the two of us, eh?"

"You bet," Georgina responded enthusiastically, helping herself to another plateful. Helen smiled privately. The girl was obviously hungry.

During the meal they talked shop. Did Georgina know

so-and-so? And is so-and-so good to you? How much do you charge for nude photos? Who are you with? Do you have any trouble with anyone 'stepping over the line'?

"No, do you?" Georgina replied.

"Oh yeah, some of 'em try it on – or used to – until I made it quite clear that they'd be in big trouble should they try agin."

"What would you do?" Georgina asked.

"I'd book 'em for sexual molestation and I've got a good lawyer."

"Oh, that's awful. So far, everybody's been admiring, but no one has come too near yet. I've always appreciated this."

"I bet!" Helen said firmly. "Would you like some wine, Georgina? I'm the proud owner of six bottles of a 1947 Borgonne-Sameau. It's cooling in the fridge." Georgina knew nothing about wine, drank alcohol very rarely but acquiesced with a smile.

"Good! You'll love it," Helen said and rose to fetch it, waving aside Anna's wish to help with a pleasant gesture. "Thanks, I'll get it," and returned from the kitchen with a bottle pearling with condensed water. "*That's* something good, believe me, and I think you'll like it," she said placing it in a receptacle.

"I'm sure I will, and it's very nice of you to offer me such an expensive accompaniment to the meal."

"Accompaniment to the meal," Helen echoed, smiling broadly. "How lovely to hear you English guys speak. It's great. I love it."

"And I like your voice," Georgina returned with admiration.

"You do? Lots of folks have said the same thing, and you know, I've never heard myself speak."

"Well, I tell you it's absolutely super, take my word for it," Georgina said warmly.

Helen was clearly moved by this remark from another woman and felt very complimented. After a few more minutes, they moved off into the lounge where the fire still blazed up the chimney. "The wine mustn't get too warm," Helen said reaching for the bottle and pouring out a glass for her guest. "Taste it and see for yourself."

"You were talking about men taking advantage of situations," Georgina reminded her friend.

"Oh yeah, but it doesn't happen very often, since there are other people around, and you put 'em off by being nice, but firm. Best to be pleasant, otherwise things could escalate." Helen sipped her wine. "You like it?" Georgina nodded and admitted to herself that she enjoyed it. Normally, she drank any kind of alcohol with reluctance, and generally to please others, but this indeed was something different.

"Yeah," Helen continued, "you gotta admit that's all in the natural way of things, and the fact that I'm black is something special here of course. I can understand it, and I don't blame 'em for it either; that'd be crazy."

"I wonder then why I haven't had trouble in this direction. Perhaps I'm not so desirable."

Helen laughed heartily at this remark, "Oh, that's ridiculous! No, I think something else plays a role with me and that's not so nice: some think because I'm black I'm easy game or because they're under the impression that coloured girls are more sexy than their own. Whatever it may be, it's the unusual that attracts them."

"You are phenomenally beautiful," Georgina said. To her surprise, Helen said nothing to this, but smiled graciously at the compliment. Helen liked her young guest. There was something charmingly innocent about her, something childlike and sincere, and Helen prized sincerity above everything else. The consequence of this conviction was that she detested all forms of guile and dissemblance. In matters sexual, she told her companion that even as young girl she had quickly developed an unerring sixth sense whereby she could immediately detect the difference between self-interest from appreciation. An approach from a man who appreciated her for what she was could be warded off by preserving his ego. She would give him a smile and gracefully accept his compliment, at the same time making it quite clear that this was all in the artistic game of producing a good photograph, and praising him for his acumen in this. There were to be no scenes offstage. That was not in the scheme of things, which, of course, he would understand. And usually he did. It was easy. Only a few persisted after this move. These were like leaches that needed effective discouragement, like the stinging threat of public exposure or a call for help. The danger was that things could turn out to be nasty in cases like these and it was important to be able to assess the possibility of harassment before this became an ugly fact. Georgina listened with interest. "What do you do if they actually lay hands on you?" Georgina asked anxiously.

"Then it's teeth and claws and kick 'em where it hurts"

"Wow!" Georgina exclaimed.

"But since you're not alone in the studio, other guys would intervene in a case like this."

"Has that ever happened to you?" Georgina asked.

"Yes, once. He was a particularly unpleasant character. I screamed. He had actually made his way into the changing room, and nobody had seen him. I was still completely naked."

"Heavens! What did you do?

"I grabbed his balls and squeezed as hard as I could. It worked. He yelled as though he'd been shot and the others came running. He lost his job, but continued to stalk me for a year after that, threatening to kill me and all that."

"But that's dreadful!" Georgina put in.

"Yes, it was. Eventually, I contacted someone in the Mafia who managed the situation. He just disappeared from the scene after that."

"So you don't know what happened to him?"

"No, and I don't care either." Helen took her glass and drank deeply. The wine was having its effect. She felt good.

"God! I hope I never have anything like that happen to me," Georgina gasped.

"Well, thank goodness, it's not so frequent. The first technique works for most males. They remain 'intact' so to speak and leave you alone."

"Helen…" Georgina paused for a second.

"Yes?"

"Can I ask you a question? It's a bit personal."

"Well of course, dear, ask away."

"You talk of pushing off all these hungry males. Do you find any nice ones, I mean, men you'd like to get to know better?"

"Of course! I've slept with quite a few."

Georgina was silent at this for a moment, and Helen answered what was in her mind. "You're thinking about marrying someone, having gone so far, is that it?"

"Yes."

"No, that's not on the books yet. Blacks marrying whites and vice versa is even difficult in the USA today, let alone down here. Sure, Italian folks are a thousand times more tolerant than over there, but that's because black folks are few and far between. People here still look at me in the street as though I'm a nine-day wonder. That's OK. I'm used to being looked at, clothed and unclothed. That doesn't bother me, but if I had a white on my arm, there'd soon be trouble of some sort, I'm sure."

"But that must be pretty frustrating for you, mustn't it? Not having a husband and so on?"

"I manage. I'm happy. My money is a big help. In America I'd be the poorest, oppressed, even hunted woman. That's no life. When I was there as a young girl I was ranked as what they call a 'nigger' like the rest of the native population, but my folks came from Ethiopia. That's quite another part of Africa where people are genetically different. We weren't imported as slaves. The Italians colonised our country, and we grew up speaking Italian and adopting their culture. As you can see, I have your features, and my hair, although curly, is not the tight cut that most African folks have. We have our own distinctive culture."

"Yes, if you'll forgive my saying so, I've noticed the similarities and differences between us. It's interesting, really interesting. How did you come to Italy, then?"

"My father had connections in the US. Because I began to get pretty when I was about fifteen, he said that he might be able to find me a job in Italy. This would get me out of there. The man took me on and here I am," Helen laughed.

"Do you ever see your parents or this man?" Georgina enquired.

"Oh, yes, I go across there every eighteen months or so and also supply them with money. They're happy about my position and I love them. My brother and two sisters benefit, too, but I don't want to stay there."

"Why?"

"I don't want to be part of their hate laws. We live in the south and it's pretty rough down there, honey. I don't think of myself as one of them anyway. I was glad to get away and haven't regretted it for one second, believe me. No sir! As for Leon, my father's contact here, well he's very good to me. He and his wife treat me like a daughter. They're great folks. I see them right whenever the need arises."

Georgina felt that she had gone too far, so she changed the subject.

"I wanted to ask you about this man in the administration here. Is he to be trusted?"

"Who? Toni Caletti?"

"Yes."

"I'd trust Toni nude in a dark cellar!" Helen cried, "He's a great guy. The nicest. And you can trust him with your money as well. He seems to be a kind of wizard in this respect. He's helped me financially several times since I've been with the firm. He's attractive, kind, civil, never, ever takes advantage of a woman, however favourable the situation may be for him. He's absolutely honest and reliable. I can't praise him enough and I've known him now for four years. Now that's a man I'd like to know better."

Georgina was amused and relieved at the same time to hear this news, but she was curious as well.

"What do you mean exactly by 'better'?" Georgina probed.

Helen smiled demurely as though to say, 'so you can't guess'?

"I hope I'm not being too personal; I wouldn't want to do that," Georgina apologised.

"Oh, you're so sweet," Helen replied. "You're not being 'too personal' as you put it. Don't be silly. What I mean is that if I like a man and he likes me, we could come a little nearer to each other – literally – if you see what I mean."

"Of course I understand", Georgina said, feeling just a little uncomfortable. Perhaps she had gone too far, she thought, so she reformulated what was on her mind. "It's just that you wouldn't want to marry him, then?"

"Why, no." Helen answered quickly. Her expression became earnest. This was the crux, Georgina thought, and she dared to probe further, "Why not?"

"Well, perhaps it's because I'm not geared to thinking about marriage, especially not to a white, since this could bring all kinds of disadvantages for both parties in the world we live in at present, including the children that emerge from such a marriage." Here, Georgina nodded slightly, and after a short interval Helen continued, "I don't think we humans are advanced enough yet to accept unions of this kind. It's a mad, dangerous world, and I wouldn't want to add to the general suffering. There's enough of that already."

It was typical of Helen to speak plainly and truthfully, and Georgina was affected by her frankness. She surveyed the woman in front of her and could only feel the warmth of admiration. Helen's face and her general composure were not only beautiful, but also dignified. The years of experience she possessed, her tolerance, good humour and her common sense had combined to fashion a being of rare maturity. Above all, Georgina thought, there was an abundance of love and compassion that emanated from the person opposite now about to light a cigarette.

"And what about yourself, Georgina? Do you have a partner?" Before answering, Georgina took another swig of the excellent wine at her side.

"No, in fact I've never had much to do with men at all. My mum and dad were steering me towards what one might call 'an arranged marriage', and I didn't want that for one single second. There was one man who lusted after me while I was on holiday in Ireland, but his selfishness and roughness put me off for quite a long time."

"Heck, how awful! Poor girl. Well, at least you're out of that wood here – or what?"

"Yes, I think so. I fled to France and was taken care of by a very good friend, then I had the good fortune to get a job down here. I've worked like a slave for four years and just haven't had the time for even a flirt."

"Yeah, I know the routine. It's hard, but I've managed to even things out a bit with a man here and there. Takes the tension out of things. When I need 'em, I go get 'em."

Georgina couldn't help but laugh at this. As she sampled the wine, she said, "You're a little older and probably much more experienced in this field than I am, Helen."

"Well, maybe, but it depends a bit on what you're looking for, what you want. I don't want to be tied down, for example, and I make that clear to them from the very first. They can enjoy my body, and I can enjoy their company and their affections, and sex, but the settling down bit isn't for me. I value my freedom, my liberty of choice to do what I want when I want.

"Is that a bit selfish to your ears, dear Georgy?"

"To tell you the truth, Helen, I don't know. I simply don't know what to say, because I've never been so near to a man. I just know that they're quite another species than we women."

"Oh, you can say that again," Helen put in.

"They seem to have different values and they certainly have different interests, and what annoys me is that they don't seem to see or to care about our 'different-ness'" Georgina concluded.

"Yes, exactly, I know just what you mean. We women take the trouble to understand them, but they just go their own way as if there were only one sex and no differences at all." Helen agreed.

"But that's just their weakness in a way, you see," Helen smiled wickedly. "just because they're so concerned about themselves, they leave loopholes for us to take advantage of their selfishness. All too often, it's we that steer the course of things, and they haven't the slightest clue what's happening. It's easy!"

Georgina and Helen both laughed heartily at this likelihood, and Helen poured out more wine for them.

"I've never tried it," Georgina admitted, "and that's because I've never got too near."

"What! You've never had a boyfriend, is that what you mean?" Helen asked incredulously.

"Yes."

"Well, I think it's about time you did."

"I think so too, but there just hasn't been anyone, and I don't go looking for a man," Georgina added.

"OK, you're right there, too. Should happen naturally. I'm just surprised that's all, a beautiful girl like you," Helen remarked.

"Oh sure, they look. Both sexes look." Georgina said hastily. "I'm so used to being looked at that it's part of my daily routine, but I've made no acquaintances."

"Perhaps it's time to work a bit less and do a bit of looking yourself," Helen suggested. "After all, you tell me you don't need to work so much as you have been doing in the last few years."

"Theoretically, I could retire," Georgina said with an embarrassed laugh. "I would have enough money to live on, but it seems crazy to give up working at such a young age. I wouldn't know what to do."

Helen looked serious. "Work is much more than earning a salary. It's a way of life, isn't it? I wouldn't give up work, dear, but perhaps work less."

"The thing is what would I do with my time?" Georgina asked.

"Precisely. I guess you have to find a new dimension,

something else to fill up your life," Helen, said, "You'll have to think about that one." She smiled kindly.

"What do you do with your time?" Georgina asked. "I hope you don't mind my asking."

"Of course not. I read a lot and regularly. Do some posing here and there, of course, and I mix with people. People are interesting. There are always problems and if I can help, which I usually can in some way or other, I do just that. It makes me happy and it makes them happy. And that's a good thing. I love it. Brings folks together, and you never ever get bored. There's always something or other. Life seems to be made up of problems. No problems, no life," Helen added with a laugh

"Have you got any problems yourself? Oh I'm sorry, Helen."

"No need to be sorry. Yes, I've one problem. I'm human aren't I? So it has to be." She laughed.

Georgina was still not totally relaxed with her older colleague, despite the wine, and despite the warmth she felt for her. She felt she had gone a bit too far in asking Helen such a question. To her surprise, Helen did not seem put off by her remark at all. Without the slightest pause, she said, "Yes, there's a problem. It concerns a man, not a particular man, but a man who doesn't exist. At least not yet. It's not an actual problem, but a potential problem." Georgina looked perplexed, and Helen laughed lightly and continued. "Let me try to explain. It's not that I'm lonely, you understand. It's not really that, no. How shall I explain it?" Helen looked wistfully into the fire for a second or two. "I can live quite well without a man. I'm self-sufficient. I'm rich. I have my own circle of friends, can manage the everyday part of my life pretty competently, and as I've said, it's good to feel you can help other people from time to time. And as far as sex is concerned, I can take a man any time I feel like it, and I do just that, but there's something missing, and for a long, long time I didn't know what."

"And do you know now?" Georgina asked gently.

"Yes, I think I do," Helen replied. "I feel I want to support someone, but that someone has to need me, not just lust after my body and ignore my mind, my personality." Helen paused again. "The right man doesn't have to live for me either. I'd hate that. He must have his own interests and his own personality, but he *must* be an inalienable part of me, so that when I'm not there he's not complete either, do you see what I mean?"

"Yes, but that's marriage isn't it?" Georgina asked.

"I guess that's what it should be," Helen replied, "but it so often happens – oh so often – that the man's not a companion in the real sense of the word, but a piece of furniture or in the worst case a mere name on a formal piece of paper and not much more – on the marriage certificate I mean."

Georgina nodded. "My mum used to say that 'little girls are there to help' and I'm certain there's something in that," she said.

"Oh sure, there's something in that," Helen agreed. "We've gotta help or there's no point in our existence, but we've gotta be appreciated as well, and that's where a whole lot of men just fall on their noses. When we leave 'em then, they're left wondering what went wrong, the stupid fools."

There was a pause while both women took a sip of the rest of their wine.

Georgina after a moment: "Why do you think that is? Is it because they're so egoistic?"

"Yeah, sure. Most of 'em are egoistic all right, but the point is, I feel, that they're ignorant, too." Georgina was listening intently. Noticing this keen interest, Helen continued. "I don't necessarily mean ignorant in the bitchy, vulgar sense, or even in the sense of sheer stupidity. I mean that they just *don't know* how we feel and function." Georgina nodded. "*They* are convinced that we think, feel and function like they do, but we don't, you see. We look different, walk differently, breathe differently, see differently, judge differently, react differently: We live in a cycle; they live in 'straight line', so to speak; they use their heads and we use our hearts; they want change and we want to preserve – it's a different species!"

"And you feel that they ought to know," Georgina proposed, impressed by Helen's oration.

"Yes, dammit, I do," Helen said emphatically. "Instead of the bullshit they teach, say, as 'religious education' or one-sided 'national history', they could instill mutual respect for the differences between the sexes *and* for each other in schools and do something really useful. They could teach human anatomy, the art of working together, mutual respect, how to judge without prejudice, learn meditation, for example or a form of this while learning an art or craft. This would gradually produce real men and women, not exploiters, moneygrubbers, leg-straddling machos, whiskey bibbers, torturers, political ego freaks and warmongers, rapists and murderers."

"And the women?" Georgina asked.

"Yeah, and the women would learn not to go along with their dirty work, stick together and enlighten the men, make sure they receive a good education, learn something other than merely trying to get a man and finally free themselves from this innate slavery and win their independence."

So saying, Helen piled two or three light logs onto the fire, which then huffed and sparked up the chimney. Georgina noticed the long, red-nailed fingers expertly grasping and throwing the wood accurately into the flames. Georgina wanted Helen to go on. She had never heard anyone talk like this before. Suddenly, the woman she once knew, the 'African' the one who 'flowed' passed you in the corridor or made you feel 6ft tall somewhere else with her smile and her general ease had become a burning apostle for a new social order. Then Helen turned from her work and smiled warmly and directly at her guest. Georgina was a little surprised at this, since it seemed incongruous with her previous remarks. It said quite simply, 'Oh, but we're not of that crowd, are we?'

"I find what you say very interesting, Helen. To tell you truth, I'd never thought of these things."

"No, my dear, I suppose not, "Helen responded with a sigh and another irresistible smile. "I really must be getting older."

"But not all men are as you describe them, are they?" Georgina probed, avoiding comment on age. "I mean they're not all exploiters and brutes, still less murderers and rapists."

"No, of course not, but it's these that win the day. Look at history, kiddie, just look at it, not only political and social, but look at man's religious history as well. It stinks."

Georgina had to admit that she hadn't read much history and said as much.

"That's sure a damn pity, Georgy, 'cos our history is what we are: a pretty despicable animal not far removed from the apes we come from, but nevertheless despise. What an irony! But I reckon apes are morally superior." There was a pause and Georgina felt a little embarrassed at Helen's downright assertions. Weakly, she asked, "How do you make that out?"

"Well, they don't organise great armies of other apes to go out and kill their fellows, using all the skill their rampant intelligence can supply, do they?"

"No," Georgina said quietly, "I suppose not."

"But we do, don't we? Every few years and that for centuries," Helen asserted, and then, noticing Georgina's embarrassment, veered a little from the subject, "Perhaps it's the opposite of sex," she said, shrugging her shoulders at the theory.

"The opposite?" Georgina queried.

"Yeah, I mean it keeps our numbers down," Helen said simply.

"Heavens!" Georgina gasped, "Do you mean that war is a kind of divine plan, then?"

"Looks like it," Helen said with an expression that asked for a reaction from her guest, but there was no comment forthcoming, and so Helen continued. "And as far as sex is concerned, you have to see what it means against the background of our evolution." Helen paused to ask whether she was boring her friend, "No, no, do go on, I'm fascinated," Georgina said.

"Well, if you consider Nature, it's clear at first glance that we seem to be at a disadvantage compared with the rest of the animal kingdom: we have no claws or teeth worth anything in competition with other land-roving creatures, and no speed, no camouflage, no eminence at climbing, no weight, no horns and no acute vision for locating and hunting down our prey. We've no fur to keep us warm during the winter either, and to live alone thousands of years ago meant certain death. Without the technology we've slowly and probably painfully created for ourselves and passed on from one generation to another, we'd have been lost to the rest of creation in a very short time on this planet. We depended on each other and that's why we lived in communities. But we are also blessed with intelligence to combat the problems of cold, for example, by wearing clothes and living together in some kind of housing, and through the discovery of fire could keep ourselves warm and relatively safe warding off other animal intruders with this at night. What I call 'technology' was everything in those rude times, and still is."

"Still?" Georgina enquired innocently.

"Yes, sure. We don't have to go looking for food and water, fear the elements for lack of shelter, and in the last two centuries, we've even managed largely to fight off many diseases, allay the effects of accident and roughly double our lifespan into the bargain. These are the main things; the rest, like architecture, communication of all sorts, including roads, shipping, rail and flight are improving all the time and are the flower of this basic intelligence we had then and still have."

Georgina listened intently to all this and sat very still, having quite forgotten her wine. Helen went on, "And we had something else which, ironically enough, was able to help us overcome the problems and dangers inherent in or environment in those far-off days, and that was that we were able and free to breed at any time. And so our numbers increased, despite the presence of disease all around us, aimed at reducing them. This ease in reproducing not only helped us to gain an upper hand in the game of survival, but it's also a counter to the ravages of war."

"That's quite a new way of looking at things," Georgina said.

"Well, it appears to be true," Helen replied. "You have to admit that this urge to reproduce is always at hand in both sexes. I can see this, and have no qualms at all about indulging in it. Once you can see the plan behind it, it becomes perfectly natural and absolutely beautiful. Have you never thought that our bodies – our skins – are all part of this plan to reproduce? In the old, old days, it was reproduce or perish. Today maybe it's different, but this and our native intelligence have been the keys to our survival."

Georgina gazed into the fire with a pensive expression, saying nothing.

"Oh, I can see what's worrying you, I think," Helen said, "it's the old religious thing probably... ?"

"Georgina nodded.

"Well, don't, honey," Helen declared decisively. "That's all a shameless interference with a private activity that has absolutely nothing to do with the Church. Nothing. The old church fogeys who advocate abstinence and tell healthy-minded people what to do and what not to do are only too often themselves perverts on the quiet. I've come across quite a few of them in my time."

Georgina raised her eyebrows.

"Sure," Helen went on, "but we don't want to get onto things like this, do we, and I'm talking too much anyway."

"Oh, don't say that, Helen. I love to listen to you, and I've never heard anyone talk like you do."

At this Helen laughed her inimitable laugh. "Oh, my goodness! What a compliment!" She laughed again.

"I wanted to ask you about sex, Helen," Georgina hazarded.

"Sure, you go ahead. Ask away!" Helen said encouragingly. Georgina paused and cleared her throat before proceeding.

"What's it like?" she asked quickly.

"It's great, simply great," Helen said promptly. "But two things are necessary: the first is that neither of you start wanting things from the other, and the second and just as importantly is that you respect each other. Without mutual respect it can become horrid."

"Oh?"

"Yes, it has to be thoughtful and loving, and entirely free from the chains of any conditions. Then it's splendid and liberating."

Georgina thought about this for a moment, and Helen regarded her thoughtfully from her vantage point on the settee.

"What are you thinking about?" Georgina asked with a smile.

"I'm thinking it's time you found a partner, someone you'd feel easy with, and then you could come and tell *me* things!" She laughed at this proposal, and opened a box of chocolates that had been lying on the small table at her side. "Want one? Sinful, they are, but ab*solute*ly scrumptious," she added with emphasis as she handed Georgina the box. Her guest indulged in two and found them good. "Yum," she concurred.

"Swiss." Helen said with her mouth full, "Can't beat 'em for chocs." A moment or two followed while these two enjoyed one of the distinctive fruits of civilisation, and their evening together came to a natural intermission.

Realising this, Georgina suggested by her manner that it was time for her to leave. "It's getting late," she said, looking at the face of the golden pendulum on the wall.

"It never stops. It's always getting late," Helen replied in fun, pulling a face at the chronometer and putting her head on one side as though the clock were in some way responsible for the implacable march of time. Georgina giggled.

Helen's lean body had snaked to the standing position as she gave Georgina her hand. "Come again, honey, and come again soon. You're always welcome – and especially when you want to talk to me about something. And if there are any problems – anything – just come over. You've got my number, I think… ?" Here Georgina nodded. "So just don't hesitate."

The chauffeur appeared at the door as though bidden, and the two women parted on the warmest of terms. It was then 11.30 pm. A few minutes later, Georgina, tired and happy, flopped into her bed at last and fell into a deep, dreamless sleep.

Shakespeare once spoke of a 'time and tide' in human experience, *'which, taken at the flood'*, he said, would lead on to fortune, implying thereby that this was largely a constellation of happy circumstance rather than man's ingenuity. Who knows?

Toni and Aldo stood together in Aldo's office on the first floor of Alberto Mori Street, waiting tensely for information to be supplied to them from a screen on Aldo's desk. It was relatively early in the morning and Aldo's muscular body was still sheathed in a pair of shamelessly pink pyjamas. His face was dropping with sweat as he announced that they would soon know whether they would have to leave the country or quietly retire to a rich suburb.

"'Ere we go, lad, another couple of items and we'll be there," he proclaimed to a nervous Toni who had reached for a cigarette to calm his tortured nerves. He lit it with trembling hands as he watched the inexorable passage of statistical information travel with insouciant regularity across the screen.

"Ere! NOW! Here it is! Hey look at that, you monster! WE'VE MADE IT! We've made it! Fifty fucking million!" With this pronouncement, Aldo fell into the arms of his accomplice, taking him along in a dance through the room like a mad thing, kicking chairs and disturbing furniture, shouting "BALLY HO!" at the top of his voice and repeating the sum cited above at least a score of times until Toni had recovered himself enough to issue a locomotive like "Sshhhh!" a hissed warning that if Aldo went on like this, the police might arrive at their neighbours' request

"We need champagne, you bastard." Aldo spluttered, quite out of breath now from his athletics, having paused for a moment from sheer exhaustion to collect himself, adding, "Out with it lad, (pointing to a bottle of champagne in a glass vitrine) I got some in last night. The best, kiddie, the very, very best. Cost me an arm and a leg, you bet, but it's worth it, aint it? Here, open the bloody bottle! I'm too much on edge." Toni gladly opened the bottle with his own shaking hands, and the liquid frothed into their respective glasses.

"To you, you old bugger," Aldo yelled at his companion, and tossed back his glass. "Aye, and to you, too," Toni rejoined, "Today, we're rich, thanks to you."

"No, no," Aldo Donati said expansively, "No, mate, you did all the bloody groundwork, and then our hunch proved to be dead right, didn't it? Imagine! Fifty mil." Then, changing the amplitude sound of his enthusiasm to one of normal expression, he went on, "Let's have breakfast at the Crowne Plaza by God, and consider what we're going to do with it all." There was the tiniest of pauses before he asked, "I suppose you have a plan or perhaps two, Signore Caletti?" Aldo was at his best. This last was asked with the sophisticated unctuousness characteristic of a waiter they both knew and was brilliant. Toni laughed heartily at the accuracy of the mimicry, "You bet," he agreed, "but we can consider that over coffee, and I'm just ready for a cup."

"Me, too," Aldo agreed in the same falsetto tone he'd used before in mocking the waiter," I'll just go and see to the horses," he added with a flourish in the manner of exaggerated eighteenth century dignity. "Won't be a moment, old boy." He disappeared towards the bathroom. Toni was left to grin, finally sitting down on their modest balcony to look down onto the street below at the first of the town's citizenry making their way to work. To be frank, he hadn't the slightest idea of what he would do with such an enormous sum. Some of it would be inevitably taxed, he mused, and of course he would keep his promise to Signora Hennessey. He wondered what she would say when he informed her, and hoped she'd be pleased. What a beautiful person she was! He mused. Not only remarkably beautiful, but a person of very nice character as much as he knew of her. For a second or two he dwelt on her image. What was she like to talk to, I mean, not only about accounts and that kind of thing, but about her likes and dislikes? Toni imagined her sitting opposite him in a restaurant. He would ask her out to the best restaurant in town, yes, and soon. He couldn't get her out of his mind. Could it be that he was falling in love?

"Right, mate, got that over," and changing his tone to one of high dignity, Aldo declared, "Let us now repair to the best breakfast house in this city," and ceremoniously taking Toni's arm, flounced to the door and from thence to stairs leading down to the street below. On the way down they met a sixty-year-old neighbour coming up holding a bag of bread rolls, and, typically, Aldo greeted him with generous cordiality to which the neighbour instantly responded and in the same tones. It was so extraordinarily amusing for Toni that he had a hard job negotiating the next few steps without collapsing with laughter. Aldo was in top form today. They emerged on the pavement, "And 'e aint got nuffin' to be pleased abaht 'as he?" Aldo asked his companion in the local dialect, changing his manner and mien again to one of serious concern. This was just too much for Toni who stopped in his tracks for breath while Aldo walked on.

Once at the Crowne Plaza, they ate their fill, rejoiced over the superb coffee and accorded the waiter a handsome tip, closing their repast with the best of white wines available in the hotel and leaving the building around 10 am.

During this beano they had debated how they should distribute their enormous gain and how it should be administered and by whom. Once deposited as anonymously as possible at a bank in another city, they agreed to take separate holidays to separate places for a week or so to let things blow over, as it were. Discretion and secrecy were the key themes of their deliberations, and since they got on extraordinarily well with each other and trusted one another, there were no disagreements. Aldo went swimming and Toni turned in for work as usual at eleven at *Mode pour Toi*.

It wasn't until two weeks had passed success, that Toni encountered Georgina again to inform her of her own, relatively smaller financial benefit from the transaction. Sitting in Toni's small but immaculately furnished office in black and silver, she received the news of her advantage with a burst of astonished pleasure, "What, $258,000! But that's wonderful. Thank you so much!"

"Well, I did promise something of a gain, but didn't count on so much," Toni explained truthfully in his modest way.

"But the capital has nearly doubled!" Georgina insisted, "And I can only put that down to your skill and knowledge. That's wonderfully kind of you, and I want you to know that I appreciate your kindness," she said warmly.

"Oh it's nothing really," Toni replied, knowing inwardly that it required the most intense research and courage to make such coups, but he waved the matter aside with a smile.

"Nothing!" Georgina protested, "Well if that's nothing,

I'll be here again tomorrow." They both laughed at this suggestion, while Toni privately hoped that destiny would bring about just such a situation.

Then, returning to the details, he said seriously, "There's the 'gains tax' that you'll have to pay, Miss Hennessey; we can't avoid that, I'm afraid."

"Of course, I've come across that before, and please call me 'Georgina'; everyone else does."

"You honour me, Miss... er, sorry, Georgina," Toni murmured, ever so slightly embarrassed.

Georgy smiled. He was sweet. She sized him up, this finance officer. His dark-blue suit was finely tailored and sat on his shoulders to a tee. He had nice hands, too, she noticed and she liked his gentle, sincere manner as he thumbed through her documents, doing the sums in his head which she had never been able to do properly at school.

"Well," Toni said at last with a tone on finality, handing her a file across the desk for her to check. "I think everything's complete and in order. I hope you'll enjoy your little gift! I need your signature... ah... here."

"Toni," Georgina said, rising, " I know it should be the other way round, but I'd like to ask you to dinner; I'm so deeply grateful for your efforts and you should a least reap some reward."

"I'd be glad to," Toni cut in before she could say more. "I could manage it this evening, because I have the afternoon off on a Thursday. I could arrange it all."

"Well, of course that would be lovely," Georgina replied. "I'll leave it to you, then."

"Let's say eight at *Montefiore's* in Avenue Galatea. I'll be there to receive you, and send a cab to pick you up at 7.45 pm," Toni added, graciously opening the office door for her.

"Super," Georgina said, smiling and disappeared down the long walk towards to the lifts.

"Toni Catelli? Well, well!" Helen's voice, delighted, enthusiastic, thundered down the telephone line. "Why, that's just great! I'm so pleased for you, dear, and for him, too. He's about thirty I'd say, and you're five years younger, that's perfect, "Helen gurgled. "I hope you have a whale of a time, girl, and let me know how it goes, yes?"

"Oh, I will, I will," Georgina agreed happily. "I just thought I'd let you know."

"That's dead right," Helen replied, "and you keep me informed now! Bye, dear." The phone clicked.

The evening with Toni was spent happily talking about their mutual interests, their childhoods, friends at work, their respective jobs, their ideals and wishes and much more. Time passed very quickly and at 10.30 pm Toni rose to fetch her light coat. They did not go to their respective homes immediately, but wandered down to the river's bank together and carried on their conversation until it was midnight when Georgina received her first kiss. Much later, they decided to walk home, and Toni gently escorted her to the door of her apartment, and here they blissfully kissed each other again in the darkness of the landing.

"Good night, dear Toni," Georgina whispered, gently unwinding herself from his embrace."

"Good night dear Georgina," Toni replied, "see you again soon."

Georgina nodded, gave him a loving smile and placed her key in the door. Squeezing her arm again, Toni turned to descend the steps to the street. The lift had been so noisy, they agreed, giggling. He switched the light on and they waved to each other. The door closed loudly. The automatic light went out and a very happy young man leapt down the stairs to the street below three steps at a time.

Four months after this they were married. Aldo was their best man and never were two people happier. It was a large affair. At least 150 guests came to the wedding reception at the stately home of a friend of theirs south of Milan. The sun shone. Pure joy.

They had agreed to use Georgina's commodious flat for the first months of their marriage as a home before moving into something larger – with a garden for their prospective children to play in, they said – on the outskirts of the town. Georgina had already agreed on the course of their lives. Toni was to keep his job at *Mode pour Toi* and that he go off with his comrades every ten days or so into the mountains, since mountaineering was his favourite pastime and "a welcome counterbalance to his sedentary profession", he was fond of saying. On two occasions he took his wife along as well, but Georgina, although she loved the scenery and the outdoor activity, couldn't compete with the burly young females who usually made up part of the teams, let alone the men and so finally gave up. Toni was disappointed, but accepted her decision. It must also be added that Toni's team also eagerly explored the region's underground lakes, and it was this which ultimately put paid to any expeditions of this kind, as Georgina hated being underground.

And so it was that, two years after their marriage, Toni's team, Monte Tora, found themselves confronted with an interesting challenge. During their clambering activities they had stumbled across a cave opening, which had been boarded up and securely locked against intruders. Toni and some of the others in the team were all for breaking down the door and taking a look at what lay behind it, but Luigi Cordini, their leader, decided that the best thing to do would be to first make enquiries of the local authorities before entering. The barricade was pretty substantial. It could be that it had been boarded up during the Second World War and that explosives were stored inside, he said. Accordingly, the team put off its exploration until more information was available, and another month went by before they found themselves in front of the gated entry once more. The team had officially received a key to the heavy padlock, which it was to return after it had made its reconnaissance. Toni helped two others remove the wooden planks, puncturing his wrist on one of old nails that had held it in place as he did so. He cursed vehemently and the others laughed. At last the young people gained entry and were obliged to claw awkwardly over rubble that seemed to have been deposited there for a purpose. What they found after another 15 metres or so was not a store of explosives, but a terrifying, sheer cliff falling away abruptly at their feet to a watercourse a good 200 metres below, a fatal trap for any unwary pioneer. Each team member gasped as torchlight illuminated the spectacle. These powerful torches also showed them clearly that there was no alternative passage through the rock and no way down that was not fraught with acute danger, so, sobered by their experience, the company scratched and scrambled its way back to the entrance, where three of them replaced the boards and locked the steel grating.

About a week or so after this event Toni complained of stiffness in the neck and chest.

"I feel OK in every other way," he said in answer to Georgina's enquiry, "it's just this odd feeling, a kind of numbness."

"You should have it looked into," Georgina suggested.

"Oh it's nothing. Doesn't hurt. The wrist hurts more. Look, it's swollen and very red." Georgina looked. "Well, *that* definitely needs attention," she diagnosed. "You'll have to have that seen to soon." Toni withdrew his stiff wrist, said nothing and made himself ready to go to work.

"Why don't you go to see the doctor now?" she urged.

"He has a surgery at six. I'll go on the way back from work," Toni replied. Georgina acquiesced to this and, after warmly hugging his wife, set off for the town centre by tram.

Georgina thought nothing more about the situation and shopped at her leisure for food an hour later in the city, returning about 3 pm to her apartment after a protracted lunch with a woman friend.

To her surprise, the door was open. She hesitated. A burglar? Frightened by this possibility, she very slowly pushed the door open a little more and peered into the sunlight parlour. There was no one to be seen, but she then heard footsteps. She waited in the corridor, ready to run and fetch help, when Toni's figure appeared, making its way to the window in their living room. Georgina entered. He turned. What she saw at that moment never left her memory. It was Toni, yes, it was Toni all right, but another Toni. The face that leered at her was not that of the man she loved. It made incomprehensible sounds through its twisted lips. One eye seemed unable to move naturally. She made to embrace him, but the figure immediately withdrew like a shy child, still uttering these strange sounds that tore her heart in two. "Toni! Toni!" was all she could shriek. He had taken up an odd, defensive position in one of the armchairs, shaking and mewing as though he were a stricken animal, his face contorted, his arms shooting spastically into the air. Stricken with terror, Georgina reached for the phone.

Within minutes two ambulance men arrived, literally cornering Toni and professionally overpowering him, gave him an injection and laid him on the floor while the other fetched a stretcher. Georgina looked on hopelessly, cold with fright and incomprehension. One of the men nodded to her while busy strapping her husband to the stretcher.

"What?" More she couldn't utter.

"Probably tetanus," the man replied shortly. "I'm not a doctor and can't diagnose. We're taking him to hospital. You should come with us. Know more there." With that the two of them capably moved Toni towards the door. His body was still and his face pale. Georgina moved down the stairs and into the ambulance like an automaton. The ambulance careered off, its siren wailing like something out of hell.

The first doctor to attend Toni was a man in his fifties, white-haired, bespectacled, practical but friendly. "Looks very much like a tetanus infection," he said to Georgina, leaning his head to one side. "Has he been immunised against this risk?" he enquired. Georgina didn't know.

"Probably not," the doctor surmised with a sigh. "He'll have to stay here of course where he'll receive special attention in the next few hours. We'll do our level best to relax the muscles of the chest and face and simply hope for the best, dear lady, more we cannot do at the moment," the doctor explained kindly. Then, turning to a nurse, he said, "Sister here will show you where to register and the like and which ward he'll be in. You look as though you need to rest for a moment yourself," he added, looking at Georgina. "Sister, take her to Ward 10 and see that she has something to drink – not coffee, please." And with that he nodded to Georgina courteously and moved off with Toni and two younger medical men.

Toni died in the same night of heart failure. He would have been thirty-one next month. Georgina was paralysed by the news, quite incapable of being able to do anything at all apart from sitting in her lounge next to the telephone, which had relayed the news from the hospital. She could neither speak nor walk nor think, but simply sat where she had placed herself hours before. What was there to do? Where would she go? Why did she have to live at all?

While in this inert cocoon, the phone rang again. It was about 3 pm. It was Helen.

"Hallo, there, honey, how are yer?" She went on immediately to relate an accidental encounter with *Mode pour Toi's* boss in a café in the town, but after receiving no response after a moment or two, said, "Hey, Georgy, you OK? What's on?" Georgina murmured something and then was still." "Hey, is everything all right?" She persisted but after receiving no reply replaced the receiver. Within fifteen minutes of this call, Helen knocked on the door of Georgina's apartment. For a time Georgina refused to move and it was only after Helen had fetched a neighbour for assistance and after both had banged violently on the door that Georgina moved stiffly from her seat to answer.

"Hey, hey!" Helen said, taking her friend into her arms, "What's up?" The neighbour mumbled something and retired discreetly. Helen moved inside half carrying her friend into the room. "What's wrong, girl, what's on?" she said again and again. Eventually, Georgina gathered enough resources to say weakly, "Toni died last night in hospital. Tetanus."

"My God!" Helen muttered, "my God!"

"Yes, it was this injury he had. It turned bad."

"What injury, dear?" Helen asked, and Georgina recovered sufficiently to explain what had happened in the last few days.

Helen immediately proved to be very helpful in her innate, practical way. First, she phoned a friend of hers, Claire, who turned up a few minutes later to take care of Georgina, while Helen made tea and a light meal. With Georgina's help, Helen then rang Georgina's in-laws and the boss of the firm whom she'd met earlier in the day.

Since she had been bi-lingual all her life, this presented no problems and her communications were couched in considerate terms. Aldo proved to be on holiday; nobody knew where, and Helen reflected what a shock it would be for him to learn that his friend had died in his absence.

From that day on, Helen, together with Toni's relations, undertook all that is necessary when someone dies. Claire remained at Georgina's side, even sleeping in the same apartment.

The funeral service, the condolences, the burial, the later reception and the meal afterwards, all these melted with the trees and the stones of the cemetery for Georgina. She only recognised her parents and her sister from a distance as though they were the moving figures under water. Her beloved friends, Evelynne and Jean-Luc were among the mourners, but she herself seemed only to be half alive in their black, consoling embraces. She was aware only of Helen's loving presence and care and it was this, which helped her through the August days that followed.

September announced itself with clear, silent, blue skies. The dusty leaves on the tired city trees were beginning to change colour and one day Georgina felt strong enough to visit Toni's grave. Helen accompanied her. It was as though the world had 'popped' and she had surfaced to the real world again. Wordlessly, the two women stood before the black-and-gold stone tablet bearing the details of Toni's brief sojourn in this world. A small, metal-framed photograph of him had been placed to one side of it.

"We wanted lots of children," Georgina said, turning tearfully to her companion. Helen simply put her arm round her. After a moment she added, "How utterly stupid that this idiotic bug could end a human life." But Helen, who in her early childhood had seen much of Nature's careless distribution of death, remained silent. They stood there for perhaps twenty minutes before turning to leave the brightly-lit cemetery for the shadow of the city's buildings. To their surprise, they met Jean-Luc at its entrance. He had flowers in his hand.

"You, Jean-Luc! What are you doing here?"

Jean-Luc, impeccably dressed, tall, confident smiled at them both, gave his hand warmly to Helen and embraced Georgina.

"I thought you'd returned to Bordeaux after the funeral," Georgina exclaimed. "And where's Evelynne?"

"I had work to attend to in Rome, and Evy's still down there for a day or two," Jean-Luc explained.

"Oh – and by the way, this is my friend, Helen," Georgina said, indicating Helen.

"Yes, I've seen the lady from time to time," he responded with a good-natured grin.

"Can't miss me or you need an optician," Helen said wrily. They all laughed. It was the first time in weeks that Georgina had laughed. Somehow, the ice had broken. Some of the unbearable tension she had endured recently now fell from her shoulders. For the moment she felt relieved. She looked at the flowers in the crook of Jen-Luc's arm, and he at once understood the question in her eyes. "Yes, they're for Toni," he said simply, "I'll put them…" he began.

"We'll come with you," Georgina suggested.

"Er, no, dear ladies; I prefer to tender my respects alone, if you understand." They did, and the three of them said their farewells. Once out of earshot, Georgina confided to her friend, "That's damn nice of him, isn't it? I mean, coming alone to see Toni like that. I wouldn't have expected him to do such a thing on my behalf. That's great, isn't it?"

"Sure is," Helen agreed and the women took the bus to the town centre where they sat down a few minutes later at a pavement bistro. The autumn sun shone benevolently. They ordered something light to eat, and Helen felt relieved in realising that her friend was feeling much better than in the previous weeks. At last, she thought to herself, they could talk about other things than her loss and her pain and Helen was at the same time glad that she had been able to help her.

"Who is this guy, Jean-Luc?" she enquired with interest.

"He's Evelynne's boyfriend," Georgina said with a smile.

"Boyfriend? He's a lot older than she is isn't he?" Helen emphasised the 'boy'.

"Well, he's a lot older, but he's OK," Georgina replied.

"He's OK all right," Helen warmly concurred. He's *whamm!*"

Georgina was amused by Helen's sudden enthusiasm and felt the need to enlarge. "He's a real gentleman, wonderfully kind and very knowledgeable."

"You bet!" Helen readily conceded, her almond eyes opening wide. This tickled Georgina, "Hey, Helen, have you fallen in love? Well, well!" she cried.

"No, I don't think so, "Helen replied, "But I *do* like a bit of class from time to time." She said this with such sincerity and depth of feeling that Georgina could only laugh. It seemed so at odds with Helen's usual level-headed composure and good sense. Helen changed the subject. "How come you speak French like that, Georgy?" she asked. Georgina told her.

"Wow!" was all Helen could bring forth for the moment. Georgina laughed again.

And it was just at this moment, although we know that such things only happen in fairy tales, don't they that Jean-Luc appeared, newspaper in hand on the other side of the noisy road. Georgina called over to him loudly. Two buses passed. He vanished and then he was at their table.

"How nice to see you again," he said cheerfully to them both in Italian. Helen answered first and it was clear to him right away that she was a native speaker. He made an effacing gesture with his hand, which apologised for any mistakes he might make in the conversation that would follow.

"I can speak English as well," Helen interjected, "so don't worry."

"Ah, Eenglish," Jean-Luc replied, "er, not so good, but I weel try, you know."

To Georgina's delight, the method of the one speaking his or her own language and the other answering in theirs worked perfectly.

"Oh yes, "Jean-Luc recalled, "we 'ave tried this before, I think," and winked at Georgina. She had remembered their arrival in Milan some years before.

"And how's Evelynne?" Georgina asked.

"She will be 'ere tomorrow, I 'ope," Jean-Luc said. "She wanted to surprise you with a sudden, er, drop-in, but now I can tell 'er that I've seen you."

"Good, I need to see her again," Georgina said, and Jean-Luc smiled his diplomatic smile, courteously ordering an espresso, while Helen busily sized him up.

"How are things in Bordeaux, then?" Georgina enquired.

"Oh, pretty good recently. I have luck. The board officially promoted me to vice-chairman, so these days I'm directly under Courelle. That's why I'm 'ere on business in Italy. The firm 'as expanded as you probably know."

Georgina didn't know. "I'm not into the firm's business anymore, Jean-Luc, I gave in my notice just before I got married to Toni, as I wanted to become a mother."

Jean-Luc's handsome face clouded just a little, "But what will you do now? You are still very young."

"Oh, I like that, that's very nice of you, Monsieur

Beremont," she said with exaggerated appreciation. "You're in my good books now, you know."

"Well, you are still a young, beautiful woman, are you not?" Jean-Luc persisted, appealing to Helen who was also laughing. Jean-Luc gave them a quizzical look and then, changing his expression then to one of serious concern, he said, "Ah, per'aps I need a pair of spectacles? I will see to it tomorrow." They laughed heartily at the earnestness of his mien.

"So I'm retired, you see," Georgina confirmed.

"Umm," he said, and it was clear now that he was no longer joking. "Are you going to remain in retirement?"

"Well, I suppose so. I have enough money, so why not? Helen here's been semi-retired for some time."

At this Jean-Luc adopted his attitude of mock concern again. "Forgive me, madame, I was really not aware that you were so old." he said most deferentially, "You don't look a day over sixty-five."

"Sixty-four," Helen corrected.

"Ah yes, sixty-four," he echoed, appearing to confirm by his manner that he had heard something to that effect elsewhere. "Seriously, Georgina, you're a little younger than Evelynne, aren't you. She'll be twenty-nine this year."

"Yes, I was twenty-seven in August," Georgina said.

Again, Jean-Luc's face dropped. "All these old people," he murmured uncomfortably, looking over the road as though for confirmation of his remark. However, though intending to make them laugh, Jean-Luc's real concern was Georgina's future. Privately, he asked himself whether she really wanted to pursue a life of leisure at her age. He cast his mind back to the young woman he had accompanied to Milan on that rainy day so long ago, or so it seemed. After a moment or two of reflection, he decided to ask his protégée what her plans were. Tactfully, he began, "Er,

Georgina, seriously now, and I know that this is neither the time nor the place to ask such a question, and so forgive me. I ask since I'm here and could perhaps be helpful."

"What, then?" Georgina prompted kindly.

"Er, well, I was wondering where you go from 'ere?"

Georgina was suddenly serious. "I don't know, dear Jean-Luc; I just don't know. There's just a big hole in my life. It's horrid. I'm just dead inside. There's just nothing." And tears welled up in her eyes.

Jean-Luc nodded understandingly. Helen wiped Georgina's tears away gently.

"Please forgive my asking," he said sympathetically. "I just want you to know that I, er, – *we* – are 'ere for you. Bordeaux is not that far from Milan."

Georgina continued to weep. Helen, who had been mostly silent since Jean-Luc's arrival, supplied another paper handkerchief. The waiter appeared again to ask whether he could bring them anything more, and this was interpreted as a sign for them to move on. Helen rose first and Jean-Luc assisted Georgina out of her seat and offered them both a lift in his car to their respective apartments. It was midday and the church clocks all over the town were faithfully registering the hour.

"Thank you, I'd be glad of a lift, M Beremont," Helen rejoined, and as Georgina didn't react to the invitation, she was accordingly ushered into Jean-Luc's large automobile, which had been parked in a neighbouring street.

Once settled, Jean-Luc concentrated wordlessly on his driving. The girls were also quiet until Helen suddenly cried out that they were nearing her street and that she would get out now and so help avoid further hold-ups. Smiling and waving at Jean-Luc and Georgina, she said, "Georgy, now, you keep in touch *today,* please." Georgina nodded that she would and the door slammed as the lights changed.

She waved her friend out of sight. More negotiation and the two arrived at a quieter street where Georgina lived and Jean-Luc drew up at the kerb. To Georgina's surprise, he switched off the engine. "Come and sit with me at the front," Jean-Luc said. Georgina joined him. "I want you to know that I feel for you," he announced firmly. Georgina was surprised by his tone and wondered what he intended to say or do next.

"Yes, I know you do," Georgina replied and there was a short pause before her companion continued. "You may well be surprised at what I am going to say, but I want you to understand that what I say is absolutely sincere and expressed in your interests, not mine. Do you understand me?"

"Well, of course," Georgina replied.

"Well, it may not be so self-evident as you perhaps assume."

Georgina waited.

"It's like this: you've suffered a terrible loss, and I just want you to know that I appreciate this."

"As my friend, I assume this," Georgina said patiently.

"Yes, but, if I may say so, I would like to put the tragedy in a wider context."

Georgina just looked. "Hateful and absurd as it is, these things happen," Jean-Luc continued in French. He paused a moment. "These things as I call them are just part and parcel of living. They can happen anytime, anywhere, are wholly random, and wholly 'unfair' from our human point of view." Georgina looked at him. "Little children go down with diseases that either kill them or render them later as twisted adults. Stupid flies transmit bugs that murder the best of us or we fall prey to accidents that maim or cripple and are entirely unforeseen. Any time. Anywhere. Always." He paused again. "There's no justice, no divine interference and no end to it." Georgina listened, spellbound to a Jean-Luc she didn't know.

"We've recently completed a repugnant war started by a raving maniac that has cost the world millions of lives and billions of francs. Innocent people were shoved into gas chambers, hanged, knifed, tortured, burned alive, murdered *en masse* for one slobbering, little snipe determined to distribute his poison all over the world. Those who hit back died in their millions in the very attempt to put an end to it all. Where, I ask you, is the moral justice in that? The fact that we won? Perhaps. But the conclusion you have to come to in all this, *chère Georgine,* is that there is *no* justice, no God-up-there that might curb our insatiable desires to murder and exploit, and no brake on Nature's nature's inexorable drive for change. And of course, where there's constant change there's no security either. Everything changes. Now and forever.

"To be here on earth is to find oneself in a kind of madhouse full of murderous traps and dangers, both within us and without. That's the true, though unacknowledged nature of this universe of ours. It is as it is. Our religions and philosophies are mere sandcastles set up against a terrifying tide of sheer power."

Georgina sat as though paralysed. Jean-Luc had expressed these ideas in French, but in such precisely chosen words and phrases that she had no difficulty in understanding him. He smiled very slightly and she indicated that he go on, saying, "I see what you mean, but how can this knowledge help me?"

"*Ah, bon!*" he began. "You must understand *why* I say these things. You, dear Georgina, are no exception in this dangerous free-for-all. While I sit in this car I could be next. None of us is immune. The stage is lit, the play is on; we must hope that we'll be all right and be ready for anything!" For an instant, Jean-Luc seemed to be inspired. "It's like something I once saw in a cartoon film," he went on. "The character was in a train and the train was passing through a tunnel. Then, suddenly, there was light, the sun shining down on green fields, cows browsing, a dog barking near a fence, a jolly man on a red tractor, woods, birds, fleecy clouds – and then nothing again. Darkness, the tunnel, noise. That's how life is; it opens up to us for a brief span, and then it's over. And that's why it's so important to recognise this very fact. *Tu me comprends?*"

Georgina nodded. "Now, young woman, I *don't* want to bore you," Jean-Luc continued, "that's the last thing I want to do, but please try to understand."

"God forbid! You're certainly not boring me, Jean-Luc, and I'm moved by what you say. I understand you, too. Thank you."

"*Bon.* I'll finish what I want to say, and then I'll shut up. Having said this, it might help to view this scene, this life of ours as a truly magnificent pageant, full of the most incredible, multifarious, incomprehensible possibilities. It is so inconceivably diverse and great that the human mind is incapable of even conceiving an atom of it. It cannot even be spoken about. "However, like the wind that cannot be seen, we can see what *it* does. And what it does is remarkably positive. It simply goes on and on and on, or, seen in another way, this life of ours, is an enormous, inconceivable, marvellous potential. Realising this, and here's the point I want to make, we either choose to go with it in all *its* incongruous, mind-boggling, impenetrable, infinite mystery or we go under. It's like an unchallengeable imperative. We must go on, whether we want to or not, and *that's* what I want to say to you. *Don't* give up. As for Toni, poor chap, he's passed on into the tunnel; that was his fate, but *you* are still part of the pageant. You must go on! I'm here to help. Helen apparently, is a wonderful friend, and there to help you, too. Evelynne is another, and I'm also on your side. I'm older, OK, a kind of elder brother if you like, but we're all behind you, Georgine, so go on! Don't give up."

Jean-Luc then apologised for having "gone on and on" himself, and switched on the ignition. The powerful engine purred.

"Oh, how can I thank you, Jean-Luc?" Georgina said. "You're so kind. Your description of 'how things are' has helped me. Thank you so much."

To this, Jean-Luc nodded understandingly, *"Rappel!"* he said, smiling faintly.

"How could I ever forget?" Georgina replied, opening the car door. *"Au revoir! Au revoir!"*

The dark-red car drew off. Georgina stood waving in the early afternoon sunshine before the small garden gate of her apartment.

# 6

## *The Going On*

The nineteenth century figure of Signore Latta sat before his serious assembly. He was dressed in black tails, the collar to his immaculate white shirt turned up to reveal the rest of the black bow tie round his neck. His gestures were neat and careful. Before him were four members of Toni's well-to-do family, also in black, Aldo, Toni's friend and a distinguished looking woman of forty or so with a much older husband whom Georgina didn't recognise, and, of course, Georgina herself and her interpreter.

Signore Latta began:

"Ladies and Gentlemen,

"We are gathered here today to hear the will of the late Mr Toni Catelli, who, regrettably, has gone from us so early in life and whose will and testament I am here to read to you on his behalf. Welcome."

At this, Signore Latti smiled briefly, sat down, and continued. "Signore Catelli was a very thorough individual of which as most of us present are aware, and so we may assume that the distribution of his will and testament have been carefully considered. Thus, as follows: Mrs

Georgina Catelli, formerly Miss Georgina Hennessey of Great Britain, whom I recognise as present here among us, together with her interpreter, is to receive the largest share of the inheritance, er... a total of 62 million lire, which at present is lodged at Signore Catelli's account at the Banca Italia in Rome."

There was a gasp from those present at hearing this and an excited rustle of exchanges among the party followed before Signore Latti, clearing his throat, continued, "er, and will be subsequently transferred to Signora Cattelli's personal bank account in Milano in due course. The house and the car also fall into her possession as was previously contracted by him before his decease." Latti looked up for a moment above his steel-rimmed glasses, as if, it seemed, to make sure that everyone was still there, and then moved on.

"The estate, both house and land at Parco Landi falls to his parents as does all the furniture, pictures, and all other household accessories therein contained. Signore Catelli was also at pains to include his sister, Signorina Isabella Catelli, in his will and this includes his coin collection of which she, he reports, was very fond. Since she is still under age, her parents will undertake to look after the same until she reaches the age of eighteen." Latti looked up again and smiled in the direction of Toni's parents who nodded. "Signore and Signora Catelli are to receive all or any other values left in his estate at his (and their) former home in Via Spaldini No. 5 in this city, as well as any other dividends, interests, dues and the like which would normally fall to him as a result of his recent business transactions as well as the office furniture, equipment and others connected with it.

"Signore Aldo Monte, should he require some or any of this, is required to negotiate with Signore Catelli's parents on these matters." Aldo acknowledged this from his position on the second row by nodding briefly.

"And that, Ladies and Gentlemen, is all of that which I have in my power to disseminate and bequeath. I thank you for your kindly attention." Signore Latti nods, shoves papers into his briefcase, smiles and leaves. Gradually, the little party disbands, Signora Catelli in tears.

Helen caught Georgina's arm as the party filed out of the room. The two exited the building without a word before they reached the pavement where the early afternoon sunshine beat down upon them. Here the others of the party dispersed, and after their goodbyes, Helen and Georgina were left standing there in the brilliant sunlight.

After a moment, Helen broke the silence by saying, "Over there. Look!" and pointed to an inviting café in the distance. Georgina followed wordlessly.

They took seats opposite each other. Helen looked wrily at her friend.

"Well, there you are. You're a very rich young woman! What does it feel like?"

"Awful. Just awful!" Georgina replied emphatically, looking angrily at her colleague. Helen raised her eyebrows in surprise.

"Awful?" she said, unbelieving.

"Yes," Georgina went on in a tone that was almost petulant. "I don't want to be rich and I don't want the money. All you Americans think about is money. You forget that I've lost my husband; I've lost my future, the prospect of a family and my happiness. These are the most important things in life, which your damned money can never buy, and you talk about it all the time." Georgina raised her voice, "The whole thing's embarrassing. I don't know where to start."

"Well you can start by calming down." Helen interrupted her gently. Then their order came. The waiter arranged the cups, plates, cake forks and serviettes with dignity on the table. After he had left, Helen began again. "I guess you're all strung up, Georgy, honey. I would be myself with such a dollop like that suddenly on my plate."

"There you go again," Georgina said irritably, "Well, it's ridiculous, I tell you. Just ridiculous. Far too much damn money. I'll give it all away. I will." Helen had never seen Georgina annoyed before at any time and was a little dismayed at her friend's aggressive manner. Feeling that it was best not to say anything in reply, she turned silently to her cake. There was silence between them. After a long time, Helen ventured a question. "What do you intend to do, dear, I mean where do we go from here?" she asked quietly.

"Oh, I don't know. Don't really care. Kill myself or something and you can have my money." This was said to hurt, but Helen was mature enough to disregard the slight, and smiled ever so slightly. She realised finally that her friend was not going to say anything further about any subject, and resolved at that moment not to say another word. Twenty minutes passed in which all the cake and all the tea were quietly consumed in tense silence.

Then they paid and each rose to leave. "You needn't accompany me home," Georgina announced firmly as they left the table.

"OK." Helen replied in a subdued voice and halted in her step to wait for confirmation.

"It's all right; I'll find my own way home," Georgina continued uncharitably, and at this Helen nodded and turned without saying another word towards the bus stop where she would catch the bus home alone. Georgina gave her friend a formal nod and pursued her own way homewards in the opposite direction.

In the months that followed, Georgina gave official notice to her employer, renovated her flat completely, changed her telephone number and her bank, made no calls and visited no one, discouraged friendly overtures, both male and female, lived as a recluse, ate little, dressed simply and poorly, took long walks on her own and went to bed early. For a long time she wore black, which, though she would have staunchly denied it, only enhanced her good looks. In the spring of her twenty-eighth year, Evelynne insisted on seeing her, and the two young women spent three days together as the trees began to find their leaves again, and this morning in mid-April found them sauntering along Gran Via. Evelynne is the one person that Georgina is glad to see, for Evelynne is part of her. Evelynne is honest. Evelynne doesn't flatter her. Evelynne doesn't tell tales, and Evelynne says what she thinks. Georgina trusts her implicitly. Above all, she doesn't talk too much. She can be silent and she has been now for at least a kilometre. Then she says tentatively, "You haven't told me much of Helen; she was a good friend, I think?"

"Yes, she's fine, but I haven't seen her for months. Independent spirit." There was a short pause while Evelynne digested this remark and its possible implications, before she went on, "I liked her when I met her."

"I like her, too," Georgina rejoined coolly.

Evelynne in that second felt daunted by Georgina's remoteness. Her dark-brown eyes glinted in the sunlight as she sized up her friend's manner. "I don't know what to say," she added. Georgina, knowing that this was uttered in complete sincerity, came to her aid. "Well she's all right. She's mighty generous. She's open and honest and has a wonderful sense of humour. No, don't mistake me; I like her all right. I like her maturity, too."

"But you don't want to see her?" Evelynne pursued.

"Well, with all that praise, I still think she's a bit materialistic and this irritates me a little."

"Materialistic?"

"Yes, she's got that bug they all seem to have over there; money's the root of everything, a kind of holy common denominator, the sacred cow of their society, so to speak, something that's so sacrosanct, thou shalt not for a second dare cast doubt upon it."

"But Helen has lived away from the USA for decades. I'm sure she very well appreciates that there are other values as you call them."

Evelynne's objection was met with an indifference that hurt her.

"Maybe," Georgina said icily, and Evelynne was brought up short. She didn't recognise her friend anymore as they stood gazing together at a wedding group leaving a nearby church. Neither of them spoke for several minutes, and during this interval it was clear to Georgina that alienation had taken place, and at this her eyes filled with tears. Understanding, Evelynne guided her friend wordlessly to a bench.

"I don't want to go on," Georgina sobbed. "I want to die. Soon. Now."

Evelynne said nothing to this, but stroked her friend's back, pulling her close. Georgina felt relieved not to need to justify her feelings or her conduct. She just sat there and wept and wept in Evelynne's arms like a infant. Evelynne, still silent, rocked her gently. Two women and a man stopped by to ask if they could be of assistance, but were assured in French by Evelynne that she had everything in hand. The wedding group had long dispersed in several waiting cars. The morning crept on and Georgina continued to cry. After an hour or more, Georgina, still in Evelynne's arm, finally stopped crying and accepted a handkerchief to wipe the last tears away. She smiled apologetically.

"It's all right, Gee," Evelynne said, dabbing her friend's

cheeks without adding anything more, and Georgina loved her for it.

"I don't know what's happened to me in the last year," Georgina said.

"It's all right," Evelynne said again comfortingly. "Come, let's go on; you don't have to say anything. Just walk." And so they did. Gradually, Georgina felt better and better. In the moments that followed, it was as though she were suddenly well again after a long illness or had passed through a door that had been locked hitherto, but now was suddenly open and she was free at last to leave the dark cell of her mental imprisonment.

In the afternoon, the two visited Toni's grave, and Georgina laid the flowers on it, which Evelynne had selected and bought that morning. Strangely, and from that moment on, Georgina's life began anew.

"I feel better," she said to Evelynne as they took the tram back to her apartment. "I don't know why or how. Perhaps it's your coming, dear Evy; you've brought the sunshine back into my life. Oh God! I'm happy again!"

Evelynne was speechless for a moment, but the expression of happiness on her brown face was sufficient for Georgina to know that her friend understood completely. She threw her arms round little Evelynne and kissed her right there on the tram seat with the tram bell ringing impatiently and the wheels whirring, grinding and clanging over the points, and the old thing swinging and jolting drunkenly round a corner. The conductor was yelling the stops and the people were staring at the neat figure of Evelynne sitting there dressed in white who had blushed when the golden beauty kissed her so boldly, so fervently, so uninhibitedly like a happy child, and who looked away in embarrassment at the blurring, merging figures waiting to board at the next stop, and the adverts and the newest colours of the spring fashions.

Evelynne had only come to Milan for three days, and on the following Thursday she left for Bordeaux, feeling that her journey had been well worthwhile. It proved to be the impetus that changed the course of Georgina's life.

A day or so passed and she looked at herself naked before the mirror combing her rich corn-coloured hair, that had now grown to her waist, and it crossed her mind that it was time someone else admired it, someone personal, not a photographer, an agent or some other commercial jerk out to make money from her curves, but someone who would take it in his hands with interest, admire it and tell her so. After all, she thought, that's what it's there for, and she turned from the mirror dressed and went in search of breakfast. Today, she promised herself, today she would find that someone and felt assured that it wouldn't be difficult. But he had to be right. She didn't want some fawning slave that couldn't look beyond his sexual desires. She wanted a real man, as Evelynne had called her ideal, a male that had other interests than women, someone with humour and independence of mind who had achieved something in life and could manage on his own if need be, but whom she would persuade to need her. Returning to the mirror that evening, now fully dressed and in high heels, she put red lipstick to her lips in that careful way women are wont to do, peering into the mirror to scrutinise the application and pursing her lips in final approval of the war paint before critically reviewing her face and general appearance with a brief flourish. Satisfied, she donned her, light-grey coat from the coat stand in the hall and left the apartment.

Enter Enrico Trotta. At this very moment he's to be

seen as they say, propping up the bar at Paganini's, a bar for Milan's rich clientèle. He's bored. He looks bored, and that's perhaps why no one, neither male nor female, has so far shown interest in him this evening. He fondles his glass of Coca fortified with Jack Daniels whiskey. He is thirty-three, fair-haired and blue-eyed, well formed, tanned, handsome, the male counterpart of a Georgina, one could say, and, like Georgina, he's done quite well for himself financially in the motor industry over the last few years. He wears light, tailor-made casual trousers immaculately creased and a fine pair of brown leather shoes and an open, light green sports shirt. In the breast pocket is a pair of pilot's sunglasses. His brown wrist sports a Rolex, which looks as though it had been bought yesterday. But he's bored, poor thing, he's bored. His expression is one of studied indifference, as he looks around the room at those present, mostly people of his own age involved in conversation, talk and body talk, the speech given to man (and woman) to hide thought and here to cunningly disguise the sexual desire, but, at a deeper level, a level never or rarely uttered, to disguise the need for another's understanding presence. Enrico has seen it all before or so he thinks, and sits alone, pan-faced, seemingly unconcerned and yet taking it all in.

Georgina has arrived with an acquaintance she recognised the day before at the baker's and whom, she knew, also worked at *Mode pour Toi*. They had exchanged the time of day with one another and then as they left the shop they very soon began to talk intensively about all kinds of things. Their liking for each other was immediate and mutual, and during the conversation, Jennifer, for that was her name, mentioned Paganini's as a place worth a visit. Georgina had been intrigued by her account of the place, and so it was spontaneously decided between them that they go together that night to this particular bar.

Jennifer, too, was an attractive blonde of about forty and Enrico also instantaneously assessed this, but his eyes were fixed on Georgina. His boredom evaporated as quickly as steam in the air and he concentrated his whole attention on Georgina. 'Surely, this was it?' he said inwardly to himself, this is the woman I've been looking for all my life! He got down from his high stool and moved a little nearer the two ladies who were ordering at the other end of the bar.

"And I'll have a Martini with ice," Georgina said with a smile at the barman.

Enrico moved nearer. The crucial opening move was now at hand, but watch. Our young man is a master at this game, "That's on me," he said with his mega smile, moving even nearer and winking at the barman.

Jennifer, the oldest in the team, replied, "That's very kind of you, Mr…"

"Enrico," said Enrico modestly. "Enrico will do." Then, move two.

"Enrico." The lady echoed, just a trifle bewildered by this spontaneous, unsolicited generosity.

"Oh don't think it's free," Enrico then said airily. Move three. At this both women looked at him questioningly. The whole episode lasted not more than five seconds, but was played with an unerring sense for correct timing:

"It's paid for by your company, ladies," Enrico said, clinching the matter with another angelic smile. The barman noticed and noted, but appeared not to notice or note anything, since barmen as a breed are, as we know, the very soul of discretion. The two women laughed at this, and Enrico knew he was already on the winning side. Now was the moment to turn to off-hand, but silver-lined platitudes. "Do you enjoy a good Martini, ma'am?" he asked, looking pointedly at Georgina. It was Georgina's turn to smile, "Yes, occasionally," she replied, looking him in the eye as he did in hers. Enrico was moved. Enrico was in his element. "I think they're particularly well-stirred here," he added, distancing himself just a little from his counterpart and looking in the barman's direction at the far end of the bar. The gesture, though slight, carried a maximum effect, the effect he wanted. Georgina came just a little nearer. Jennifer sipped her Martini and looked on.

"Do you live in Milan?" Georgina asked lightly.

"Live here," Enrico replied simply.

"Here?" Georgina queried.

"Yes, upstairs." Both women laughed at this.

"In the hotel above this building, you mean," Jennifer said, the penny dropping.

"That's right," Enrico answered simply. "It's very convenient to come down to this bar in the evening, the hotel bar being a bit of a bore," he added.

"A bore?" the women said in unison.

"Yes, lots of old people in their thirties and forties. God, some are even older: mummies of sixty and *more*!" The girls laughed. Enrico said all this in the manner of a man giving an interim report; the voice level, the tone factual.

This amused Jennifer and Georgina, but little did Enrico know that in all this amusing banter he had been carefully analysed by both females. They knew what he was made of and consciously submitted to his blandishments an hour later. A small band struck up with a slow waltz and Enrico announced that it was time "we danced", by which he really meant dance with Georgina, but was equally pleasant to Jennifer, with whom he danced first. No, no, I will not say in the sense, "to get it over with."

No, that would be unfair. Enrico, if a playboy, was not a bounder. He calculated that he would give more time to Georgina later. Meanwhile, she could stew in the mistaken assumption that he was more interested in her companion. Strategy, he called it. Thus, a few minutes later, he had Georgina in his arms. He looked deep into her green eyes. "God," he said ardently, "are *you* beautiful!" Georgina was used to such compliments by now of course, but she had to admit that it was still a pleasure to her to receive them. Moreover, Enrico's enthusiasm stirred her. Returning to the bar, they ordered another round of Martinis and Jack Daniels and all three learned to get to know each other better as the evening went wore on. Jennifer had found someone who interested her and this gave Enrico and Georgina the chance to deepen the acquaintance. Both were willing to. Both knew that what would soon follow was an adventure in bed, but Enrico took his time. For the moment, he told his companion what a lovely skin she had and that he had never seen a more beautiful shape even enter the bar. He complimented her on her breasts, to which she promptly replied, "How do you know, you've never seen them!"

"Oh yes I have. No amount of textile can disguise the design within," he asserted with a smile. She laughed outright, blushed just a little and earnestly returned to her drink.

"And then there are your beautiful arms, so superbly rounded, so stylish; not too thin and not too much adipose tissue."

"What?"

"That's the tissue inside that gives the roundness. Excellent, divine idea," he concluded. Georgina laughed again.

"And beautifully manicured hands." Enrico took her

left hand into his. "Not only the manicure, but how nature formed them. Yes. Beautiful." Enrico studied the hand carefully like a doctor making a diagnosis. "They tell me something about you – quite a lot in fact."

Georgina was intrigued to have her hand taken and read. She smiled unbelievingly.

"Oh yes," Enrico affirmed again. "Now I don't know anything about you other than what you've told me this evening, but I can look into your personality and tell you true things about yourself, which you haven't mentioned," Enrico continued.

"Go on, then, tell me," she said with interest. "Well, in the first place I see a practical person. You're not a dreamer, that's for sure." Georgina did not want to divulge too much to this charming stranger. She hesitated in telling him he was right. If anything was true about Georgina, it was this steely practical streak in her make-up, but she would wait and see what else he could divine of her nature. "Oh, yes, pretty practical," she admitted.

"Umm, let me see," Enrico said seriously, turning her hand in his and gazing intently at it. "And allied to this practicality, is a very sharp sense for weighing up matters correctly and then coming quickly to a decision," he added.

"Well, you might have deduced this from the fact of my practical sense," Georgina objected, trying with this remark to deflect him.

"Oh," Enrico exclaimed with an exaggerated expression of hurt dignity. "No confidence in me, then? And when I tell you that you love animals and are extremely tactful in your dealings with others. That's another piece of baloney or what?" His eyes sought hers for an answer, but she said nothing for a moment or two. In all his statements he'd been right; this she had to admit. These features were undoubtedly important aspects of her personality, and she had said nothing of them during their previous conversation. Instead of saying anything this time, she gently took both his hands in hers and smiled warmly at him. His face came nearer hers. His nose caressed her cheek. "Boy, I like that scent. It sends me!" he said, looking heavenwards. Georgina smiled, and Enrico suggested they dance.

This time, they danced for ten golden minutes, an interval in which the two of them shared the same wavelength. Their clasp was closer, their voices lower. Enrico's body was on fire, while Georgina's tingled delightfully all over, a sensation she had never experienced before. For a fleeting moment, she wondered whether it was the unusual amount of alcohol she had taken, but she didn't care. After the dance, they returned to the armchairs placed around the dance parquet and there met Jennifer and the friend she'd angled during the evening. They were laughing happily. Georgina, too, was happy.

Looking at Enrico's handsome, friendly face, she suddenly found that she could say nothing. Seeing this, Enrico smiled as he guided her to her seat.

More drinks were bought, but Georgina, used to this tactic elsewhere, declined to drink more than one, and merely sipped at her glass, glad of the fact that she could still make conscious decisions. They all talked gaily, then danced again until well after midnight.

"I'd like to see you again," Enrico said sincerely at the end of the evening. "I'm here practically every evening after 8 pm, so just drop in for a chat." He made it sound casual, as though they had made a mere brushing acquaintance with each other, but he knew and she knew perfectly well that there had been more than a spark of intimacy between them and this casual manoeuvre of his only heightened the sexual tension between them. At 1 am they said their goodbyes and the women departed for home. Jennifer chattered jauntily about this and that as they travelled home by taxi. Her experience of the evening had been a playful flirt for the most part, which she had enjoyed immensely, which threw Georgina's evening into sharp, emotional contrast. While Jennifer chattered on, Georgina resolved that she would certainly visit the bar again, if not tomorrow, then within a day or so.

Alone.

Before the next encounter with Enrico at Paganini's two days later, Georgina took special pains to make herself as desirable as possible. She knew she didn't have to do much in this direction, but made sure that her partner would have a tempting view of her breasts by selecting a low-cut dress and painting her fingernails red. This time, she would wear her hair long, she decided; she would give him the pleasure of seeing it at its best. What would he do? How would he react? The time could not go by quickly enough for her.

He was there as she had hoped when she entered the bar at about 8.15 pm, and she went up to him, ready to give him her hand, but he took her gently in his arms and kissed her on the cheek, a surprise that thrilled her with happiness. They spent the next few minutes talking about the events of the last two days and he asked after Jennifer. Georgina liked that. For her, it showed that he was not an egoist and they spoke kindly about her for a moment or two. Enrico then ordered the drinks and after a further ten minutes of banter, it was time to dance again.

This time, Enrico took the liberty of holding Georgina much closer to his body than before, and Georgina enjoyed the embrace, firstly because she was glad of it, and secondly because he showed self control in that he didn't go too far. In short, the encounter was very satisfying. After the dance, they returned to their seats on the edge of the dance floor and indulged in a little more alcohol. Georgina felt herself shifting, sailing, slipping into an all-embracing haze of comfort and well-being. Enrico was talking about something, but she was more aware of his voice than what he was saying, and looked at him without comment. He laughed and she smiled, not knowing why. By the time the sounds of the third dance had ebbed away, she knew she was drunk, but didn't care. During the music she only knew that his caresses had become a little more daring, and that he had navigated her into a corner of the bar where he had kissed her very gently on the face and finally on the lips. She responded to his ardour.

Just how she landed in this bedroom some time later in the evening she couldn't fathom, but she was aware that she was quite naked, that it was very warm in the room and that Enrico, was holding her in his arms and that she was being penetrated. She didn't resist, but gave herself up to him willingly. What she was experiencing was good, very good. It was even better than Evelynne's touch, she reflected. In the next few minutes both came to their respective climaxes and rolled over, sighing and grateful into a deep, dreamless sleep.

It was already broad daylight when they awoke.

Enrico proved to be a virile lover. His thirst for sex seemed to be unlimited. They came together not only in bed, but also on the living-room carpet of his flat, over the sofa, on the stairs, in the kitchen, on the balcony, in the bath, under the shower, once in the park and – God help me – once in a lift. There were no taboos in their embraces, and they proved to be a perfect balance for one another, enjoying every position for coitus in the book and were so free in their lust for one another that Georgina began to have qualms about pregnancy. It seemed odd that she had not conceived during their wild copulations. For the most part, Enrico was careful not to embarrass her in this respect, for at that time there was no reliable means of preventing a pregnancy, but there were moments in their joy for one another when she received all that he had to give her. On the one hand, of course, it was a huge relief to see her period when this appeared. On the other, it was just slightly disappointing, and she wondered whether she was infertile.

Their flight into paradise lasted exactly ten weeks. Although Georgina had been able to give herself to Enrico sexually, she didn't share his interest in expensive, fast cars, his enthusiasm for the local football team, his superficial social life with other rich folks or in the long hours at the billiard table which played a significant part in his life. Enrico was kind, it was true; he was handsome, had a perfect manly, 'six pack' physique of which he was very proud; he was also considerate, gentle, even-tempered and generous. He sat easily to life, nor did he easily lose his composure. Added to this, he was very wealthy and nothing seemed beyond his financial means. Yet for all these virtues, Georgina did not fall in love with him, and after a time and to her intellectual astonishment, she didn't want him either. She sat one day before the mirror in her apartment after their informal estrangement and concluded that the image in front of her was rather an odd kind of person. Later that week she and Jennifer met up in one of the city's parks, and Georgina related her short but intense encounter with Enrico. The older woman listened with interest and smiled. "It happens," she said by way of consolation, "there's something missing in the mixture, that's all. You know, you can have a highly explosive chemical mixture, but if the essential spark's not there, the thing won't go off!"

Georgina laughed at this metaphor. "Yes," she objected, "but whatever could it be? The man's perfect. Everything a woman could wish for, but…"

"A healthy young animal. A stag." Jennifer concluded laconically. Georgina laughed again, much amused at Jennifer's simple wisdom. "And I'm not a bit sad at letting him go either; it's funny" she added.

"Don't worry about that," Jennifer advised, "if you've not intentionally wounded him on parting that's OK. He'll soon find another; he's got the means!"

Georgina agreed and they both found themselves admiring the deep-blue clematis that had decoratively wound its way over and along the wicker archway ahead of them. "What a wonderful blue!" Jennifer exclaimed. "Yes, superb," Georgina concurred, glad now that she had related her experiences to Jennifer. The feeling was almost 'cathartic' one could say.

"And what about – I've forgotten his name – the friend you met on our first night out?" Georgina asked.

"Oh, Alfredo. Yes, well, a good companion, Alfredo, but an inveterate smoker, and I can't bear smokers. Sorry. Just the way I am." Georgina looked at her friend in disbelief. "Yes, it's true, dear," Jennifer went on, "I don't want to live in a cloud of smoke for the rest of my life. From time to time I have attacks of asthma, and that's enough to put up with I can tell you, without having the condition exacerbated by his daily bellows of tobacco smoke. So I opted out of the relationship as tactfully as I could." They walked on in the early summer sunshine, Jennifer with an uncomfortable memory, and Georgina recalled Evelynne once objecting to Jean-Luc's smoking habits. How was Evelynne? Georgina had not heard from her in an age. What would she think of Georgina's sexual excursions? Would she laugh or would she censure her? However, Georgina knew that she would understand. For the moment Georgina was glad she was free from her relationship with Enrico. It had fulfilled a purpose, but was not meant to be long lasting. Looking back, it was not so much a relationship, as an escapade, a release of emotional energy. Somehow, she felt, it had been necessary in order to place her on an even keel again after her husband's death, and she didn't regret it.

The next man to appear three months later in Georgina's life was an influential diplomat, Roberto by name, fifty-one years of age, highly educated, distinguished, greying now, dignified and kindly. He was everything that Enrico was not, Georgina reflected after their first encounter at a reception given by the American Consulate in Milan that summer. Helen had invited her after her associate there had found a very attractive photograph of Georgina, which Helen had with her and had made him curious to see her. Helen thought this very amusing and rolled her eyes heavenwards in supplication to the Divine to bring more discrimination to the male mind, but she was somehow glad to show off her friend and enjoy her company at the same time. How simple it was to negotiate these men! She concluded. What simpletons they were! Complete slaves to their eyes, for normally it was by no means an easy matter to worm one's way into diplomatic circles, but this had done the trick immediately. Ha!

"Good day to you," diplomat Sulla had said on that occasion as they stood on the lawn of the consulate. "Sulla," he added, nodding courteously towards her. Georgina smiled sweetly and they raised their respective glasses in greeting. While Helen's friend, Glenn, a young American in the diplomatic service who could hardly take his eyes off Georgina, she for her part interested herself in the older diplomat. Like Jean-Luc, she noticed, he had impeccable manners and after a few minutes of conversation with other ladies of rank and substance in the company, turned his friendly attention to Georgina. "Sulla," the man said, offering her his hand. At this, poor Glenn realised he had no chance at all, and retreated in orderly fashion to the end of the garden, leaving the field open to his older colleague.

"I hear from Helen that you worked at the same fashion company together," the older man said, opening play.

"Yes, but I've since retired," Georgina replied simply. To this our diplomat burst into laughter. "Retired?" he echoed, "Rather young for that, what?"

"Well, I got married, you see," Georgina answered, modifying the reply.

"Oh, I see," Orlando Sulla said, smiling. "Good for you."

"But then my husband died from an infection," she added.

"Oh, goodness me, I'm sorry about that. May I ask what kind of an 'infection'"?

"Tetanus."

"Oh dear, that's awful," Sulla commented. "I'm very sorry to hear that. So young, too, I assume."

"He was twenty-eight," Georgina said.

"Gracious me! I'm so sorry," Sulla said again. Georgina received this not as a mere superficial commiseration from a stranger. His manner was too sympathetic for that, she felt. She sized him up as he looked away across the lawn as though he were searching for someone. His next question was again put to her with the same sincerity. "Is there anyone to look after you? I mean does this mean that you live alone? More specifically, are you managing?"

"Thank you. Yes, I'm managing," Georgina replied truthfully, inwardly aware for the first time that the pain of Toni's death had metamorphosed into a sad memory.

"Um," he mused. "Very regrettable." Without warning, the small band which had assembled a few feet away from them now struck up 'Happy Birthday to You' for someone in the crowd, who was then ushered forward from the group to stand in front of a microphone to 'say a few words'. There was much gaiety and laughter and someone looked their way in recognition. Sulla responded to this and hurriedly but courteously took his leave from Georgina, but not before presenting his visiting card and assuring her at the same time of his assistance, should she ever need it. With that he left, smiling at her kindly as he did so. She steered clear of Glenn and walked on through the crowd towards the bottom end of the lawn where, to her surprise, she discovered that there was a small river running along at the end of it, and, sitting in a punt waiting to have her photo taken was Helen, full of goodwill as always. "Hi there! She shouted across the water to Georgina. "Stay there! I'm not gonna get wet." Gina was pleased to see her, and a moment later they joined each other.

"Hey, you scooped a big fish there, my dear, what happened to him?" She asked in a way that might have indicated his having got lost like a small child or that she had possibly murdered him on the quiet.

"Dunno. He suddenly felt obliged to join the gang over there," Georgina replied offhandedly.

"Gang?" Helen repeated, reiterating Georgina's casual manner. "That's the boss himself, girl, and the 'gang' you speak of is the embassy staff."

"Oh," Georgina said almost apologetically, "I didn't know, but I should have thought of it. Silly me." Helen smiled, adding, "Yeah, we're especially privileged to be here and this time by no means the focus. We – I mean that *you* – should mingle. There are some very important folks here on the lawn, sweetheart."

"I'm not particularly interested," Georgina said, and Helen looked hurt.

"I mean I don't want to offend you and thanks very

much for inviting me. No, it's just that I don't seem to get the right connection, that's all."

"What!" Helen exploded, "The guy you were talkin' to was the ambassador himself. He's a really nice guy. Did you quarrel or somethin'?"

"No, not at all," Georgina said hastily. "Like you, I think he's nice, but as I say he had to go away."

"Pity," Helen said reflectively. "Could have been a good contact."

"Well, he gave me his card," Georgina replied without much interest.

"His *card?* Hell's bells, are you lucky!" Helen almost shouted.

"Why?"

"Oh why, you dear, simple little English girl, I know for sure that he doesn't give his card to every pretty face, and the fact that he gave you his card means that he definitely liked you. Take it from me, honey. I know," Helen declared emphatically.

"Well, all right, he doesn't give his card to anyone and now he's gone and that's that isn't it? I don't want anything from him. He's nice as you say, but he's over fifty!" To this Helen said nothing, but with a gesture urged her friend in the direction of music and laughter. "And the food's damn good here, Kiddie, I assure you, so don't you go anywhere," she warned.

Well, the band played, the sun shone, the banquet consumed, the week passed, leaves fell, skies greyed, the wind blew, snow fell, and thus, to shorten the passing of time, it was not until the following May that something happened to prompt Georgina to hunt for the visiting card again, which had lain unread at the bottom of her summer handbag for nearly a year.

Her permission to live in Italy had run out by two

months, and Georgina had quite forgotten to renew it. She knew that her forgetfulness would incite a wave of administrative fuss and red tape, but, when she at last visited the authorities, she was stunned to learn that her residence permit would not be lengthened.

"But I was married to an Italian and I have property here!" she protested on hearing that her stay would not be tolerated more than a week longer.

"Yes, you *were* married, Signora Catelli, but you are no longer married and you still have a British, not an Italian passport," she was told by the fat woman in charge.

"And I've lived here for twelve years on top!" Georgina proclaimed. "I was never informed by the Italian Consulate that I have to be naturalised!" she added.

"Well, I'm sorry," the fat woman retorted, "that's not my fault. Next, please!"

And seizing a small bell at her side, she rudely summoned the next visitor from the many who were waiting there. Georgina, considerate as ever, ceded to the next in line and returned home. She had exactly six days to arrange her things, pack and leave the country. It was infamous, she thought. She rang Helen to explain the situation, but there was no one at home. She rang Jennifer with same result. Finally, after much inner struggle, she summoned enough courage to ring the manager of Milan's *Mode pour Toi*, Signore Denti to ask what she should do. After two secretarial barriers, she was at last put through to him, and explained her situation.

Denti was kind and sympathetic, but as he said himself, not of much help in such things. However, he would ring the Italian Consulate himself and obtain information, he told her. He would ring back, he said. Two hours or more passed before he rang back.

"As I see it, there is only one satisfactory way to get

round this embarrassing situation," he began. His voice was authoritative and encouraging, "I suggest you take a train back to Britain and stay there for a week, then come back into the country on a new visa. This is a bit of a nuisance, I know, but it is the simplest way round the problem in that it won't lead to any diplomatic complications. From the moment you return we can then go about the business of assuring you a permanent stay here. Believe me, I'm very sorry this has happened. "

"Oh dear," Georgina sighed into the phone.

"Don't upset yourself, dear lady," Denti continued in friendly tones, "Regard it as a week's holiday. When you get back, come and see me personally, and we'll get the rest of it settled for you."

"Thank you. Thank you!" Georgina said warmly as she replaced the phone, but somehow she was loath to return to Britain. She would have to stay in a hotel, since she had no desire to descend on her family just for a week out of reasons of expediency and then go away again. That wouldn't be fair, and now so much proverbial water had passed under the bridge of time that she would be something of a foreigner in her own country. It was odd what a protracted absence could bring about, she thought. It was at the moment that she remembered her brief contact with the ambassador some months previously. Would he be inclined to help her? Could he help her as the representative of another country? Time was short. It would be wise to ring Helen first, she considered.

"It's me, Georgina."

"Hi, there. How you doin'?" Helen asked, friendly as ever.

Georgina explained.

"Oh sure! He's the kindest of guys from what I hear; he'll help you. By all means, give him a ring." Helen then went on to talk of this and that and little by little Georgina grew restless, yet remarking to herself how relaxed her friend was.

"But Helen, dear, I must ring off and get something done." She cut in at last, "I've got exactly six working days left to save myself!"

"Yes, honey, I know. I'll let you go – and give the boss my kindest regards!"

"Yes, I will, I will," she assured her friend and rang off. A moment later, she carefully tapped out the number on the card she'd been given only to be fobbed off by an unctuous secretary who explained that Dr Sulla was away until Tuesday and whether she, the secretary, could do anything for her. "I will tell him you rang. What was the name again, please?" (Pause while the name was noted.) "And I'm to remind him of the 'garden party last May', is that right?"

"Yes, please, and tell him it's urgent, and that I'm sorry to have to encumber him with my troubles, but would be very grateful to him if he could help me."

"Yes, I'll do that," said the voice at the other end. "Thank you," it said, and the conversation ended. Georgina replaced the receiver hopelessly. Tuesday. That would give her just three more days' respite. "Damn!" Georgina exclaimed and wandered into the bathroom, although she didn't know why. Perhaps it was the sun that had attracted her which was now pouring in from the upper window filling the room with light. She looked critically into the mirror over the sink. Her anger and frustration looked back at her, as she peered closer at her face and then at her hair. To her consternation, she discovered one small but distinct silver hair among the unruly, golden mass surrounding her face and falling carelessly over her shoulders. "That as well!" she cursed. And this year I'll be twenty-seven on top. Damn!" The idea of reaching thirty without being married chilled her. She cursed again. She meticulously removed the offending hair, examining it with the greatest care before tossing it contemptuously into the waste bin. Then she recalled Jean-Luc's anecdote about the train and the brevity of life. The hair seemed to be compelling proof of what he had said. It was depressing.

Two days before she would be officially ordered to leave the country, a Saturday, the telephone rang about 9 am as she was busy packing, and Georgina assumed it was Helen, but instead a male voice addressed her. "Signora Hennessey?" the deep, oily voice enquired. "This is Sulla. I have news for you, which is not really suited for a telephone conversation, and wonder if we could meet somewhere? I can then divulge what I have to tell you."

"Yes, why not?" Georgina rejoined, not fully orientated.

"Then I suggest we meet for lunch. Would that suit you?" the smooth tones continued. Georgina concurred.

"Let's meet at midday in Giuliani's Pizzeria in Strada del Motto, a side street off the Piazza del Santo Marco. Do you know it?"

"Yes," Georgina replied almost mechanically.

"Good. See you there, then," the voice concluded and was gone.

Georgina arrived just on time, having twice missed the bus to the city centre, and was a little out of breath when she finally entered the restaurant. This was a very well-appointed emporium, she noted as she went in through heavy brocaded curtains to its interior. Sulla recognised her at once and stood to receive her light coat from her shoulders and show her her seat. Georgina noted the light grey suit and the blue tie, the large, leonine head and greying hair, but more than she had noticed at her first meeting, the kindly, large grey-blue eyes.

The waiter arrived and they ordered. A moment

later, the two fell to talking about generalities before he announced that he had good news for her.

"I have managed to secure an extension of your residence permit here, young lady," he said, and noted her pleasure at hearing this with amusement.

Raising the forefinger of an immaculately manicured hand, he then said, "Oh, don't think it was easy, dear lady, but hearing of your problem, I was obliged to make enquiries about you, and everywhere received only good reports." He said this, imitating a schoolteacher's manner and laughing lightly as he did so. "And I'm very glad to have been of help to you, and glad, too, to further our acquaintance." She believed him. The meal was good and they both enjoyed the conversation that followed which turned on Britain, her family, the current world situation, rising prices in Italy, her work at *Mode pour Toi* and more. It was lively and amusing for them both. His comments, she noticed, were sometimes brief and ironical, and she liked this, impressed by their accuracy, and assumed that this was his experience of people and of the world. Vaguely, and at the back of her mind, Georgina wondered whether she would have to acknowledge his kindness to her by sleeping with him. She hoped not. Yes, she intensively hoped not, but her fears in this direction were relieved some forty minutes later by his rising to go. At this, Georgina objected, "Dr Sulla, please allow me to invite you to the meal; it was lovely, and I feel I owe you this at the very least for your kindness in helping me." Sulla laughed his kindly laugh. "No, no, my young friend, there's no need to trouble yourself about that. It's all taken care of anyway," he said jovially. "I enjoyed your company. That's acknowledgement enough," he added, winking at the waiter as though in connivance with him as the latter stood by, exchanging pleasantries, ready to accompany them to the door.

"Thank you, signore," the waiter said. Once on the pavement outside the restaurant, Sulla turned to Georgina with an outstretched hand, "Thank you for coming," he said, his light jacket blowing slightly in the wind of that moment, "I have to go in this direction. Goodbye, my young friend," and he was off towards the crowds moving townwards. Georgina stood quite still, the same light wind of a moment ago playing with her hair and the hem of her flowered summer dress.

It was the first time in months that she had been for a walk on her own in the city, and she knew very well that she would have to walk resolutely to somewhere, in order to avoid being enticed off route by young men out to bait her. Sure enough, after covering a few metres or so she recognised the lustful swains of the city were already at work with their adolescent guffaws, their catcalls and whistles. Georgina found all this irritating, and eventually found refuge in an ice cream parlour, where she considered what to do next. "It's a rotten shame that girls can't feel free to walk and enjoy the park without these fools ruining it for them." It wasn't easy, being beautiful, she reflected. While licking her ice cream, she thought of the past hour or so in the diplomat's company. She had felt free to chat about things in general, without being forever complimented. Her lunch companion had been charming, a good listener and interesting.

She was to see him often in the months that followed. He would call her and ask whether she would like to accompany him to the theatre or in enjoying a good meal or visit an exhibition. The calls came after fairly long intervals, say of three to four weeks or even more. On these occasions, he would often pick her up at her home, sometimes by taxi or sometimes by private car. His manners were always impeccable. He was always courteous, always interesting, and never insistent, always charming, good mannered, friendly and yet never intimate. Their friendship deepened. But, in a phrase, he never made a pass at her, so that she wondered at last what his intentions were.

"Are you married?" she asked him after they had been to an especially interesting exhibition of art in the old part of the town, and were sharing views on it in the museum cafe.

"Yes," he said with a smile and added, being far too intelligent not to discern that there was a reason for her enquiry, "Would you like to meet my wife?"

"Why, yes," Georgina replied.

"Very well," he said, "On Wednesday next week, I have time, so that we can call on her."

Georgina felt that the wording was strange, since he was always very articulate in all that he said. Thus, she concluded, there must have been a reason. 'Did she live somewhere else than at his home?' Georgina queried to herself. What did he mean by "call on her"?

A short time after this, he excused himself and left after seeing her home with his usual gentlemanliness. Wednesday came and he picked her up in his car at about 2 pm. They drove a long way through the town to the outskirts a good ten miles distant, and to Georgina's surprise he drove through the gates of a large, spacious park to what was clearly an institution or other. They drew up and it was clear straightaway that he was known to the premises as a uniformed man directed him to a parking lot. The two men exchanged a few friendly words before Georgina and her companion passed through the arch of the large entrance hall and beyond.

"Is this a hospital?" Georgina whispered as they entered the building.

"Sort of," Dr Sulla answered as he directed Georgina up

some steps to the first floor, "It's the third door on the left," he added quietly when they had arrived at the top. They entered the room. In it, there were two beds, one of which was occupied. Orlando Sulla approached this and gently touched the head of the woman lying there, stroking her hair tenderly.

"Oh!" Georgina said, seating herself uneasily on a chair near the wall.

After a moment or two, her companion turned to Georgina sadly with a gesture of hopeless resignation, sitting on the only other chair in the room next to the bed. The two whispered across the room to each other.

"What's wrong?"

"Nobody knows. Nothing organic. Just this." He looked at his wife.

A nurse came and greeted the diplomat, briefly glancing at Georgina and assuming what most people did in these last weeks that Georgina was his daughter. After the nurse had left, the two remained there with Sulla's wife for perhaps half an hour or more, saying nothing to each other. Every now and again, he would rise and talk to his wife, holding her pale, limp hand in his, while Georgina looked on helplessly. Finally, realising that the situation was becoming too hard for Georgina to bear, he signalled for them to go and they left together quietly. At the bottom of the stairs, Sulla left his young friend to attend to some matter at the office there and joined Georgina later in the grounds just outside. For the next minute they walked on silently over the grass of that place. Georgina felt that he should speak first and waited patiently for him to do so.

"I'm sorry if this visit has distressed you," he said at last. "But I know that you will have certainly asked yourself from time to time what role I play in your life." Georgina didn't answer, and so he continued.

"You see, I love my wife and my friendship with you is simply that of a loving friend. I am glad to have helped you, enjoy your company and am always pleased to see you enjoy yourself in mine. In any case, I'm much too old to be considered as anything else than an elder mentor." He smiled slightly.

"But what has happened to your dear wife?" Georgina asked, choosing to ignore his explanation for the moment.

"I can only tell you that one day she was at home with me. It was a Sunday, I recall; and Ilona – that's my wife – said as she sat down on our veranda, 'That's odd Orlo, I feel as though I'm going to faint,' and she did just that. I caught her as she was about to fall, took her up and placed her on the sofa in the lounge, fetched a blanket and called the emergency medical service. The men who arrived couldn't establish any injuries like an insect bite or whether she had eaten anything that might have disagreed with her, and so it was decided that she be taken to hospital forthwith where they could find out more." He paused. "They've found nothing and to this day, no one can say what the matter is, despite the fact that she has undergone all kinds of medical examinations. She seems to be in a permanent sleep – a coma, though why God knows."

"That's dreadful," Georgina put in.

"Yes, isn't it? I feel so useless. I want to do something to help and can't. All I find that I can do is to visit her every few days and just sit for hours with her. I talk to her and don't know whether she understands or even hears me. She lies there like a corpse. It's agonising.

"How long has she been in this condition?" Georgina asked.

"About a year now," Orlando replied and added, "only a few people know that she's in this home. You are one of them. I just want you to know, Georgina, that I greatly appreciate your company when I see you from time to time. Somehow, it does me good, and relieves me from constant concern with Ilona. I can only hope that you can put up with me from time to time."

"Well, of course," Georgina replied warmly. "To be there when you want me is the least I can do to help whenever I can."

Orlando was quiet for a long period. His handsome face assumed a gaunt expression as he looked hopelessly over the park into the distance. Georgina remembered what Jean-Luc had said about life being 'a dangerous free-for-all'. Anything could happen. Anytime. It was true. We were good for a few decades in which time we could mature and healthily reproduce our kind before those same forces which brought us to that point went on to destroy us sooner or later, but in either case with implacable certainty. In this cycle of birth, maturity, eventual decline and certain death, she mused, there were occasions for disease and earlier demise. Little children, for example, could fall prey to accident, crippling diseases, suffer and die long before their time or later in life, odd quirks of tragic circumstance could take place like the one Orlando was faced with now. Or there was the incidence of war like the one that had just finished before her birth, the internal forces of destruction in man that seemed an ally to the planet's general, innate plan of seemingly senseless, eternal creation through destruction. And not only the human world, Georgina went on to contemplate, what affected the human animal also affected the animal world in all its incredible variety of course, of which the human was a fully integrated part. While sitting there she saw all this quite clearly. Jean-Luc in his earnestness to cheer her after Toni's decease had been right: life was a risk, a tightrope of chance and murder, a brief pageant of beauteous savagery set against an eternal, inscrutable backdrop of impenetrable darkness lit here and there by sparks of light. The two, the fifty-year-old and the young woman sat there on the park seat, each enwrapped in their individual thoughts. It was Georgina who spoke first.

"I don't know whether I can make this clear in my simple Italian", she began, and he looked up from his sad reverie to listen to what she said.

"I understand something clearly," she continued "and that is that we're in this life together, not separate and that love binds us. Or should do. When we can experience this, it makes us truly human. In reality we are all part of each other's lot and can therefore never really be alone. I feel deeply sad about your present situation and also for that of your dear wife, and I want you to know this. I can't say more."

Orlando turned to her and smiled. "Dear Georgina, you couldn't say more to comfort me, and because I know that you understand I'm made happy at this moment. Thank you." And he laid his hand gently for a moment on hers.

After this, they walked back to the waiting car and so drove back to the city, said their farewells and each returned home.

The months passed and from time to time they met each other. Orlando Sulla introduced her to influential circles in Milan, supplying her with free tickets to concerts, exhibitions, soirées and invitations to all sorts of social gatherings, and on most occasions he accompanied her. Thus, he remained a good friend and the two enjoyed that rare and yet deeply satisfying platonic relationship based on mutual understanding and respect. Later, Georgina would look back on this association as one the best things she had ever encountered in life.

But for the present there was Dario Campa. Signore, Dario, Ernesto Campa, journalist, sharp-witted, bearded, just beginning to grey at forty-three with two light blue eyes that never missed a trick, that indeed were very used to discerning and isolating tricks of all kinds, quick on the uptake, supremely aware of every minute that passed, artless in dress and manner, so that you would easily consider him heedless of the things that matter in life, but there you would be so very wrong. He would lounge, sprawl like an octopus over everything and drink – usually something hard enough to drive – his legs thrown carelessly over this or that, his tired blue jeans ending in brown, incongruent boots that he never seemed to take off, his loose, white shirt blowing about him summer and winter. "No, never feel cold, do you? It's all in the mind anyway," he would say if you asked him during the cold months of the year. When he talked to you it was in a bantering way that asked questions in reply to your enquiries such as "And how's Dario today?" "Who cares a fart how I am?" he would retort. "You can see for yourself, can't you?" And then he would smile that engaging smile of his, which you could never take amiss, for if you did that, it would immediately make you look like a small-minded quibbler. His remarks were generally good-natured enough, but you were never quite sure, for such was his way. Everything about him, his movements, his winning smile, his gait, the way he spoke to you was loose and set easy to life as though it were a lazy dream. And yet others would report at times that he was as quick as a tiger when it came to taking the photograph of the year, that in argument he was as sharp and deadly as a falling sword, succinct, acid and biting in presenting the truth of a case in his articles or defending moral principles and the rights of underprivileged persons. He lived simply. Like the composer, Johannes Brahms, he would drink inordinate amounts of the blackest coffee, eat minimally, but also read the news of every paper avidly in Italian, French and English every day with an eagle eye, work all hours God sends at his clack-clack typewriter, the second most treasured possession after his camera, wind his way each day through narrow corridors of paper four to six inches high on a living room floor, strewn with journals, magazines, reports, booklets, folders, notebooks, all of them keeping company with other books piled by the score near your feet, having coloured stickers in their pages locating the ruminations of yesteryear, laid aside for future reference in a still sea of recollection, lying there like a rarely used horizontal library and not very different in character from the rows and rows of other books which lined every wall from floor to ceiling.

Then he'd be away at some dangerous war, which threw up sand and dirt from a mine or a bomb into his truculent face and from where he would coolly tilt his camera in the direction of the disturbance and take a picture as soon as the rain of muck had subsided, bear his camera to his encampment in triumph, down a bottle of smuggled wine and write his report for the day.

At home, this courageous man would charm Georgina into intimacies, which she never really enjoyed. His seduction was irresistible, it was true, but his performance was like the man: headstrong, forceful, direct, yet without tenderness, so that sometimes she thought an ape would do better! Though full of energy, he was nevertheless impulsive to an extent that was finally inconsiderate, and yet he never noticed this failing. Georgina for her part was left strangely unsatisfied both sexually and emotionally. Then he'd be off again, this time trailing the jungles of Ecuador where there had recently been skirmishes between the local population and gangs of marauding militia armed to the teeth like the pirates of old. It was while he was on one these excursions that she decided to leave the flat she had shared with him over the last six months and seek solitude in her own apartment. Leaving her luggage in the hall and slumping into her favourite armchair, she had to admit that she was glad to be alone. Dario was not for her. No, never.

A further six months passed alone. One wet and stormy night in a station waiting room, she met a British entertainer called Mick Hallerson and was glad to speak her own language in all its rich, humorous, idiomatic diversity, share opinions, laugh while listening to his anecdotes gathered on his way through dozens of continental cities. He was an excellent raconteur, charming, engaging, supremely self-confident without for a moment being arrogant, a wonderful partner for an evening at dinner, but, like Dario, ever off somewhere keeping appointments to sing and accompany himself ably at the guitar. She attended two of his concerts and was for a week or two caught in the noise and whirl of public entertainment. The two enjoyed this social acquaintance and both benefited from it. She basked in his tactful compliments, delighted in the warmth of his companionable, brotherly hugs, laughed heartily at his bawdy jokes and generally took pleasure in his company. She remembered his large, bantering blue eyes and his greying beard, for he was well over forty, but above all appreciated his manners and his gentleness. But then he, like his forerunner, was much more interested in the fun life offered him than in taking his female counterpart seriously as a companion for life. And so he, too, left for London by train on a dank February afternoon, she waving him off and thankful for their brief, chummy association, promising to meet him again one day soon and in the sure knowledge that nothing 'tangible' as she called it could develop from their friendship. She was beginning to ask herself whether she was right in looking for the right man. Perhaps there was no such thing, but she was sure that the last few encounters were certainly not meant to be permanent for her. The contemplation worried her. Something was wrong. Her physical attributes were perfect, despite the fact that she was now moving towards thirty. Neither was she foolish nor frivolous, she assured herself. She had enjoyed her sexual adventures and given pleasure in turn, but this was all very well. The truth was, she concluded to the mirror when she arrived home, the truth was that she needed something else and was not quite sure what that something was.

Two more suitors followed. The first was a man she met at a dance during one of Evelynne's occasional visits. As ever, Evelynne had been a veritable bastion of moral support and entertainment, and they decided between them to visit a local dance hall. Here, the two of them became acquainted with a German engineer working in Milan. On the evening in question he had charmed them both with his open joviality and generosity and all of them danced happily into the early hours. It had been on this visit that Evelynne had said something which disturbed her and she thought of this again as she danced with a certain Dr Herman Wittig the engineer. Evelynne had suddenly fallen quiet and had observed, "I've heard somewhere that it very often happens that the most beautiful women never marry," and naturally Georgina had given this some thought.

Herman proved to be an excellent companion for them both that evening. Both women were delightfully amused by his gift for mimicry and by the way he laughed. This was a small explosion, which in its turn set them laughing all the more. Two days later, Georgina, to keep a promise, turned up alone to meet Hermann again at the dance hall, Evelynne having returned after her short stay. During the late night waltz, Georgina, tight in Herman's embrace, looked beyond him to the others seated there and thought again of what Evelynne had said. She remembered what she had said in reply: "But you're beautiful yourself, Evy." This was uttered more as a question than a statement to invite comment, but to which Evelynne had answered wistfully, looking away slightly, "Ugh, ugh, I suppose so," and had not enlarged on the subject. Georgina asked herself at that moment whether she hadn't seen a tear in Evelynne's wonderful dark eyes.

Hermann proved to be very good company. He talked in an interesting way about his work, which apparently was very dear to him, and by the time they had danced enough and drunk enough to become a little less inhibited than by day they found themselves sitting next to each other like old friends. She was glad of his company and listened with interest to all that he told her about the engineering project he was working on. After some time, and noticing the gold ring on his finger, she asked him, "Are you married?"

"Yes, married with two children, a boy and a girl," he replied simply.

Georgina's face fell. Seeing this, Hermann, who happened to be a kindly, sensible person, guessed what she was thinking and was saddened.

"Ah, Georgina, my girl, wonderful woman that you are, I'm not taking things any further. I'm happily married, love my wife and kids and wouldn't dream of leaving them. However…" and here he said like a public lecturer, resorting again to his gift for mimicry, "however," he repeated, then immediately assuming a serious expression again, "I do want to say that I enjoy your company, Georgina, and am honoured to be with you." He paused to assess Georgina's reaction to this. She merely raised her blonde eyebrows.

"Yes, what I say is the truth. You honour me by your company." Georgina relaxed visibly, and he continued,

"I may admire the flowers in the other man's garden, may I not? Do not touch or steal! But I can admire them nevertheless or what?" He paused. She was glad he was honest, said nothing, but smiled. There was a longer pause. "Anyway, I'm thirty-seven," he added. "You must be much younger."

"I'm twenty-seven." They both laughed for some reason unknown to them both. Perhaps it was relief on her part that he had been frank with her, and on his that he hadn't upset her.

They met again that week on a Wednesday after he had finished work and at 8 pm they were having dinner together. He was as ebullient as ever, generous as ever and beguiled her the while with all sorts of stories aided by his histrionic talent so that she could hardly keep a straight face. He himself only smiled now and again, evidently pleased that she found his tales so amusing, but for the most part keeping a poker face during his relations that only caused her to laugh all the more.

"Ah," she said, catching her breath after another bout of laughter, "Ah, it must be good to live with you. Your wife must be the happiest soul alive, if you keep her supplied with anecdotes like these."

"Oh, she's happy enough," Hermann remarked, "and she has a lot to do with two small children," he added. Then he asked, "Do you intend to marry yourself one day, or is that a silly question?"

Georgina then told Hermann that she had been married and what had happened. Dr Wittig's face clouded. "I'm sorry about that," he said.

"It's all right; it took me a long time to get over it, but I'm OK now," Georgina replied, "but I'm still at a marriageable age, and am in fact looking round for a meaningful relationship, but I don't think Mr Right has come my way yet. So far, there has been a string of them – men, I mean – but always there's been a false note in the association – or they're married, like you."

Hermann was still serious.

"Well, if you are looking for someone with a set list of characteristics, it's a pretty hopeless pursuit," he said. "Somehow it gets in the way of the natural flow of events."

"So if I don't try either, it's going to be sure failure that's certain," she said quickly.

"Well, I'm not sure about that. Depends on the way you go about it," Hermann assured her. "It's important – I mean the way you tackle it," he added, and his features were set as he went on, "No, the right way to go about finding a right mate is to sit quietly one evening and say to yourself: 'I want this, and it's coming my way without the slightest pressure from me,' and then forget all about it. The forgetting is absolutely essential. If the problem crops up in your mind again, just say to yourself: 'That's all been taken care of, and I'm glad about it,' and go about your business normally. Whatever you do, don't force anything. Just let go and the right person will come along and you'll be astonished." She hadn't seen Hermann so earnest before, and smiled slightly, a faint doubt on her handsome features.

"I'm not kidding you, Georgina," Hermann insisted. "What I say may be difficult for you to accept, since it appears so simple, but it works perfectly. As an engineer I know what works and what doesn't," he concluded.

Georgina pondered this for a moment. Then she said, "Are you sure that's all I would have to do? It seems so facile, almost childlike."

Hermann said neither aye nor yea to this, but looked at her frankly. The look said everything, and after a few seconds they fell to eating again. The subject was not brought up for the rest of the evening. At 10 pm he took her home by car and as this stood outside the apartment, her engineer friend said: "The firm has another project afoot in Dubai and I must fly there to see what the folks there are up to, so I won't be around for the next three or four weeks. It was lovely to have your company, dear Georgina, and I wish you luck in your search, and you'll be lucky I'm sure; I feel it in my bones somehow. And I feel very close to you, though I don't know why. After all, we've only known each other for a few days. The chemistry is right, I suppose."

With that, they said goodbye to each other and in settling himself to drive off he proclaimed facetiously: "Hermann the German! Don't forget now, Georgy. Beware of imitations!" And he was off round the corner in his super car, Georgina turned and let herself into the building.

The next day the telephone rang before 8 am. It was her mother.

"Georgina, dear, your father died last night in the Goscote Cottage Hospital."

"Oh God!" was all that Georgina could say, and tears welled up in her eyes. It was difficult to say anything more. After a silence, her mother, seemingly composed, went on: "I think you should come over as soon as possible, dear, if you can. There's a lot to do before the funeral, so I won't ring again."

"Yes, of course, mum, I'll catch the next train."

"Well, love, I'll expect you, then…" her mother replied in concluding tones.

"Hold on a moment," Georgina interrupted, "what did dad die of?"

"Heart, dear. He'd been ailing for some months as I told you in my letters."

"Oh God," Georgina repeated. "I'll see you as soon as I can, mum."

"Very well, Georgina. Till then. Goodbye."

"Goodbye, mum."

So her father was dead. With him died a generation, the last of England's Old Guard, the final defenders of an England that once ruled the world's waves and spoke of India and "our colonies" as if they represented the God-given right of a small island to 'rule the world properly', since there were no others who were worthy of such a responsibility. Of this he was convinced and joined the British Army in 1920 as a lad of eighteen and enlisted in the Royal Irish Guards, had taken his commission at twenty-one, had risen from there to become a colonel at forty-five, and later, at fifty-five, retiring with that rank to the territorials. During this career he had seen service in many places in the world, but, like his kind, spoke none of their languages and knew little or nothing of their cultures. Such was not necessary for practical military or administrative purposes. To enquire too closely into these things in his time was not regarded as seemly. After all, the peoples conquered were required to aspire to the values approved of by the victors. At least in part. But they were never to come too near, these brown people. To have them as friends was not encouraged, and generally looked down upon, while intermarriage was not only tacitly forbidden, but meant certain social death for anyone daring to break this taboo. Hennessey's world was a white skinned one, peopled by human beings from northern Europe and preferably from Britain where the arrogant assumption of superiority in all things was generally accepted. Then came the Second World War and the stiff class society to which he belonged was slackened and later radically modified to accommodate the realisation that there were nations beyond these shores that could compete with Britain in other fields of human achievement. He never really accepted that, in his later years, the world had changed so much as to render practicably obsolete all that he had lived for, but so it is in life: the one undeniable truth for us all is change and decay, and yet are we not forever seeking security in some kind of inviolable set of beliefs that counter this fact?

So it came to pass that on the 24th of June of that year, Lt. Col. Henry Hennessey was borne to his grave in a Gloucestershire country churchyard by six, straight guardsmen and lowered into the earth for ever. He was seventy-three and his passing marked the end of an era.

Georgina's reaction, standing there with her mother among the grey stones with the nearest of her relatives and the throng of mourners in the early summer sunshine, felt not only a deep sadness at her father's demise, but, to her surprise, an equally powerful need to honour his memory by bearing a child. After all, he deserved such recognition, she told herself. Patrick, as far as she knew, was still busy with his career, had no intention of marrying for the moment, and sister Sarah was as yet too young for motherhood. Georgina brought herself up sharply at such a thought in such a place, but knew, too, that it was the best homage she could make to a good man and a beloved father.

Gina kicked off her high-heeled shoes in the hall before picking up a quantity of mail lying on the black-and-white tiles behind the door of her apartment in Milano. She had stayed two months with her mother and sister in Britain. It had been a harmonious sojourn and she was able to entertain them all on many occasions, not only with meals out and many an anecdote, but also buy Sarah several pairs of new shoes, as well as clothes, which had absolutely delighted the younger woman, managing as she was at the time on a meagre university grant from her local authority. Even Patrick had benefited from her wealthy presence, since she had been happy to clear a couple of bills for his car that had been tearing at his pocket for a month or so.

And now she was home, in her own home, among her own things, free to do as she wished, although, she had to admit, she had not felt at all restrained in her former home. It was just that she could now enjoy her independence again. "Phew!" she gasped as she threw herself into a chair and indulgently sipped the hot green tea she had made for herself a few minutes before. She looked over the rim of the cup at her reflection thrown onto the glass of a piece of furniture in her room by the late afternoon sun. The tea was good that Helen had bought for her some months ago. 'I must give her a call this evening,' she thought, 'and tell her how good the tea is.' Georgina was something of a connoisseur of tea in general, but she had never tasted such good tea as this, and it occurred to her to try and find the shop where it could be bought and so put a bit by for guests. Then she fell to thinking how much better the weather was here compared with the so-called summer in Britain. Just before she left, the temperature there had dropped to a mere 15 degrees C, while in northern Italy it was still 26 degrees C and sunny. She looked back on her stay with satisfaction. Despite the sad occasion, she had got on very well with everyone at home. There had been no bickering and no selfishness, only an open friendliness, which had made her very happy. She had even slipped into the English style of living for a few weeks and that, too, had been a pleasure. It had been nice to see so many people she once knew as neighbours and friends at school. 'Are you going to stay there forever?' some of them had asked incredulously, and she couldn't give them an answer, for frankly she didn't know herself. After a few more minutes of such introspection, she realised that her cup was empty and that the pale visitor to the furniture had vanished. At this she suddenly felt a pang of horror. It was the sudden, poignant, realisation that time was implacably moving on and that she was part of this movement. It was so clear to her in that instant, that she compared the insight later to somebody as a tearing rip of lightning that for one, vivid moment rudely exposes the countryside. She saw quite clearly that she and the plants in the garden, the clouds in the sky, her friends and relatives, the folks in their cars beyond the window, the rolling sun and the moon themselves were each a part of a universal, unhampered, inexorable urge to move and change, all of them mere ciphers in a grand drama of inconceivable dimension that would break the head even to contemplate. It scared her.

Not long after this experience she and her friend Helen were asked to a soirée held to collect funds for the worldwide humanitarian foundation Bread for the World, and while there she came into contact with one of this organisation's employees, an American called Dr Harry Coates. Georgina found this man's company most absorbing. She learned that he had once been employed by the organisation as a doctor working in Africa for little or no pay, but for the ideal of helping less privileged people in rural areas there. His descriptions of life spent with the country folk at this time fascinated her.

"And what do you do today?" she asked him.

"I work with the mentally ill," Harry replied, "here in the city."

They met twice after that, and after about ten days or so had passed and they were sitting over coffee in his office, he asked her whether she would like to accompany him on his rounds through the wards of the psychiatric department. Georgina accepted this invitation, donned the white coat he handed to her and they left for the long passageway that would lead them to the wards.

*"What! Did the Hand of the Potter shake?"*

What she saw there was to change her life forever. First, there was the men's ward No. M 224. She was introduced to other members of staff, who, she noted, were polite enough, but who all wore a similar expression in manner and mien that she found difficult to describe exactly. It was a mixture of earnestness and wary efficiency. There was none of the encouraging persiflage she had come across in her other brief contacts with hospital life. "Here, we have patients suffering from minor psychoses," Dr Coates said with a wave of his hand as if he were an estate agent indicating space and facility. Faces and bodies wrapped in pyjamas and bathrobes leered at them. They moved on. More faces appeared, many of which were uncomfortably hostile and looked at her and her companion as though they were unwelcome intruders. She smiled, but her smile was not reciprocated. Coates, on the other hand, received the occasional grimace in response to his cheery greetings. As for the rest, these were only faces of deep distrust at the presence of a beautiful stranger in their midst. Georgina felt very uncomfortable. She thought briefly of her school, and of her teacher who once asked the class in an English lesson what they considered of Shakespeare's observation that "there is no art to find the mind's construction in the face" and caught herself thinking now how very wrong the poet was at this moment. The faces here were windows upon tortured souls, avenues full of hate and suspended frustration.

But she was to experience that discomfort giving way to fear as their advance was suddenly checked by the presence of steel bars reminiscent of the junctions to passage in a prison. "How now?" Georgina enquired nervously. "The more serious cases are accommodated in this ward," her friend replied.

Georgina looked suspiciously at the bars and beyond. She saw two sturdy male nurses robed in green in the distance. The gate clanged behind them.

After a few steps, a few voices greeted them, "Is she your new assistant?" a large man in grey pullover and baggy trousers asked cheerfully. "In a way, Uncle Joe," Coates replied jovially, "Got a nice uplift – and that bum! Now that's something good to take to bed!," the patient said appreciatively and smiled. To this, the doctor reacted at once, "Oh come now, Joe, that's not the nicest way to greet a lady is it?" Joe looked Georgina up and down and she felt that she had no clothes on. He came nearer, his hand raised to touch the merchandise. Georgina shrank from his intention and in taking a step nearer, Dr Coates was there the next moment to dissuade his patient from his desire. "Come, now, Joe, tell me about last Saturday's lottery. Did you win?"

"Yes," Joe replied with enthusiasm, "I got four out of six."

"Why, that's a splendid result, lad!" Coates said warmly. "That'll bring at least £400, all for you."

Joe, diverted just for a second or two from his frank assessment of Georgina's form, went on,"Yeah."

"And what are you going to do with it?

"Dunno. Gotta think about that one," Joe said simply to the air and returned his concentrated, lascivious gaze to Georgina. What happened next Georgina was to remember all her life. In less than a second, the patient had both his hands on Georgina's breasts in a grip that made her scream with pain, and before she realised what was happening, the monster had thrown her to the floor and was on top of her. There was a violent, undignified scuffle, screams, bruises, and fingernail scratches. Within less than a minute, two staff members joined Coates, and Joe Shaw was torn from his victim and held down on the floor by all the main force the three men could muster, while Georgina freed herself with difficulty from her assailant and adjusted her clothing. With tears in her wide-open eyes, Georgina stood up shivering with fear, removed herself as far she could from her would-be rapist. Her left cheek was scratched, her hair awry and she had a large bruise on her arm, which she nursed as she stood there in terror. Her doctor friend ushered her away into the open ward without a word and from there back to his office. Georgina declined the cup of coffee he then offered her, and said in a voice a little louder than normal to conversation, "All I want is to go home!" Coates drove her home, despite the fact that he was on duty, and for that reason was obliged then to leave again immediately. Still shaken, Georgina fumbled for her keys and let herself into her apartment, hardly saying goodbye to her friend. The door slammed firmly behind her. She phoned Helen, who arrived a few minutes later. In the afternoon while Helen was still with her, Dr Coates rang. "How are you now?" he asked, concern in his voice. "I'm OK." He made to speak, but she interrupted him. "I'm all right, really I am, just a bit nervous still, but I'm OK. My friend Helen is here."

"It's very good that she's there, Georgina; she can do more for you at present than I can." Georgina said nothing to this and so he continued. "However, I feel it's my duty to see you again soon." He paused.

"Yes," Georgina replied without much enthusiasm.

"Good, then see you soon. I have a patient to attend to at the moment. So, see you soon, then." The phone clicked.

"Are you going to see this fellow again?" Helen asked incredulously.

"I don't know yet," Georgina said miserably; "it isn't his fault, is it?"

"No, but I don't find the idea too joyous," Helen commented.

Harry Coates and Georgina did meet each other again a few days later, and it was then that Georgina's mind cleared in the conversation that followed.

"You feel better these days, I hope?"

"Yes, I've got over things. It's just a horrible memory, that's all."

"Yep, Joe is an unpredictable character," Coates concluded.

There was just a crumb of indulgence in this remark. It wasn't an excuse for his patient's conduct. No, that would be too much to accord to it, but there was the physician's detachment about it, and worse, Georgina thought, a leaning towards his patient's well being, rather than an intimate concern for hers. True, he had gone through the motions, so to speak, had said the right things, followed up matters, had seemed to be considerate in a routine kind of way, but there was no deep concern, she detected. Suddenly, she felt cold inside. A moment later, her suspicions were concerned. The main course was served.

"Mr Shaw is generally a congenial guy, friendly enough on the whole, a bit tactless – doesn't care much for what folks think – but we know him as a non-violent individual…"

"I think he's a monster," Georgina retorted.

"Oh, I wouldn't say that," Dr Coates countered. "But I can understand your feelings."

"Can you?" Georgina asked sceptically. There was a brief interval. An awkward interval. Then he began again. "These fellows are sick. They need to be treated, and someone has to look after them. Fact is fact. We can't have such people loose in our society. And on top of that they are cooped up for months and even years and their sexual potential is frustrated. Then a beautiful woman like you suddenly appears and the fuse blows. You see what I mean?"

"I couldn't give a tinker's for his bloody 'fuse'," Georgina remarked icily, emphasising, the last word with poisonous sarcasm. Coates shut up and their repast continued in silence. He had enough tact and sensibility to remain silent except for a few insignificant remarks about this and that. Georgina felt wretched. She was absolutely convinced that Dr Coates was certainly not the man for her, but that was not to assert that he was dishonourable in any way. She had to own that he was courteous and considerate, and very generous. These reflections made her miserable, and that night, alone and warm in her silk bed, contemplating the events of the last few years, she decided not to try anymore to find the "right" man. Those eligible, she mused, were either matadors like Enrico – and there were plenty of these around and all of them younger than she – or they were egotistical, testosterone-drenched cowboys like Dario who didn't really need a female for anything other than sex, or they were much older like Orlando or divorced, or happily married like Hermann. Where were the normal young swains? And it occurred to her that she was no longer 'young'. The eligible category for marriage she deduced in these moments was between eighteen and twenty-five. Would she end up, then, an old maid, 'a spinster of this parish'? She didn't know and so, peevish, disappointed and discouraged, she fell into a deep sleep of resignation.

# 7

## Tom Cullen

A year passed in which she took up an extended course in first aid together with Helen, which both women had enjoyed very much, and it was already springtime again.

One ordinary kind of Tuesday morning in April sunshine, found Georgina whirring along Via de Milia on her Vespa scooter to fetch vegetables for lunch. She parked in front of Barbaroni's Fresh Produce, turned off the motor, and hitching the machine onto its stand went into the shop. Seven or eight minutes later or so, she reappeared, loaded the wares into the scooter's pannier, pushed the Vespa into the driving position and kicked the start pedal. A cough and then nothing. Surprised, she tried again. The same willingness to oblige, but nothing more. The sun poured its careless light onto the street. Cars flitted by. A bus stopped. Someone called to a child.

"Damn!" Georgina said, "What now?" She got off and looked at the machine helplessly as women will when faced with a technical problem beyond their ken. Then she threw her right leg over the saddle again and thrust a foot at the start pedal for a third time. Nothing. Again, she received a cough in return for effort, but nothing more.

She looked round. Should she ask Signore Barbaroni for assistance? She could see from the road that the shop was full as usual at this time of the day. It would be an imposition to ask this busy man to help her, she concluded, but what should she do?

It was at this moment that she heard an Irish voice from behind her ask in English. "And what seems to be the trouble?" Surprised and flustered, Georgina smiled weakly and pointed to her Vespa. She hadn't the slightest idea what the 'trouble' could be.

"Um, with these things it's usually a matter of a flooded carb," the young man said moving towards her scooter, his mind bent on finding out whether his surmise was correct or not. He took not the slightest notice of Georgina, who, we must admit, looked lovely this morning in her full, pale yellow dress with its bright red sash round her tight middle and her bright hair falling almost to her waist. No, this fellow gave her not so much as a nod. She watched him with a touch of alarm as he bent over her scooter and efficiently removed the outer housing of the engine and peered at a spot that meant nothing to her, but which was the focus of his attention. Then after a little fiddling and banging, screwing and unscrewing in which his fingers were dirtied, he then swung his leg over the seat and kick started the machine. It roared into life. "Oh that's wonderful. Thank you so much." Georgina cried with relief. She turned to her knight in shining armour and was surprised for a second time. "No it isn't," the young man contradicted, hitching the bike on its stand again. "How often do you have it inspected?" he asked pointedly, like a sergeant major, she thought. Her dad used to ask in this manner and it never failed to irritate her.

"Why, I've never had it inspected," Georgina said honestly. As he stood up from the purring machine, she could assess him better. He was not well dressed as most people were these days in Italy. His jeans hadn't seen the cleaners for years, she concluded to herself. His heavy jacket was too warm for the weather they had been enjoying recently, and this, too, was not the cleanest of personal apparel. He sported a reddish beard as well. She wasn't certain about bearded men. He had dark blue eyes, she noticed, that surveyed you, but not at all with that note of appreciation she had been used to for more than a decade. These eyes appraised one as an object within their purview, noting everything without emotional reaction. Briefly, she had the feeling that he was talking to another man. "Do you clean your teeth regularly in the morning?" he asked with a hint of a smile. She laughed, unintentionally flashing her own regular, white teeth at the moment. "Of course!" Georgina returned, a little taken aback by this intimate enquiry.

"Well, your two-wheeler needs regular care as well, young woman," he replied conclusively. Again, Georgina felt very strongly that he was addressing a man. "Well, thanks very much for your help, Mr…" she said sincerely as she mounted the scooter again.

"Cullen, Tom Cullen," he said and added, "Anyway, my help's only temporary; this little thing needs an overhaul," he said, pointing to the scooter and raising his hand in a half-hearted salute. She nodded in understanding and drove off.

Despite his rough-hewn manner and appearance, there was something else about this individual that, she had to admit, was strangely attractive. In these last remarks and the dismissive gesture, which had accompanied them there was a deeper element, which she could not fathom.

And in all her doings with menfolk this something was a trait she had never come across before. As she got into third gear at the next corner, she concluded that he was perhaps not quite the boor she had at first taken him for. He was conceited of course. They all were. She had hated the phrase 'young woman' and his admonishing manner. He might have used 'young lady' or omitted the phrase altogether, Georgina assured herself. That had more style. He had no style. Funny bloke, she concluded as, a minute later, she approached the turning, which would lead her into her own street. Anyway, what the hell? He had helped her and she felt she could not condemn him for his lack of polish and deference. And yes, she would follow his advice and take the scooter in for a check-up very soon. Georgina brought the motor scooter to a halt outside her apartment. There was a lot to do today in preparing for this evening's party.

Not many days after this, a week or so perhaps, Georgina had business at the same grocer's when she caught sight of Tom Cullen again, this time sitting alone in the sunshine outside a café two shops away from hers. He was sprawled in his seat, she noticed, his feet on another wicker seat, apparently in deep thought. She wondered in a split second that followed whether he had seen her and whether she should catch his attention and wave, but a second later abandoned the idea and went into the shop. Afterwards she felt a bit mean about the matter. However, it so happened that as she turned to the door after paying a good ten minutes later his broad form almost bumped into hers.

"Hello, there, dear lady," he said, and added, "hey, let me help you with all that," and he immediately relieved her of some of her purchases. They walked together to the motor scooter at the kerb. On the way he asked, "And is your pop-pop bike behaving these days?" It was true that the engines of the Vespa models of those days made a soft, pop-popping sound.

She liked his Irish accent.

"Oh, yes fine, thank you; I took your tip and had it inspected. Thanks. And thanks for your help the other day, and here you are helping again."

"Believe me, it's a pleasure to help a fair maid in need," he said, smiling. The eyes, she noted, were not so searching as before, and she even detected a wicked twinkle in them, which, she had to admit, delighted her.

"May I invite you for a cup of coffee in the modest circumstances of this café here?" he asked, the twinkle now quite distinct in the dark blue eyes, and in the rhetorical tone and obsequious attitude of a Shakespearean actor, his tall body bent slightly to escort her and waving his arm in a generous sweep towards the three or four simple pavement seating accommodation of the café like a sixteenth century gentleman to the table seat nearby. No boor could avail himself of language and gesture such as this, she conjectured, and accepted right away.

When they were seated, Georgina protested that it was really she that should be inviting him as acknowledgement for his assistance.

"Yes, that's true," he shot back, his face suddenly earnest as if he had forgotten the fact. "We'll settle that later." This was said so soberly that she almost took his remark seriously. "And since you're paying, I'll have a croissant as well," he added with childish eagerness. Georgina smiled. 'This fellow's a wag for sure,' she noted.

"Of course!" Georgina said, laughing.

"Don't laugh, young woman. You haven't seen the bill yet." That Irish burr enchanted her. So the coffee came – and the croissants, and they stretched their legs in the early summer sunshine while the plane trees played with their new leaves high above in the light, spring breeze.

"Do you come here often?" Tom then asked, placing his cup in its saucer to add significance to his query and with that same serious mien as before, his attitude this time more that of a doctor inquiring after a symptom. The silly, threadbare ploy, the accent and his general bearing thrust her into a fit of laughter in which she was also aware that she would have to be on her toes with this one. Tom merely smiled indulgently over his cup as if in doubt that there was so much to laugh about. "No," she responded after finally recovering herself, "but you do apparently; you know your way around and the waitress knows you, too."

"Oh yes, that's my wife," Tom declared in a way that was superbly attuned to the accents of one who had been married for fifty years. For one, short moment, Georgina was caught again, and this time they laughed together.

Then Tom said quite simply, "No I'm not married yet, are you?" Georgina rightly discerned this time that he was no longer joking. She replied with the same simplicity. "No, nor I." Tom said nothing to this and changed the subject.

"What do you do in life, Miss... ?"

"Georgina. I modelled clothes at one time, but now I'm, I'm retired."

Tom, without a moment's pause for reflection, said, "Well, you're managing well without a stick these days." He smiled. She laughed and wondered why he didn't pursue the line. Instead, he took a long swig of his coffee and finished the cup with a satisfied "Ugh, good." After a moment or two, Georgina felt moved to ask him the same question.

"I'm a taxi driver. Off duty at the moment. My mate's in there," and Tom signalled towards the café, "he does the cooking from time to time on a Saturday like today. His wife does the waiting. That's the young lady who brought us the coffee."

"Oh," Georgina, said, just a trifle disappointed that this obviously gifted individual couldn't boast of a more elevated profession. But he was quick, this Irishman, and he noticed her reaction, and added, "I studied in Rome for a bit, and then gave it up."

"Oh," Georgina said again, this time with interest. "What did you study?"

"Oh, it doesn't matter," Tom replied, dismissing her query with a brusqueness, which clearly indicated that he did not want to talk about the subject. Georgina was at once curious and piqued by his manner, but before she could consider what this might imply, her thoughts were interrupted.

"Is it not a lovely day Miss Georgina? Now I'm sure you'd want to accompany me down to the riverside over there where we could discourse upon a variety of matters, and we could feed the ducks into the bargain since, I am sure, as a retired person, you have time on your hands."

"But allow me to pay for our coffees first, Mr Cullen."

"Oh, that's all taken care of, dear lady," he said, his hand waving carelessly towards the café's entrance. "And 'Tom', please; it's not hard to remember." He rose from the table and put out a strong, arm to help her up from the seat. 'That voice of his is irresistible,' she thought at that moment.

"Thank you," she said.

Now the psychological sciences are not wholly in agreement about just how the human mind finally makes its decisions. What exactly is it that prompts us to choose this and abandon that? All of us will offer some reason or another for our decisions and summon the angel of logic to our side, talk about sanity and rationality, common sense, appeal to our listeners to recognise the cogency of horse sense and calculable reaction, the obviousness of the only conclusion in the circumstances or insist on common human experience, history, tradition, feasibility, imperative tendencies, emotional antecedents necessarily governing behaviour, the past, habit, urge. Take your pick, but all of them fall short of our really knowing for sure why we do this and not that.

And so it was and with no further debate on these things and on this sunny Saturday, in the burgeoning month of April, the sun having climbed to its zenith and the time being 11.45 am that Georgina decided to accompany this stalwart, Irish taxi driver down to the river Naviglio Grande to feed the ducks.

Once there they walked along, talking of this and that and yes, they fed the ducks that waddled up to them in scores, fed them with bits of bread and other fragments they bought from a stall. And yes, the ducks were happy and they were happy, and neither knew why. He beguiled her with amusing anecdotes and as for Georgina, she just felt free, light and buoyant. Somehow there was nothing else better to do in in the world than simply to wander along, her gay straw hat in hand, the sun in her eyes, skirt blowing in the breeze, happy just to wander along with this funny man telling her about the origin of the bridge nearby or the church over there. And as for Tom, he was glad, glad in the company of a beautiful young woman who was so natural and so ready to laugh with him and would she like to take a trip on the riverboat with him? And yes, she would, she said, and so they paid for the ticket and went on board, these two, and watched the superior swans glide disdainfully, and smiled at the children licking their ice creams scrumptiously and at the dogs happily wagging their tails, and laughing and chatting under the fleecy white clouds as the vessel bore them over the water towards the town centre.

Georgina listened with interest as Tom pointed out places on the skyline. "Look! That's the Giacattolo Museum! We'll soon be there."

"Where?" Georgina asked innocently.

"I suggest we disembark soon and then we can wander towards the Parco del Basiliche; it's nice there, and if you like we can have a bite to eat at a small bistro belonging to a friend of mine. Afterwards, we can set fire to the park if you like."

Georgina did like. They found the bistro open and were joined by Tom's friend, another Irishman and another charmer, Patrick O'Neil. The conversation, which then ensued, was something she had never experienced before. Their reacquaintance began not with warm handshakes or an embrace, but with a curt nod and an exchange as though they had both spoken to each other a minute before. Then Patrick looked up to greet Tom's companion. "How d'ye do, young lady," O'Neil said with great courtesy, ignoring Tom and shaking her hand.

"This is a lady I became acquainted with this mornin' at the grocer's," Tom said honestly. Patrick O'Neil received this information with a serious air.

"A ye sure it was the grocer's?" he asked with a poker face.

"Yes, the grocer's," Tom replied.

"Not the haberdasher's?"

"No."

"And not the post office?" Patrick enquired suspiciously, as though assailed by another grave possibility.

"No, 'twas the grocer's," said Tom with certainty.

"So, the grocer's," O'Neil repeated in a confirmative tone, satisfied now that all doubt about this detail had been resolved. He raised his eyebrows and winked privately at Georgina. "Well, all I can say is that you were damn lucky," O'Neil continued flatly in the same voice while laying a crisp, clean cloth on the table. "Damn lucky."

"Yes, I think we can say that," Tom replied philosophically and in the same, serious-minded key. He then sat at the table and indicated to Georgina to do the same. Georgina was much amused at this ridiculous exchange. After handing them the menu, Patrick returned inside with the comment that he might be back later. In the meantime Tom and Georgina considered what to eat.

"There's one thing I'm insisting on, Tom Cullen," she said across the table.

"An' whaat is thaat, Miss Hennessey?" So he remembered her surname, she reflected in that moment. Probably because it was an Irish name. The brogue continued to intrigue her.

"I insist on inviting you," Georgina said emphatically. Tom merely smiled.

"I mean it," Georgina protested.

"You don't owe me a meal. You don't owe me anything Forget it all and just enjoy yourself – and enjoy your meal," Tom said, tucking into the salad on his plate.

"Patrick seemed to know what you wanted," Georgina said, changing the subject.

"Yes, he knows I'm a vegetarian."

"Oh, are you?" Georgina said, surprised.

"I'm a funny feller altogether," he added, smiling.

"I didn't say that, Mr Cullen."

"Oh yes you did," he answered playfully and the brogue came through again.

"No I didn't," Georgina countered half seriously. "Are you a vegetarian out of principle or for other reasons?" she pursued.

"Both," he said simply.

"Both what then?" Georgina asked.

"Well, I don't think it's moral, and I don't think it's necessary – either as food or for health. It might even be harmful in the long run."

"Goodness! I've never heard that before. I like a bit of steak now and again I must say," Georgina said.

"You wouldn't if you knew where it came from," Tom said cryptically. For once he was serious, she noted.

"Enjoy your food," he said. It was just like him, and she smiled again, noting the irony. She turned things over in her mind, but refrained for the moment from going into detail. After dessert, they said farewell to their host and sauntered through the park together without saying anything to each other for some time. Georgina appreciated the fact that they could be together without needing to say anything, and for the first time in her life she felt at home with this situation. She loved Evelynne's presence of course, but Evy twittered like a bird nearly all the time. Helen and Jennifer were good companions, too, of course but with this man she felt especially relaxed and couldn't fathom why. When they did come to talk again it was somehow natural. She realised that with a man things are different for sure, but it wasn't just because he was a man. It was as strange feeling of mutuality and inexplicability so that when he said that he would have to be off to drive his taxi at 6 pm, she felt disappointment, but knew somehow that she would see him again, although nothing to that effect had been arranged. Disappointment and assurance, and yet she hardly knew the man.

"It's early, I know, but there are things I have to do," he said, "our meeting was quite fortuitous, thank God." She knew he wasn't bantering this time as was his wont with his 'thank God', and she felt complimented. The phrase, although unusual, was sincere. She interpreted it as destiny as they walked together towards the park gate and she wondered at the same time if that's what he meant." Yes, it's its been a lovely afternoon, Tom. Thanks," Georgina said. "That's fine, then, and if you've time and interest, we can paint the town red another day; I can show you a lot if you're interested in history and culture and so on. I have access to most of the buildings, as folks know me. Could be fun."

"Oh, that sounds interesting; I'd like that," Georgina agreed.

"OK, we've come a long way from our grocery shop, I fear, so I'll call a taxi and you can take it from there, as you have to pick your scooter I suppose?"

"Yes, I can take it from there as you say." Once outside the park, he waved down a taxi and she turned to him as it stopped. It occurred to her that she had not given him an address or a telephone number. The taxi's engine turned over. On the spur of the moment, "Let's make it next Monday at the grocer's," she suggested, "about midday, if that's convenient," she said.

"OK," he replied, "and if not, I'll leave word with Signore Barbarone," Tom replied hurriedly, and the taxi was off. Ten minutes later, Georgina located her Vespa and, once astride, set off for home as she arrived a minute later at her apartment in via Crollalanza. 'Its been a nice day,' she said to herself.

Monday arrived and this time, since she had no shopping to do, she walked to Barbarone's and was pleased to note that he was already there when she arrived. Smiling, he greeted her and shook her hand, which she thought a little formal and yet at the same time rather charming.

"Where shall we go?" Georgina asked.

"I'd like to take you into town and show you the chapel

*Santa Maria delle Grazie*, but before that we can have a coffee and you can tell me what you think of the idea". This pleased her, the idea of being asked and she readily agreed.

"Let's take the bus," he suggested.

"The bus?" she echoed, a little surprised, "we could go on my Vespa, and it's just two streets away."

"And to the bus stop as well," he said.

"All right," she said, "you show me where," and the two of them walked off. As they went along, he said, "No, your machine is OK, but I think it looks inappropriate when a big bloke like me sits on the back while you drive me around."

"Well, you can navigate it if you like and I'll sit on the pillion," Georgina suggested.

"The bus," Tom said, having stopped to consider this possibility and now resuming his steps in that direction. Georgina, smiling, caught him up.

"You look very nice, I must say," Tom said appreciatively.

"Thank you, sir," Georgina returned airily. He said this in a way that was quite different from the way other men had paid their compliments, she noticed. With all the others, perhaps with the exception of Dr Sulla, there was always a sexual innuendo, however slight, which, she had to admit, was a gentle thrill, but with this man, it was a cool, objective appraisal. It was like the assessments made by her dressmaker and her designers, a friendly, matter-of-fact observation, and she liked this, too.

The bus came eventually, and they alighted five minutes later in the city centre.

"Good," Tom announced as they stood on the crowded pavement and added, "it's lovely weather, so let's sit outside and have a cup of something or other until the building opens." Georgina agreed. They made their respective orders and then fell into conversation.

"Do you come here often?" Tom enquired in a snooty tone. This time Georgina was ready for him.

"Not if I can avoid it, "she countered. They laughed.

"But seriously, Gee, you don't seem very familiar with the city's tourist attractions from what you told me the other day."

"I'm afraid it's true, Mr Cullen. For me, the city has always been primarily a place of work."

"Yes, but there were all the weekends. I mean, how did you spend these?"

"At the weekend I used to go to friends, do necessary housework or simply rest up and read."

"Read?"

"Yes. I mean a woman usually needs an escort to visit places of culture, go to the cinema or other places. I've seen one or two places, of course. For a year or two I belonged to a fitness studio which kept me in touch with people at large and of course I've got one or two special friends and have often been out with them." Tom lifted his cup pensively, considering what she had just said, then, like a teacher, he asked, "But I take it you've seen the cathedral here?" She wasn't sure whether the raised eyebrows expressed censure or whether he was playing again.

"Oh yes, I told you the other day that my friend Evelynne and I were there once."

"Yes, you did; I'm sorry," Tom concurred. Then, changing the subject, he asked, "You said then that you're twenty-seven. When will you be twenty-eight? I mean in what month?"

"In August, – on the 7th."

"Ah-ah, a Leo, in other words?"

"That's right." She smiled and looked at him. His

grey-blue eyes surveyed her kindly. I bet you're a pretty independent being. Leos are leaders, and there cannot be two kings!"

"Oh, well, I'm not the bossy type, if that's what you imply," she replied.

"Well, you had courage enough to leave home at seventeen and go to another country to live, I think you told me? That was pretty plucky, especially against the will of your dad."

"That's true, but I owe a lot to my best friend for that."

"Evelynne, that's her name, isn't it? By your report she sounds a nice person."

"Oh, yes, she's a wonderful person."

"I'd like to meet her."

"Well, perhaps you will one day. And what's your zodiac sign?" Georgina enquired, changing the subject herself this time.

"Aquarius, 25th January – exactly a month after Christmas and all that," he replied.

"Arty, creative people. Tolerant. Independently minded," Georgina commented. He uttered nothing by way of a reply to this, except to say, "I see you've swatted up on your astrology," and immediately added, leaning back in his seat and sizing her up, "Georgina. Posh name, that. Goes very well with Hennessey, and its regal echoes suit you, too."

"Thank you, sir," she said for the second time that morning.

"Not at all," he said formally, with that humorous glint in his eye again. She found this to be another charming trait in his general manner, like the brogue, and couldn't refrain from smiling inwardly at her reactions to them. Tom, too, liked his companion. He liked her naturalness and her independent air. She had soon cottoned on to his playfulness. He liked that. That showed intelligence, he concluded, and she laughed when she was caught out swallowing his blarney for truth, instead of pulling a face or putting on a mock countenance of being hurt when outwitted. Then she hit back in his own vein especially at their last meeting when they were looking at some swans on the river Ticini, "Look at them ducks on't river," Tom had said, imitating the voice of an untutored northerner, when she had replied in just the same tone as though they were a couple of buddies on tour, "Them ain't ducks; ducks ain't white." He had liked that: the readiness; the initiative.

The sun shone on their table, and he noticed her perfect complexion, the full lips and the clear, green eyes, and he liked what he saw.

"You told me you live not far from the provisions shop where we first met, but you didn't say what street exactly," he said.

"Via Crollalanza."

"Nice district," he noted.

"And where do you live?" she enquired.

"Oh, a long way from here. I'll show you one day. Awful place. I'm thinking of moving soon, but just can't bring myself to take the step. Too idle, I suppose."

Georgina nodded and thought no more about the matter.

"I think we can go now," Tom suggested, "The place opens at 10 am, and I believe we'll be among the first visitors this morning. Get a better view and all that."

"OK," Georgina agreed lightly, "let's go." They rose and walked leisurely towards the capella. They entered and were relieved to see that there were only a few people already before them. "That's the famous *Last Supper*, painted by Leonardo da Vinci between 1495 and 1497. Not bad, eh, in two years?" Georgina looked. Tom talked. "The colours haven't faded in 460 years – well, a bit of course. That's inevitable, but the depth and warmth is still there. Amazing." Tom moved a little nearer, Georgina at his side. "The makers of colour in those days certainly knew their stuff, and Leonardo knew how to mix them and apply them." The two studied the portrait carefully for a while before Tom continued, "See how these thirteen figures are presented, all of them with feeling and movement. The men are alive."

"And the suggestion of an expansive countryside behind them," Georgina added. Tom enthusiastically agreed. "Yes, it's marvellous." They continued to view the masterpiece for a few moments longer. Then Georgina said, "Have you noticed?" she said, pointing, "no one has begun to 'break bread' yet, so we assume that the prophecy that someone was present who would eventually betray Jesus on this occasion must have been made before they actually started to eat."

"Do you know, I've never thought about that one?" Tom replied and looked closer at the piece. Turning to Georgina, he added, "Good for you, girl!"

Georgina smiled," Perhaps it's because I'm a woman that I notice such a practical detail," she commented.

"Maybe," Tom agreed appreciatively, clearly impressed by her power of observation.

After a few minutes, Tom began again, "This bloke, Leonardo, this 'leading light of the Renaissance' as he's been called, was a bit of a crank, you know, not in the negative sense, not sick in the head, but very unorthodox for the time he lived in. He didn't care a tinker's cuss apparently about what folks – even the big fish – thought of him. Very 'independently minded' as you would say, Miss Hennessey," and here he smiled at his companion. The hint that he, Leonardo, might have been an Aquarian wasn't lost on her. "Well, who knows, Mr Cullen?" she said with a wry smile. Tom was beginning to like her more every minute. "Fact is," he went on, "nobody knows for sure exactly when he was born. We know that he was left-handed and he may even have been homosexual."

"Homosexual?" Georgina chipped in. "Well, well, I didn't know that. Don't know much about that kind of thing anyway. I've met a few of the 'other kind' and have found them very nice people. At least those I've met."

"Oh yes, why not?" Tom elaborated; I share a flat with one. In fact, he owns the property under whose roof where I live. He's a great guy. Spanish origin. Works here for a Spanish fruit juice firm, *El Janta*. Works like a horse all day lifting crates of fruit juice and piling them up for the lorry. He's really strong. Funny, ain't it?" Georgina considered this for a moment.

"I suppose we all have our preconceived ideas and our funny little prejudices," she returned. "There's no reason why he shouldn't be strong, is there?"

Tom liked the way she viewed things, this young woman. He liked her objectiveness, the frank way she spoke, her openness generally. Then there was something else about her, which he appreciated. It was difficult to pin it down. Was it a certain friendly freedom of mind, a happy equanimity perhaps? Yes, yes, but there was something else, too. There was something about this young woman, which he could only describe as 'noble'. She was not only beautiful outside, he assured himself, but inside as well, but he kept his thoughts to himself.

"Yes, he was a many faceted man, this Leonardo," he continued, returning his glance to the painting, "seemed to be able to put his mind to anything and turn it into a success, although in his time he would have been reckoned by the elite around him as an *homo sanza lettere*, an illiterate. As far as we know, he was illegitimate, spent his early life in relative poverty, never knew his father, somewhere learned to paint well and, from what we can ascertain, a stickler for detail. Just why he left Florence for Milan at thirty-years of age we don't know other than that we *do* know that he had a letter of recommendation in his pocket for the big boss of the times here, Ludovico Sforza. We know, too, that he had plans to augment that gentleman's military repertoire with ideas of his own that included a cannon that could rain metallic horror on his enemies and potential enemies, a kind of tank, horrendous catapults and God knows what to murder and maim other human beings, since he was not only a painter, but an engineer to boot, had done his homework in mathematics, learned Latin at forty so as to familiarize himself with the works of Pliny and also knew some Greek."

"That's amazing," Georgina said, finding all this very interesting.

"But that ain't all," Tom continued, "he had an intrepid, eagle's eye in everything he beheld. He studied the human body and made accurate records of human anatomy, although he risked punishment from the Catholic Church for doing so. But that was typical of him. He didn't care a damn for authority; he was his own authority. He probably knew too, that the folks in power then were indebted to him for his ingenuity. He made plans for the city which also included waterways. He studied the flight of birds very minutely and recorded everything very carefully, so that he was able to try out the first parachute – and much, much more. I do hope I'm not boring you, Miss Hennessey, he said with his wicked smile."

"You're certainly not boring me, young man," Georgina rejoined with a smile of her own. Secretly, she just loved to listen to him.

"Where shall we go now?"

"The Museo Bagatti Valsecchi is just over there. We could take a look at Andrea Previtalis's *Portrait of a Man*, it's worth it. So they went. And they looked, and he supplied all the information about the building, the date of its erection, the kind of people who had lived in it for the last four centuries, its peculiar decorations and the reasons for their application, its development and the dates of its several renovations and recent history as a museum. Georgina, who had never been particularly interested in architecture or painting for that matter, was enthralled by it all, and listened now more intently to the content of what Tom related to her rather than the music of his voice. She was impressed.

They lunched at an especially expensive restaurant that he knew of not far from the cathedral, because, he said, they shouldn't miss a visit to this 'Christian monument' as he called it.

"Well, at least I've been there," Georgina said confidently.

"Good," Tom said, and they drank the especially good wine the restaurant and were a just slightly tipsy even before the first course arrived.

"Do you come here often?" Georgina asked facetiously, while surveying the menu, but nonetheless maintaining a serious countenance, and for once, Tom, at that moment being deeply involved with cost/hunger considerations, was caught for once. He looked up from his calculations and suddenly replied, "No, not very often…" before realising that he had fallen nicely into her trap. All he could do then was to laugh outright. "So you got me there, you devil!" he said, "Just you wait, young lady."

When their food came they ate it with relish.

"I'm amazed at how much you know about all this

surrounding culture," Georgina ventured, keen to know more about this man who had entered her life and who was very different from all the other men she had encountered so far.

"Well, it's interest, I suppose. I can't live here and ignore it all," he said modestly, while Georgina for her part thought that was precisely what she *had* done in the eight years of her residence, and felt very much at a disadvantage at that moment. She looked at her companion's hands as he tackled the food on his plate. They were strong, capable hands, and as she glanced at them, she was also struck by something else which she could not quite determine. The only word of description she could bring forth from her mind was 'knowing'. They were 'knowing' hands, she noted inwardly and there she was nonplussed.

"I think Milan must be a regular treasure box for you," she remarked.

"That's a very good term," he replied, "I love the place," he added as he earnestly applied himself to the potatoes. It was clear that he was very much enjoying his meal. At the same time Georgina noticed that the cuffs of the shirt he wore were a little frayed. Such an observation could only have come from someone who had been long concerned with human apparel, she noted to herself again, and it occurred to her that he hadn't much money. And indeed, this restaurant would have been foreign to most taxi drivers – at least to dine in, she concluded. Like him, she was enjoying her meal. It was excellent, and the wine was good, too. It was this latter perhaps which urged her to probe a little deeper into this man's past.

"What made you come here in the first place?" she asked, "to Milan, I mean?"

"Work," he said simply, and seeing that this was not a satisfactory answer, he went on, "I'm just another Irish immigrant seeking employment; there are lots of us here, you know."

"And there are no taxi drivers in Dublin," she surmised almost primly. She knew he was hedging.

"I don't hail from Dublin," he corrected her, again sidestepping the issue. It was a little disappointing for Georgina to realise that he was keeping something from her. It had been the only false note in their association so far, but she submitted to his tacit refusal to tell her more with a smile of resignation. After all, we know, don't we, that Georgina was a well brought up young woman who didn't pry into the private life of others, and she was far too intelligent not to have sensed the nuance of his resistance on his part.

"No, I come from Connaught," Tom announced, and in the country at that. "No work. No future. But the countryside is wonderful. You'd love the scenery," he said grandly, and she wasn't sure he was being ironic or not. She said nothing to this last remark and smiled her gentle smile, courteous as she was. However, Tom sensed her need to know more about him, since he was no fool himself and so teased her with a morsel of further information.

"But you might be interested to know that I've lived in Dublin and therefore know the city well, and I think it was this experience that finally decided me for the continent as it has many another Irishman before me. A kind of springboard, you know. I left and then I think you can say that my troubles began."

"Troubles?" Georgina queried.

"Well, I was no better off materially than before, but I could wallow in all this culture at little expense and I was happier. It's a funny thing, isn't, it, all these folks jumping ship like James Joyce, Samuel Beckett, Oscar Wilde and George Bernard Shaw and all of 'em living elsewhere and yet remaining as Irish as a shamrock?"

At this Georgina smiled again and noticed this time that the collar of his shirt had seen better days, too. She sensed the same feelings as before about him and was still as curious as ever to know more about the individual opposite her. She tried another tack.

"And what are your ambitions for the future, Mr Cullen?" she asked in the manner of a bank manager enquiring of one's financial well-being.

The humour of this wasn't lost on him and he appreciated her initiative for the umpteenth time that day.

"Oh, just bum around, you know," he replied with a laugh, and received a look of slight disdain from his table partner. Then, seeing this and taking it seriously, he added, "Well, no, I have pretty serious plans, but if you'll forgive me, dear Georgina, I'd like to outline these to you a little later." There was the slightest of pauses. "If I may?"

Georgina admitted the change of key, appreciated the courtesy of this and they ordered the dessert.

"I'm going to have a banana split," Georgina decided.

"And I a peach melba!" he said with enthusiasm.

An hour passed very agreeably.

"Have you any brothers or sisters?" Georgina asked over coffee.

"Yes, three sisters and two brothers."

"That's nice," Georgina commented.

"I suppose so," Tom said resignedly. "I love them all, but don't see much of them nowadays. I'm here and they're there."

"Do you miss them?" Georgina then enquired.

"Yes, it'd be nice to see them more often, but..." He hesitated.

"But what?"

"I don't think they would have much time for me. They think I'm a bit of a renegade, I'm sure. My new world is not their world. None of them would have much patience or interest in the things I'm interested in. No understanding and so no appreciation. It's akin to fearing what you don't know. As a consequence, we'd only be able to talk about the things they are familiar with, and these topics either bore or irritate me."

"Does that include your mum and dad?" Georgina pursued.

"Oh yes, those two in particular. They're furious that I don't go to church anymore, that I've given up the Catholic Church and it me, but I can only laugh about that. That is, laugh and cry at the same time."

Georgina wanted to know more.

"Well, laugh, because I'm free from all that medieval bilge, but sad to realise that they are truly unhappy that I'm so inclined. They can't see that they are bound, hand and foot by an uncompromising, outrageous power machine."

Georgina listened. Tom went on, seeing that she was interested. "You see, the poor folks can't see beyond the garden fence. They've never known or wanted to know anything other than what this organisation dishes out to them. It's both sad and ridiculous at the same time." He raised his shoulders and hands and looked at the ceiling.

"And how did you escape the shackles of the Church?" Georgina then asked.

"I read."

"Is that all?"

"Yes, this and travel. I went to Britain on a shoestring once, about five years ago, and the trip opened my eyes."

"How?"

"I found the Brits all right, I must say. They have their funny little ways of course, but they can think for themselves and I like that. Whereas I was able to smile at their crass class system, which is *their* bondage and one to which I didn't belong, since I was a foreigner, they could look at *my* particular tight shoe and smile. Altogether, it was an enlightening experience. When I got back to Ireland, I was a changed man. It was a lot like the bird and the egg; I couldn't get back into the shell!" He laughed.

"And then you decided to leave?"

"Well, it wasn't quite like that. There was a lot of digestion to be done if you see what I mean. I couldn't just go off like that straightaway, but the England experience did me a lot of good. I couldn't get rid of the memory either. It didn't fade. What you know, you know. This wasn't a matter of believe this and believe that. And do this or that to save yourself from hellfire. I was faced with facts."

He took a long draw at the rest of his coffee.

"Good for you," Georgina said with admiration. "It's not everyone that can break away from a form of conditioning that has been with them since their earliest years, even if they know the 'facts' as you call them. It takes a bit more to actually break away and forge a new life."

Tom thought this a wise assessment. 'This kid knows something', he thought to himself. 'Mind you, she's older than most of the chicks I've had to do with up to now,' he figured. He looked at her. 'Yes, there was something noble about her, too', he went on thinking, 'but just what was it'? he wondered.

"Time now to take you to one of this church's most distinguished fortresses," he proclaimed, and seeing that she had finished her coffee, he called the waiter. Georgina watched as he parted with his money, and there was just the slightest pause between what he calculated as adequate for a tip and his offering the notes from his wallet. In it, Georgina knew for certain that he was not very well off. Wealthy people, she knew, proffered their money differently. Her observation lasted but a fleeting second, but was conclusive.

"Thank you," she said.

"It's a pleasure," he replied and they slowly made for the door amid friendly good wishes for a pleasant day from the restaurant's employees.

"So, we've got a bit of a walk in front of us," Tom said, putting a friendly arm around Georgina's shoulders as they walked uphill towards the cathedral.

When they arrived, there were many before them, and they were obliged to queue, but it wasn't long before they were standing in front of the famous stone effigies depicting the Christian martyrs as conceived by various masons in the 14th fourteenth century. They stood there for several minutes, not so much in awe of the remarkable crafted stone before them as in stark dismay that man could be fascinated by such horrid detail. Here was one man hanging head down in boiling water, and there was another enduring disembowelment, while yet another was about to have his brain ground by millstones, and St Sebastian in anguish as he suffered the slings and arrows of the heathen. Georgina spoke first.

"What did they want to carry across with all this?" she whispered to her companion.

"Fear." Tom whispered back.

"Why?"

"Because that's a great way to govern," he replied simply and added, "Very effective." And as Georgina said nothing to this, he continued, "Folks in those days couldn't read at all, let alone the Latin in which Christianity was embalmed, so they were obliged in good faith to believe those who could, poor devils."

"You're on your hobby horse again, I fear," Georgina warned and smiled.

"Not half!" Tom concurred, smiling himself. She liked him for this. He didn't jib at her mild censure, but could laugh at himself and yet at the same time confirm his views. For his part, he liked her independence of mind. Independence! Yes, that was what he'd been searching for in her manner. She was independently minded, this woman, and said what she thought without deference, but not tactlessly.

"But let's move on now to our next station and leave these fellows to wallow in the muck of their subconscious minds," Tom said in that adopted superior English, upper-class voice of his, as though he were an official ecclesiastical guide. Georgina smiled and was charmed. Realising this, Tom continued in the same tone, waving his arm loftily to the right as they walked on for a few steps. "There used to be an opening to the west here and onto the street so that folks actually traversed cathedral premises, and not only people, but horses and carts and God knows what went from one side to the other before it was finally walled up. Imagine!" Georgina looked. They then looked at Visconti's famous 14th fourteenth century portrayal of the devil. "I'm always amazed by the energy their belief endowed them with," Tom went on. "Artists in stone came from all over Europe to contribute to this holy monument, from Flanders, Germany, France – everywhere and they did a good job and all."

Georgina nodded in agreement.

"But it never finishes, you know. Work's been going on since the 13th thirteenth century to maintain the glory of this place."

"Really?" Georgina was interested. "Yes, by Jove, there's always work to be done. In a way, you could say it's an unending contest against the implacable, primordial forces of change and transmutation in one form or another.

"Tell me more, Dr. Cullen." Georgina was interested to learn.

"Well, there are the usual forces in the service of entropy; heat differences during the seasons, for example, evaporation and condensation helping to erode and deface stone exposed to the elements, which is going on all the time, every day, every hour of the day and night and which, if left entirely unattended, would bring the building to certain ruin within a few years. "Then there are the living forms of destruction all busy doing their own thing, the weeds and other plants taking advantage of every hollow and crevice providing water for them to flourish so as to express their own form of the joy of life in light and then the birds that scratch and pick, build nests and leave their excrement to devour wall, roof and turret. Then there's the woodworm and his associates slowly digesting rafter, beam and stair. And not content with these, there is our own breath rising to pollute the wonderful frescoes and paintings on the ceilings above. Slowly, slowly, but surely. All the time. Every day. Every hour that passes."

"Phew!" Georgina gasped," It's not safe in here!" Tom smiled. "Well, in a way, you're not entirely wrong about that, my lady, because the underground route runs directly below us, and this, too, causes reverberations that gnaw at the very foundations of this distinguished edifice."

"Heavens!" Georgina exclaimed.

"Yes, Line 1," Tom added, smiling.

They moved towards the cathedral's magnificent chancel.

"It was here that Napoleon allowed himself to be crowned 'King of Italy' in 1805," Tom explained.

"Napoleon?" Georgina asked, astonished.

"Yep," Tom confirmed, "the little gangster got around quite a bit in those days. Insatiable, infantile appetite for power, you know. Huge ego, no soul."

Georgina had never heard Napoleon defamed so thoroughly before, and she had heard Jean-Luc refer to him in almost reverent tones in an aside he had once made to someone. This Irishman was of quite another persuasion apparently, she thought to herself. But then weren't these Irish inherently against everything? She thought fondly of her dad and his prejudices, bless him.

"I've heard that he was a clever strategist," Georgina objected.

"Cunning is to intelligence as ape is to man," Tom retorted oracularly.

"Wow," Georgina said, and there the issue ended. They walked on among the great columns of the cathedral to a kind of annex where there were as many as 3,000 statues of famous men and women, which both found most impressive. "Many of these are copies," Tom noted, "a whole lot of the originals are in the nearby museum."

"There's one here of Mussolini!" Georgina cried. Tom nodded, "Another gangster."

"Well, it shouldn't be here, should it?"

"I suppose not," Tom agreed, "must be some kind of administrative hiccough," he added. "Funny things like this do happen from time to time."

Georgina stood before the figure disbelievingly, a smile of amazement on her face, her lips slightly parted as though she wanted to add something more to her discovery, but they left that place to discover more of that awe-inspiring place, eventually to reappear outside, blinking, in the sunlight of late afternoon. Once in the forecourt of St Mark's Square, they looked up and back towards the magnificence of this architectural tribute to God in wonder and appreciation. After a moment's respect, Tom spoke again. "Took a long time to complete. The last stone of the façade was set in 1813, some 600 years after the building's foundation. Think of that!"

"And thereafter all the maintenance," Georgina put in.

"Sure."

After refreshing themselves with an ice cream, these two wandered casually through the old town, admiring the wares in various shops and discovered that they had the same tastes in colour and design. This pleased Georgina.

Later, they visited a funfair and competed with one another at the shooting stand where Georgina realised for the first time in her life that she had a good eye with a rifle, earning for this attribute a large white, fluffy teddy bear. Tom was much amused at his own clumsiness with firearms and didn't do half so well, either with the pistols or the rifles. He scored just one bull's eye after fifteen minutes and the stall keeper threw him a bar of chocolate for his trouble, which only made them laugh all the more.

While wandering around there, they came across donkeys carrying small children in a ring of sawdust.

"What a bore that must be for them!" Georgina exclaimed, watching the dainty feet trudging forward in unison to a command from their warder.

Tom looked on without comment.

"They're well cared for though," he said after a moment. "They may even enjoy it," and after the round had finished, he went up to the man in charge and asked if he might stroke one of the animals, at the same time pushing a few coins into the man's hand. This was met with a warm invitation to do so, and Georgina noticed how lovingly Tom did this. It was as if he knew donkey language and was able get his feelings across to them. In fact he did talk to them, and funnily enough, she noticed, they seemed to understand him. This short communion impressed her, because she had a long association with horses herself.

It was 4.30 pm by the time they left the fairground to take the bus back to where they had boarded that morning.

"I'm on nights this week," Tom explained." If we want to meet again, things will be easier for me next week."

Georgina nodded, "Here's my telephone number," she said in answer to this and jotted it down on a piece of paper she pulled out of her handbag.

"How can I reach you?" she enquired.

"I haven't got a personal phone," Tom replied, "but you can get me in the taxi," and so saying he wrote down a long number for her, which was clearly a firm's number and its extension.

"Good," Georgina said happily, tucking the shred of paper into her handbag, because she was very happy. It had been a wonderful day. The sun had shone on them, and she had not laughed so much for a long time. This man and his fascinating brogue, his wealth of knowledge, his anecdotes and his pithy conclusions on life and people had been for her like a tonic. It seemed strange, aye, very strange, but she seemed to have known him all her life, so that it was easy to acquiesce to his tacit invitation to go out with him again. He accompanied her to the bus stop, got off with her, shook her hand there, said farewell in fun to the white teddy in her arm, and turned to go on foot to wherever it was he lived. Making her way home, it occurred to her then that she had not asked where he lived, but she would learn that in time, she assured herself as she finally mounted the steps to her apartment.

Filipe Santos girded his loins for another workout that morning at the fitness studio a mile away. He was of the opinion that the obligation to lift crates all day long at work was only one-sided exercise and took the training of other parts of his physique seriously. So to this end he regularly trained his already well-formed body to breathe and pant and sweat every Thursday on the walkers in that place by pacing off the miles for an hour or so before showering and dropping into the bar, there to sip at his favourite milk shake and relax for a while before returning home. He was always made welcome in the 'bar', which only sold non-alcoholic drinks and it was here where he met friends and acquaintances. One of these was Franco, a giant of a man who shared Filipe's propensity for physical exercise and the development of the body.

"Mornin' Franco."

"Morning, Filipe, lad. How goes it?"

"Oh, not bad. Can't complain. How's yourself?"

"Good, good, thanks." For a moment or two the men quietly enjoyed their respective beverages. Then Franco continued. "Saw your roommate the other day – with a woman."

"Oh?"

"Yeah, and what a woman! Looked like a film star," Franco enthused.

"Oh," Filipe said again, but this time with a different intonation. Women didn't interest him too greatly, but he was surprised that Tom had said nothing to him about a new acquaintance.

"Yeah," Franco repeated with emphasis, "bet she costs him a packet to take out. Looked like something out o' the top drawer."

"Oh," Filipe said for the third time and in yet another key. As Tom's closest friend, he knew that Tom had known only a few women, and that these few had not meant much to him, since they hadn't shown much interest in his work. That was important for Tom.

"Is he still pushing that taxi around, by the way?" Franco went on, taking another swig of his apple juice.

"Yes, brings in the millions he needs," Filipe said, smiling and adding, "yes, he's very generous, our Tom; even pays me for the sessions he needs for a drawing, and I think that's very nice."

"What, nude, you mean?" Franco asked incredulously.

"Yes, why not?"

"Well, well, "Franco maintained, laughing, "it's an opportunity to show off your six pack, I suppose!"

"That's right," Filipe shot back. "I'm only in it for the money, you see."

Franco laughed outright. "You old rogue!" he said, clapping Filipe on the shoulder and the two collapsed into laughter at the counter like a couple of rag dolls.

Tom and Georgina met each other again a week later. On this occasion, Georgina needed to go shopping and so the two decided to shop together, eat out for lunch and wander through the town. The weather was beginning to be even warmer and for Georgina the meeting was particularly enjoyable, because she found to her pleasure that her companion shared her taste in colours and that, even more importantly, he had good taste in general. In a way, this was surprising, since he himself wore the simplest clothing, and seemed to always wear the same things. These were always clean, admittedly, but not the newest and certainly not the most expensive, she noted, but what of that? Not everyone was in the business as she was, she told herself. She had remarked on a number of occasions that he was not very well off, and sometimes she had been obliged to help him out. There was the trip to the cinema, and once they had been in a hotel bar, which she knew, was expensive but for all that a secluded place where they could talk and where he had been a trifle embarrassed by the bill when it arrived. But Georgina, we know, is generously minded. She smiled and was glad to help out. For her, it was the company that counted. She was glad of his company as now, listening to him tell her about Milan's canal system, about how these were founded in the twelfth century, about many that had since been filled in, that there was a time when the inhabitants of the city could actually catch a boat at their doorsteps, and about others that had been replaced in 1920 by concrete at the behest of the dictator, Mussolini, to create space for wide boulevards where the fascists of the time could conduct their histrionic parades and marches. It was all very interesting.

April passed, and then May. During this time they saw each other at least twice a week and undertook trips to Helen's friends, excursions into the countryside where they picnicked, climbed hills together, and once sailed over a lake together, he sturdily at the oars and she reveling in the sunshine on her face and where, later, they stopped at an inn and fell into conversation with the owner. On this occasion she was interested in how much he knew of the landscape and of the villages round about and his ease in carrying on long conversations with people versed in their particular cultural heritage. She was impressed, but observed at the same time that he was never conceited in airing his knowledge and retained his usual modesty. Moreover, he was always courteous to her and to whom he spoke and his good humour seemed to be inexhaustible. This pleased her greatly. It crossed her mind now and again how her father would have received this young man in his time and what both he and her mother would have thought of him, and indeed what he, Tom, would have thought of her father. By what she could gather from their conversations, Tom was no great lover of the army – and especially of the British army – so that of course would not have gone down well. But all this in any case was speculation, a mere mental excursion. He had never made a pass at her at all in the month that had elapsed during the acquaintance. Perhaps she was not his type. Most of the men she had known were all too ready to say how much she pleased them. In one way this pleased her, and yet in another she missed such blandishments – even the covertly sexual asides. Was she no longer so attractive, she wondered, but then dismissed the idea altogether. Tom was a good companion and she enjoyed being with him. Moreover, her friends and acquaintances had liked him; Helen got on very well with him, for example, Jennifer, too, and Jean-Luc had spoken well of him on his last visit to the city. The funny thing was, though, she had never met any of his own friends. He never talked of his friends either, and they had never returned to eat at Patrick's place either. Somehow, it was odd.

One day, he suggested they might visit Rome. Georgina was delighted with the idea and a day and time was arranged. They travelled by train in mid-June and arrived in scorching sunshine, found a small hotel almost immediately, as they had planned to stay one night there. He did the arranging and had booked separate rooms. She was somehow glad of this, since, as I say, there had been nothing of a sexual rapport between them, and yet at the same time surprised that he had not taken advantage of the opportunity for a closer relationship. Other men, she assured herself, would have jumped at the chance.

They visited a number of sites while they were there, among them the Colosseum, and this especially was long to stay in her mind. Afterwards, in the late afternoon, they sat outside one of the nearby bistros for a drink. The many steps in the Colosseum had been a strenuous undertaking.

"What do you think of it?" he asked when they had settled in their seats about 400 yards or so from the amphitheatre where the building could be viewed as a whole.

"Breathtaking."

"Yes, isn't it just," Tom agreed.

"But incredibly sad," he continued, "In my opinion, it should never be a tourist attraction, but a place of devout pilgrimage where men and women should be reminded in humble silence of what hateful beasts men have been in the past and basically still are at heart."

Georgina nodded at this; from the rounds they had made this morning, she knew what he meant. "You haven't got to look back much further than fifteen years for the same bestiality," he added. "Not in the interests of public entertainment recently, but at the instigation of one man's hatred for other human beings."

Georgina considered this. "Hitler, you mean?" she said.

"Yes." They sat together contemplating this for several minutes as they watched the massive architecture of the Colosseum collect the first shadows of the afternoon. Their beer was brought to them, and Tom changed the theme slightly.

"In the 18th eighteenth century farmers grazed their cattle in the central section, which at that time was overgrown with weeds and grass. Apparently, the vegetation did very well; it had received so much nourishment from being soaked with human and animal blood over several generations!" Georgina pulled a face, and Tom veered again. "And later generations regularly nibbled at the ruins, you know, taking away what they could of the heavy stone to use for their own buildings, but they didn't completely succeed in destroying this monument to human wickedness."

They sipped at their cool beer. It was especially good today. Georgina was moved by the philosophical tone of Tom's remarks and remained silent for some time, haunted by ancient horror. Finally, having slaked their thirst, the two of them walked on again towards the city's centre to visit the Trevi Fountain, the Spanish Steps, the Vatican and St Peter's Square. Once more, Tom proved to be an interesting, veritable encyclopedia of information. During this particular afternoon for some reason, Georgina and her companion came closer together than ever before. They agreed with each other on many topics, found themselves enjoying the same food, laughing at the same things, observing the same things, so that it made her happy when, from time to time, he slipped his hand around her waist, ostensibly to guide her up the steps of a bus or into a shop or through the crowd. And so it seemed the most natural thing in the world later that day for him to hold her hand and as they sauntered along, admiring this or that, commenting here and there on what they saw or appreciated.

Occasionally during that afternoon, they looked into each other's eyes. It was only fleeting, this look, almost shy, self-effacing, accompanied with a smile on every occasion and with some banal remark like, 'Oh me, too,' or 'Oh yes, I love red and black' or 'Do you think so?' or 'Really? Lovely', but each time both knew that a spark had been struck between them, that their nearness to each other had been informed with a delicious tension.

In the evening of their last day in Rome they caught the last train back for Milan, and as the train forged its way northwards and homewards, Georgina fell asleep around midnight, her head falling on Tom's shoulder. He, too, was happier than he'd ever been before and put his arm around her and clasped her to him. They knew they had fallen in love.

After an hour or so, the train stopped for some reason that was clear to no one, and Tom took his friend into his arms and kissed her tenderly for the next few minutes before the train clanked forward once more. From that moment, their lives changed.

They took a taxi home, she to hers and he to his somewhere in town. He accompanied her to her door, and they embraced once more, before he descended the steps to the waiting cab purring gently in the street. They waved. What a wonderful day it had been!

That was a Sunday. Tom was obliged to stand in for a sick colleague during the day that week, which meant longer hours for him, so he and Georgina were only able to meet after 6 pm.

"Where shall we go?" Georgina enquired when they met in the city.

"Well first of all, I'm hungry; I've not eaten all day, so let's do something about that, and then I've a suggestion."

Georgina happily agreed, and with his arm round her waist, he steered her towards a popular and very high-class pizzeria which happened to be only a few steps away.

When they were seated, they ordered wine and he smiled lovingly at his companion. This made Georgina very happy. The truth was that she had waited all day for this moment.

"And after we've eaten our fill, we could go dancing if you like at Tattini's. It's a wonderful place and the band there is really top notch – what do you think?"

"Oh, that's great!" Georgina said. "I've not actually been there, but Jennifer has told me a lot about it."

"Good," Tom said with his mouth full "You won't regret it," he added, still chewing. Georgina smiled; he was obviously hungry. 'Perhaps he hasn't eaten all day' she thought to herself. She tried one of the delicious pizzas that the restaurant offered. "Good," she confirmed, and he laughed. The day had been warm and now the balmy evening was closing in on the city. The dance hall opened at 8 pm. They took their time and both of them lounged in their wicker chairs after their meal and idly watched the evening crowds drift by. It had been very warm for the time of year. Georgina knew that she had not felt so happy for a long time, and could not formulate in so many words why this was so. She knew she was in love and bathed in her elation as she sat there with this man whom she hadn't known long and yet knew that this liaison was somehow right. What did he think? Did he feel the same? Yes, she assured herself, he felt the same, and he probably couldn't say anything about this strange 'rightness' either. It was a miracle.

At last they paid, rose and took their way slowly to Tattini's.

To tell the truth, this was actually the first time that these two had willingly given their tacit consent to physical contact. The embrace in the train and their holding hands had been Tom's initiative. In the first few seconds before the band struck up and as the two stood opposite one another on the dance floor ready to take up the first figures of the dance, there was an exchange of profound, mutual understanding between them as they looked into each other's eyes, a communication that neither of them had ever experienced before. The wonderful thing about this moment was its mutuality. All egoism had vanished. They were at one in their shared respect and appreciation for one another. Neither had the slightest urge to change the other, still less to exploit, and it was this trust, which gave their contact a depth and a fineness that both of them sensed to the full, standing there ready for action. As they waltzed and whirled, tangoed and cha-cha-ed, through the evening to the rhythms of the music that only heightened their joy for each other, they saw their love happily woven into the faces of the bandsmen smiling and laughing over their instruments, and gaiety of the other dancers who themselves were thoroughly enjoying the universality of it all.

At midnight it was all over. The lovers, tired and happy, took their leave of Tattini's and met the moon high above the now empty streets on their way home.

"Shall we walk or are you too tired," Tom asked.

"Yes, the fresh air will do us good," Georgina answered, so they walked some of the way home, and then caught the last tram for the rest of the way. They were the only passengers and the interior of the tram seemed especially light. At last they came to Georgina's stop, and Tom accompanied her to the door of her flat.

"It's 12.45 am by golly," Georgina remarked as they reached the door, and she looked at her wristwatch.

"Aye, time goes by quickly when you're happy," Tom said, smiling, and gave his companion a long kiss.

"Thank you, Tom; it was lovely," she whispered. They stood there a moment before she put the key into the door. "We'll do it again soon, girl," Tom said enthusiastically, hugging her once again, "but from tomorrow I'm on night shift, so we'll have to think of something to do during the day," he said with a short laugh. "Good night, darling."

"Good night, Tom, dear, and sleep well," Georgina said quietly, and squeezed his hand. Tom waited until she was inside the hallway and then set off along the moonlit streets to his digs in the Vicolo del Lavandai about a mile away.

The following week they met twice to picnic in the countryside around and were as happy as any humans could be, and in the week after Tom was on holiday for a few days, and so they took advantage of their free time to see each other more often. It was during this week that they consummated their love.

They had reached a small lake after a hike of about three miles or so, and since it was particularly hot, they sat down for a moment or so. They looked longingly at the cool water shimmering in the hot sun before them. To

Tom's utter surprise, Georgina suddenly said, "Shall we swim?" Flummoxed by this candid suggestion, Tom didn't know what to say for once and looked at her questioningly. Before he could answer, Georgina had disposed of her frock and was busy undoing her bra. Tom looked on wonderingly. Her fine breasts appeared from their armour and in the next second, she had thrown her slip to join the rest of her clothes and was on her way to the water like a Grecian nymph. Tom was so astonished by this that all he could do in the few seconds that all this took place was to – well yes – goggle like a fool. But not for long. By the time he, too, had divested himself of his garments, she was already languishing in the water and he was still overcome by the speed she had put her decision into action. The image of her departure and her entry into the water had cast a spell on him. They joined each other a moment later.

"Hey, you're a one," was all he could say as he caught his breath on surfacing from an underwater swim as he approached her. "Why not?" she asked with an engaging smile when they were together. "I've no inhibitions about the body."

"Apparently not," he rejoined, still a trifle embarrassed by her unselfconsciousness. She laughed and struck out for the open lake. She was pleased with his body. He was muscular and well built she had noted as he had made his way to the water's edge. Somehow, this made her happy, too. Tom caught up with her in mid-stream. "It's super isn't it?" he shouted. She smiled, nodded and slid under water like a mermaid, her hair streaming and he following, hoping to catch her, but Georgina was an accomplished swimmer and nimbly avoided his attempt to grasp her, coming once more to the surface and laughing at his gaucheness. Then they swam to their heart's content for forty minutes or more before joining each other on the lake shore and wading together up to the welcoming grass beyond. Tom was enthralled by her shape and took an early opportunity to clasp this wonderful creature into his arms and kiss Georgina passionately.

"We haven't got any towels," Georgina noted practically as their wet bodies met.

"Don't want any," Tom said, bending her towards the grass at their feet.

"Not here," Georgina protested, "it's too exposed. Let's get dry and then move to a more secluded spot. So they took up their clothes and sought a space nearby that was not so exposed either to the sun or to eyes that might be in the vicinity. Once sure of their safety, they settled to making love for the next two hours. Their unions were very gratifying for them both, and they returned to the city of Milan like conquerors. Strange to say, neither of them spoke much either on their way home or when they had reached the outskirts of the town. There seemed nothing more to say. Their tender glances and kisses sufficed. Tom got off the bus a few stops before her to wash and 'freshen up for dinner', declining her invitation to do that at her place. She travelled on to Via Carlo Torre in a kind of delectable dream, happier than she had been before in her life. When her washing and changing were finished, she rang Evelynne to tell her of her happiness. They spoke for thirty minutes.

"That's the right one for you," Evelynne assured her friend. "You've found Mr Right at last, you lucky thing. How wonderful! I want to see him. What do you suggest my pet?"

"Give me a little more time, dear. I seemed so muddled at the moment, but I'll definitely let you know shortly."

"Oh, do. I'll come over shortly, you bet. I have to anyway."

"Oh?" Georgina enquired with interest.

"*Bien entendu* – for the final certification. He can't marry my Georgy without consent and a blessing from me." Georgina's eyes moistened. "He hasn't said anything about marriage. We haven't got as far as that yet," she said, half smiling, half crying.

"Oh, he will, if he's got any sense," Evelynne pronounced with confidence at the other end, "You'll see!"

Georgina and Tom spent a lot of time with each other over the next few weeks. They visited the city jewels of Florence and Siena, revisited Rome, spent a weekend on the coast, and even took a trip to Lago Maggiore and peeped at Switzerland during the hot weeks in August when business was slow at the taxi rank. In all this, they got to know each other pretty well, both mentally and physically. What pleased them both was that they seemed perfectly adapted to each other. Georgina was confident in the knowledge that he didn't just love her for her physical qualities, but treated her as an equal in every particular. She was overjoyed about this. Tom, for his part, was delighted with a partner that could match him in conversation, was educated and had the same sense of humour. They met Georgina's friends, Helen and Jennifer, and also Jean-Luc, with whom Tom got on very well, despite some language difficulty. They returned to Patrick's emporium and spent a very happy afternoon with him and his wife and rehearsed 'old times' that were scarcely four months away. Yet it seemed to them both that they had known each other for years, laughing the sunny hours away. It was just now and then that she wondered again why Tom didn't introduce her to some more of his acquaintances. One day soon she would face him with it, she promised herself. Oh, and yes, they frequently revisited the countryside, loved each other passionately in its folds until one afternoon as October was busy repainting the trees, she whispered, "Why don't we go home to my place? You know, I always feel a little uncomfortable. Someone may come along." Tom smiled at her by way of concession.

"I mean, it's wonderful to shed your clothes in the open air. It's so natural too, but when we come together, I'm not completely relaxed, you know?"

He raised his eyebrows and smiled again, adding nothing, but looking down at her lovingly.

"All right, we'll go to your place. Less breeze," he added as a balmy wind got up to disturb their activities. Georgina laughed lightly. They got up, dressed and left to walk the long mile to the bus stop on the road.

When they finally arrived at the city's centre, Tom excused himself to make a call from a public telephone box, while Georgina stood by waiting a few feet away. Her manner enquired who was on the other end, and he explained that he would probably have to work that night to stand in for a colleague unable to report for duty. "They did mention the possibility," Tom said as they walked along towards the bus that would have taken them to her apartment, obviously disappointed.

"These things happen, "Georgina acquiesced, as he shrugged his shoulders questioningly.

"We'll see each other tomorrow, if you like and if you can," she suggested.

"I sure like, but I'm a bit under pressure at the moment, Gee. 'Twill be all the better when I'm relieved of it."

"Yes, of course," Georgina said sympathetically, but wondered at the same time what might have caused 'pressure'. The fact was, she reflected, he had often been taken up with something else that, despite their eagerness to see each other, had consumed time other than his preoccupation with work. Then she dismissed these thoughts. They had arrived.

"Thank you, darling for a wonderful afternoon," Tom said, taking her in his arms.

"Thank *you*," Georgina said sincerely. "You'll give me a ring then later today or tomorrow morning?"

"Yep," he replied. They kissed. The bus drew up. She boarded and waved. It left and Tom went off to the office of his employer in another part of town. He would just make it, he thought. Tom rang his lady as promised the next day, Sunday, but only to announce that he would be free on the following Friday. Georgina was disappointed, but was obliged to accept the fact. She wondered again, but again passed the matter off.

In the meantime, Georgina looked up her friend Jennifer, enjoyed the day with her, went shopping the next day, phoned Jean-Luc to ask after his welfare and tell him of hers, dined with Helen on Thursday evening, phoned her mother and was told that Patrick would be in Italy 'soon'. She didn't quite know when. And then it was Friday. At last! Tom agreed to come over at 7 pm or thereabouts. "Depends a bit on custom, but I should be able to make it by 7 pm," he assured her.

The doorbell rang at seven 7 pm indeed on the Friday in question and Tom was warmly welcomed and ushered into the cosy, friendly warmth of her apartment. The nights were cooler.

Tom looked round like a man in a museum. "Nice place you've got here, Madame," he said in affected awe, looking at the expensive furnishings and decorations, which Georgina had acquired in setting up a home of good taste and comfort for herself. In this, she had always maintained the principle that her home should be a safe den to which she could retreat after work and close the door on the world. In furnishing this home, she had not considered cost but only quality. This need to get away from work and 'turn everything off' was important for her mental and physical well being and something she treasured. So, from her point of view, Tom was a privileged intruder, as it were.

She had prepared a first-class meal for them both, and this, too, much impressed her guest.

"Heck! That's a feast for the eye and the palate," he exclaimed with genuine appreciation.

"I'm glad you like it," Georgina said with that simple sincerity he so much loved about her. In so much of her presence and her doings there was a naturalness and honesty.

"Well, everything's ready except for the coffee," she said in her uncomplicated way, "so please do sit down, Mr Cullen. Tom seated himself slowly at the table as though at royal invitation. His keen eye admired the cloth, the cutlery and the crockery, assessed the value of these things and admired the polish and precision of its presentation. That same keen eye noted the painting on the wall. "That's a Bruno Lucci, isn't it?" he remarked, not as a question, but in the tone of someone needing confirmation of his observation.

"Don't know," Georgina replied, "I just bought it because I liked it."

"Because you liked it?" This time it was a question.

"Yes, I like portraits; that's why I bought it," this with that same simplicity as though she had said, 'it's raining today.'

"Damned expensive," Tom commented, "Is it genuine?"

"Well, I suppose so. The man at the shop said it was anyway," Georgina said, surprised at his knowledge and interest, and a trifle amused. "I'll bring the soup before it gets cold," and with this she disappeared into the kitchen, returning a moment later with two bowls of soup.

"Just like that," Tom said, continuing the theme and thanking her for the soup. Georgina did not comment on this, but instead asked him if he liked what she had set before him. He nodded enthusiastically between mouthfuls.

"Ginger's not everyone's taste," she said, watching him devour the soup with relish. 'Seems hungry' she noted to herself and was secretly pleased.

"Like some more?" she enquired a moment later, rising to fetch the rest from the pot in the kitchen. As she did so, Tom rose and quickly went over to the painting, briefly inspecting it like a professional art connoisseur before leaping back to his place at table.

"I've been particularly careful about choosing the best ingredients for your vegetarian taste," she said. "I didn't want to bang on the cheese idea, so I've bought some special stuff from an Asian shop in Via Grande. I hope you like my concoction," Georgina ventured.

"Of course I'll like it," Tom said. "If it's anything like the soup, then it'll be five-star."

Georgina ushered in the main dish, and they both set to with gusto. Truth told, it was delicious. After the sweet, Georgina scuttled the dishes into the kitchen sink and, coming into the lounge, turned the record player to soft, background music.

"I'll help with the washing up," Tom obliged, but Georgina held up a hand in protest. "Then I won't know what to do with myself tomorrow," she said jokingly. With that, the two settled into the settee and put their feet up. Georgina had lit a fire an hour or two earlier, which was now burning cheerfully. Hardly two minutes passed before they were in each other's arms, and hardly ten before they were both quite naked.

They made love there in front of the hearth until about 10.30 pm, when the fire in the grate began to wane, but not the fire they had within themselves. Tom had never known Georgina to be so passionate and uninhibited, so much so, that he was a little startled by her ardour. It was clear that she felt much freer to express her feelings than outside, and this only increased his desire for her. They retired to her bedroom then and continued their love-making there until about 1 am. As sometimes happened in the fields, the two of them 'let go' in a huge explosion of semen, joy and relief, but leaving her to wonder again later whether she would be pregnant by him, but this had not been the case, so that she wondered once again whether she was fertile. It troubled her ever so slightly. She wanted a child and she wanted Tom, so that tonight she didn't care anymore about the consequences of his ejaculation and abandoned herself to him completely. Ecstasy overtook them and, a minute of so later, they both fell into the deepest and most delectable of slumbers until dawn touched the rooftops of the town and the first trams began to rattle by outside the window.

Tom was first up and after washing and dressing, and seeing that Georgina was still fast asleep, he took the opportunity to look into the kitchen. Here, too, he admired the quality and cleanliness of its fittings and accessories. Seeing the washing up still in the sink, he then set about washing the dishes of last night's meal. He ran the water, found washing-up liquid and a brush and began placing the pots and cutlery in a container to dry next to the sink. There was still no movement from the bedroom, so he took the opportunity to quietly inspect the other rooms of the apartment where the doors were open. In each he discovered opulence and taste, and then returned to the lounge where he pulled up the blinds and looked out into the street below, unsure of what to do next. Then he decided to return to the bedroom where he found

Georgina still sound asleep. He looked long at her, and felt suddenly uncomfortable. He would not wake her; that would somehow be wrong, and yet he didn't want to stay in the apartment where he felt himself to be something of a ghost. He considered for a moment. Then, finding a piece of paper and a pencil in the hall, he sat down in the lounge and wrote a short note:

> Dearest Gina,
>
> I didn't want to wake you, dear, so I've left to get to work on time. Will ring later.
>
> With a big hug and lots of love,
> Tom.

He placed this on the bed next to her and tiptoed out into the hall, unlocked the front door and welcomed the sunlight of the morning. Once on the pavement, he was assailed by the thought that he should have woken her. Somehow, it seemed mean, and yet leaving like this gave him the chance to think. He needed to think. Walking along in the early sunshine, he wondered how Georgina had come to live so luxuriously and was troubled. 'Did she really own all this?' he asked himself, and if so, how did she come into so much wealth at her age? He knew that an original Lucci would cost at least a couple of hundred thousand lire today, and there it was on the wall of her apartment as though it were a barometer or something. He thought, too, of the bedroom where everything was of the very finest, and in thinking of this, he was disturbed by the reminiscence of her total abandon during their lovemaking. There was something professional in it, he convinced himself. It was deeply disturbing. On the one hand, he welcomed her lack of restraint. He had been totally committed to her; that was sure. But was she just playing a professional game? Perhaps he was being grossly unfair. He shunned the idea as he walked on. No, Georgina was genuine. He was prejudiced, just giving way to an unfounded suspicion, but then… What if his suspicions were justified? What if she had been a prostitute up to the time she met him? How would he react then?

He reached home to find Felipe brushing the yard outside.

"Ah, there you are!" he announced meaninglessly.

"Looks like it," Tom said. He looked up, noting Tom's manner.

"What's up, mate?"

"Oh, nothing."

"Didn't go well, then, last night?" he enquired. Felipe was an understanding person and was not given to probing, On receiving no answer and no further development of the theme, he remained silent. Ten minutes passed. Tom made himself a cup of tea and sat down at the plain wooden table in the kitchen. He sipped the hot tea and pensively watched Felipe continue working. After a further minute or so of committed activity with his broom, Filipe put it in its corner and sat by Tom at the table.

"Er," he gurgled.

Tom looked up.

"Was talking to Franco-bear yesterday, and he told me he'd seen you a few days ago with what he described as a 'film star'.

Tom sat unmoved. After a longish pause, Felipe cranked up the conversation again. "I'm sorry, lad," he said,"seems to have gone wrong. Eh?"

Tom looked at Felipe squarely. Over the years of living in close association with Felipe he had learned to respect his flatmate. Outwardly, Felipe was a cynic. His observations were pithy and to the point. Moreover, he was a very good judge of character (and not only in assessment). A scornful remark from his direction could be truly annihilating, and all those who knew him feared his tongue, but Tom had come to know this as hard shell round a compassionate core and valued the man's humanity and integrity.

"Ugh," Tom said, taking a swig at the tea, which seemed to soothe his nerves just at this moment. Felipe waited patiently, and brushed the breakfast crumbs from his bright-red pullover. Then Tom opened up again, "Yes, last night I was at her place in via Carlo Torre."

"Wow, man, you're rocketing to stardom," Felipe remarked. Having worked as a taxi driver himself, Felipe knew exactly where the street was.

"Yeah, nice place." There was another short pause.

"What happened?" Felipe asked.

"Nothing really," Tom replied

"Now I'm not going for that one, lad. There was a crisis, don't tell me."

"Well, yes and no. She's great, but I'm a bit concerned."

"About what?" Felipe pursued.

"It's tricky, mate; I don't know really what to say," Tom stumbled on.

Felipe had plenty of patience. He waited.

"It's just that I've got an awful feeling."

"About what, feller?" Felipe was much older than Tom and could allow himself various familiar appellations of this sort.

"Nice as she is, I think she's spent her life as a prostitute."

"Get away. You're kidding?"

"I hope I'm kidding, but I've got a funny feeling," Tom added.

Felipe was quiet for a moment. "What makes you suspect her of that?"

There was another pause while Tom collected his thoughts and tried at the same time to be as objective as possible.

"Well, I'm wondering where she amassed all the wealth she has. Her apartment is a veritable treasure house and I reckon I came across a real Bruno Lucci hanging on the wall there."

"Christ!"

"But apart from that, she seems to have endless amounts of money."

"You must introduce me," Felipe said, raising his eyebrows.

"OK, OK, but she's only twenty-seven," Tom went on, ignoring the remark.

"Perhaps she's inherited a lot, who knows?" Felipe suggested.

"Could be," Tom agreed.

"And then…"

"Then what?"

"She was so uninhibited last night; I began to wonder."

"Whether she isn't a professional you mean?" Felipe ventured.

"Well, God, I hope not." Tom felt miserable. "Damn!"

"Maybe she was at one time and has now retired," Felipe suggested, "That could be the case. The girls picking up wealthy businessmen outside the Star and Meridian Hotels must be getting quite a screw – if you see what I mean?" he added mischievously.

"I'm not amused," Tom said with a glare at his companion.

"I know, I know, but you need a bit more proof than what you've told me in the last few minutes," Felipe concluded firmly.

"Yes, you're right – and I love the woman. Hell! What a

bloody rotten situation!" Tom declared, throwing his empty cup into the sink.

Tom did not ring Georgina back as he had promised and not three days had passed when he happened to deposit a customer outside the five-star Meridian in the town centre, and while negotiating the change for this passenger who should he see but Georgina warmly greeting a young man in front of the doors of the hotel and then proceed with him into the hotel, She was obviously very happy. Tom boiled within, and wondered whether he should get out and accost her, but the hooting, tooting traffic situation at that very moment outside the hotel was extremely cramped and he was obliged to move off. However, he managed to park the taxi awkwardly in a side street nearby and retraced his way back to the hotel where he looked around the lobby for Georgina. Neither she nor the young man were to be seen. Tom was shattered, but both duty and his outrageous parking manoeuvre strongly urged him not to look further. He left the hotel with an appalling conviction. Horrified, he returned to the taxi.

"Two-three-two, two-three-two come in!" Tom switched in. "Where the hell have you been?" a crackling voice demanded over the intercom as he positioned himself into the driver's seat.

"Trouble with a customer," he replied into the mouthpiece.

"OK, but come over here. Three customers for Albino Park. Make it snappy!"

With a heavy heart and his mind elsewhere, Tom drove to the taxi station and picked up three people and accordingly steered his vehicle in the direction of the park.

Georgina awoke, found the note and waited for his call. After three or four hours, she called the only number she had, his cab number, but for some reason she didn't get through. Subsequently, she looked up the taxi station number and the manager there informed her personally that Tom had reported for work and that as far as he was aware, he was hale and hearty. In the evening she tried to contact him again, but was told that he had gone off duty. Could he relay a message?

"Er, no, don't bother," Georgina said and replaced the receiver. The following hours were a torment, but she decided there and then not to contact him again. The ball was clearly in his court. At 11 pm she rang Helen and explained the situation.

"Heck, that's odd," Helen declared in her husky voice at the other end.

"There was no row between you, then?"

"No, not at all. The only thing I noticed is that he felt a bit… how shall I say, out of his depth," Georgina explained.

"How? Out of his depth?"

"Well, he looked around the place as if he were in a royal palace or something."

"Umm, odd." Helen breathed, clearly trying hard to grasp the affair at a distance.

"Do ye wanna come over, my love?"

"It's 11.15 pm, Helen, I don't want to put upon you at this time of night, but can you make head or tail of this very odd behaviour?"

"Damned if I can. Men are funny creatures sometimes; I know that. Different wiring. But I had the firm conviction when I saw him that he loved you very much and that both of you were happy," Helen said with conviction.

"Well, I don't know what to say now," Georgina replied. It was true that Helen could not fathom what had happened and agreed to talk to Georgina about the problem the next day over lunch.

"Yeah, Franco brought this along today, Tom, lad. Hope it doesn't fit, but I thought you would like to know, should it be 'applicable', if you see what I mean." By this time, four days had elapsed since their last conversation. Tom took the glossy front cover of a magazine Felipe offered him. Tom scrutinised it for a full minute without uttering a word. Then he let the paper fall onto the kitchen floor and collapsed into a chair. Felipe retrieved the sheet and held it before him.

"It's her, that's for sure," Tom said hopelessly.

Felipe looked again at the photo, "You sure?" he asked seriously.

"Yep, that's her all right. I know the curve of her neck and her breasts, the way the hair meets the forehead and where. The legs and feet are exactly hers as well. No doubt about it. No doubt at all."

Felipe, for reasons we'll learn of later, made no objection to Tom's certainty, and put the offending photo back onto the table and said, "Shit, man, that's tough. I'm sorry about that. I really am." Tom just looked at him. There was a long, long silence between them before Felipe tentatively suggested they eat something before he went to the gym. "Come with me, Tom," he said, "I'd feel better if you were around and not on your own."

"What would I do there, mate? I'll be OK, don't worry and I have to stand in again at midnight anyway," Tom said.

"Somebody else ill?" Felipe enquired.

"No, not this time, the bloke gets married tomorrow."

"OK, then we'll have a snack and I'll go off, if you feel all right?"

"I'll be all right, thanks," Tom assured his friend. At 8 am Felipe had gone.

"I'd be inclined to find out where he lives and talk to him directly. There's more in this than meets the eye," Helen assured her friend, "It's not normal. There's no rhyme or reason in it, unless, of course, he's mental," Helen continued. To this, Georgina smiled wanly. "He seemed to be OK to me," she replied.

"Sure, I'm only kidding, but it's very peculiar if you ask me. 'Irrational' is the only word that keeps popping up in my mind, girl. It's just mad."

"But it is as it is," Georgina corrected her, "mad or not."

"Righty, then I'll find out where the gentleman lives and you must summon up enough nerve to make the trip into the lion's den. We don't want to go on like this, living in the dark. The darned thing needs clearing up. You deserve to know. You've a right to know." Helen's hackles were up.

But before a visit could be arranged, it was Tom's fate to see his beloved again, this time in front of another hotel in the company of another man, someone he vaguely remembered from some party or other. He observed the two carefully from the relative security of his cab. They were obviously on the best of terms. That much was clear from their amicable gestures. This couple, too, passed into the sheltered portals of the hotel lobby. Tom was simply enraged on this occasion and jerked his cab to the right, away from the scene as soon as possible. What further proof of her infidelity did he need? These accidental glimpses of her were a godsend, he affirmed to himself real, indubitable, yet sad evidence that she was a whore. In that moment he hated her.

The phone rang. "He lives in Vicolo Lavandai," Helen said loudly, without introducing herself. "I'm quite certain. Number twelve. Ground level. Do you want me to come with you?"

"Yes, something might go wrong and I don't want to be

in a district like that if it does," Georgina replied, "Suggest you keep at a safe distance, but be near."

"Okey-dokey," Helen agreed. "We'll go tomorrow in the afternoon around four. He'll probably be off duty then."

"Good, that's that settled. We can go together on my Vespa. I'll call for you."

"Wow!" Helen said, "Now that'll be just swell!"

And so it was. Under Helen's direction, Georgina drove down narrow lanes until they came to No 12. Both women had dressed simply, so as not to attract attention. Georgina wore a headscarf into the bargain. While Helen kept the rearguard, Georgina knocked on the simple door. This was answered by Felipe, cool as the lettuce he held in his dripping fingers.

"Does a Signore Cullen live here?," Georgina asked bluntly. She was a little unsure of the reaction she would receive.

"Yes," Felipe replied, "but he's not at home at the moment. Work." Georgina noticed a neighbour staring from a window out of the corner of her eye. She and Felipe stood for a moment opposite each other, neither knowing exactly what next to say to each other. Then Georgina: "What time is he likely to be home, do you think?"

"About 6 pm. Why don't you come in for a moment?" Felipe said, recognising his opposite number instantly. Georgina hesitated, looked in the direction where she had left Helen, but could not discern her just at that moment. "Do come in and sit down," Felipe said civilly, "I can make us a cup of tea if you like." Georgina hesitated again. "Do, please," Felipe urged gently. Georgina entered.

"It's not much of a place, I own, but we manage quite well," Felipe commented when Georgina had accepted a seat at the bare table. She felt uneasy and looked around circumspectly. 'What a dump!' she thought to herself and her heart sank in contemplating the modesty of the place while Felipe rattled with things in the kitchen. 'At least it's clean,' she noted as she waited nervously.

"There we are," Filipe said as he placed a chipped cup of tea in front of her, taking another for himself and sitting down. The two were silent as they sipped the hot water, and Georgina vaguely wondered where Helen was at that instant. And again, Georgina didn't know what to say to this womanly man beside her, and now she felt even more insecure. Felipe came to the rescue.

"I hope you don't mind my asking, but can it be that you are Tom's lady?" he said, coming straight to the point.

Georgina nodded. "You're as beautiful as he said you were," Felipe noted with a friendly smile. "Pity things don't seem to have turned out right recently, but pardon my observation. I don't want to be nosey. I just feel sorry, that's all." Now Felipe, apart from his other virtues, had another attribute. He had an artless manner that intrigued others when he talked to them, so simple and honest was this way of his that Georgina found herself all too ready then to divulge more of her errand.

"Thank you," she said, "Yes, and I don't know why he's jilted me," she said forthrightly, surprising herself in so saying. Felipe looked earnest. "Well, I don't know for sure either," he said honestly, "I must let the two of you talk about that, my dear." They continued to sip their tea and when they had finished, Felipe stood up and said ceremoniously, "Well, dear lady, I could show you round the premises. To our right we have our sleeping quarters and the bed in which, it is said, that Napoleon Bonaparte slept during his siege of the city in the year 1798, a room which, incidentally, also serves as the morning room of a distinguished artist dwelling in this city," and he pointed to two mattresses covered with carelessly spread bedding lying on the floor at either end of the room, a plain wicker chair and in one corner an easel surrounded by a great many brushes, rags and painting materials together with small pots of paint. Small plates and saucers used for mixing paint littered the room. A stack of paintings stuffed into a primitive rack near the wall was the only other item lit by the afternoon sun above them. Georgina wept.

Felipe had taken one recent drawing from a pile to show his guest, but when he stood up and turned towards Georgina, he saw that her eyes were already filled with tears. Sobbing, she sat down on the one and only chair in the room. As she did so there was a gentle knock at the kitchen door. Helen had come to enquire about the welfare of her friend. "Do come in," Felipe said kindly, opening the door to the street, "Your friend is here," and he pointed to the entrance to the second room. Helen's shiny high heels clicked over the rough boards of the room, "Whatever's the matter?" she asked, leaning over Georgina, at first suspecting foul play. "It's all right; it's all right," Georgina said, blowing her nose. Helen looked round her and immediately understood.

"Oh God," she said quietly.

Felipe had followed her and was looking on like a confused child, clearly embarrassed, the pictures still in his hand. Inappropriately, he asked the newcomer whether she would like a cup of tea. Helen shook her head without saying anything. It was then that Georgina asked her host if she might look at the work he had in his hands. She dried her eyes and looked in wonderment at the first, a landscape sketch and the other depicting what must have been a street scene of the locality in front of the door. With tact and gentleness, Felipe showed her others. There were a few nude pencil sketches of himself, for which Felipe self-consciously excused himself, and at this Georgina couldn't help smiling through her tears at Felipe's girlish manner. Helen, too, had to laugh. "Er, two against one," he said, referring to them both, and hurriedly found another painting of a cardinal or some other prince of the church against a dark, ecclesiastic background.

"But that's brilliant!" Georgina exclaimed. "And the others are good, too!"

"Well, I did say that we had a distinguished artist in the family, didn't I?" Felipe maintained, for a moment quite naturally exhibiting that feminine manner of his, which then made both women laugh. Minutes passed while Georgina and Helen looked at other drawings and paintings in the rack, before they returned to the kitchen.

"I don't know when he'll be back," Felipe said for a second time that afternoon, and the girls took this as a signal to leave. "That's all right," Georgina said, "You've been very kind, Signore Filipe, thank you very much. Please let Tom know that we were here."

"Of course, of course," Filipe replied, "I'll tell him and I hope that everything'll be OK with you two. Oh hell. Please take care. He's a bit of a Caravaggio, you know." They didn't know. The pair walked towards the parked scooter, which was in the process of being admired by about six young children. As the women appeared, one of these urchins blatantly proclaimed, "Coo! Look! She's as black as coal!" Helen and Georgina mounted the little scooter which was navigated down the shaded, narrow ways and out onto the main highway back home.

"Depressing wasn't it?" Helen said as they parked outside Georgina's home.

Georgina was near to tears again, and Helen put her arms around her friend's shoulders. "Let's go up," Georgina said, and they turned to the steps leading to the front door. Once inside, tea was suggested. "I guess we need something a bit stronger than that," Helen said.

Whiskey was brought on to the low table in the lounge and the friends sat without saying anything, staring into the empty fireplace. Finally, Georgina spoke up:"That's why he never asked me to his place, but I wouldn't have minded. I love him."

"Sure. I know what you mean."

"And those paintings. They were good, weren't they?"

"Just great, kiddie," Helen agreed. "Now you know what he did with his spare time?"

"Yes, I almost suspected him of cavorting with someone else at one moment," Georgina admitted. "How absurd!" There was a pause.

"Felipe's a nice guy, isn't he?"

"Yeah, he's a genuine guy. I like him."

"So do I."

Tom's reaction to the women's visit three hours later was furious.

"Why did you let them in, you fool!" Tom roared.

"Do you think I'd receive them on the street and everyone learns of your business there, ugh? They'd just *love* that!" Felipe retorted.

"You had no right to let them in, you idiot!"

"And don't call me an idiot. Whose place is it then? And look in the fucking mirror if you want to see a fool!" Felipe almost spat the words.

"You shit head!" Tom shouted and turned to walk into the other room. It must have been about 8 pm.

"Hey" you cretin! Did you show them my work, you bastard?"

Felipe said nothing to this. He was very annoyed himself and turned to the sink where he mindlessly toyed with the cups and plates waiting to be washed up. He could hear a determined rustling next door. Shaking his hands, and briefly wiping them on a towel, he went into the other room where he discovered Tom raging through his pictures and systematically destroying them.

"Hey! What the fuck? Are you out of your mind?"

Now it's a strange thing in this life, but sometimes events take on an unsuspected pattern that might suggest there's sense in it all, for at that very moment Franco the Strong happened to knock on the door. As was his custom, this knock was merely a courteous formality before marching in.

He heard the scuffle next door as Felipe grasped Tom's shirt collar like a sack of potatoes and flung him backwards. Felipe was older but strong. Tom was strong, too, but smaller but, unlike Felipe, out of training. And there, suddenly, was Franco happily in the fracas with a placed punch here and a vicious dig there, coming to the aid of his fellow gymnast. In seconds Tom was pinned to the floor. If the truth were told, Felipe disliked physical violence, and he was glad when Franco had managed by sheer brute force to control the situation.

"MARCO!" Felipe thundered up the stairs. "Marco! Come!" His neighbour was by his side in seconds. Others followed.

"Tom's gone stark raving. We need your help." They went inside the 'morning room' to find Franco blithely sitting on Tom, awaiting further instruction. Filipe gestured that the game was over and he could stand again. Tom unrolled and stood up himself, rubbing his ribs where Franco had landed one or two of his punches and all four men went into the kitchen. Tom took the chair and buried his face in his hands while the others sat around on the floor.

"Tea? No, I don't want bloody tea, what are you thinking of?" Franco said loudly in reply to Filipe's invitation. "What we need is a good swig of grappa. All of us. Does the soul good. Surely you've got a drop somewhere in this hole?" he asked, looking round for confirmation among those assembled. There was general agreement on this suggestion, and Felipe went to a cupboard and brought forth a green flask, and poured the liquid into various cups and glasses, since by this time there were about ten people in the room, some standing, some sitting. Only Tom was excluded. He continued to look at the floor between his knees, head in his hands, and no one felt the need to disturb him. "Let's drink to more harmony in this place!" said Franco in the manner of a man about to lead his army once more into the battle. They lifted their different vessels to this and gulped down the clear, fiery liquid.

It was 11.30 pm before the last of the coterie dispersed.

Two days after this episode, the phone summoned Georgina's attention as she was dusting her bookshelves.

"Why did you come?" the voice on the other end stormed without introduction. It was Tom Cullen.

"Oh Tom! At last! What's wrong?" Georgina cried.

"Why did you come over to Lavandai?" he asked strictly.

"I came over, because you didn't contact me and I wondered what had happened," Georgina replied.

"You rummaged through my stuff, too. That's illegal entry and no business of yours," he went on coldly. Georgina stiffened.

"I was asked in," she said soberly. "And I noticed the pictures and drawings myself. Filipe was kind enough to show me them."

"You didn't have my permission."

"No, that's true. I'm sorry," Georgina replied with dignity, "but they're wonderful."

"That's none of your damn business!" Tom shouted.

"I'm sorry. I just wanted to find you, that's all, dear," Georgina said quietly.

"Well, you can leave me alone and go and fish for a man outside the Meridian!" Tom retorted and slammed down the receiver.

Georgina slumped into a chair. What could he mean?, She asked herself over and over again. Meridian? Because it was impossible for her to ring him back and demand an answer, she was obliged to think hard and reconstruct what she knew of the Meridian Hotel. Eventually, she cottoned on to the fact that she had once met her brother there and that they had gone inside together for a drink. Could he be implying that she worked outside on the pavement as a prostitute? The idea was abhorrent. Is that what he thought her capable of? Is that what he thought of her? The very idea! 'He must be out of his mind,' she concluded, and wept tears of sorrow and horror. How heartless he had been to her over the phone! She collapsed into despair and ate nothing for the next two days. That was in mid-September. In the next month she knew for sure that she was pregnant. She rang her mother.

"I think you should come home, dear," her mother advised. "You will need someone's help and guidance." On the one hand, Georgina was happy to be with child; on the other, the circumstances were not, to put it mildly, very propitious. It depressed her to realise that now she would have to capitulate and return home after all these wonderful years abroad, but more than anything else in this sad season was the realisation that the child would have no father. As she thought of these things, she rued the hour that had prompted her to make love with Tom on the very day she knew she was fertile. She had only herself to blame. This reflection did nothing to improve her state of mind.

The months passed. Tom spent more and more time with Andy Brennan at King Edward's pub in the scrubby end of the town, where he deliberately went to eat these days, seeing Felipe only on occasion or in passing during his shifts. Felipe was a well-balanced individual and not given to bearing malice. Things were cool between the men, Tom being convinced that Felipe had betrayed him, and Felipe convinced that Tom had made the mistake of his life. They moved about their small apartment when together like two pious monks.

One evening in December found them both over a mutual meal of spaghetti. It was cold outside and the cold air breathed below their simple kitchen door. The spaghetti was especially good, and Tom said as much.

"Good. I'm glad you like it. I think I've found a shop where I can regularly buy this brand. I've got a good bottle of wine here, too, which I can vouch for," Felipe announced. They drank. To be sure, it was of the very best.

"Umm," said Tom, "goes down well with the spaghetti. Have you got a sweet by any chance?"

"Well, as it happens, my boy, I have."

Tom always had to smile at Filipe's father-like condescension, and he enjoyed what followed.

"Shall we go out for a pint?" Tom asked to Felipe's considerable surprise. "We can go and see your crony at King Edward's if you like." Felipe and Andy Brennan were the closest of friends, and he did like.

They took the half-mile walk from where they lived. "We needn't lock up; Marco will look after any folks that might drop by," Felipe muttered as he closed the door of their modest dwelling.

The King Edward was warm and inviting after the cool winter air of their walk, and they settled down opposite each other in one of the cosy booths that particular tavern boasted.

"What ye havin', mate," Felipe asked. "This is on me."

"Oh, don't mind if I do," Tom laughed, pleasantly remembering the old days in his hometown with a wisp of homesickness. They sipped their cool beer in the warmth of the bar and talked of a dozen things. Finally, Felipe, swallowing his third, belched gently, and wiping his lips, said, "Look, mate, I'm sorry about what happened a couple of weeks ago, I really am."

"And I know you're sorry," Tom replied. "I'm sorry about the whole fucking show." Felipe nodded. Silence for half a minute, then, "I reckon the whole business was damn sad, if you ask me," Tom continued. The beer had created the excellent effect of bestowing peace and mildness of disposition on these protagonists.

"You know something, feller?" Felipe asked suddenly.

"No, what?" said Tom with faint interest.

"There's two ways to get here."

"Now fancy that," returned the other, ready for a lark.

"Yes, two paths."

"You're not kidding," Tom countered.

"No, be serious for a minute, mate. Two ways to reach my friend Andy's."

"OK, so what?"

"Well, I always take the other one than what we took tonight."

"Oh, can you give me chapter and verse on that?" Tom enquired playfully. Felipe ignored the remark.

"I take the one that's a stone's throw from the Meridian, you see. "

"So what?"

"Well, Andy and me see each other every couple of days or so, you know that." Tom nodded.

"And?" he probed.

"Well, mate, I've never seen your queen selling herself out there. Never. And I know 'em all by sight and some of 'em to talk to."

Tom fell silent. For a moment, Felipe anticipated a row. Indeed, he was ready for it, but Tom simply sat there, fingering his mug and looking out of the window at the winter's leafless trees. For his part, Felipe thought it best to leave his observation at this point and wait for a reaction from his comrade. There followed a long, quiet but comfortable interval between them. Felipe downed his fourth glass, gasped and ordered another. He was a quarter way through this when, to his surprise, Tom said in a small voice, "OK, I may be wrong." Felipe just looked at his friend for a long time, then he said, "Yes, matey, I think you were. And *are*."

"She's no pro, my friend," Felipe went on. "She's a good one. Not that the other gals are bad. I don't mean that, but I knew the moment I set eyes on her. She's of gold. And both ladies had the best of manners. That counts with me. They weren't acting it out either. They were genuine. I know." For Felipe, this was quite a lot to say, and he waited for a reaction from his fellow boozer.

It was soon evident to him that Tom was at that moment under great stress. His partner looked up hopelessly, saying nothing. Andy Brendan refilled their glasses. "That'll have to be the last, good friend," Felipe warned, "otherwise I'll have to go home on all fours!" Brendan grinned.

Felipe waited a long time before he uttered anything else that he could consider sensible in his present state, and seeing Tom so downcast, he finally hazarded. "It ain't too late, Tom. Tell the lady you love her and that everything was an appalling cock-up. She'll understand. You'll have to do your homework, though, my lad and be ready for some resistance after all she's been through."

"Me, too," Tom added miserably.

"Sure."

Around 11 pm they rose with difficulty from their places and stumbled towards the door and into the cool night.

Tom chewed on Felipe's good advice and another week passed before he could overcome his ego and summon enough courage to make a visit to Georgina without prior warning. In the end, with great self-control, he managed to spruce himself up in a new suit, buy a huge bunch of flowers, rehearse what he was going to say with Felipe and set off on the first day of February in a cool, sobering breeze which helped him clear his head.

He had ascended the steps, rang the bell, and Signora Trasti, a large, gentle woman of broad bust and kindly eye, opened the door. Tom, surprised by her appearance, enquired whether Georgina was at home.

"Oh, Signora 'Ennessy has been gone a month," she assured Tom, as he stood there limply.

"Gone?"

"Yes, she' gone home to England. The place here is empty, Signore. Sorry."

Tom dropped the flowers and stood there like an imbecile, unable to say a word. The woman picked up the bruised flowers and remarked on their beauty, adding as she did so, that she was terribly sorry to have reported bad news. He merely nodded, and, broken-hearted, retraced his steps towards the road. "Oh God!" he said as he walked along aimlessly under the cloudless sky. "Oh God!" Later that day, Tom wrote a letter to Georgina, which contained everything his heart wanted to express, and hoped it would be forwarded, but it was never answered.

In the weeks that followed, Felipe and even Franco were a great support to their friend, and very slowly Tom recovered enough to accept the new situation and curse his own suspicions. After a much longer time still, he went back to his painting in his free time, and when the flowers were a riot in the plant pots that hung in the sun at every window in that modest alley, he decided one bright morning that he needed to replenish several colours. Accordingly, he informed his flatmate that he'd be away for a while in the town.

"Great, man; I've got enough to do to clean this place," Felipe replied.

Tom set off for the bus stop. For some reason today, Georgina didn't cross his mind. He was preoccupied with the subject he wanted to convey to the canvas, nearly missed his bus, dropped in at the shop, made his purchases, had a word or two with the owner, narrowly missed being run over on carelessly crossing a main road and, realising that the bus home would not be due for another thirty minutes, decided to drink a cup of coffee before returning. On his way to this particular bistro near the cathedral, he saw Helen, and wondered for a moment whether he should greet her, as he had not seen this lady in the months that had followed their visit to Vicolo della Landavai. For seconds his mind raced as Helen's tall, queenly figure moved in the crowd. Then, without further mental debate, he made for the figure.

Catching up with her at last, he said, "Hey, Helen!" Helen turned and paused.

"Oh, Hi," she said with her large, toothed, red smile. "How ye doin'?" she asked cordially. "I just spotted you in the distance," Tom said, a little breathless from his sprint to catch up with her. "Yeah, I'm not easily overlooked," Helen replied mischievously. Tom laughed at this. "That's wonderful!" he replied, delighted with her answer. "Come, let's sit down for a coffee, it's a while since I've seen you."

"OK," Helen complied, drawing out the last syllable of the word in an American intonation, which for other English speakers suggested final conviction after some consideration. They soon found a place and settled themselves at a small, round table outside.

"You look ravishing!" Tom said with enthusiasm.

"Thank you, sir," Helen returned happily, "and how are you these days?"

"Life goes on; no great events," Tom said evenly. Helen nodded. Under the incredible wealth of deep-black hair, there was a remarkably keen mind and flashing eyes that never missed a nuance, however slight.

"You seem to have recovered," she said, coming straight to the point and knowing that she would be understood, hoping, too, that she would not open old wounds.

"Ugh, I'll never recover from that," he said conclusively.

"Yeah, bad time for you both." The coffee arrived. Helen was also wise. She made up her mind then and there not to mention that Georgina was to have a baby. Tom, for his part, noticed that Helen's movements were superbly relaxed and economical, that his opposite number was exquisitely well groomed. Every part of the woman reflected good taste and care.

"I don't know how our mutual friend is faring," she said tactfully, aware of the fact that Tom would be interested. "I'm hoping for a letter any day now."

"Would you do something for me?" Tom asked, looking at her squarely.

Helen nodded again. She anticipated what it was that her counterpart wanted. "Would you send her a letter from me? The other one never got there. Perhaps she never received it."

"Possibly." Helen agreed. "These things happen."

"Or she just didn't want to reply… ?" Tom ventured.

"I really don't know, Tom. I can't help you, as I don't know much myself."

Tom looked glum. "Anyway, I'll be glad to send on the letter you want to write," Helen said.

"You're an angel," Tom said.

"A black angel, now that's something new," she countered with a laugh that showed her superbly white teeth again. Tom smiled coyly. Helen rummaged in her handbag. "Here, it's on this card. Just send the letter in another envelope and I'll send yours on. Promise."

"Thanks a million, Helen," Tom said jubilantly. Helen laughed. '*Oh what fools these mortals are!*' she declared, quoting Shakespeare. Tom understood, smiled to himself, paid and they took their leave of each other. "Gotta a lot to do this morning, my friend," Helen said as she squeezed her way out of the closely set tables. "See ya!"

"God bless," Tom said and they went their separate ways, Tom forgetting his paints, and having to return to collect them. He missed his bus, but didn't care for that. He would walk home and write the letter this very afternoon. The next day, he did write the letter and, as he had been arranged with Helen, placed it in a larger envelope and posted this to her.

Dearest Georgy,

I don't know whether you received my last letter written some months ago, and I can only hope that you will receive this one day. There are only three things I want to say: I am deeply sorry that I caused you so much pain and sadness, that I'm to blame for everything and that I still love you. I cannot hope for forgiveness, but I do think it is my responsibility to make things clear to you and to admit my folly. I am so very sorry about it.

I trust that you are well and happy,

With all my love,
Tom

The letter remained unanswered. Anticipation waned over the weeks to disappointment and finally to forgetfulness.

# 8

## *Intervention*

Now Dr Sulla was a man of considerable discretion as I have already suggested. His actions, like his views, were well considered, his manner tactful and considerate of the feelings of others, his judgement on matters generally one of unerring perception and accuracy. Moreover, he was well liked and respected by all those who came into contact with him, a man appreciated for his humanity and an urbane frankness tinged with humour. As a rule, he was to be found moving in the higher administrative and cultural circles of the city to which he was usually conveyed by chauffeured vehicle, so that it was a strange sight to see him now on this Wednesday morning walking alone in an impeccable light blue suit along Milan's 'washing street' at ten o'clock in the forenoon of the 14th of September. Folks peered from their small windows through the hanging washing between their respective residences and wondered what such a toff was doing in their quarters. But Dr Sulla, discreet and well-prepared as ever, knew in which house he would be likely to find the person he wished to meet. He had already rung the central taxi station to ascertain whether he could expect to meet Tom in his lair. Locating house number twelve, his manicured brown hand knocked on the door. Felipe responded.

Sulla, a trifle surprised not to find Tom answering the door, hesitated. "Er, is Mr Cullen at home?" he enquired.

"Just a sec," Felipe said and retreated nimbly into the kitchen. "Tom! Gent for you at the door." Tom appeared in his smock and with paint-smeared hands. He recognised the man at the door immediately. "Doctor, er," he stuttered.

"Sulla. Good morning, Mr Cullen. I hope you'll forgive my sudden appearance like this, but not knowing quite how I could otherwise contact you, I decided to run the gauntlet as it were and look you up personally." Neighbours stared and listened.

"Sure, Dr Sulla, come in and I'm sorry you find me ill-prepared for your visit. This is my roommate, Signore Brasa." Sulla nodded politely in Felipe's direction.

"Well, Mr Cullen. First of all, I have to crave your indulgence for simply dropping in on you like this. Not very mannerly, I know. The fact is, I did try to contact you at Busoni's taxi central, but they were very discreet and refused to divulge your address, which, I must admit, was wise. One never knows these days."

"Well, well," Tom said, removing his smock and proffering his dirty hand, which Sulla received warmly. "Then how did you manage to find me?"

Dr Sulla hesitated before saying, "Well, do forgive me for not answering that question directly, Mr Cullen, but there are ways, you understand. I do apologise." Tom was puzzled, smiled at this, and offered his guest a cup of tea that had just been brewed. Dr Sulla took the browned mug in his hand and looked around for somewhere to sit. Felipe seized the one chair and placed it for Dr Sulla to sit on, winking wickedly at Tom as he did so. Sulla sipped the hot tea and looked at Tom over the rim of the mug.

"You will wonder why I'm here, of course?"

"Well, yes, I'm honoured by your visit. Is there anything I can do for you, Dr Sulla?"

"Yes there is, but first let us enjoy our tea together. It's a wonderful morning, is it not? But I do believe that the leaves on the trees are turning colour. Have you noticed it?"

"Indeed I have," Tom acquiesced. His artist's eye never missed anything.

They talked thus for the next fifteen minutes when, without advanced allusion, he came straight to the point.

"I understand I'm in the presence of an artist of considerable acumen?"

"I don't know about that," Tom said self-effacingly, laughing away the title with a gesture of disdain.

"Oh yes he is," Felipe cut in, "Please come and see for yourself," and so saying, he indicated the neighbouring room. Sulla rose, returned the mug to the table and followed Felipe into the room next door, Tom hanging behind.

"I take it that these are they?" Dr Sulla suggested, indicating the pile of work crammed into the rack, looking at Tom as he did so. Tom nodded and came forward to select a few that might interest their guest. Sulla looked at the first two or three, holding them in front of him for inspection silently and critically.

"Ah yes," he said slowly, reviewing one painting after another and now and again umming and ahhing with apparent satisfaction. "Can you also show me a portrait or two, young man?" he asked after a few minutes of further investigation. Tom obliged, rustling through his work and handing irrelevant creations to Felipe to hold for the time being.

"Now this one is interesting!" their guest pronounced,

almost with a cry of triumph, holding up the picture of an old woman sitting in front of her house decorated with geraniums at a window. "That's what I want!" he said.

"And this," he added, holding up the painting of a warrior on a chariot drawn by two wild looking horses. "Would you be willing to exhibit these two at least on 14th October at the Museo della Arte?" Sulla asked, his clear blue eyes alight with interest.

"Oh sure," Tom said, "of course."

"Good, then you will have to contact the procurator there, Herr Simones. I'll inform him of my visit, and he will arrange the details with you. If there are any other matters that may arise, contact me through him." He paused to allow Tom to add something himself, and seeing there was nothing to add, smiled kindly and said, "Well, I think it's time for me to go. There's a lot to do today, and to tell the truth, that's why I descended upon you so early," and turned towards the door. "Just one moment, please," Tom interjected. "May I ask you, sir, how you came upon my name?"

Sulla turned. "Oh yes, I should have mentioned this right at the outset. I do apologise. The recommendation came from an acquaintance of mine. More I cannot say, you understand? One must be discreet in these matters." Tom looked dumbfounded. Seeing this, Sulla continued, "There is also the fact that your name is on the lists of those who studied here in the fifties and also the fact that you exhibited some of your work at the La Gata Studio some years ago."

"Oh that," Tom said, the wind taken out of his sails for a moment. "I'd completely forgotten about that."

"Well, you see, institutions don't forget," Dr Sulla replied, waving a finger in mock admonition. Felipe opened the door for their visitor, and the figure in the immaculately blue suit, shiny black shoes and tie stepped into the road.

"Thank you for the tea," he said, waved and set off. People looked as he leisurely walked along the sun-soaked alley toward the waiting limousine about a hundred yards away.

"Well, fancy that!" Felipe exclaimed as they retreated into the kitchen.

"Like some kind of dream," Tom concurred, "but who could have recommended me?" Tom asked the roommate.

"There could only be one person if you ask me," Felipe guessed, "your friend Georgy, mate."

"But she didn't even answer my letters."

"Umm," Felipe murmured.

The next few weeks and months passed very quickly. The press approved Tom's exhibits, and later, following Mr Simones' advice, Tom was asked to set up an exhibit of his own and informed that the institute would put up the money for this. It was a risk, but Simones was confident that, following the recent press applause, this was precisely the time to 'strike while the iron was hot' to use his own phrase. His speculation proved correct and won Tom a large article in *Corriere della Sera*. Ticket sales went to defray the institute's expenses, and Tom saw practically nothing for his efforts. However, shortly after, he was asked to take part in designing the scenic setting for a performance of Shakespeare's *King Lear* to be held in December of that year. This particular performance proved to be a great success in Milan on that occasion, and for the first time, Tom could take a considerable sum of money home. The following year, another company employed him to be responsible for the scenery for the film *Jane Eyre* and this also helped him along financially. Perhaps more importantly than the salary paid for this was that he came into contact with the world of art around him, met influential people and was generally encouraged to be creative. Some years before this, he had painted a market scene in one of the much frequented, historic quarters of the city. It had been painted at the time he had first fallen in love with Georgina, and yet he had never even mentioned the fact to his love, much less ever shown her the painting. It was this painting that attracted the notice of a certain Signora Trotta, herself an artist and very rich patroness of the arts in Europe. She purchased Tom's creation, and in one stroke changed his life.

He was able to move out of his premises, since these had become quite incompatible with his new way of life. He bought Felipe a scooter, which, for Felipe, was a godsend, allowing him to go to his work seven kilometres away with much less inconvenience than by bus. When Tom moved out, he parked it in the kitchen to avoid possible theft. Tom cherished Felipe's friendship and regularly supported him financially. He was also able to help his friend, Franco pay hospital expenses incurred by an accident earlier in the year.

"What's the stuff good for, if not to help others?" he would say when they thanked him for his generosity. Tom meant it. Money had no deleterious effect on his character, even when, later, he reached the point where he often did not know what to do with it.

I suppose it was around this time when he was very busy and involved with an important vernissage in Milan. This time, he wished to exhibit all his work for a two-month period. It was a daring venture, and opened on the evening of the 4th of June at the Instituto Cultural in the city's centre. Many of the town's political and economic eminence were there to applaud its inception and Tom was required to reply to a speech given by the mayor.

The speech was given in English and simultaneously translated into Italian as the room occupied by about 150 people fell silent to listen to what he had to say.

*My Lord Mayor, the Officers and Advisers of the Cultural Institute, Friends, Ladies and Gentlemen:*

*I shall be brief.* [Gentle laughter] *But the brevity of my words may not overlook the debt I owe to those who have helped me in the past two years and whose appreciation of my work I am glad to humbly acknowledge this evening. 'No Man is an Islande unto Himself', an English poet noted some 300 years ago, and I must agree. No one goes through this life unaided, and each one of us owes a debt to many others. All of us. Every day. With this knowledge in mind, I want to avail myself of the opportunity now to say how grateful I am to you all for your support, principally to Dr Emanuel Sulla, who has been unstinting in this regard, to Mr Alberto Simones for his guidance and infallible good advice, to Signora Dottore Trotta for her mature criticism and her excellent judgement, to Mr. Adrian Hutchinson for his unerring good management and, not least indeed, to all those of you who have said an encouraging word here and offered help there to realise the exhibition which is to open tomorrow. To you, I say most warmly, Thank you, and God bless you all!."*

After the applause, the assembly disbanded to mingle with others and head for the buffet, Tom among them. It must have been about 9 o' clock when he spotted the rear of a woman with long, fair hair talking to Dr Sulla. He moved slowly through the crowd in her direction. Dr Sulla, facing his way, nodded, smiling in friendly recognition. His partner turned. It was Georgina. He dropped the glass he was holding, drawing attention to himself. Unable to speak, and disregarding the broken glass on the floor, he flung his arms around her. "Georgy! You! Oh God how I've missed you!"

Georgina merely stood and smiled, quite overcome by his show of emotion.

People cheered, glasses clinked. Someone shouted

"Hip-hip!" and the whole distinguished company joined in. Georgina cried and Tom continued to hug his loved one. The entire assembly began to sing "For he's a jolly good fellow!" Strangers and friends came by in turn to congratulate them, exchange words of encouragement and it was some time before things returned to the normal chit-chat of social behaviour.

Words failed both Georgina and Tom, and here Dr Sulla was at his best in exercising tactful assistance. "You forgot to mention one person in your tribute, young man," he said, indicating Georgina, "It was she that suggested I visit you on that memorable morning."

"What!" Tom burst out. Georgina nodded shyly.

"So you got my letters?" he cried.

"Yes, I received them both, thank you," she said, her eyes still filled with tears. Dr Sulla bowed slightly to them both and withdrew. "I'm sure you have one or two things to talk about," he said, underlining the understatement of his remark by his deferential manner. He flowed into the chattering crowd. But the truth was that the pair just stood looking happily at each other, before it occurred to Tom to ask his girl where their mutual friend, Helen, was on this august occasion.

"She's at home with my mother, looking after Alexandra," Georgina stated simply.

"Alexandra? Who's that?" Tom asked, surprised not to know a common acquaintance.

"That's your daughter," Georgina said in the same manner.

"My *what*?" Tom demanded.

"You have a two-year-old daughter, Mr Cullen. She has black hair like you. Quite unlike her mum in other ways, too."

Tom stood there flabbergasted. What he had to say to her comment was not very original either.

"You mean I'm a father?" he sputtered over the second glass of champagne he'd been given.

"I'm afraid so, lad," said a voice behind him. It was Aldo. The same larking, teasing Aldo as ever with a fine-looking woman on his arm. The two men shook hands and greeted their respective partners. "So you knew about this as well before I did, you bugger," Tom declared. "Hey, you watch your language, young feller; we don't use that kind of talk here," he warned, his rubber face adopting an expression of grave censure. Everyone laughed at Tom's ignorance

"So what ye gonna do about it, young Cullen?" Aldo asked provocatively, his expression having now changed to that of an irate father of a generation before his. Once more, Tom found no words to retaliate, which was very unlike him, but stood there stupefied at the question. Aldo, however, was master of the situation. There was just the smallest of pauses before he advised the nincompoop that stood in front of him.

"You ask her to marry you, you idiot!" Aldo said, turning his head away in disgusted desperation at such obtuseness. This time, though, Tom caught on, and turning to Georgina before the group, said, "Will you marry me after all?"

Georgina was quite overcome by this and lost her composure for once. Falling into his arms, she nodded affirmatively several times.

"Good, then, that's settled, Dad," Aldo concluded cheekily.

# Epilogue

Well, and that's how Georgina became an important mum. She had two other children, a boy and a girl, Tom and she having married in the meantime, and they live now in the Tuscan countryside on land that supports a small farm for animals that are allowed to enjoy the full cycle of their existence, and where Tom still successfully paints.

Patrick, Georgina's brother is securely cemented in the British Navy, and I've heard recently that he's risen sky high in its ranks, so that his late father would have been proud of him. Sarah is a neuro surgeon at a famous London hospital.

Evelynne eventually married her Jean-Luc and the two moved long ago to Paris from where they still keep in contact with Tom and Georgina.

As for Helen, well, she married the most unlikely of men at forty-five years of age, a jazz man with a three-day beard, unkempt, loud, jovial and lacking all taste in clothes and education, but a veritable wizard on the saxophone. I saw them a week ago after eight years of marriage, and you'd think they'd met yesterday!

Jennifer got married, too, as little girls do and went to live as a sheep shearer's wife in New Zealand. Felipe and Franco now run the King Edward together while Aldo of all people is the president of a bank! Think of that!